FOREVER IN TIME

Ben stood up and walked to the back of Maddie's chair. He set his wine glass down and put his warm hands on her neck, moving them slowly, seductively, over her bare skin. "I've missed you," he said, bending to kiss her ear.

Maddie shivered at his touch. She had missed him, too; missed him and longed for him. She drew in her breath, fighting her undeniable desire, but it was no use. Ben was standing behind her and she felt her whole body respond to his seductive touch. It was like magic.

Ben pulled her up and turned her around in his arms, kissing her passionately. "I've missed you," he whispered as he swept her into his arms and carried her to the bed.

He undressed her slowly, caressing her as he did so. She in return kissed him and unbuttoned his shirt, longing for the feel of his broad chest against her own flesh.

At that moment she thought of home; of what she had left behind when she was transported back in time. At first she had been frightened, then it had become something of an adventure. But here in Ben's arms, it seemed as if fate had somehow granted her an unspoken wish—she had been delivered into the arms of a man to whom she felt overwhelmingly drawn.

"You're silent," Ben whispered, nuzzling her ear with his lips.

"I was thinking," Maddie said. "Thinking I want to stay here. I want to stay in this time."

A
TIMELESS
TREASURE

JOYCE
CARLOW

PINNACLE BOOKS
KENSINGTON PUBLISHING CORP.

PINNACLE BOOKS are published by

Kensington Publishing Corp.
850 Third Avenue
New York, NY 10022

Pinnacle and the P logo Reg. U.S. Pat. & TM Off.

First Printing: September, 1995

Printed in the United States of America

Chapter One

The sleek motor launch cut across the choppy blue waters of Mahone Bay, leaving a trail of white foam in its wake. On the shore she had left behind, Maddie watched as the brightly painted houses seemed to grow smaller and the tall pines blended into a spectacle of green hues above the blue water.

The ocean spray lightly showered the eleven passengers who sat on a wooden bench that circled the perimeter of the small vessel. Though the sun was warm, the combination of cool water and crisp sea breeze caused Maddie to shiver. She pulled her cotton sweater together, covering the thin material of her summer sundress, and folded her arms tightly as if to hold in the warmth.

If Chip had been sitting next to her, his warm, tanned muscular arm would be around her shoulders and she wouldn't be cold. She frowned slightly as the thought of the comfort he might offer faded, and was replaced with the memory of their most recent argument. It was because of that argument that she was on this boat—alone among what were obviously five couples.

Maddie inhaled of the salt air deeply, then let out her breath slowly, letting her thoughts wash over her just as the ocean spray washed over her. *Damn him,* she thought angrily.

Damn Chip! Well, I'm going to enjoy myself anyway, she vowed. *Just let him stew. It served him right.*

Not that he *would* stew. He made that plain before she left. That wasn't like Chip at all. No, Chip would find a bar and he would stew there. He would drink, he might even pick up some woman, if there was a woman available. No, regrettably he wouldn't have any problem at all. Women adored him. He attracted them like a magnet. No doubt he would enjoy this weekend and she would be the one who would be miserable.

Whatever made her agree to come on this vacation with him? Maddie silently asked herself for what seemed like the hundredth time. Didn't she know what he would demand?

"C'mon," he'd urged, looking at her with his deep blue eyes. "It's not like I'm suggesting we make off to some shack-up resort in the Caribbean, or anything. Hey, Nova Scotia's a rugged holiday—at least that's what I've heard. Look, we'll drive. We'll hike, and walk, and go sailing. We'll stay in motels and you can have your own room. We'll share expenses and good conversation. Honey, we'll really get to know each other. No pressure, I promise."

They hadn't done any of the things he promised. And there *was* pressure. She most definitely had taken her own room, but he kept trying. He kept wanting to sleep with her, and in the beginning she had thought it might come to that. No, she hadn't been sure what would happen at all, and so in a sense she supposed she might have led him on. But now she sadly knew for certain that she did not want that kind of relationship with Chip. In fact, she was reasonably sure she didn't want *any* relationship with Chip.

Oh, Chip was attractive. In fact, he looked like a movie star. He was tall and blond and had deep blue eyes. He had a dark, even, golden tan, and well-developed muscles rippled under his smooth skin. All women seemed drawn to him.

But no matter how physically attractive she found Chip, warning bells kept going off. She knew full well that a relationship should be based on more than mere physical attraction. For one thing, in spite of his professed desires to have an "outdoor" holiday, he complained bitterly when they were outdoors, and always seemed to be trying to steer her toward bars and dark hideaways. He wanted to dance, hold her close, and he never ceased trying to seduce her. He was always making suggestive comments, and the more he drank, the more suggestive his comments became.

Yesterday, they had come to Nova Scotia's South Shore. She had read about the tour of Oak Island and the "Historic Mystery Weekend" on the island in Mahone Bay. It was a special tour and a special island—an island where there was supposed to be some sort of buried treasure. And the idea of the mystery weekend intrigued her. She had read about such weekends and had always wanted to go on one. And this one had the added feature of being "historic." The brochure promised eighteenth century costumes, food, and a realistic atmosphere.

"It's a beautiful day and there are wildflowers everywhere," she had enthused. "Oh, Chip, it'll be fun! We'll take a boat over to the island, and then walk around and look at the excavations where they're trying to find the treasure."

"I'd say 'yes' if it were only one day, but hell, Maddie—it's for the whole weekend."

"We'll enjoy it. The Inn provides box lunches for a picnic, and the brochure says there are lectures about the island, and then we all dress up in costumes, have an eighteenth century feast, and there's a make-believe murder which we all try to solve."

"Just another damn hokey tour of nothing," he had answered sarcastically. "Geez, Maddie, pirates and treasures are kid stuff."

"I want to go, I think it sounds interesting," she maintained stubbornly.

In truth, she hadn't thought it all that interesting. But they'd been together for over a week, things weren't working out, and as she spoke to him, it occurred to her that a weekend apart might improve both their humors. She waited for him to answer, but he didn't. Then she announced, "I think I'll go alone, then."

"Do that," he retorted meanly.

"I will," she had answered defiantly. And so she had, noting that he didn't hesitate one moment in letting her know he didn't care. He took the rented car and headed off toward Halifax, doubtless to pursue a weekend of drinking in one of the city's many pubs.

That was the real problem. When Chip drank he became someone different, someone she didn't know, someone who made her feel vaguely wary. He had not been abusive with her. It was just that when he drank, he revealed a greater degree of temper, and she suspected that in time, if he continued to drink, his temper might easily result in hurtful behavior. His heavy drinking was the main reason for her warning voices . . .

"Here we go!"

Maddie snapped out of her reverie as the young guide made his announcement. He turned the motor off and let the launch move slowly under its own power toward the old wooden wharf where an elderly man with a flecked gray and black beard stood, ready to throw out a rope. Maddie smiled, pushing all the unhappy thoughts about Chip from her mind and once again she vowed to enjoy herself.

The guide was no more than seventeen or eighteen. He had unruly red hair and freckles, and his nose appeared to be perpetually peeling.

The guide stood up and caught the rope. Then he expertly pulled the boat in alongside the wharf where the older man stood, ready to assist the passengers, most of whom were middle-aged, though two passengers were decidedly elderly.

"Let's have your names as you disembark," the man on the wharf asked in a voice that sounded as if he must sing bass in a barber shop quartet. "My name's Henry—Henry Standard."

"Florence Eldridge," a woman with tightly curled grey-blond hair said, as she allowed Mr. Standard to take her hand.

"Frank Eldridge," the portly man who followed her added. "We hail from Indiana."

"Right nice place, that," Henry Standard commented with a grin. "And you folks take up this good man's idea, give your name and your place of origin."

"Jessie Anderson and this is Andy. We're from Georgia." It was hardly necessary for them to say they came from Georgia once they had opened their mouths. Their slow southern drawl was all too obvious to another American, though she supposed a Canadian might not be able to pinpoint the exact part of the South from which they came.

"Eliot. James and Martha Eliot from Boston."

The Krammers, Gladys and Hershfield, from New York followed, and then the Kingsleys, June and Rodney, from Ontario.

"Maddie Emerson," she said softly as she stepped onto the dock and stretched. "I'm from Boston, too."

"Alone, eh?" the old man said, grinning. "Well, you can just walk along with me while the young'un here conducts us on our tour of the money pit. That's what they call this here place, the money pit."

Maddie smiled. "Sounds intriguing."

"Now all stay together," the young tour master asked. "In case you've forgotten, my name's Tim MacLean, but you can all just call me Tim. Now it's real important that we all stick together 'cause parts of this island are honeycombed with excavations and walking around not knowing where you're going can be right dangerous."

They set off across a field, then walked along a path under the trees that paralleled the shore.

"For about two hundred years folks have been digging up real interesting stuff hereabouts," Tim MacLean told them as they approached a square wooden structure that only half hid a large excavation. "First stuff they found was plank flooring,

tnen some old oak chests. Then this here main shaft was uncovered in 1795."

They gathered round the shaft and peered into its murky
depths.

"Eventually it was found to be over a hundred feet deep.
It had been booby trapped, too. There's an elaborate series of
flooding tunnels."

"Seems pretty complex," Mr. Eldridge commented.

"Well, for sure whoever built it knew what they were
doing," Tim allowed.

Maddie stared into the pit and felt a slight chill run through
her. Chip might think that buried treasure and pirates were
kid stuff, but she didn't. She loved pirate stories, and often
when visiting the beach she had dreamed of finding buried
treasure.

"This is one of some three hundred islands in Mahone Bay.
It's only a kilometer and half long and about a tenth of a kilometer wide. As you can see, the digging—maybe I should say
hunting—is still going on."

"Who would have hidden treasure here?" Mr. Krammer
asked.

"Well, some say it was Captain Kidd and others say Henry
Morgan or Blackbeard. Still one college professor—well, he
thinks it might have been Inca refugees fleeing from those
conquistador fellows in South America. He says they were
the ones who had the technology to build the flooding
tunnels—'cause they were miners."

The group whispered among themselves, then Tim continued.

"See this old oak tree was the first clue. There was a de-
pression in the ground—of course, it's all dug up now. And
there was evidence that a block and tackle had been used on
the tree. When they started digging, they found a pit with
platforms at three meter levels. In 1804, another group dug
down to the thirty meter level. Then the whole thing filled up

with salt water. Later they discovered this here pit was connected to the ocean by these here flooding tunnels."

"To protect the treasure," Mrs. Eldridge breathed as if she suddenly understood something very important.

"That seems the likely theory," Tim answered nodding. "Anyway, six people lost their lives looking so far. Mind you, once lately, they lowered a T.V. camera down there and they think they saw the outline of three chests. For sure they found a dismembered human hand."

Mrs. Kramer winced and covered her mouth with her hand.

"Anyway folks, we have a picture presentation in the hall over there, and we've also got some artifacts found hereabouts. After the presentation, you can all head over to the picnic grounds and eat your lunches. After that, you can select the costumes you want to wear to the historic feast and then we'll show you to your cabins."

"When's the murder?" Mr. Eldridge asked.

"Could be anytime," Tim answered with a friendly wink.

With those last words, Tim led them toward a wooden hall that sat in a small clearing.

"Isn't this exciting? I think it's really fun!" Mrs. Eldridge gushed. She tilted her head of tightly-curled grey blond curls and studied one of the dresses. "There's a lot to choose from. I was afraid they wouldn't have anything in my size, I'm so hard to fit!"

Maddie didn't comment, though she was sure Mrs. Eldridge was hard to fit. She was pear-shaped, and not much over five-foot two. She wondered how Mr. Eldridge was doing. He was quite a large man and would no doubt require a Henry the Eighth sized outfit. She mentally visualized him, and a smile crossed her lips.

"Is something funny?" Mrs. Eldridge asked.

"Oh, no. I was just wondering where all these costumes came from."

"From the look of them I'd say some enterprising Nova Scotian went to a fire sale at a Hollywood studio." Mrs. Eliot said, holding up a fluffy gown that looked more antebellum than early eighteenth century.

"I'm sure that was in *Gone With The Wind,*" Maddie laughed.

Martha Eliot held it up and circled around, "I do believe I feel like Miss Scarlet," she intoned in her crisp Boston accent.

"But you don't sound like her," Jessie Anderson drawled in her Georgian accent.

Maddie laughed. She felt good now. Lunch had been a little awkward because everyone else was part of a couple—but the Eliots had taken her under their wing.

She had enjoyed the Oak Island lecture, and after that, the women had been brought here to this warehouse building to select their costumes while the men had gone to an adjacent building for the same purpose.

And this, Maddie thought, was really fun. It was nice to be with a group of women—albeit women older than she— trying on clothes and good naturedly joking about bygone styles. It all seemed natural now, and she felt better than she had before when she just kept feeling like some sort of third wheel.

"I wonder if the murder will take place at the feast," Mrs. Krammer said, thinking aloud.

"I should think not. It ought to occur when we're in our cabins or on our way, or something," Maddie suggested.

June Kingsley turned to Maddie. "You're the only one here without an escort—are you perchance the victim?"

"Don't you dare take all the fun out of this!" Mrs. Eliot said. "If she is the victim, I don't want to know."

"I'm not! I'm a genuine tourist just like you," Maddie insisted.

"Oh, look at this!" Mrs. Eliot said, taking a fire red taffeta gown from the rack. It had this traditional low cut bodice and was trimmed in white lace. She held it toward Maddie. "You're the only one who could get away with this one!"

"If you ask me, that's asking to be the victim with the murderer being a jealous wife," Gladys Hershfield from New York said, lifting a dark brow.

"It's you!" Mrs. Eliot proclaimed. "You have those black Irish looks—the dark hair and green eyes—you can wear this color!"

Maddie took the gown and held it up in front of her. It certainly looked as if it would fit. But it was very sexy and it seemed silly to look sexy when there was no one for whom to look sexy. Yet the dress seemed to call out to her. She felt drawn to it and she bit her lip. "I do like it," she admitted.

"Aren't we all supposed to gather at four to be taken to our cabins?" Jessie Anderson reminded them as she consulted her watch.

"They can't give women all these clothes to chose from and then expect them to be on time," Mrs. Eliot joked. "Even if they are fashions from another century."

"I'm wearing this one," Mrs. Eldridge said holding up a golden gown.

"And I want this one," Mrs. Eliot said, holding up a gown in blue.

"If you're taking the red one, we're all ready," Mrs. Krammer announced, looking at Maddie.

Maddie nodded, and they all headed out into the afternoon sunlight, their costumes draped over their arms.

"I'm going to look a proper swashbuckler," Mr. Eliot announced.

"Let's stay together," Tim MacLean said. "Now it's important that you stay on the path when you're walking between buildings or are coming and going from your cabins. These here lights are lit at night and as long as you stay on the path, you're going to be safe and sound."

He led them away from the two small warehouses and down a winding path into the northern pines. "The hanging stuff is Northern moss—not unlike Spanish moss in some ways. Both of them was once used to stuff mattresses and the like."

Maddie looked up at the Northern moss. It hung like torn lace from the trees and she could only imagine that on a foggy day it gave the trees an eerie appearance.

But it was not foggy today. Nor was it silent. The whole group carried their overnight bags and their costumes. The men clanked along as their swords and other paraphernalia hit one another with each step.

They rounded a bend. "This is the main lodge. At eight o'clock you'll come back here for the historic feast."

"And murder . . ." Gladys whispered loudly.

Tim said nothing. "You can't get lost. The path is totally circular. Just stay on it and you'll come to the lodge. They went a bit further and came to the first cabin. Mr. and Mrs. Eldridge were dropped off. They trod on and around another bend, then the Eliots were dropped off.

Each cabin was secluded even though each was on the main path.

"Here we are, Miss Emerson."

Maddie waved goodbye and headed into her cabin. It was cool inside and she hung her costume on a hanger in the small closet and flounced on the big double bed.

The cabin was rustic and modern at the same time. The bed was a big four poster made of pine and covered with a patchwork quilt. A dressing table with a small mirror sat on one side of the room and on the other a stone fireplace chimney traveled to the ceiling. Off the one room was a small bathroom with just a shower, a toilet, and a sink.

Too bad, Maddie thought as she peered in. She had rather fancied the idea of a deep hot bath, but clearly it was not to be. In fact, water was probably something of a problem. Drinking water was provided in a cooler and a sign over the sink cautioned against drinking the tap water.

Maddie went back to the bed. She stripped down to her white lace slip, tossing her clothes over a nearby chair with abandon. Then she flopped down on the bed. There was time for a nap. Time to think some more about Chip—about what she was going to do when this weekend was over and she had to face the reality of Monday morning.

Martha Eliot was a tall slender woman with dark eyes and short grey hair. James was also tall and bean pole thin. He wore square rimless glasses and looked very much like the bank manager he was.

Martha sat on the edge of the bed flipping through a magazine while James sat in the only arm chair with his newspaper.

Martha looked up, a frown covering her face, "I wonder why that young woman is alone."

James answered without lifting his eyes from the paper. "A lot of women travel alone."

"Oh no, not women that age. Women my age, women who are divorced or widowed. No, that Maddie Emerson is young and very pretty."

"Well, sometimes even pretty women are alone."

"It just doesn't seem right. No, I'm sure she had a boyfriend and she had a fight with him or something."

"Really? My, you are insightful."

"Don't tease me, James. I mean, she's more than pretty, she's beautiful and she's very nice, too. She speaks well, I think she has a good education. But she does seem preoccupied. You know, as if she's trying to work through some kind of problem."

"I'm sure she'll be fine. And I'm afraid there isn't anyone you can fix her up with—not this weekend anyway."

Martha Eliot smiled. Her husband knew her well. But he was right. There wasn't anyone on this weekend trip for Maddie. "I'm not really insightful," she said, "I saw her last night at the Inn on the mainland. She was with a young man—but he wasn't her type at all and I'm sure they were arguing."

James folded his paper and laughed. "I'm sure you'll solve the weekend's mystery, Martha. You never miss a thing."

Martha smiled and went back to her magazine, "I hope it's a good mystery," she said finally.

Maddie tossed and then with a sudden awakening, looked at her watch in panic. "Seven o'clock. Perfect," she said, as she sleepily forced herself up.

Perhaps it was all that ocean air on the way over to the island; perhaps it was walking around most of the morning and afternoon. Or, more likely it was her troubled sleep last night that caused her to lie down for a short nap and drop off into a deep sleep, Maddie decided.

Then she shrugged. "I'm on vacation!" she said aloud, reminding herself that the essence of a vacation was not having to do things on schedule. It was being able to sleep when you felt like it. She would be a little late, but what did it matter?

She went into the small bathroom and took off the rest of her clothes. Then she ran the water till it was warm, and stepped into the shower, scrubbing herself from head to toe.

She toweled herself dry and then examined her costume. There was no way to wear a bra under the dress—not that it was necessary. And panties weren't necessary because the costume included pantaloons and slips.

With the towel wrapped securely around her, she sat down to do her hair and makeup first. She peered into the mirror. Usually she didn't wear much makeup but tonight she applied a little foundation and some eye shadow. Her lashes were naturally long, thick, and dark so she needed no mascara. She did put on a little green eye shadow and just the tiniest amount of blusher.

Then she set about to tame her hair. It was long and thick

and raven black in color. It was in marked contrast to her milk white skin.

Maddie skilfully wound some of her hair into a large back bun, but allowed the rest to tumble down over her shoulders with wisps falling about her face.

When satisfied, she turned to her gown. She put on the pantaloons and the slips, then she put on the red gown and laced up its tight bodice. No, there was certainly no need for a bra—in fact, had she worn it, the straps would have been quite evident.

Maddie stared at herself in the mirror. It was terribly low cut. Her ample cleavage was not simply evident, but emphasized.

"Who cares," she muttered to herself. Everyone was quite coupled off and much older than she. There was virtually no one to ogle—the tour guide was too young for her, and everyone else was married.

She smiled at her image. "Too bad," she said to herself, admitting that the gown was, indeed, quite appealing.

Maddie threw the shawl that had come with the costume over her shoulders and took one final look in the mirror.

"All ready," she said aloud as she opened the door.

Before her the narrow pathway was lit with little pagoda type lights every four or five feet. It wound off into the darkened distance.

"Not a yellow brick road," she said, but somehow as it disappeared into the trees, the pathways gave the impression of a road into the unknown, into the soft velvet darkness of the night.

An intuitive feeling swept over her, a feeling that as she walked down the path toward the hall, she was leaving her past. "Silly," she said, just to hear her own voice in the still of the night.

But wasn't it early for it to be so dark? Again Maddie checked her watch. It read ten minutes to eight.

She looked upward, seeking the sky beyond the tall pines.

Strange, there were no stars. The day had been perfectly clear and she was sure the weather forecast had been for continued balmy weather beneath clear skies.

She sighed, reminding herself that she was on an island off the East coast of Canada. Weather by the ocean was always changeable—and perhaps an unexpected storm was headed this way.

She lifted her skirts and headed off down the path, following the narrow row of lights.

"Shouldn't I have come to a cabin by now?" she asked herself in a whisper. She sighed again. Very likely she had turned in the wrong direction and was headed for the lodge the long way around. But no matter, the path was circular and she would end up in the right place no matter where she started. At least that is what the young tour guide had told them.

She walked on, wondering to herself. She was really quite sure she hadn't turned the wrong way—but still she passed no cabin.

Again she checked her watch. She had been walking for five minutes! She knew she had come a goodly distance since she was not walking slowly, but still she passed no cabins. "Good thing I'm not wearing heels," she murmured, grateful for the fact that the shoes that had come with the costume were soft and comfortable, rather like ballet slippers.

Then, quite suddenly, the wind began to blow. Not a mild evening breeze, but a real wind—a high wind. Maddie's hair whipped in the strong gusts, and she clung to her shawl. There was a dampness in the air and then a great lightening bolt split the dark sky. Maddie sucked in her breath—in a moment a loud thunder clap shattered the silence.

Maddie glanced backward. Should she turn around? The wind was terribly strong, it whipped down the pathway as if it were following her—seeking her out. She grasped her shawl more tightly now. No, better to go forward, the lodge must be very near now. She hurried on, head down, walking into the wind.

Then there was one great gust and the lights that lit the path went out, leaving her standing in absolute blackness. "Damn!" she cursed. It was pitch black. There were no sounds save the sounds of the wind and brittle branches creaking and blowing in the wind.

Maddie stomped her foot angrily. Now what was she supposed to do? Stand still until the lights came on? Try to find her way in the absolute darkness? As if answering her, the heavens opened up and it began to rain. Not a simple summer rain, but a torrent of rain with huge, hard drops.

Instinctively, Maddie began to run. She ran as best she could, holding up her skirt. Then she heard it rip as it caught on a bit of brush. Surely she was off the path, the brush and woods seemed to be closing in on her.

She shivered as she continued on, feeling her way as best she could. She was drenched and part of her skirt had been left on some bush. She felt like crying—she had tried to get away on her own for a little adventure, a pleasant weekend and now it had turned into a nightmare. Why didn't the lights go on? Perhaps then she could see something—find her way back to the path at least.

She plunged forward, not daring to stand still as another crack of lightning temporarily lit the night sky. Nothing! In its fleeting light she had seen nothing. She plunged on and then something caught her foot and she tumbled down— down without warning, without even time to scream.

Maddie felt sensations before she was actually able to open her eyes. She shivered and tried to draw her shawl around her neck. But it didn't help. She was wet and she was cold.

Maddie forced open her eyes despite her desire to remain unconscious. It wasn't quite as black as it had been, the sky above her was a kind of purple color, as if it were close to sunrise. Yes, that must be it. It was always colder just as the sun rose on the horizon.

She moved carefully—slowly, testing her arms, stretching her legs. Then, with sudden horror, she realized there was nothing beneath her right foot. Was she on a ledge of some sort? As she moved her foot back onto the ledge, she winced in pain. "Oh, dear," she gasped, reaching down to massage it. It began to throb dully. Not broken, she thought, but no doubt sprained.

Carefully, she eased her foot onto whatever she was on, and just as carefully, she pulled herself into a sitting position.

She shook her head as if to clear it. How could it be dawn? She had been on her way to the historic feast at the lodge and it was only a few minutes to eight when the storm started, the lights went out and she had gotten lost in the woods. Could she have been unconscious so long?

Maddie blinked. It was getting lighter and her eyes were getting used to the light.

She looked upward. She could make out the sides of the pit into which she had fallen. And she realized she was on one of the wooden platforms. Why hadn't they found her? Surely she had been missed. Surely they had sent out search parties.

She ventured to lean down. Beneath her was the blackness of the hole—a hole so deep she couldn't even see the bottom in this light. She shivered in fear, it seemed truly a bottomless pit.

Again she looked up. Hadn't she been in the woods? There seemed to be no trees surrounding this pit, yet she had been deep in the woods and there had been trees everywhere when she fell.

Abstractedly, she touched her dress. Yes, she was still quite wet from the rain. She squirmed slightly in her clothes. They were uncomfortable and clung to her.

"Help!" she called out as loudly as she could. "Help! I'm down here! Help!"

Her cry echoed off the sides of the damp pit, but they were greeted only by complete silence.

She called out again to no avail. Where was everyone? This was unforgivable! They should be searching for her.

She struggled with her torn shawl pulling it closer and covered herself as best she could with her ragged torn gown. For a long while she just listened, straining her ears, hoping for the sound of a human being.

Within the hour, the island was alive with sounds, but they were not human sounds. They were the cries of a hundred birds. Frightening black crows—one of which swooped dangerously close to see if she was alive—curious gulls, circling, gliding, and seemingly playing tag as the sun came up and at least offered the comfort of daylight.

Maddie called out again. Still there were no human sounds and no one answered her.

She studied the walls of her prison. They were too steep and slippery to climb. If she slipped, she would fall all the way to the bottom, which she assumed was full of water.

Again and again she called out till her voice was hoarse. She shivered again, even though now the sun was fully up. The absence of human sound, the locale which appeared different than yesterday—it all combined to fill her with fear.

When she had first come to, she had assumed she would be found right away. But now at least two hours had passed and she was still here on her precarious perch and there wasn't even the sound of another human being.

Maddie closed her eyes and tried to concentrate on pleasant thoughts. But her discomfort wouldn't allow her to be distracted. Then she heard something . . .

Again she strained to hear. It seemed to be laughter—raucous male laughter. By this time everyone must know she was missing. How dare they laugh! She might be dead. "Hurry up!" she shouted, aware of the anger in her voice.

No one answered.

"Help!" she cried out loudly. "Help me! Please, I'm down here!"

Chapter Two

The morning sun had just risen in the east when the long boat, propelled by twelve oarsmen, hit the shallow water of the place they called Hidden Cove.

"Over the side lads, that's as far as we row," Samuel Harrowsmith called out, even as he secured his oar and jumped from the boat into the cold water. The other eleven followed, each man grasping a part of the boat in order to haul it onto the pebble strewn beach.

"Damn cold water," Black Henri commented. "You'd think it would be warmer this time of year." He was a brawny black man dressed in black breeches and an open necked white shirt. Round his waist he wore a red cummerbund, into which a vicious looking twelve inch knife was thrust. He wore a red scarf around his forehead too, and from his right ear, a large gold earring caught the light of the newly risen sun.

"Pull her in and turn her around!" Black Henri ordered. "That way it'll be easier when we leave."

The men pulled the heavy boat onto the shore and turned it about. Black Henri stared out to sea, out to where the *Wilma* lay peacefully at anchor. Between the shore and the larger vessel, another long boat bobbed in the choppy water. It held another twelve men, one of whom was their captain, Ben York.

"The storm last night made the water choppy," Gabriel Vagas commented as he stood by Black Henri's side.

"It's not bad," Black Henri said. "By noon it will be calm. We'll probably have to wait for a good breeze in order to set sail."

"Aye," Gabriel agreed.

Black Henri turned to the huddle of men, many of whom were emptying water from their boots. "No need to wait for the captain. Get those chests out of the long boat and divide them up. Half of you head for the West Pit and half for the East Pit."

Grumbling, Riffen positioned himself at one end of a chest while Digby took the other. On the count of three they heaved the chest upward and then trudged off to the east.

"You had to pick the heaviest one, didn't you?" Digby complained.

"They're all heavy," Riffen spat. "Just stop your blabbering and move along."

Riffen and Digby were strong and they strode well ahead of the others who stopped now and again to readjust their load. In moments they were well out of earshot.

"This voyage could have a fine ending if we knew where the hell we were," Digby muttered. "Then we could get back here and dig this up for ourselves."

"Well, we don't know where we are," Riffen grumbled. "Neither of us could ever find this place again—not in a million years."

"Gotta be over two hundred islands in this one bay," Digby said, and yesterday we sailed past more than one bay."

"We're almost to the pit," Riffen reminded him.

"Fourth time we've been here and we still don't know where 'here' is," Digby went on.

They trudged forward, then in unison they brought the heavy trunk down. "I could sure use some rum," Riffen said, wiping the sweat off his brow.

"Help! Please help me!"

"What in the name of the King is that?" Riffen thundered. He was a squat man, whose girth made him appear even shorter than his five-foot five-inches. Not only did his weight subtract from his height, but his build was deceiving in other ways as well. He was, in fact, not really fat. He was solid muscle, a bear of a man who could, and had, broken the neck of more than one man who crossed him.

"Sounds like a woman . . ." Digby answered, as he stood up straight and rubbed his stubbled chin.

Both men were sweaty and tired from carrying the trunk. Both wore heavy boots, grubby skin tight breeches and both had discarded their tunics and jackets when they'd come ashore. Both had bad rotting teeth, and both smelled of stale tobacco and filth.

"She calls in English, it ain't no Indian woman," Digby added.

Riffen scowled. "Best look into this," he muttered as he strode off, following the sound of the plaintive cries.

Digby followed and from further down the beach several others watched, then they too began walking in the direction taken by Riffen.

Riffen paused at the edge of the pit they had dug last time they'd been on this island. He stared in, a look of disbelief covering his face. "What have we here!" he shouted, just as Digby arrived.

"God save me!" Digby said, suddenly crossing himself. "It must be a she-devil!"

Maddie looked up into their faces. One was leering at her, the other looked almost frightened. "Get me out of here!" she demanded. "Where is everyone! I don't recognize you! You weren't in our group!"

"What's she babbling about?" Digby said, recovering himself slightly.

"Who cares?" Riffen muttered. "Look at that length of thigh, me boy! If that's a she-devil then I say let's get her out of there, tie her down, and have ourselves a devil of a time!"

"She does look like a comely wench," Digby agreed.

"Lie down, Digby. I'll hold your ankles and you grab her and pull her up. She looks light enough."

Digby didn't hesitate. He knew Riffen far too well to argue. He lay down and Riffen seized his ankles, then he allowed himself to be lowered into the pit.

"Isn't there a rope ladder?" Maddie asked.

"Shut up, beauty!" Digby seized her round the waist and Maddie screamed as he held her tightly and shouted, "Pull away, Riffen!"

Held by the waist and suspended over a bottomless pit. It was as terrifying a moment as Maddie had ever known. She wanted to struggle and resist her unkempt, disagreeable deliverer, but sheer terror kept her from it. So instead she closed her eyes tightly until she felt herself dragged none too gently over the edge of the pit and deposited on solid ground. But even as she was so deposited, her ankle gave out and she buckled, falling to a sitting position with a small shriek of pain.

"Oh, it must be sprained," she gasped.

"We want you down in any case," Riffen roared. "Immobile and ready for us!"

Only then did Maddie take a good look at the two. The one who had lifted her had scrambled to his feet and now stood looking down at her, his narrow mouth twisted slightly.

Maddie yanked at the neckline of her all too revealing gown, and pulled her torn dress down over her leg. "Stop joking!" she said sternly. "Your costumes are great and you sound authentic, but I've been on that ledge all night! My ankle's sprained, and I'm hungry!"

"Costumes!" Riffen shouted. He leaned down and looked into her face. Then in one swift movement, he wrapped her long dark hair in his hand and yanked on it, jolting her head up, so that he was nose to nose with her. "This is no joke, wench! We mean to strip you and have you! Right here!"

Maddie felt stunned. He smelled foul, as if he hadn't

bathed in a month. The knife by his side and his sword were both real, his rotting teeth were real, too. It was then that she realized with a chill that whoever these men were, and regardless of how they were dressed, they were dangerous.

"Who, who are you?" she stuttered.

"Privateers! And whose thieving little spy are you?" Riffen asked, still holding her hair.

"Blimey! Where did a wench come from!" Samuel Harrowsmith shouted. There were others behind him now. All wide-eyed and staring.

Maddie looked back at them in terror—was this some sort of gang?

"Wherever she came from, she's welcome!" another laughed.

"Must be a spy!"

"I found her!" Riffen said menacingly. "She's mine first. Stake her down! Let's have our way with her and then throw her in the pit!"

Maddie covered her face with her hands and screamed. What nightmare had she awakened to?

"Aye!" another said, looking around for something that could be used for stakes.

"You found her, but I brought her to the surface," Digby said sullenly.

"Then you can have her when I'm done!" Riffen laughed. "She looks enough for all of us."

Maddie could feel the color draining from her face. She began to tremble uncontrollably. This couldn't be real— privateers? These men looked and spoke, and indeed smelled as if they were right out of the eighteenth century. But there was no use puzzling over that. Regardless of the mystery of them—they intended to rape and then murder her. She looked up into their faces, only one looked as if he would even hesitate.

It was at that moment that she heard a silence breaking pis-

tol shot. The men who surrounded her parted, and Riffen
looked up, even though he did not loosen his grip on her hair.

Maddie looked, too. Down the center of the path made for
him strode a tall, powerful looking man. He was well over six
feet, his shoulders were broad and even though he alone wore
a shirt, she could see he was muscular and well-built. He had
sandy brown hair and brown eyes. He stood with his legs
apart and his eyes rested on her. For a long moment she forgot the man who so roughly held her hair. She was absolutely
transfixed. The stranger's eyes bore through her, she felt as if
he were mentally undressing her. She felt exposed and naked.

Then he turned. "Unhand the wench, Riffen! You know
full well I have first pick of any women who come our way!"

The man called Riffen let her hair drop and stepped away
from her.

"Stand up woman!" the man demanded.

"I can't. My ankle's sprained."

"She was in the pit. Says she fell," Digby revealed.

The captain looked back at her, and a smile twisted round
his mouth. "Aye, but the question is, how did she get to this
deserted island in the first place?"

"Deserted?" Maddie said. "It's not deserted."

"Maybe it wasn't when you came woman, but it is now,"
he answered.

"Maybe she was left here to spy," Riffen suggested.

"Maybe," the captain agreed. "In any case there is no time
to question her now. I can make her talk later."

Maddie started to open her mouth, but he looked at her
sternly and she held her tongue half out of fear and half because she wasn't sure she could speak even though questions
formed in her mind, her voice seemed lost to her. Who were
these terrible men and what was happening—if this were part
of what was supposed to happen, then it was all frighteningly
realistic.

"Black Henri!" the captain shouted.

From the periphery of the group came a hulking black

man. His skin glistened in the sun, he was naked to the waist and he wore an earring.

"Row this tasty little bundle out to the ship. Tie her in my cabin, lock her in, and come back here. See that young Will feeds her."

Maddie had no time to say anything. Black Henri was at her side in three long steps, and in an instant he had slung her over his massive shoulder and was carrying her down the beach as if she were a sack of flour.

After what seemed a fairly long walk, they came to two beached boats. He dumped her unceremoniously into the smallest of three rowboats, shoved it in the water, jumped in himself and in moments they were headed out across the water. Maddie squinted into the distance, staring disbelievingly at what she saw. At anchor off shore, was a galleon of the sort she had only seen in old Hollywood films. Could a replica look so real? She had seen one once at anchor in a pond at Disneyland—but it was obviously a replica. The closer they rowed to this vessel, the more real it looked to her.

Maddie closed her eyes. Was this some horrible dream? What had happened to her? What had happened to everyone? And above all, who were all these horrible men? These men who threatened her and who was the one who now ordered her to be tied up?

Maddie struggled to sit up straight. She looked into the intent black face of the man who rowed the boat. "I know this is Canada," she said, trying to sound a good deal more calm than she felt, "and I know I'm not Canadian—I, I demand to know who you are? I want to speak to the American Ambassador."

The black man stared at her, then his face broke into a wide grin and he laughed loudly.

"Why are you laughing?" Maddie demanded.

"America be this whole place and Cajun people speak French. I never hear of an Ambassador man. The sun must have touched your head."

Maddie stared at him and again she trembled with fright. What was happening?

Maddie couldn't think of anything else to say. She clung to the side of the little boat as Black Henri rowed it across the choppy waters. For a moment she considered jumping overboard, but to where would she swim? The men—the privateers they had called themselves—were still on the island. And it was certainly too far to swim to the mainland. These waters were rotten cold even in summer and, truth be known, she wasn't that strong a swimmer in the first place. A mile tops—and certainly that would be in warmer water, water in which she didn't run the risk of cramping. Besides, she thought miserably, her ankle was beginning to swell.

Maddie watched Black Henri as he rowed. Somehow he seemed less menacing than the others, at least in the sense that he didn't leer at her. In fact, as he rowed, his dark eyes had a faraway look and somehow his seeming lack of interest in her gave her strength. Perhaps she couldn't escape these terrible men, whoever they were, but perhaps she could find out something that would help her.

"Where are you from?" Maddie suddenly asked.

He turned his dark eyes to her and smiled. Unlike the other crewmen, his teeth were large, pearly white, and when he smiled he looked almost friendly. "Martinique, Mademoiselle. *Parlez-vous Français?*"

Maddie shook her head. "Don't you speak English?"

"Oui," but I always hope to find someone who speaks French beside the captain."

"But he isn't French, is he?"

"No, *Mademoiselle*. Captain York is English, even though we sail under a Dutch Flag."

Maddie frowned and considered her next question. But she didn't have time to ask it. Black Henri brought the rowboat alongside the galleon.

"Ahoy!" he shouted loudly. A young boy and two older

men peered over the side. "Throw over the ladder for me, and lower the basket for the woman, here."

A flimsy rope ladder came tumbling down the side and then, a basket suspended from three ropes. Black Henri held it steady. "Climb in, or I shall truss you up and throw you in."

Maddie was sure that in spite of the fact he seemed less menacing than the others that he would do as he threatened. She climbed in. There simply was no choice. She closed her eyes, sucked in her breath and held on tight as she felt the basket being hoisted aboard. In a moment it landed on deck with a dull thud.

Maddie made no attempt to get out, and neither the young boy nor the two older men urged her to move. Black Henri climbed over the side, his cutlass held between his white teeth.

With no explanation whatsoever, he lifted her out of the basket, "Come, Will!" he ordered.

Once again Maddie was hoisted over his shoulder. "Put me down! I can walk!" she shouted even before she remembered her ankle. What a silly thing to say, she probably couldn't walk.

"Be still!" Black Henri replied.

Maddie ceased struggling. His grip was like iron. She tried to see where she being taken. If this ship was a replica of some sort, it was certainly the finest she had ever seen. Black Henri climbed a short outside staircase, rounded a part of the deck, and then stopped in front of a heavy oak door. He withdrew a key and opened it, carrying her inside. The boy, Will, who followed, waited outside.

Black Henri walked through a second door and still carrying her, took her to a wide bunk. There he tossed her down.

"What are you doing?"

He had grasped her wrists and seemed ready to tie her with a rope which hung loosely, at the moment, from a iron handle on the wall at the head of the bunk.

"I was ordered to tie you," he answered. "Don't worry. I'll tie you loosely so you can rest easy."

"I have to go to the bathroom!" Maddie protested.

"Ah, yes."

He dropped her wrists and yanked her to her feet. "In there," he pointed.

Maddie struggled to her feet and painfully limped, following his direction into a small room. There was a mirror, a metal basin, a pitcher of water, and in the corner, a wooden toilet seat with a bucket underneath.

"There's no lock on the door, *Mademoiselle*. And there is no place to run."

Maddie went to the bathroom and then poured a little water into the bowl. She splashed it on her face, washed her hands, and then patted dry with a cloth that was hanging nearby.

She paused for a moment to look in the mirror. Her hair was a tangle, her dress was torn. Any trace of makeup she had worn had been washed off in the rain. She struggled to pull up her dress a little more, then curiously, she peered out the porthole.

She froze as she stared out toward the mainland—yes, that was the mainland, there could be no question about it. That was the way the ship was facing. That was the direction this porthole in this cabin would be facing. And yet there was nothing! There were no buildings on shore! Not one!

But the buildings on shore had all been visible when she had motored to this island yesterday! Where were they? Where was she? Maddie shuddered, then feeling fear and bewilderment and a bit like she might faint, she turned, just as Black Henri opened the door.

"Do not waste my time, *Mademoiselle!*"

He pulled her back to the bed, threw her down and quickly tied first one wrist to a length of rope, then the other to another length of rope attached to a handle on the wall at the far side of the bunk. Then, just as quickly, he tied one ankle to one side of the bunk and one ankle to the other side. Maddie winced in pain.

He paused and looked at her swelling ankle, then without a word he untied that one side.

"There you are," he said grinning. "Ready and waiting for the captain's pleasure. It don't look like that leg can do no harm," he pointed to her swollen ankle.

Maddie wiggled. As promised he had tied her loosely enough to move about. She bit her lip, realizing the utter helplessness of her position.

"You don't look so comfortable," Black Henri grinned.

He went to a cupboard and returned with two big pillows. He pulled her up and stuffed the pillows beneath her head. "There," he said with satisfaction. "When Will comes to feed you, you can eat better."

With that, and without even turning back to look at her, he left, locking the door behind him.

Maddie struggled only a little. It was no use. The iron handles were clearly there for the very purpose of trussing a woman to the bed. This Captain York was going to come back—he was going to take her—and she, she was quite helpless to do anything. And when he was through with her? Would he give her to the others? She shuddered and closed her eyes. How had this happened and who were these men?

Again she opened her eyes and looked around the cabin. This simply could not be a game or a ruse of any sort. What had happened to the buildings on shore? And how could anyone build a replica of such a ship as this. The timber wasn't new—everything looked handmade, or close to it. Even the fine furniture in this cabin had a handmade antique look. The lamp was an oil lamp, and the toilet was primitive.

Maddie lay on the bed for what seemed a long time. Her ankle throbbed and her head hurt. Then she heard the lock on the door being turned, and looked fearfully toward the door. But it was not the immense Captain York who entered, it was the boy the Black man had called Will.

He carried a tray. "Ma'am?"

He was certainly no more than ten, Maddie decided. "Untie me, please."

He shook his head. "The captain said you were to be tied. I can't go against Captain York, ma'am."

He seemed so polite. And he was a nice looking boy. He had red hair, blue eyes, and freckles. He had an open face. "What's your name? I mean, what's your whole name?"

"Will, ma'am. Will McNab. I've brought you some dinner."

"I can't eat it if I'm tied."

"I'm to feed you. Black Henri gave me strict orders."

"And do you always do as you're ordered?"

Will nodded. "If you disobey orders you can be beaten or even made to walk the plank. Yes, ma'am I always follow orders. Anyway, Captain York is always good to me."

Maddie frowned. The boy's loyalty was obvious. She watched as he pulled a little table over near the bunk and then set the tray down on it. He sat down on the edge of the bunk.

"Does the captain have women brought here—ah, to his cabin often?"

Will shook his head and then grinned. "He doesn't have them brought at all. They usually come on their own. Ladies like Captain York."

Maddie wanted to ask why, sarcastically, but she knew the boy wouldn't understand. He seemed strangely naive about her position.

"Soup first," he said, lifting a big spoonful toward her mouth.

Maddie hadn't intended on having any till she smelled it, then she realized she was, in fact, quite hungry. She took the soup and Will smiled with satisfaction. He continued feeding her, one large spoonful at a time. When the soup was finished, he wiped her face and chin with a damp napkin that had been folded on the tray.

"I'll butter you some bread," he said.

Maddie watched as he buttered some bread and held it up for her to take. She bit off some and chewed it. She had a little more, then she shook her head.

"I've had enough," she said.

Will nodded. He held up a goblet, "You're to have this."

He lifted it to her lips and Maddie drank. It was wine, a fine dry wine and she felt it warm her chest. It also seemed to dull the throb of her ankle. Again Will held it up and again she drank, feeling slightly more relaxed with every mouthful.

When the goblet was empty, Will again wiped her face.

"Can you stay and talk awhile?" Maddie asked.

Will looked dubious, then he nodded cautiously. "Only for a very little while."

"Tell me what day it is," Maddie asked. "I was marooned on the island, I've lost track of time."

"Wednesday," Will replied.

"And the month?" Maddie pressed.

"Wednesday, August first, the year of our Lord, seventeen hundred and two."

Maddie's lips opened slightly in pure shock. Yet everything seemed so real she could say nothing. Was she so surprised? At first she had thought this was all part of the historic feast, part of the mystery weekend. But those thoughts soon fled to be replaced by unanswerable questions. Now the fear she had not allowed to surface seemed to come to full blossom. Was it somehow possible that she had traveled through time? That she was now in another century and truly among privateers—a genteel word for pirates.

She looked at Will steadily. "You wouldn't lie to me, would you?"

Will shook his head. "Captain York taught me never to lie—unless it was to save our lives."

Maddie nodded dumbly. But she couldn't let this boy know how terrified she was. She forced herself to ask more, to try to discover what she could. Perhaps a little knowledge would save her.

"Where are you from, Will?"

"London, ma'am. Me father sold me to a Captain Pike who almost killed me, but Captain York saved me. He made me his cabin boy, he did. He's been like a father to me, ma'am. I'm sure he won't hurt you."

Maddie thought of her short encounter with the captain. He hadn't seemed at all kind. Besides, if he were so kind, why was she tied to his bed?

"And what are you doing here?" she asked. "I mean here, off this island."

Will seemed to look a trifle afraid. "I can't say, ma'am."

"How long will we be here?"

"We set sail tonight, ma'am."

"For where?"

"You'll have to ask Captain York, ma'am." Will stood up and picked up the tray. "I have to go now. Black Henri will be expecting me."

Maddie nodded and watched as Will left, then she sunk back against the pillows allowing all her conflicting emotions to wash over her. *Could this all be true? Could such a thing happen?* She felt fearful as well as intrigued and curious, while at the same time she was acutely aware of the danger she was in. If this had truly happened to her, she thought with sheer panic, how would she survive? She didn't know how to survive in this century—she couldn't do anything useful. And what of men in this time period? There were no constraints on them as there were in her time. They could do as they wished with her. Maddie shuddered and clenched her fists and closed her eyes, praying, and wishing to be transported back to the familiar, to what she knew and understood.

"Please don't leave me here," she whispered. But it was no use. When she opened her eyes she was still very much there—tied to the bed of a stranger, and very much at his mercy.

Maddie thought and listened for a long while after the door closed behind young Will McNab. Then, feeling the wine take effect, she closed her eyes, surprised how comfortable she was leaning up against the feather pillows, even though she was bound hand and foot.

She slipped easily into a deep dreamless sleep and it was the feel of a hand on her throat that awakened her suddenly, so suddenly that she started and let out a half scream.

"Easy, wench. I'm not going to strangle you. I was just admiring your lovely long white throat."

Maddie stared up into the dark eyes of Ben York. He was sitting beside her on the bunk, looking down at her. "Of course I might strangle you, if you don't tell me the truth, woman. How did you get on that island? Who brought you, and who are you? I have important business. I cannot tolerate a spy."

"I'm not a spy," Maddie protested. "I don't even know you. I haven't the slightest idea why you were on the island . . ."

He stared hard at her, as if he were trying to see through her. As if he could read her mind. "I could have you taken top side and beaten till you tell the truth. And you've seen how hungry the crew is for a woman. It would be more than a little unpleasant for you, I assure you. Tell me who you are and how you got to that island and tell me now!"

Would he do such a thing? At this moment she felt he would. "My name is Maddie Emerson."

He looked at her skeptically, then again touched her throat, moving his hand up to her mouth. To her surprise he forced her mouth open with his hand and looked inside, "Good teeth," he said coldly. "It would be a waste to give you to the crew. I could sell you for a pretty penny as a slave to some rich man."

Maddie shuddered as he moved his hand from her mouth back to her throat. His fingers moved sensuously back and forth, first across her throat, then up to her ear which he circled slowly even though he never took his eyes off her cleavage. "Yes, a lovely piece of goods, you are." His voice was low and his finger moved slowly, slowly toward her cleavage, then across the top of her breasts. Maddie felt her face flush a hot red, and she shivered. He was hateful and she was tied up. But she couldn't help responding to his touch. It was taunting and his eyes seemed to burn through her, to command her.

"I'll ask you one more time before I cease being gentle, my girl. How did you get on that island?"

Maddie shivered. He could certainly do any or all of what he threatened. She had to keep her wits about her if she hoped to survive.

"I was at sea with my uncle. On my way to Boston. He was angered because . . ." she paused and then let the tears she had been holding in for so long fill her eyes. "Because I wouldn't willingly yield to him."

As she recalled, it was the plot of some old movie—she met his eyes and hoped she was convincing. His face seemed to soften only slightly.

"And where, pray tell, was this uncle sailing from?"

"Portsmith, England. He kidnapped me."

He leaned close to her face, his fingers on her throat again. "Now you wouldn't lie to me, would you?"

Maddie let out a real sob and shook her head.

He drew back. "You're an unexpected burden," he muttered. "Women always cause trouble. Always."

"I won't cause you any trouble."

He pressed his lips together. "No, you won't!" he said, firmly. "You'll do as you're told, you're my property now and I expect obedience!"

"I won't yield to you, either," she said, looking back at him through her tear-filled eyes.

"You will if I desire it, woman! But right now I have no desire to take you by force."

He leaned over and untied her arms, then he untied her foot.

"Can you stand up?"

Maddie struggled to her feet, but she could put no weight on her sprained ankle.

He pushed her back down on the bed, then drew the nearby stool closer. He sat down lifted her leg into his lap, examining her foot. "I'll have to bind it."

"I think I twisted it when I fell into the pit."

He didn't answer her, but went to a chest, returning with a long length of cloth. Again he lifted her leg, and this time he bound her ankle tightly. When he had finished he looked at her. "Now stand!" he commanded.

Again Maddie staggered to her feet. Her ankle felt better now and she realized she could lean on it ever so slightly.

"Your dress is a mess. Take it off."

"No! I just told you . . ."

He advanced on her and she looked up. He was a huge man. His hands grasped the side of her torn gown firmly and he tore it off in one sudden movement. It came down, torn bodice and all.

Maddie stood before him naked to the waist. Her hands flew to cover her breasts and she knew her faced was flushed. She felt as if her skin were burning under his steady gaze. He did not make the slightest attempt to hide his thoughts.

Though his eyes devoured her, he did not reach out to touch her. "I suppose you might be worth a little trouble when you're tamed."

Maddie stared back at him defiantly.

Then surprising her, he turned away and strode to the closet. From it he withdrew a dress. "The bathroom is in there. Wash yourself and put this on. And, my girl, try to develop some sense. Had I intended forcing myself on you, I would have taken you when you were tied up."

With that, he turned and left her. Maddie heard him lock the door and she sat down on the side of the bed. He seemed cruel, yet not as cruel as the others. And though to her he seemed brutal, he had handled her sprained ankle gently. What manner of man was this?

Did he own her? Were there no laws to protect women?
She closed her eyes and clenched her fists and whispered,
"Oh, please let this be a terrible nightmare! Let me return to
my own time! Please . . ."

Maddie opened tear-filled eyes. She was exactly where she
had been and it all still seemed frighteningly real. Dejectedly,
she grasped the dress and went to the bathroom.

Maddie stood in the tiny bathroom once again. But this
time she poured a goodly amount of water in the basin and
washed herself thoroughly.

The gown he had given her appeared to be a nightgown. It
was floor length, white, and made of soft cotton. It was a
simple nightdress in the empire fashion and its low neck left
as much revealed as had her tattered gown. Not that it mattered. He had disrobed her already and she knew she was at
his mercy.

She found a brush on the shelf and brushed out her long
dark hair and then returned to the cabin. She went to the porthole and once again looked out toward the shore. All was in
darkness. The populated South Shore of Nova Scotia which
she had left yesterday had seemingly ceased to exist. It was
no more. In its place was a beautifully rugged coast; a virgin
wilderness.

Maddie went to the bunk and sat down on the edge of it.
It was all inexplicable. But somehow, someway, she had been
cast back across the centuries. She had to believe it was all
real. This man, this, Captain York, was different from any
man she had ever encountered before. She shrugged, knowing
she could not predict what he might do. He had disrobed her,
but he also seemed to have some code of honor. He was
strange . . .

Just as she had once again conjured him up in her mind,
she heard the door latch and she looked up just as the door
swung open.

Ben York paused in the doorway, his eyes once again studying her.

"I see you've readied yourself to sleep."

Maddie drew the blanket around her. "Yes, I'm quite tired."

"You shall be well-rested when this voyage is over."

He had stepped into the room, and now bent over, lighting the oil lamp. "Do not use this lamp if the seas are rough," he cautioned.

"Are we sailing tonight?"

"No, Lady. At dawn's first light. I'll have young Will bring you some supper."

"Where are you going?"

He half grinned. "To that first room. I've strung a hammock there. Why had you rather I warm your bed?"

Maddie shook her head.

He walked over and stood in front of her, then he reached out and pulled her off the bed and to her feet as the covers fell to the floor.

"No!" she said, even as he pulled her into his arms.

"You're a pretty wench. I can see why your uncle wanted you. Are you really a lady?"

He was holding her close and she could feel him pressing against her through the thin material of the nightgown.

"You're black Irish, aren't you lass? I've always fancied that thick black hair and those green eyes."

He was looking down into her face and she turned trying to avoid his eyes. But she couldn't look away. She was as a moth to the flame, drawn to him. But just as she couldn't keep her eyes from locking with his, she also couldn't find her voice.

He held her fast round the waist with one hand, then with the other he touched her neck, stroking it gently. "Lovely white skin, yes, you're a beauty."

"Please don't hurt me—please leave me alone," Maddie said softly. For the moment her temper had fled. The realization of where she was—the fear of this man and his unsavory crew—made her realize that for the moment it might be wise to be prudent, at least until she knew more about this Captain York.

His eyes softened ever so slightly, but he held her no less tightly. Then he bent and kissed her lips. It was a hard, passionate kiss—a kiss she responded to in spite of herself. But as his hands began to move across her back, she summoned herself and pushed him away. "Please . . ." she said, "I don't . . ."

He smiled at her. "You don't want me to take you—I'm afraid I don't quite believe that, my girl. I think you want it very much indeed."

His eyes were twinkling now and Maddie stiffened as she found her anger once again. "You're arrogant!"

He pushed her back down onto the bunk and stood looking at her, hands on his hips. "I'll have you if I wish, but now I have better things to do."

He turned suddenly and left as quickly as he had come, latching the door from the outside, locking her once again in her prison.

It was half an hour before young Will appeared with dinner.

"I see I don't have to feed you now," he smiled.

"Thank you for doing so before," she said. "Can you stay?"

Will shook his head. "No, Lady. But the Captain says I'm to bring a quill and paper in the morning and some sewing so you won't get bored."

"Where are we going?" Maddie asked.

Will shrugged. "Perhaps to Havanna, perhaps to Curaçao— maybe we'll stop in New York first, or even Boston."

"It sounds like a long journey. Will you come and talk with me?"

"If I can."

With that, he tipped his cap and left, locking the door behind him.

Maddie looked at her food. There was bread, fish, and some kind of greens. Perhaps, she thought, dandelion greens. In any case, she felt too hungry to care. She sat down again on the edge of the bed and patted it with her hand. It was not uncomfortable.

Ben York passed through the outer cabin, then out onto deck. The two rooms that made up his quarters were one flight of stairs above the main deck and underneath the pilot house. He went to the rail and leaned over, staring absently at the sea he loved so much.

Then, in frustration, he kicked the rail. He had terrified the woman in an attempt to find the truth. But if she were a spy, she could jeopardize everything! His own crew didn't even know where they were. But if another vessel had followed him—if she had been put ashore on purpose—no, he was certain she would have confessed. There was no denying her fear. Was her story believable? He wasn't certain. But what troubled him most was her manner of speech. She did not sound English and although she spoke English, she did not sound like anyone he knew. Where was she from?

Questions about her filled his thoughts and so, alas, did guilt. He knew he had been very hard on her in search of a confession, but she stuck to her story. Furthermore, her reaction to his pulling down her dress and humiliating her, was clearly not the reaction of a loose woman. When he had seen her in that dress he had assumed she was a harlot, but she had certainly not reacted like one. Moreover, however odd her speech, it was somehow refined, as if she were educated, as if she were a lady.

Was he rationalizing because she was so very beautiful? Did he believe her story because it was believable or because he wanted to believe it? Her lips had been delectable, and he had felt her return his kiss even though she had pulled away from him.

"An enigma," he whispered, even as he vowed to be careful with her till he found out more.

Chapter Three

It was the general stuffiness inside the cabin which finally awakened Maddie. Restlessly, she kicked off her covers, then she sat up, rubbing her eyes.

The bright sun shined through the window but since it was not open to let the sea breeze in, it was airless inside.

She sat absolutely still for a long moment till she determined the fact that they were certainly underway. At anchor there had been a gentle sway, but now the galleon cut through the water moving the ship up and down. Maddie went to the window. This cabin was not below deck so surely there was no reason why it could not be opened. She studied it for a moment, then moved the handle and released the catch. The window opened and she pulled it up, inhaling deeply of the fresh salt air that suddenly filled the cabin, relieving the heat and sweeping away the stale air.

For a moment she closed her eyes and tried to imagine how this vessel must look, cutting through the water at full sail. Then it occurred to her that this was the first time she had ever been on such a vessel when it was sailing. She had been aboard one in Halifax, but it was at anchor at the dock adjacent to the Hotel. And that vessel had been a replica of a sailing ship. But this was no replica! This was a full sailed galleon—a pirate galleon! A little chill of excitement surged through her, in spite of her lingering fear.

At that moment there was a tap on the door. "Are you awake?" Will's voice asked.

"Yes, come in," Maddie called out.

Will came bearing his usual tray. This time there was some sort of gruel and bread.

"Can you stay and talk?" she asked.

"I'm sorry I have no time now, ma'am, but Captain York says I can come this afternoon and talk with you."

Maddie smiled, "Tell Captain York I want to see him."

Will tipped his cap and was off. As usual, he dropped the bolt into the slot.

Maddie noted that it was well over an hour before Captain York deigned to appear.

He seemed a trifle irritable and he was certainly in a hurry.

"I've little time today. What do you want?"

"I want to be let out! I want to go outside and breathe some fresh air. I can't stay in here for the whole voyage—wherever it is we're headed."

His brow furrowed, "I could allow you into the outer cabin."

"No. I want fresh air. I want to go outside. We're under sail, where can I run to?"

"That's not what concerns me, woman. You saw my crew yesterday. You should know full well what a gang of pent up men desire. They desire you, and given the opportunity you would be raped by them."

"But I want to go outside—just for a little while."

He sucked in his breath and nodded. "You must promise to stay in the area just outside this door and on this deck. I can allow you out for an hour or so in the afternoon. It's sheltered and I'll issue orders that it's off-limits to all crew. But remember, the rest of the ship is off-limits to you."

Maddie smiled. "I'll remember." Then she looked down at her nightgown and fingered it self-consciously. "I have nothing to wear," she reminded him.

"In the outer cabin there's a closet with women's clothing. I imagine some will fit your fine figure."

"I assume that means you make a habit of kidnapping women."

He laughed at her. "I did not kidnap you, lass. I rescued you. I've never had to kidnap a woman, but true enough, I've enjoyed the company of many women—some of whom have left their clothes behind."

"How fortunate for me," Maddie replied, aware of the edge of sarcasm in her voice.

"How fortunate indeed," he answered with equal sarcasm. "I've no time for this repartee, woman," he said as he whirled around and in one step was through the door.

Maddie watched and listened as he closed the heavy door behind him. The bolt was left undone and in moments she was in the outer cabin, examining the dresses left by the unknown woman or women to whom he had referred.

All of them looked expensive. One was green taffeta with an ecru lace bodice and lace trimmed sleeves. One was blue with a daring filmy bodice, another was brown taffeta and appeared to be more prim and proper, perhaps it was for afternoon, she pondered. The last was also green, but it was silk and its skirt hung in soft folds rather than being extended by paniers or stiff petticoats held out by whale bone. All of them had daringly low necklines and were most certainly designed to emphasize the bosom. She sighed, resigning herself to the fact that it was the style of the day and there was really nothing she could do about it.

She further explored the closet and found a box of lacy undergarments packed in rose petals. Finally she selected the green silk dress. Taking it, she returned to the smaller of the two rooms of what she now assumed was the Captain's suite. She put on fresh undergarments, adorned the green silk dress, and brushed out her hair, scooping it up and tying it with a ribbon she had found among the undergarments.

Her rich wavy black hair fell down her back, but wisps escaped to caress her bare shoulders and frame her face.

When she was finally dressed, Maddie opened the door of the outer cabin ever so slightly and looked out. No one was about and the whiff of fresh air was tantalizing. She stepped out into the afternoon sun and looked about, taking in her amazing surroundings.

Above her the sky was a cloudless blue. Below, the sea was also blue, but white caps gave contrast in spite of the fact that the water was relatively calm. In the distance, she could just make out the shoreline.

But it was the ship itself that amazed her. She had seen it when she boarded, though then it had been at anchor. It had a peaked prow, a high square forecastle that rose behind the bow, and the four masts carried both square and fore-and-aft sails. Below she had noted tiers of guns broadside. The rails and the brass trim were highly polished, but the deck was worn and weather-beaten.

It had looked like a beautiful ship at anchor and she had thought it was beautiful then, in spite of her fear and the way she had been treated. Still now, under full sail, it was more than beautiful. It was absolutely breathtaking.

She moved carefully a bit closer to the edge of this elevated portion of the deck. Clearly, the captain's rooms and the pilot house were all that were on this raised portion. The crew's quarters were no doubt below.

Maddie leaned back, craning her neck to take in everything. In spite of her predicament, she felt adventurous. She lifted her head, seeking the highest mast. From it, a flag fluttered in the breeze. It was a Dutch flag, not a skull and crossbones. So, she thought, this Captain York was not a pirate, but in truth was a privateer. A privateer flying under the Dutch flag as Will had said. Not that there was so much difference. A privateer was really—as far as she knew—a kind of pirate who was licensed to steal by some country. And the victims, as she recalled, were usually the vessels of nations unfriendly to the nation which had licensed the privateer. Which was to say that French privateers preyed on British ships, while British privateers attacked French vessels.

Maddie frowned. It was 1702. Wasn't there some kind of war going on? Of course the eighteenth century was, in her foggy memory of history classes past, one long war with a few time-outs. The fighting was primarily between France and England and it involved all their colonies, and in America, various Indian tribes as well. She tried to remember what this war was called, although she knew full well that various people called the wars of this century by various names. Was it the War of The Spanish Succession? Yes, but in America it was called something else. What she needed was a little more information to jar her memory. And then it came to her, Queen Anne's War. That was it!

Again she glanced upward at the flag of the Netherlands and wondered where they stood in time. She frowned, trying to remember tidbits of information. When did New York become a British colony instead of a Dutch colony?

"And are you enjoying the air?"

Maddie turned around. Captain York had rounded the elevated portion of the deck and stood only a few feet from her, his dark eyes examining her.

"I hoped you'd choose that dress," he said, taking a step toward her.

Maddie didn't move. In fact, to her surprise she discovered she felt quite unsteady.

Another wide step and he was right next to her, looking down at her, commanding her to look back into his dark eyes.

"The color is good for you," he said, touching the sleeve of her dress slightly, then allowing his finger to move slowly across her bare shoulder.

Her lips parted to protest, but he stopped, lifting his hand while still looking deeply into her eyes.

"Your eyes are like the sea, lass. Green with circles of gold around your pupils. A man could lose himself in those eyes."

Maddie stared back into his eyes and her skin felt flushed and hot. She took hold of her long silk skirts and lifted them. She whirled around and fled back into the cabin, her heart beating wildly.

What's wrong with me? she asked herself again and again. She turned around cautiously, afraid he had followed. But he had not. *Why do I react that way to him?* She stomped her foot in anger at herself. His voice was—almost hypnotizing. His eyes demanded her attention, his strength seemed to embrace her. "Oh, damn," she whispered. It was imperative she not let him get the upper hand in any emotional sense. She didn't know enough—she hadn't the foggiest idea how to behave in this century.

Ben York lifted the telescope to his eye and slowly scanned the horizon. To the east and south only empty ocean revealed itself. Across the vast distance, a slight fog and overcast skies caused the sea and the sky to blend together. It was nearly impossible to tell where one started and the other stopped.

He moved slowly around, pointing his looking glass westward, toward the jagged rocky coastline. Before this day was finished, they would round the Southern Horn of Nova Scotia and enter a bay well-known for its high tides. By this time tomorrow, they would be headed south along the Atlantic Coast. The bay of high tides was as weird a place as a man could want to see. When the tide was out, whole vast areas became instant mud flats, their bottom exposed and any vessels grounded. But then, when the tide flowed in, it came to heights he personally knew equalled nearly seventy feet. It flooded the flats, refloated vessels, and was once again reclaimed by the sea.

He knew this area and its strange characteristics from experience. Once he'd sailed the *Wilma* into a seemingly deep river and anchored at nightfall. By morning, the *Wilma* was mired in mud, aground in what seemed a helpless quagmire.

Then, with a frighteningly sudden quality, the tide began to rise, and within the hour, his ship was once again afloat. His men had thought it a miracle such as those recounted in Biblical tales, but he knew better. He knew there was something special about this great bay that separated the huge peninsula called Nova Scotia, from the mainland.

He put down his looking glass and consulted his maps. Almost one hundred years ago exactly, the great French explorer and map maker Samuel de Champlain had charted these waters for the first time.

He smiled to himself. Although he sailed under a Dutch flag, he himself was English, one of the few English captains who dared sail these predominantly French controlled waters.

On occasion the English and the French had been allies, but more often they fought. Well, ill feeling or not, the French devils deserved their due, most especially Champlain, in Ben's opinion. No one had much improved on the French maps of this area. Champlain was a genius, and Ben admitted to himself that he owed that particular Frenchman a lot. Indeed, by a quirk of fate, his family owed Champlain a lot.

Most English seamen were unaware of Samuel de Champlain's diaries and charts. That was partly due to the simmering animosity between the English and French, and partly due to the fact that many Englishmen did not read French.

Not that his own discovery of Champlain's documents had come about as the result of research. No, the fact that he knew the waters off Nova Scotia, had sailed in and out of the many hidden bays, and visited hundreds of small islands unknown to many, was due to a strange personal—though second hand—contact he had with the great French explorer who had died some thirty-seven years before he himself had been born.

His parents had left him nothing much in the way of material goods, but their legacy had, nonetheless, proved valuable. Fate, Ben contemplated, worked in mysterious ways.

In the year 1629 when Charles I ruled a troubled England,

Samuel de Champlain had arrived as an unwilling visitor to London. He had been taken prisoner by the Kirke brothers when Quebec was seized by the English. But when The Kirkes arrived in Portsmith with their prisoner, they discovered the war between France and England had been over for nearly six months.

Champlain thus found himself a free man in London. He had immediately realized the seizure of Quebec was illegal under the terms of the peace treaty. As he was free, he remained in England to try to petition for the return of his property.

Clearly those months in England were lonely for the French explorer. He befriended a young boy—a poverty stricken street urchin, an orphan boy who followed him for days, asking for coins.

Champlain did not give the boy coins, rather he hired the lad to show him around London. Champlain soon discovered the boy had a quick mind, and he set about to teach the lad French. By the time Champlain left England in January of 1630, the boy, Richard York, and the French explorer, artist, and map maker, Samuel de Champlain, had become close. So close that Champlain took young Richard back to France with him.

Young Richard York sailed with Champlain when he returned to New France, and when Champlain settled down in Quebec, York shipped on as a crewman, sailing on French vessels, under a French flag. He made many a voyage to the new world, and he explored the northern coast with the French.

When Champlain died, Richard York obtained a copy of Champlain's diary and a sheath of his maps of the coastline of North America. He cherished them and learned from them. But the French with whom he sailed did not trust his English origins so advancement in the ranks, in spite of his knowledge, was denied. When he was twenty, in the year 1640, five years after his friend and mentor, Samuel de Champlain, died, Richard York returned to England.

His talents were recognized almost immediately and by the time he was thirty he was well-known for his navigational ability. Ben knew there were women galore in his father's life, but it was not until his father was fifty-two that he met Deirdre, the beautiful young Irish girl to whom he gave his aging heart. Theirs, his father had revealed tearfully, was a passionate, but tragically short love affair.

Ben did not remember his mother. She died in childbirth when his younger brother, Rob, was born in 1674. His father, almost driven mad by her death, took both boys to sea. His father lived and sailed for another fifteen years. During that time, he taught his sons everything he knew, and he passed on his precious copy of Samuel de Champlain's diary and maps. It was his only legacy to his young sons.

Ben pressed his lips together and stared at his maps. He'd been at sea all of his life. When he was just twenty-five, because of his navigational skills and knowledge of the coastline of North America, he had been able to arrange for a syndicate of London investors to buy him this ship, which he had rechristened, the *Wilma*. Three voyages to North America had netted a fortune in furs, the investors were soon paid off, and the *Wilma* was his alone. That was five years ago, and now he had a privateer's license, a fine home in Curaçao, and a woman in every port.

He conjured up the images of women in Boston, New York, and Cuba—none were as stunning as the one now sleeping in his cabin. She was a beauty, an exotic raven haired lovely whose heart he fully intended to capture—as soon as he was certain she was not a spy. She seemed unique, self-possessed and wonderfully proud. Yes, she was a challenge and he liked challenges.

Maddie sat at Ben York's desk. It was next to the window in the outer cabin and it had the best light in the room. Before her was a book she had found on the shelf. It was one of about forty volumes that lined a shelf behind the desk.

Most of the books she had opened had been filled with hand drawn charts and maps with commentaries. Surprisingly, there were several volumes of poetry including George Herbert, Robert Herrick, John Dryden, and the works of Milton. Novels as such, she lamented, had not yet begun to be written. So, in order to pass the time, she selected the plays of Shakespeare.

What was that silly question that was always being asked? If you were marooned on a desert island and could have one book, which book would you choose? The answer most gave, it seemed, was either the Bible or the Works of Shakespeare. Well, there was also a Bible so she supposed she was fortunate. She could alternate her reading to pass the long days between the Bible and Shakespeare. Today, she tackled Shakespeare.

Maddie looked up startled, as Captain York strode into the room. They had been at sea for three days now, and during the day he was usually on deck or in the pilot house. Only once before had he made an appearance during the day.

He stopped midway across the room and stared at her curiously. Then arching his dark brow, "What are doing, lass?"

"Reading," Maddie answered. "The days are long—I can't stare into space."

"Reading?"

He looked incredulous. "I noticed your books, I didn't think you'd mind."

"Mind? No, I don't mind," he managed. "Do you really read?" he asked, leaning over to peer at the open page.

"Of course I do." She had admitted it before she gave her own admission any thought. Now, she realized how unusual this must seem—if she knew one thing, it was that few women in this century were able to read. In fact, few men knew how to read.

He still looked disbelieving. "Read me what it says— here."

He pointed to the Epilogue of the Tempest and she knew that he didn't just own books. He too must read.

She stood up, holding the open book. "Now my charms are all o'erthrown, And what strength I have's mine own, Which is most faint: now 'tis true, I must be confined by you . . ."

"Stop! That's enough," he ordered.

Maddie stopped—it wasn't at all appropriate, but the last lines caught her eyes, "As you from crimes would pardon'd be, Let your indulgence set me free." She finished reading, and looked up into his eyes, letting Shakespeare speak for her.

"I told you that was enough."

He seemed unmoved by the literary reference she had read.

"You told me to read, I can't help it if you don't like the words."

"It's strange you can read. Reading is much reserved for women of station, breeding, and money. Even then it is rare."

Maddie was quite penniless and certainly she had no station. In this century she didn't even have a family. But she certainly wasn't ill brought up. She was a university graduate, well-educated and well-read. "Just because I was marooned doesn't mean I'm not well-bred or that I'm uneducated," she replied a bit haughtily.

He still looked puzzled and he rubbed his chin thoughtfully. Then he walked to the other side of his desk. She watched as he unlocked the drawer and withdrew a slim volume.

"John Donne, poet and painter," he said, smiling slightly. He opened the book, and again pointed with his finger, "Read this . . ."

"Thy virgin's girdle now untie, and in thy nuptial bed, love's altar, lie. A pleasing sacrifice; . . ." Maddie felt her face flush. "I'd rather not read this aloud," she said trying not to sound as flustered as the unexpected words made her feel. Did they write this way in the eighteenth century? Something in her education seemed lacking, though true enough, she had not been an English major and John Donne, though she had heard of him, had not been in her survey course.

Quite suddenly he reacted in a way she did not expect. He laughed. "Perhaps I was testing you—to see if what you first read was something memorized. A beauty like you—you could be an actress who knows all of Shakespeare from memory."

"I'm not."

"That remains to be seen. But certainly you can read, and let me say, I liked the words."

"I'm not terribly interested in what you like and or don't like," she replied, trying to sound distant.

"No matter. I have a job for you. Something to help you earn your keep since you won't warm my bed."

Again she felt the blood rush to her face. Damn this man. He was so—so earthy. "And just what might you have in mind," she said coldly.

"I want you to teach young Will to read. I've been trying, but I don't have the time. You have all day with nothing to occupy you."

"And what shall I teach him to read from? Shakespeare?"

"No, the Bible. I learned to read from the Bible. It is text enough."

"You keep him too busy. He can't even stop to talk to me most of the time. When will there be time to teach him?"

"Ah, that's because he was ordered not to stop and talk— but I'll make time for him to learn and you will teach him."

"I will be pleased to teach Will," Maddie said, "but not because you've ordered it. I'll teach him because it would please me to do so."

He pulled her close to him and again Maddie could feel him against her. Even through his clothing she could feel the heat of his body. He held her tightly and she couldn't escape him even if she struggled. He was only inches from her and she thought he would once again kiss her—but instead he shook his head.

"You try my patience, woman."

With that he released her. She started to say something but he didn't wait. He turned and abruptly left.

Maddie sank back into the chair as he closed the door. Every time she encountered him, he seemed to test her anew to see if she had changed her mind. She smiled ever so slightly and again opened the slim volume he had made her read from—"John Donne," she said aloud. He seemed quite the poet, and rather ahead of his time. A rough and ready captain—a buccaneer, a privateer who read erotic love poems—this Captain York was an odd combination, more of an enigma now than he had seemed before.

Ben York climbed the stairs to the pilot house. Black Henri gripped the wheel, his earring swinging with each roll of the *Wilma*.

"I thought you would be gone longer, Captain."

Ben grinned. "I might like to have been gone longer, but she's still distant."

"Are you satisfied she's not a spy?"

"I think so, though just who she is and where she came from is still a mystery to me."

"You think her quite beautiful, don't you, Captain?"

"Aye, she's beautiful. Don't you think so?"

Black Henri flashed his pearl white teeth. "For a white woman, Captain. But Black Henri fancies women with smooth cold black skin and dark soft nipples. She be good for you, Captain, but not for Black Henri."

"You miss Angela, don't you?"

"She hard to forget."

"We'll be making port in New York. You'll see her then."

Black Henri sought his Captain's eyes. "I want to make her my wife," he confided.

"You want to take her back to Curaçao?"

"Yes."

Ben York pressed his lips together. "Why not? She can help with the women."

"Is Missy Melissa coming aboard?"

"Yes, if I can find her? I suspect her stepmother watches her."

"Sarah Oort is a she-devil," Black Henri hissed, rolling his eyes. "She be bad luck."

"We'll be careful," Ben promised. "Here, I'll take the wheel now. You go below and get some rest."

"Some of the men are grumbling," Black Henri confided. "They covet the women."

Ben shook his head, "Women always cause trouble—but with this crew we'll have to be especially careful. We've some bad ones; I intend to leave them in New York."

"Good idea," Black Henri agreed as he turned to leave.

Ben watched him disappear down the steps and then emerge onto the lower deck. In a moment he had gone below. Black Henri was loyal and absolutely trustworthy. They'd been sailing together for some time now and he was closer to Black Henri than any other man aboard.

Then he turned his thoughts briefly to young Will. Will also had been with him for a while. He was a bright lad and Ben York intended to see him educated. Yes, young Will filled the same role in his life that his father had filled in Champlain's life. In some way, by helping Will, he felt he was repaying a debt. Like Will, Ben's own father had once been a street urchin. "You'll be an urchin no more," Ben said aloud. "You're going to learn to read, then maybe I'll be able to send you off to a good school."

Maddie lay in bed. The cabin was strangely lit from the bright moonlight that shone in the window. Her thoughts went back to the night she had become lost in the storm, and again she relived the whole experience in her thoughts, searching for clues. But no explanation for what had happened to her made any sense, save the absolutely unbelievable fact that she seemed to be in another century.

If it were true, what did those she had left behind think had happened to her? Were they searching for her? Or had she really died when she'd fallen in the pit?

Then, for the first time she thought of Chip. He'd probably gone home by now. In fact, by now he was probably with another woman. No, she didn't miss Chip because now she knew she would have left him anyway.

And her life—did she miss that? She had graduated from university three years ago and gone to work at the head office of *Multi Oils* in Boston. She was second in command in the department of Human Resources. She made a good salary and lived on her own in a small apartment. Would anyone miss her, she wondered? And then, on a more serious note, she wondered if she would miss anyone.

There were her parents, of course. She was an only child, and her parents had moved to a retirement community in Arizona shortly after she graduated. She usually visited them a few times a year, but they were independent, and she was off building a life of her own—or had been till this happened.

Maddie acknowledged the truth of her own loneliness. She had felt alone, even though she was financially independent and had lots of acquaintances. Her life, she admitted, had been adequate, but it lacked any excitement or challenge.

Would she suddenly be swept back to that life? And if she wasn't, how could she adjust to life in this century? *What do I know that could help me?* she asked herself over and over. It really seemed as if she ought to know something. True, she had an idea of what was happening in this world, but she had not studied history well enough to remember all the specifics.

On reflection, she knew she understood hygiene better than

most people in this time period and she certainly knew about all the many things that would be invented to improve life. But she didn't know enough about them to introduce them. And even if she did, she felt somehow that wouldn't be right—that it would in some important way, alter history.

At the same time, she realized that people in this time period knew far more about basic survival than she did. In childhood fantasies she had always supposed that someone who traveled from the future into the past would know more than those they encountered. But now, she realized this was not so. Almost all of what she knew—how to use her computer, how drive a car, even how to cook, depended on twentieth century technology. "Useless," she said to herself. And perhaps dangerous, too, she added silently. Her attitudes, her knowledge, so many things about her would make her stand out as different when compared to other women of this period. This had already been pointed out to her—she read. Few women seemed to read. It marked her as different and she reminded herself that she would have to be careful.

Maddie forced her eyes closed, reminding herself that regardless of what had happened to her or might happen to her, she still needed sleep. Tomorrow was another day, and unlike her twentieth century existence, every day in this time period was filled with challenges.

Ben York held the ship's wheel loosely and stared out over the black ocean. It was near midnight, near the end of his watch. At half past midnight, Black Henri would come and take over for him.

Ben turned at the tap on the door of the pilot house. He motioned young Will inside.

"I've brought your hot soup," Will announced. He carried a small metal pot with a cover on it.

"You're a good lad," Ben said, grinning. It was his habit to have a bowl of hot soup at midnight. It tasted good, and put him in the mood to sleep just about the time his watch was up at twelve-thirty.

Will put the pot down, then he slipped off his knapsack and withdrew a ladle and bowl. He ladled out a bowl of soup. "Here you be, Captain."

"Thank you. Come here, Will, take the wheel and hold her steady."

Will smiled and hurriedly slipped behind the wheel, making sure his hands were just where Ben York's had been. This was his favorite moment of every day. It was the moment when his hero, Captain Ben York, allowed him to steer the vessel, to play captain. Ben sat down on the small bench, only inches from the wheel. He began eating his soup with gusto. "You're doing fine, lad. Just fine," he praised.

Will fairly glowed, but he maintained a serious attitude.

"One day, my boy, you're going to make a fine captain. You'll have your own ship, too. I'm going to train you to use the maps and charts I use."

Will did not turn his head toward the captain, although he wanted to. "But sir, to follow maps and charts, to pass the tests necessary, I would have to be able to read."

"And read you shall."

"But you're so busy, sir . . ."

"Ah, Will, I'm not to be your teacher, lad! Fate has brought us both a present."

"There is no one else who reads," Will reminded him.

"Aye, there is. The woman, Maddie Emerson, she reads and she says she can teach you to read."

"Mistress Emerson? Captain, I never heard tell of any woman who could read."

"Admittedly, they're rare. But she does read and she reads well and to earn her keep, she'll teach you to read as well. You, and when the time comes, Mistress Melissa, too."

"Does she know she will have two pupils?"

"Not yet. I'll tell her about Mistress Melissa later. And I trust you to keep a secret, Will."

"Yes, Captain. Does that mean we'll be going to New York?"

"It does indeed. But for the time being, let's keep that a secret too."

Will nodded. He felt proud when Captain York trusted him and made him a confidant. "I hope I can learn to read," Will said, after a long moment.

"I'm quite sure you can. All I ask is that you try hard and do as Mistress Emerson tells you."

"I shall, Captain. I promise."

"And another thing, Will . . ."

"Yes, Captain."

"It's been a long while since we made port. Some of the men—some of those I hope to leave in New York—are restless. You know who we can trust, don't you?"

"Yes, sir."

"Good. But keep your eyes and ears open. Tell me if you hear anything suspicious, anything you think I should know."

"Yes, sir," Will said. He truly felt as if he would burst with pride. Captain York let him sail the *Wilma*, had arranged for him to learn to read, and had made him a special confidant.

"You know, sir, I have already heard one thing."

"And what might that be?"

"Some of the men—Digby and Riffen, well they covet the woman. They say it is wrong that you don't share her. I don't know what they want, but I think they mean to harm her."

Ben pressed his lips together. He had finished his soup now and was ready to take back the wheel. He put his arm around Will and gave the boy an affectionate hug. "Don't worry, Will. We won't let anyone hurt her."

"Yes, sir. I won't worry, sir."

Ben rubbed his chin thoughtfully, "Digby and Riffen," he said repeating their names. "Yes, they always were troublemakers. When the time comes, we'll leave them in New York for certain."

"Shall I wait for you, Captain?"

"No, Will. Get along to bed. Tomorrow will be a long day."

Chapter Four

Maddie looked at the coastline of what she knew to be Maine with a combination of distress and wonderment. Her distress grew as more and more she began to accept her reality. Even though she had considered it all at length just a few nights ago, this morning she had awoken with doubts, doubts which were soon dispersed as she stared out toward the mainland. Looking at the deserted shore of Maine she knew it was all real. The coastline of Nova Scotia had been deserted too—but it was rugged and less populated in any case. But this was an area she knew, an area she had visited many times. There were hotels, resorts, all manner of homes both permanent and summer cottages on the Maine coastline she had known, indeed had so recently driven. But now there was nothing. Nothing but dense woods, the sea, and deserted islands. There was something else, too. Wildlife was abundant, and today it was visible because they traveled close to shore. In fact, they seemed to be moving up a river. In the distance, deer could be seen now and again. Yesterday, she had watched whales—a vast number had passed the vessel on the starboard side. She had been utterly fascinated as the giants passed by, fascinated and frightened since by modern standards this privateer's vessel was reasonably small.

There seemed to be no question that it was the year 1702 and that she was captive on a pirate vessel. Someway, somehow, and for some reason, she had journeyed back over the centuries.

Almost from the beginning, the practical side of her personality had accepted what her eyes had seen even though she had then considered it a dream or illusion. Day by day their manner of travel, their clothes, and the food they ate further convinced her of the truth that she was indeed in another time period. The feeling that it was a dream or an illusion had disappeared, now she only wondered now and again if she would be taken back.

There was something else. She admitted now to feeling adventurous. In a sense she was enjoying herself, feeling free of all the shackles that had, in the past, bound her—a strange feeling for a person being held prisoner.

"I see you're enjoying the air."

Captain York rounded the deck having come down from the pilot house.

"It's very pleasant," Maddie returned. "Why are we traveling so close to shore?"

"Because we're anchoring off *Ile Sainte-Croix*. Fish are plentiful in these waters, and the island has fresh water. In any case, it is safe from Indian attack."

They must have turned inland from Pasamaquoddy Bay, Maddie thought. They were in fact where she had assumed they were, though it looked very different from the last time she had been here. This was the river that separated Maine from New Brunswick.

"Are the Indians a danger?" She should have known the answer, but she didn't know about these particular Indians so it was an honest question.

"Sometimes. In any case one always looks for three things—security, shelter, and food supplies."

'You seem to know the coast well," Maddie commented.

"Samuel de Champlain, the French explorer, first found this place. He charted these waters."

"Didn't Cabot sail here too?"

"Cabato? The Italian—yes. But he was no map maker. Champlain was a map maker and the keeper of a detailed journal too."

"You seem to know a lot about him."

"I'm an admirer, but that's another story."

Maddie felt he didn't want to talk about himself much and at the same time, she felt curious. It seemed unusual that an Englishman would be such an admirer of a French explorer and navigator, especially as France and England were so often at war. In any case, in order to know about Champlain's journal, would he not have to read French? She had been surprised enough to discover he read English and that in some ways he seemed quite cultured.

"Do you read French?" she asked.

"Yes, but as I told you, that is a story for another time."

Maddie waited a moment before changing the subject. "How long will we be at anchor?"

"Ah, lass, you're growing curious. And I might add, civil. Perhaps while you are teaching Will to read, he is teaching you your manners and your place."

Maddie looked back at him coldly. Why was it that just as they seemed to be carrying on a reasonable conversation, he had to remind her she was his prisoner. It angered her.

"It's almost time for Will's lesson," she said. This time she would be the one who cut the conversation short.

She went back inside the cabin aware that she felt a growing sense of frustration. She was his prisoner in the real sense, but she was his prisoner in another way as well. She didn't understand this world. Even if he were to set her free, she didn't have any way to survive. She simply didn't possess the skills to survive in this society—save one. Unfortunately, the one eighteenth century skill she did possess was not a skill practiced by women. In fact, she had decided not to reveal it, lest it get her into some sort of trouble.

She sat down and waited for Will. Captain York had unearthed an invaluable tool. A slate and some chalk. She wrote words out, one at a time, and she was teaching Will to sound them out. She had simply started with his name. Now she had him write different consonants in front of the "ill." He sounded out bill, dill, fill, gill, hill, kill, mill, nil, pill, quill, sill, and till. Today she intended teaching him the sound of *st* so that sill could become *still*. He seemed to learn quickly, and he perused the twenty-third psalm looking for words he could sound out. She had begun by reading it over and over to him, pointing to each word.

Maddie looked up at the sound of Will knocking on the door. "Come in," she called out. It was the third day of her lessons and each day he stayed for well over two hours. It was an enjoyable two hours for her.

"Here, sit down and let's begin by reviewing."

"Yes, ma'am."

Maddie wrote words and Will responded. He only faltered once.

"You're doing very well, Will."

"Thank you ma'am. Captain York says reading is the most important thing there is. He says you can be anything if you can read."

Maddie smiled. At least the Captain had respect for education even if he was a male chauvinist. But then, she supposed all eighteenth century men were male chauvinists. He probably couldn't be different and she didn't know if she could change her own attitudes enough to get by in a world where women were very much regarded as chattels.

On the other hand, there did seem to be a difference between the way men treated "ladies," as opposed to women in general. Money, as usual, seemed to buy respect if not respectability.

"He's right, education is very important."

"Oh, Captain York is always right."

Maddie smiled. Will's admiration for Captain York was quite obvious. "Where exactly did you meet Captain York?" she asked.

"In London. I was in an orphan asylum—a terrible place ma'am. We had to work fourteen, sometimes fifteen hours a day and the beatings were something awful. One day I ran away. I hid on the bottom of a carriage and rode right out of London holding on for dear life. I was seven then. I ended up in the countryside somewhere. I walked and walked. I stole some eggs and then I walked some more. Somehow, I ended up in Portsmith. I got caught stealing a potato pie from a street seller. The constable was about to take me off to the goal, and I was screaming and kicking in spite of being so terribly hungry. Then suddenly the Captain was there. He paid for the pie and told the constable he'd be responsible for me. He fed me good, and we've been together ever since."

Maddie looked into Will's face. The poor child! He was no more than ten now. What a terrible life! She thought for a moment of Captain York. Perhaps she misjudged him. Somewhere, at least as far as this boy was concerned, he seemed to have a heart. But with her, he had yet to reveal that soft human side. He was curt, always busy being in charge. "Is he always good to you? Does he beat you?"

Will shook his head vigorously. "No ma'am. He buys me clothes, feeds me, takes care of me, and he's good to me."

Maddie smiled. "As well he should be," she said. "Well, we'd better get back to our studies, or he'll be mad at me."

Will grinned back at her. "I think he likes you, ma'am. Sometimes he just acts mad."

"Why does he do that?" Maddie asked.

"There's rough men in the crew, ma'am. The Captain has to be strong to be in charge."

"I see," Maddie said softly. Maybe Will was right, maybe Captain York was not so terrible. But on the other hand, she had to consider the source. Will worshipped the Captain. He would always take the Captain's side.

It was nearly twilight when the vessel made anchor off *Ile Sainte-Croix*. From her vantage point on the deck, Maddie could see the shore of the island. She could also hear the men shouting as the heavy anchor was lowered. Above the din, Captain York's voice was loud, clear, and understandable. This was the first time she realized that the others did not all speak English. The crew, it seemed, spoke a potpourri of languages—Dutch, Spanish, Portuguese, with English or broken English being predominant. The crew was multinational and clearly many were multilingual.

No sooner had his orders to the crew ceased, when Captain York climbed the short flight of stairs to the quarter deck where his quarters were located, and where she was allowed to stand, just outside in the tiny area of deck between the flight of stairs leading to the main deck and the flight leading to the pilot house. He stopped short and looked at her. "Put on that green gown. I'll be back in an hour."

Maddie had no time for a reply. He scooted down the gangplank to the lower deck. Put on this—put on that. Who did he think he was? She whirled about and headed inside again. She flounced down into the chair. Should she do as he had told her? For a few moments she thought about how to respond. Then, although she still felt rebellious about being ordered to do anything, she decided there was no reason not to put on the green dress. And perhaps, she reasoned, if she tried to control her own rebellious feelings, they might at least have some sort of conversation.

The hour passed quickly. She was still in the inner cabin when she thought she heard him in the outer cabin.

She opened the door a little bit and peeked through. It wasn't Captain York. It was Black Henri and he was covering a small round table with a white damask cloth. She watched, fascinated as he set it with silver candlesticks and silver flatware. Then he filled a slim silver vase with wild roses and placed a bottle of wine on the table.

For a long moment the big black man stared at his handiwork, then he hurried away. Maddie slipped out of the inner cabin into the room. She walked to the table and examined it.

The silver service was astonishingly beautiful! It was heavy Spanish silver and each piece marked with the initial, "Y."

At that moment the door opened and Captain York stepped in. He looked quite a different man than he usually looked. He wore fresh clean skin tight breeches, a red velvet coat trimmed in gold braid, and a crisp white shirt. His dark hair was combed and he smiled bequildingly at her.

"Ah, I see for once you've done my bidding."

"There was no reason not to," she replied crisply.

"I had planned a little surprise, but our quarters are too small for that, and there is no other place than this for us to supper in privacy. So, to make up for the lack of a change of scene, I had flowers picked ashore and I've found a good wine."

He moved to the back of one of the chairs that Black Henri had placed by the table. "Please, sit down. I've decided we should dine together tonight."

"Is there something special . . ."

"My birthday and I have no one with whom to share it. In any case, the ship is at rest so a good meal is possible. Fresh fish has already been caught and I've had the ship's cook prepare us a special dish."

Moody and commanding one minute, a suave gentleman the next, Captain York was full of surprises.

He opened the bottle of wine and poured some into each of their glasses.

Maddie looked at him for a long moment in silence. He perplexed her—yet at this moment she felt deeply attracted to him. "I would toast your birthday if I knew your first name."

He smiled, a sort of appealing half smile, a boyish smile. "Ben—Ben York."

"To your birthday, Captain Ben York." She lifted her glass and smiled back at him.

"Women do not usually offer toasts. It is not the proper thing to do."

Maddie laughed. "There is no one else to offer a toast."

"True."

"May I ask you age?"

"Thirty."

"I thought you must be around thirty."

"And you, lass?"

"Twenty-four," Maddie answered.

"Twenty-four? You're a beautiful woman, how is it you're not wed? Or, are you?"

"Oh, no. No, I'm not married." He must think I'm an old maid, she thought silently and knowing full well that women in this time period married young. She hesitated, trying to think of some reason she might give him for her single state.

"I was studying at . . ." Maddie swallowed her words. "With tutors," she finished.

He looked at her disbelievingly. "You know, lass, your story has all the holes of a sieve. You say you sailed from Portsmith with your uncle—yet you speak not at all like someone from England. Indeed, you speak in an accent I've never heard before. You say your uncle put you ashore, yet almost no English vessel ever sails those waters now. We'd been at anchor for several days and seen no ship—yet when we found you, you were not dying of thirst nor of hunger."

Maddie wanted to avoid his commanding eyes, but she couldn't. "If you didn't believe my story, why did you bring me aboard."

"It would have been a waste to have left you or let the crew harm you."

"Is that the only reason?"

"No, lass. I'm a civilized man. Besides, I find you attractive. Puzzling, but beautiful. True, I did consider the idea you might be a spy, but that too seems unrealistic considering how and where you were found."

"I'm glad you did bring me aboard."

"Well, make no mistake, lass, a woman aboard is a bother. Especially a lying woman."

Maddie looked into his eyes. For the first time since they'd set sail, she felt she might cry. She felt suddenly over-whelmed with everything that had happened and was happening. "My truth is harder to believe than my lies," she said softly.

"Try me."

Maddie could hardly say the words. She had only just come to believe them herself. "I'm a time traveler, I don't know how I got on the island myself, so I can't tell you."

He looked at her steadily, unblinkingly and she looked back at him.

"I almost believe you . . ."

"It's the truth."

"Well, truth or not, I can believe you don't know how you got there. On that point you seem honest. Perhaps you've lost your memory."

"I do remember, and at first I didn't believe what happened to me myself. I thought I was in some dream."

"I suppose that could account for the manner of your speech—not that I'm saying I believe you. Tell me, lass, what's your given name?"

"My name is Maddie."

"Maddie," he said her name slowly. "This is a strange name. What does it mean?"

"It's short for Madelaine."

"Ah, well, Maddie, whether I believe you or not is irrelevant to your situation. You were on the island and you are learned enough to know where the island is—I'm sure you know full well what we were doing there or will figure it out in due course of time. That means that you will stay with me. You will become part of my entourage. And I urge you to keep your tongue in check and forget all you know about the island. I urge this for your own safety."

Maddie nodded. What difference did it make if she did have to stay with him? She had no husband, nowhere to go—and hadn't she always been fascinated with stories of pirates? But that was only one aspect of the situation. The other was her relationship with this man. What did he intend? He said he was attracted to her and so it seemed clear he wanted a liaison. But she knew she was far from ready—she knew she was far too confused about all that had transpired.

"A time traveler," he said, stroking his chin thoughtfully. "I must say it would account for a lot—your manner of speech, the fact that you seem learned."

"But you don't believe me."

"No, but your tales should be entertaining. Perhaps like Scheherazade you can weave me an entertainment for each of a thousand and one nights. From whence in the future do you come?"

"1995," Maddie answered. "And I'm not English, but American."

"American? I do not understand."

"There will be a revolution in 1774 and the American colonies will free themselves from England."

"And what of the French in this land?"

"They'll be defeated in 1764. Quebec will fall to the British forces of General Wolfe." Maddie felt wildly proud she had remembered so much. But still, she hoped he did not test her too carefully.

"Ah, lass, this is a tale! And entertaining too. Tell me exactly where you come from—tell me about this life you claim to have lived in the distant future."

Maddie let out her breath. She couldn't blame him for not believing her and for the moment it really didn't matter. She found it a relief to tell the truth, to stop trying to pretend to be what she was not. "Women in my time are equal to men," she said. "I went to university . . ."

"To university? With men? Tell me, lass, was it Cambridge or Oxford? Or perhaps your parents shipped you to Spain to go to Salmanca or . . ."

"It was the University of California in Los Angeles."

"Ah, it was a Spanish University. Not that such a place exists."

"Not now, but it will. And it is not a Spanish University. California was taken over by the Americans—it's one of the fifty states."

His face clouded over. "Your fancy is not without intriguing detail." He sipped some of his wine. "Wait here, I'll be right back."

With that, he left Maddie sitting at the table. She, too, took some wine, surprised at how good it tasted.

In a moment Ben returned carrying a large rolled up parchment. Behind him one of the ship's crew followed carrying a large tray laden with food.

"We'll eat first," Ben said as the man set down plates. "Then, lass, I will know more of your story."

"If we're to wait till after dinner, then tell me about yourself," Maddie asked.

"There's little to tell."

"Tell me why you helped young Will?"

A solemn, faraway look filled Ben York's eyes. "Because my father was once such a lad, and, lass, I owe much to my father."

"Where is your father now?"

"Long dead, but not forgotten."

"And your mother?"

"I hardly knew her. She died in childbirth."

Maddie looked down, "I'm sorry."

"Not mine," he clarified. "My brother's birth."

"And where is your brother?"

"Yes, you are curious. He's in Curaçao minding our business interests."

"I've never been to Curaçao. Is that where we're headed?"

Ben finished his meal. "Aye, eventually."

Maddie finished, too. "It was very good."

Ben stood up and began to clear the table of dishes. Then he unrolled the scroll of parchment. "And now," he said, "you will show me some of the changes you say will occur."

Maddie looked at his map in fascination. It was at once

more detailed than she had thought such a map would be, and yet also somewhat inaccurate. The continent was too small in the middle. Of course, no one had yet crossed it east to west so they didn't know how large it really was. Mexico was the most detailed area and Canada was the least detailed.

"Now, you show me what this America is to become."

"All of this part is to become the United States. In addition there will be two other states—one made up of islands in the Pacific known as the Hawaiian Islands, and the other of Alaska—this area." She moved her hand across the parchment.

"And the rest?"

"This will be the border of Mexico and this, more or less, the border with what will become Canada."

"And is this Canada independent of Britain and France?"

"Yes, but for many years it will be known as British North America."

"And when does all this happen?"

"The American Revolution in 1776—the defeat of Mexico and the acquisition of Texas and California in the mid-1800's. Total constitutional independence for Canada not until 1982."

He continued to hold the edge of the parchment, then he slowly looked up into her eyes. "You weave an intriguing and inventive tale, lass. One which is hard to ignore."

"Do you believe me now?"

He half smiled, "Not entirely, but you're very entertaining and clearly learned. But I'll hold my judgment a while longer."

"I understand. I didn't really expect you to believe me."

"I think I'd like to believe you—I'll ask more later, and I'll think on your tale."

He turned to the wine and poured some more into their glasses which he had put on a shelf. "Here, lass. We have to finish the bottle. Uncorked wine does not long keep."

"It turns to vinegar."

"As I said, you are learned."

"You seem interested in maps. I mean more interested than just the normal interest of a sea captain."

"I'm a minor cartographer. Of your predictions, yes, geography is the most interesting to me."

"If you leave me paper and a quill, I'll try to draw you a map as it was in my time."

"I will see that such are brought to you tomorrow."

He poured the last of the wine. "I must go now and make my rounds."

Maddie finished her wine. "Happy birthday," she whispered.

"Thank you. And a word of warning, lass, I advise you against confiding your tale of the future to others—I especially advise you do not tell others you're a time traveler. I may not believe, but I am tolerant and do not believe you to be mad. Others might not be so charitable."

Maddie nodded. "I shall tell no one else."

He smiled, then bent and kissed her. It was a long probing kiss and, as before, she could not fight him. Perhaps it was the wine, perhaps it was her confession. Her lips yielded to his and she felt limp in his arms. When he let her go, he looked into her face.

"A good gift for my birthday," he whispered. "With promises of more to come."

Maddie leaned over the rail and stared into the sea green ocean and the foam that met the side of the vessel as she glided through the water, her sails fully unfurled to the blue sky above.

Maddie daydreamed about last night's dinner and about Ben York. He had not tried to go further than a kiss and somehow she felt he respected her more now that she had told him the truth. And if he did not believe her, at least he didn't entirely reject her story either. Unconsciously she ran her tongue around her lips—remembering once again his long passionate kiss. Had she wanted him to go further? She shivered slightly as she remembered how it felt to be held in his strong arms.

"I'm ready for my lesson," Will said as he appeared at the top of the steps that led to the deck below.

Maddie had been so deep in thought, she had jumped slightly. Then, recovering, she smiled warmly. "It's good to be back at sea. It's cooler."

Will nodded in agreement then added, "We'll be at sea for a while now, depending on the winds."

"I've never been to Curaçao."

"It's beautiful. But when we get there, the Captain says I will have to study all the time."

Maddie laughed gently. "He only wants the best for you."

"I know," Will said, shuffling his foot.

"Will we stop before we get to Curaçao?"

"We'll dock in New York. The Captain has business there. He told me I could tell you now."

"New York!" Maddie raised her brows in surprise. She had not thought about the possibility that they might stop in New York. She had supposed that because he was a privateer they would be staying clear of places such as New York or Boston. "Is it safe to stop in New York—I mean the Captain is a privateer."

Will laughed. "Aye, ma'am. Quite safe. Even though the English have taken over, much of the city administration is still Dutch and we sail under a Dutch license and Dutch flag. Besides, Captain York was a great friend to Captain Kidd. Captain Kidd was much loved by many in New York town."

"Was?" Maddie asked.

"Aye, he was hung for turning pirate. They said he stole from his own—the British who had licensed him a privateer. But Captain York says that's a lie. He said the charges against Captain Kidd were all made up."

How limited my knowledge of real pirates is, she thought. True, she'd always been fascinated with pirate stories, but the stories she had read seemed to bear little resemblance to the realities of history. "Why was Captain Kidd popular in New York?" she asked.

"He donated the block and tackle to build Trinity Church, ma'am. He is much honored for his generosity."

Maddie knew that Trinity was one of the oldest churches in New York. But she certainly had not known of Kidd's role in building it. "It's you who are teaching me, today." She took Will's arm. "Best we get to studying."

Will grinned. "I'd rather talk about Captain Kidd."

"We will talk some more," she promised. "But after today's lesson."

Maddie awoke early the next morning. She washed, dressed, and brushed out her hair. She went outside and stretched in the morning sunshine. It was breathtaking outside, warm, sunny, and with an almost cloudless blue sky overhead. She looked about. Most certainly Ben was in the pilot house by now. She walked to the edge of the small area of deck outside the Captain's quarters where she slept, and looked over the side. Below on the main deck she could see only one crew member about. He was coiling rope and didn't even seem to notice her.

If she could just go down the stairs and walk to the bow, she thought, she could see the unfurled sails much better. Surely the best view of the ship was from the bow. She longed to see this vessel at sail, she yearned to walk free beyond the area outside Ben's cabin, an area no more than eight feet by twelve feet. Perhaps he wouldn't mind. She and Ben York were getting along better now. Most certainly he would not object to her taking just this one liberty, to see just this once how truly beautiful the ship looked under full sail.

Carefully, Maddie lifted her gown. How cumbersome these wretched eighteenth century clothes were! How much more comfortable she would be in jeans and tennis shoes or even in the tight breeches worn by the men and a loose tunic. Anything would be better than these absurd gowns. She felt certain that this one weighed a ton.

This morning she had put on the red gown. Not that its low neck and lacy trim were unattractive, nor was the color unflattering. In fact, her dark hair enabled her to wear red though she knew green was her better color because it picked up the green of her eyes. But she tired of wearing the same colors—blue and green each day. Yes, this morning she had decided it was time for a change even if the red dress did seem too dressy.

She reached the bottom of the stairs looked once again at the man coiling rope, and moved silently across the deck toward the bow of the ship.

"Hey lads! What have we here! A swan sailing our deck in broad daylight!"

"Is that the Captain's whore come to give us comfort?" another shouted.

Maddie froze and whirled around. She had just reached the bow and stood back to the rail that circled the deck. The men moved in a group. Apparently, they had been behind or to the side of the quarter deck from which she had descended. They had been out of her vision as she looked out from above and out of her vision as she came down the stairs.

"Keep away from me!" Maddie shouted as the men advanced. There were five in all.

"What a tasty morsel. Look at that dress. She's prettier than a sea siren."

"Prettier than the day we found her. She should have been ours then."

The man who spoke was short, fat, and dirty. He had dark narrow eyes and a ragged unkempt beard. Was this the man who had found her? She wasn't certain, but she was sure he was dangerous. "Don't touch me. I'll tell Captain York."

"I'll tell Captain York," he muttered, mimicking her. Then

he burst into evil laughter. "It's not fair of the Captain to keep you to himself!"

"We've been too long deprived!"

The one with the beard advanced on her. He reached out and grabbed her wrist, yanking her toward him and into his arms. "She puts me to mind of a wench I had in Jamaica. Taken off a Spanish vessel, she was—and as pretty and as nice smelling as a flower. We had her for days—she was a real pleasure."

"And where is she now?" one of the other's asked.

"Still in Jamaica, in one of the whore houses—but it's a long way to Jamaica and this one's here."

Maddie screamed as he seized the top of her dress and roughly tore it, exposing the curve of her breast.

"Let's see her! Let's tie her down and toss to see who'll be the first to lay her!"

Maddie kicked her assailant as hard as she could. "Get away from me!" Mentally she again cursed her clothing for prohibiting her kick to have a full-blown effect.

"Leave her alone! She's a lady! She's the Captain's lady!"

It was Will. He fought his way through the crowd of men who surrounded her. They had grown in number. "Get Captain York!" she shouted. "Run, Will, run!"

Will spun around and avoiding the grasping hands of one of the men, he headed for the steps that led to the upper part of the deck.

One of the men pulled a knife out of his belt and threw it. Maddie's scream pierced the air as Will, struck by the flying, well-aimed knife, fell to the deck with a cry.

"You've killed him!" Maddie shrieked. She again kicked her assailant and doubled her fists to hit him. Not aimlessly, but as she had been taught in self-defense class. She hit him in the center of his throat, and raised her knee to kick him again, hard in the groin. Again, she cursed her gown.

The bearded man doubled over in pain. "I'll teach you, wench," he muttered darkly.

"With what!" one of his cohorts roared. They all seemed to reach for her at once, but Maddie still fought. She could feel their grimy hands on her, tearing her clothes—trying to subdue her. But she kicked and hit and screamed, resisting with all her strength.

Then there was a series of shots. One of her assailants fell to the deck, another grasped his arm. Those who surrounded her parted and she saw Black Henri and Ben York, pistols drawn.

"Pick up the boy!" Ben ordered, as he pointed at one of the sullen crew members.

"And don't try anything funny or you're a dead man!"

The others started to move in unison, but Black Henri fired again. His fire was accurate, deadly. Another of the crew fell.

"There'll be hell to pay for this!" the bearded man muttered.

"Unhand the woman!" Ben ordered, then his own eyes narrowed in anger. "Get to my cabin, woman!"

Maddie lifted her tattered skirts and fled toward the stairs. She nearly tripped going up them. Ahead of her, a frightened crewman carried Will's limp form.

"Put him on the bed!" Maddie ordered as she summoned her last bit of strength.

Below, she heard other shots and shouting. Then, after a few minutes, there was nothing but silence. Silence and Will's labored breathing.

Maddie hurried to Will's side. His face was as white as the ship's sails against the blue sky. Blood covered his shirt and was beginning to soak through his leather vest. But he was alive and he looked up at her imploringly.

"You're not going to die," Maddie said firmly, although at this moment she herself did not know if that was true.

She moved swiftly to open his tunic and tear away his bloodied shirt. "Oh," she said as she looked at the wound. It was not in his chest as she had feared, but rather in his upper arm. Miserably she realized that he was bleeding more because the well-meaning crewman had pulled the knife out.

She turned to the crewman who had carried him. "Get me some boiling water immediately," she ordered. "And some alcohol."

"Only Captain York has alcohol," the young man told her. His expression was curious, rather as if he thought she wanted it to drink.

Maddie nodded. She had forgotten her time frame again. Naturally there was no rubbing alcohol, just the sort of alcohol you drank—probably rum, she thought, shaking her head. "Then just get the water, and hurry."

He scurried away and she returned to her examination of the wound. Yes, there was no question that it certainly would have been better if the blade had not been pulled out until pressure could be applied—but it had been pulled out and Will lost a lot of blood as a result.

Maddie put a pillow under his head, then she tore the sheet from the upper bunk into strips. She folded one, making a pad, then she put it on his arm and applied steady pressure, forcing the wound closed. It would, of course, require stitches to heal properly.

"It hurts," Will whispered.

"I know it hurts. Will, I'm going to have to stitch it up."

"You mean sew me?"

He looked terrified. Maddie nodded. "But we'll have to make you unconscious somehow—I promise I won't hurt you." Even as she said it, she wondered if this was a promise she could keep. Oh curse this time period! She wanted nothing more than to put Will out of his pain. But what was used? Indeed, was there anything that could be used?

It seemed like an eternity before the crewman reappeared with the steaming water. Maddie set the sterile water aside in order to allow it to cool. Then she handed over the strips of sheet. "Now take these and boil them. Boil them for ten minutes and then leave them in the bucket and bring it all back here."

The crewman looked perplexed, but he quickly left.

Maddie continued to apply pressure but she knew that when she stopped the deep wound would again begin bleeding. Her mind raced, what could she use as a pain killer?

Ben suddenly burst through the door. She didn't even have to turn about to see his face. She knew his expression still held anger. "How is he?"

Maddie looked up. Ben York glared back at her. But it was obvious that he was controlling himself because of Will.

"It's a deep wound. He needs to be stitched up. I've sent someone to sterilize bandages . . ."

"Do you know what you're doing?" he demanded impatiently.

"Yes! I need a needle and some thread. Most of all I need alcohol to sterilize the wound and I need something—something to render Will unconscious."

His eyes were still dark and smoldering with anger, but there was curiosity, too. He seemed about to ask a question when the crewman returned, carrying the steaming bucket of boiled sheet strips. "They've been boiled," he said unnecessarily. Then he saluted the Captain and backed out of the cabin.

"Why did you boil cloth? Why do you need alcohol?"

"To sterilize them, to make them clean. It prevents infection."

He frowned. "You speak in riddles."

"No. I speak the truth. There are bugs so small the human eye can't see them—they cause infection, gangrene . . ."

He still looked doubtful, but he shrugged and strode across the room to a cabinet. He took a chain from around his neck and on it was a key. He opened the cabinet and brought out a bottle of clear liquid. "Caribbean fire water. It's alcohol. It's the strongest I have."

"Just put it there on the table."

"I have a needle and thread—and opium."

"Opium . . ." Opium had not occurred to Maddie. "Do you know how much to give?"

"To induce dreams? Yes."

"He must only have it once. It's habit-forming."

"Yes, I know," Ben replied in irritation.

In a few seconds, Ben had prepared an opium pipe. He held Will's head up and induced him to inhale deeply.

Maddie watched as the pain disappeared from young Will's face and was replaced with a kind of drunken smile. Then his eyes closed as he drifted off into a deeper sleep.

"You'll have to help me," she told Ben York. "You apply pressure while I prepare things."

He replaced her holding the compress on the wound. Maddie threaded the needle and then passed it through the flame of the candle several times. She washed her own hands and wrung out and prepared the bandages. Then she turned back to Ben. "I'll sew as quickly as possible, you wipe away the excess blood as I sew."

He watched fascinated as she cleaned the wound with an alcohol soaked cloth and then soaked the thread in the alcohol. He removed the pad and she began stitching quickly, pulling the torn skin together and slipping each stitch to make it stronger. Blood oozed out and Ben patted it dry between each stitch. When the stitches were complete, Maddie wiped away the oozing blood with more alcohol and then tightly bandaged the wound with sterile damp cloths.

Then she wiped young Will's brow. "He's still asleep," she whispered.

Ben nodded and then turned to her. His eyes were cold, demanding. "I hold you responsible for this—I have to go now and make preparations to prevent a mutiny. No matter what happens, you stay by the boy's side, do you understand?"

Maddie looked into his eyes. His tone was menacing, deliberate. He was still furious and while his first concern did seem to be Will, he could not hide his anger. But what was he talking about? Hadn't the crew been calmed down? "A mutiny?" she questioned.

"Aye, we've shot one man and wounded another. Two more are in irons, but there'll be more trouble. If not tonight, then tomorrow there will be an attempt to take over this ship. You disobeyed my orders, you've threatened the lives of every loyal man on this ship and placed your own life in jeopardy. From this second on you do exactly as I say, my lady, or no matter who you are or where you came from, I'll have you in irons!"

He turned and stomped off, slamming the door to the outer cabin behind him. Maddie sunk into a chair and covered her face with her hands. Tears began to flow down her cheeks as fear, remorse, and weariness combined.

It is my fault that Will is hurt, she thought. *I should have listened. I should have realized this was no game.*

Chapter Five

Ben York moved swiftly. *Damn woman! Whoever she was and wherever she came from, she didn't have a drop of common sense.* There were crew members like Black Henri, Lopez de Vaca, Samuel Hammersmith, and Bob Tanner who could be trusted to obey orders and who would not molest a woman. But then there were others—those led by Riffen and Digby. In between were men who could be easily influenced and who, at this juncture, needed to go ashore and enjoy themselves. Briefly he thought of Riffen and Digby. They were troublemakers and he vowed to put them ashore in New York and take on two new crewmen to replace them. Men without such murdering lustful souls. Yes, that was a necessary move. Especially as when he left New York he would have two women aboard—that is if all went well.

But there was no time to think about the future. There was only the here and now, and the situation on the ship demanded he make the appropriate preparations or face the consequences—consequences which he had not exaggerated to Maddie.

Ben York rounded the upper deck. Beneath the steps that led up to the pilot house, there was a small heavy door. Again he accessed the key around his neck and thrusting it into the lock, opened the door and stepped into the semi-darkness. He quickly lit the lamp and closed the door. Inside, neatly arrayed along one wall, lined up and ready to use, were the ship's armory of guns. He selected eight special guns. They were flintlock rifles—but a special kind. They were a shoulder weapon, with a wide smooth bore flared at the muzzle to a maximum width of about four inches. The flaring scattered shot at close range. For the wide area of deck below the quarter deck, four blunderbusses would be sufficient for crowd control. Four men armed and on guard in shifts. That, he decided would keep the peace and discourage any schemes or attempted mutinies.

In a moment there was a knock on the door—one knock, a pause, and two rapid knocks.

Ben opened the door to Black Henri who slid in. He wiped his gleaming brow where the beads of sweat glistened like dew in the early morning. "There be much talk below deck," he said shaking his head.

In a moment there was another knock—the same kind. Again Ben opened the door. This time Lopez de Vaca and Samuel Hammersmith came in.

"And what do you hear?" Ben asked them.

"Palaver, palaver, palaver," Hammersmith muttered.

"Soon they'll be taking sides," Lopez said darkly.

Ben looked at Lopez. Most of the Spanish crewmen seemed happy-go-lucky, but Lopez was different. He was habitually downcast and pessimistic. His manner was as dour as a stranded sailor in Portsmith after thirty straight days of fog.

"Who else is coming?" Ben asked. He hoped he knew the answer.

Black Henri smiled. Even in the half light his white teeth glistened. "Bob Tanner, Runner Jim, Yan Ould, Juan Corso, and Jack Hacket."

Ben smiled. "Good. Four on, four off." As he said it, there was yet another knock. Ben admitted Juan Corso and Runner Jim. He handed out five of the eight rifles. "You men take up your positions now." He turned to Runner Jim. "You and the others will make up the second shift. There's a small cabin in front of mine. Those not on duty will sleep there. Food will be delivered along with water. Just in case, there is an ample supply of food and water stored aft—for just such emergencies."

"Will you be making an announcement?" Tanner asked.

"Aye," Ben answered. "I'll state the rules. Anyone who tries anything will face the blunderbuss. I'll have no mutiny on my ship. If there's trouble—if there's an attempt to rush the guns—fire. No hesitation! Understood?"

They all agreed.

"Then take positions now. I'll wait for the others and explain it to them."

They all left, and in moments the remaining three arrived. Ben armed them, went over the arrangements, and dismissed them. An ounce of prevention, he knew full well, was worth a pound of cure—especially if the disease was discontent that could lead to mutiny. He had his best men with him—but others would stand by him, as well. Those who did would sail on with him to Curaçao, those who did not could warm their bottoms on a bar stool in New York. Doubtless he could pick up needed crew in New York; if not, it was far better to sail with half a compliment of loyal men than a full compliment of men which included dangerous troublemakers.

Ben looked around the store room. He added some ammunition to his own bandoleer and further armed himself with a good pistol. Then he selected a small pistol. It was only fair to allow the woman to arm herself—just in case his worst fears materialized.

He strode from the room, turned once again, locked it securely, and then he headed for the rail that surrounded the quarter deck. There, with deliberation, he rang the great iron ship's bell three times to signal all hands on deck. Behind him, in the shadows of the overhang from the pilot house, stood his four loyal crew armed with their blunderbusses.

He smiled to himself as his full crew began to assemble on deck. The men behind him and the men below were a mixed breed. Among them were English, Dutch, Portuguese, Spanish, French, black men, and white men. Some of them were truly good men, some were truly bad—dangerous men. Most were in-between. It was to the latter he had to make his most eloquent appeal. It was they who would decide how this drama ended. He reminded himself to hold out the olive branch and to offer a future plumb in order to influence the largest number of men.

In moments, his total crew of forty-five was on deck, milling about. Ben studied the formation. Riffen had chosen a spot on the starboard side of the deck. There he stood surrounded by ten of his obvious supporters. On the aft side, Digby had taken up his position. He stood surrounded by seven men. In all, Ben York made the hard core out to be no more than nineteen men. But they had taken up positions on opposite sides of the deck in order to appear stronger and to make it seem as if there were more of them. He acknowledged it was a smart move and he reminded himself not to underestimate Riffen.

Ben picked up his horn. "I've heard talk of mutiny," he shouted.

"You've the woman!" one of Riffen's supporter's shouted.

"You're supposed to share the booty!" Another yelled.

Ben himself would not have treated the woman differently had she been a common prostitute, but the fact was that for most of his men there was a code. Common women were common property, ladies were to be treated differently—or somewhat differently.

"This is no common woman," he shouted back, "but a lady . . ." he was so angry with her at the moment he couldn't think of quite what to say in her defense; still, he had to sound right.

"So why was she out on deck?" another shouted. This time the question came from the other side of the deck.

"We ain't had no shore time in four months!" someone in the middle added loudly.

His comment was followed by a wave of low grumbles.

"She *is* a lady," Ben reiterated. "And I have good news, hear me out!"

"I say we don't need good news! I saw we need a Captain who knows how to share!" Digby shouted.

Riffen shook his fist in the air and added his agreement loudly.

"And I say any mutineer will be either dead or in irons!"

He gave a slight signal with his hand and the four men armed with the blunderbusses appeared. There was no man among the crew who did not know how effective these weapons were on the matter of crowd control. A sullen silence fell over the crew.

"We'll not sail straight to Curaçao, my men, we'll make port in New York. There will be an extra ration of rum for all loyal hands, a bonus of two sovereigns, and plenty of time ashore to love the ladies."

A cheer of approval rose from the middle of the crowd and all grumbling from those with Digby and Riffen was drowned out.

"Four days to port in New York, men. You can wait that long for the ladies!"

"Can they wait that long for us!" someone shouted back.

There was laughter and Ben breathed a sigh of relief. Not that it was over. He would have to keep the guard till they docked. Then, he vowed, it was goodbye to Riffen and Digby. Goodbye and good riddance.

After dismissing the crew, Ben retreated to the pilot house. There, he poured over his maps, made copious notes, and charted their course to New York. It was not an easy task. There were areas of high tides, and the entire coast was peppered with islands and hidden rocky shoals. If he sailed too far out into the Atlantic, he was more vulnerable to pirates and to privateers working for other nations. Then again, it was hurricane season and monster storms sometimes swirled out of the Caribbean and battered even the northern sea. On the other hand, if one sailed too close to shore, a sudden storm might cause a vessel such as his to be bashed against the rocks or be damaged by high winds, thus marooning them all on some hostile coastline or on a deserted island. Thus he took great care with his charts, planning for all manner of weather and for any other possibilities he could imagine. When he had finished, he was tired and headed for his cabin.

Maddie was reading when he entered, she looked up, as if she were surprised to see him.

"How's Will?"

Maddie could hear the control in Ben's voice. Perhaps his anger had dissipated, but it was not gone entirely. Nor could she blame him for still being angry. She was angry with herself.

"He's resting peacefully. I doubt the opium has worn off."

"I'm going to move him to the bed in the pilot house. It's more comfortable and lighter during the day."

Maddie nodded and watched as Ben went into the inner chamber and returned with the sleeping boy in his arms. He disappeared with him, but in a few minutes returned. "Now, my lady," he said giving her a hard look, "Your sleep will not be disturbed and you can have your bed back."

Maddie pulled herself up out of the chair and slammed her book shut. "I would have gladly slept on the floor next to Will, had it been necessary! How dare you be so self-righteous! I care about that boy, too!"

Her green eyes blazed at him and her lovely lower lip quivered with suppressed guilt.

But to Ben she still seemed too prideful, too self-centered, and far too cavalier. "As well you should! You and you alone are the cause of his pain. And you and you alone are responsible for the deaths of two men as well as the fact that I've had to post a round the clock guard to prevent a mutiny!"

"Those men are murderous! They tried to rape me!"

"And you asked for it! You were where you weren't supposed to be—prancing around the lower deck. Lady, you are not without your charms. I told you once and I tell you again, these men have not been with a woman for many months!"

"I did not ask for it! Men are always saying that! Men have been saying that for centuries! Well, I did not ask for 'it'!" She felt on the verge of tears she was so angry. "I wanted to see the sails unfurled from the bow! And that was all I wanted!"

She was standing now and her green eyes were looking directly into his. How she hated this time period when women were nothing but chattels. Her face was flushed with her own fury and she tossed her hair back, sending dark curls across her bare white shoulders.

"Bastards," she murmured. "I notice you have absolutely no concern for the fact that I was almost—almost . . ."

He took a step forward and enclosed her in his arms. His move was so sudden it caught her off-guard and she struggled against him.

Maddie continued to struggle but he found her lips and pressed hard on them. She was a fighter, a prize to be taken, and as angry as he was because she had endangered Will, he knew he wanted her.

It was a long kiss, a kiss to which she responded.

But then she ended it. "Let me go!" Maddie demanded. Her fists were doubled and she beat his chest. She smelled delicious; she smelled like wildflowers. He kissed her neck, her ears, then he kissed her lips again. She continued to struggle, but he paid her no mind as he moved his hands across her back sensuously and in turn, felt her begin to respond to him, unable to resist what they both clearly desired.

"You're no better than your men!" she murmured.

He drew her back and smiled. "I'm a lot better than most of them, lass. In any case you do want me, and all of your denials are turned to lies by your own reactions. I can feel the heat of your body and see the desire in your eyes. You're damp with desire, lass."

Maddie felt her face flush hot. "I'm no such thing!" she

blurted out. But before she even finished her thought, she was back in his arms, a victim of gentle prodding kisses and tenuous, erotic movements made by knowing hands and experienced fingers.

She barely felt her corset unlaced as he moved to free her swelling breasts. Undone, but not revealed, he carried her to bed, closing the door behind him. He lay her down gently and stripping quickly, he lay beside her, his hard manhood pressing against her thigh even while he kissed her again and again.

"Beneath your lacy petticoats is a treasure worthy of plunder," he whispered, as he dipped his warm hand beneath the gauze chemise of her dress to cup her breast.

Maddie moaned in sudden pleasure. His words, his movements aroused her in a way she could not suppress, did not want to suppress. She felt a passionate fury stronger than she had ever known. It filled her and every thought fled, save her physical response to his teasing touch. His thumb and forefingers gently rubbed her nipple. He moved from one breast to the other till her nipples were hard stones beneath her chemise.

She moaned again as he pushed the material aside and looked at her bare breasts.

"Like a white-breasted swan you are," he murmured as his lips fastened on the nipple his fingers had just caressed. Then his fingers returned to the other nipple and he nursed one and rubbed the other while Maddie squirmed with pleasure, arching her back, moving toward him, silently begging him to fill her.

He lifted his lips and again kissed her neck. "So filled with desire," he whispered before returning his mouth to the tip of her breast.

He pulled off her petticoat, and completely removed her chemise. She was naked next to him and she felt his slight growth of beard against her flesh. He rubbed her breast with his cheek, and this too produced a delightful sensation that caused her to move against him once again.

"Ah, Lady. You did protest too much. I shall make you writhe with anticipation. I shall make you scream out with desire."

His voice was low and deep and she shuddered in his arms because his movements, if they continued, would indeed make her call out.

Never had any man made her feel so—so taken!

Both hands held her breasts and she closed her eyes, giving in to the sensation of his fingers on her nipples even as he kissed her stomach. He slid down her body, still toying with her breasts even as she felt him, warm and darting in that place of her most intimate and treasured sensations.

He was as skilled with his tongue as with his fingers. Never had she felt so many sensations at once and she moved to reach him, to feel his fleeting movements more strongly. She was, as he had predicted, writhing in his arms as he brought her to fevered desire.

And then she did scream as she tumbled into the pit of passion, pulsating wildly with pleasure.

"Oh," she sighed. "Oh."

His gentle laughter caused her to open her eyes and look into his face.

"You're perfect," he said, again running his hand from her throat down her belly to her mount of venus. "Perfectly shaped and your skin is soft and pliable. And you, lass, are ready, willing, and able."

Maddie opened her mouth to speak, but he closed it with another kiss.

Then, again looking down at her, "I have not yet had my pleasure. But a woman can know pleasure many times. I like to watch you. I like to watch you shudder with pleasure."

Again she was about to speak. But he put his finger to her mouth. "Lie easy, lass. I'll play you like an instrument and you'll know a fulfillment I vow you've not known before.

I've sailed the China seas you know. I learned from the Chinese that a woman well-pleasured is a pleasure to her man. They have a book, lass. I'll teach you things you didn't know about yourself."

Again his voice in her ear was low, his words sensuous, and his movements matched his words. She felt unable to protest in any way, indeed at the moment she didn't want to protest or even move away from his body which pressed on hers, holding her prisoner to his whims.

He lifted himself off of her and went quickly to a chest in the corner. In a moment he returned and covered her with a length of black lace. "How lovely you look naked beneath it," he whispered. His eyes hungered for her and his hands moved over the lace, touching her through the thin material, but not touching her. Again, her nipples hardened, pressing against the lace.

He looked at her, and his look was as burning an arousal as his movements had been. She lay still, beneath her lace covering while he looked at the curves of her body and spoke softly to her about the feel of her skin and the beauty of her hair on her bare shoulders.

He sat on the edge of the bed and uncorked a bottle of wine. He poured some into a glass and sipped some, then he held the goblet to her lips and bade her drink. Maddie immediately felt the heady effects of the wine. It must have had a higher alcoholic content than modern wine, and in her present state, it seemed like a love potion. She felt almost fevered, but in the most pleasurable of ways.

"Touch me, lass," he whispered. "Touch me so you'll know me."

As if in a trance her hand closed around him and she shuddered in anticipation and in surprise at what she felt.

"Lie easy, lie still," he said. Maddie closed her eyes and she felt him remove a part of her lace covering and pour some of the red wine onto her flesh. Then his lips sucked the wine from her breasts while his leg lifted slightly to rub against her, causing her once again to feel an insurmountable passion rising from deep within her.

"Easy, lass," he whispered. "There is pleasure in waiting."

He had almost scooped her into his arms and he held her as he moved against her. She wiggled in his grasp. His hands, his mouth, even his strong muscular legs felt wonderful. He was everywhere . . .

Then she felt him part her legs. He hovered above her, kissing her nipples again, drawing them full into his mouth. Then he slipped into her, filling her with his hot throbbing member.

"Lie still, lass," he said again.

"I can't . . ." she breathed. Her back arched seeking him though he filled her, she quivered against him but he did not move, he remained still, taunting her with the pure heat of his body and the feeling of the joining.

Then, as he had predicted she would, she did cry out for him. He moved slowly at first, then more rapidly till she felt him lift her even as she felt the joyful relief of her own pleasure. He, too, shuddered against her. Then they were both panting, both bathed in perspiration. He was still joined to her when he turned over suddenly, taking her with him. Now it was she who looked down on him.

He took her breast into his mouth once again and nursed it even as his hands clasped her buttocks. She thought he would withdraw, she thought he'd roll over. But as his hands squeezed her buttocks and his lips and tongue toyed with her breasts, she felt him again grow strong.

He smiled at her. "Come, lass. You know what to do, don't you?" His eyes danced and she moved as he had moved on her. And as she moved, he continued to tease her breasts while one hand sought her center of pleasure once again.

Again, for a third time she cried out as they tumbled together in pulsating ecstasy, this time collapsing in weary delight.

Maddie lay on the bed, her hair wet from exertion, her

body still tingling from head to toe. He was, as promised, an extraordinary lover.

"I suppose now, lass, you will accuse me of rape."

"No," she answered. True she hadn't wanted it to happen, but it had and she could hardly deny she had enjoyed it—no, more than enjoyed it. She had known total gratification, complete pleasure—his lovemaking was erotic yet somehow playful—she knew she would want him again and again. She knew at this moment she might never be able to say no to this man.

"Not hard to see why my men wanted you."

She looked back at him, "Didn't you want me?"

He laughed. "Of course, lass. I'm a normal man! You've a body well worth taking. Now if your disposition improves, I may see my way clear to keeping you."

Maddie sat bolt up right. The lace with which he had covered her fell to her waist. "You're disgusting!" But the fact was, she knew she didn't sound appropriately angry or disgusted.

He roared with laughter. "Not what you thought a minute ago and not, I wager, what you would think a moment hence if I began again."

"You wouldn't—you couldn't."

He grinned at her. "Is that a challenge, lass?"

Maddie's lips parted but she couldn't find any words. No doubt he could do it a third time. She shook her head.

"Now get some sleep, lass. We're going to New York and your book learning will come in handy."

He disappeared for a moment and she heard him washing. Then he returned and stretched out next to her. "Get some sleep. I like starting my day with a woman."

Maddie lay on her back staring upward at the ceiling. He lay next to her and in a moment she heard him snoring lightly.

She couldn't even think how she should feel, she was so confused. Never in her whole life had a man made love to her that way. Never had she known such exquisite pleasure. Yet he was a pirate! Perhaps a murderer! What did she know about Ben York really—save what an admiring young boy had told her.

She forced her eyes closed. There was no place to run and she wasn't sure she would run if she could. If only he weren't so—so sure of himself.

Go to sleep, she told herself over and over. Finally, weariness overtook her and she fell into a deep dreamless sleep.

Beneath his strong hands, Ben York felt the fine, highly polished mahogany of the ship's wheel. He held it tightly, keeping the _Wilma_ steady on her course despite the brisk wind which had arisen out of the Southwest. "Steady, on course," he whispered to himself. Yes, in spite of a life of adventure, he had always kept "on course". His brother Rob had veered off course many times in his young life, but Ben had always been there, playing big brother, getting Rob out of trouble, setting him straight once again. "Rob takes chances," Ben said to himself knowing that he took a few chances—at least with his emotions. With his emotions, he played it safe, avoiding permanent involvements, avoiding complications . . .

He shook his head, trying to shake his thoughts. He looked around, checking his reality instead of checking his beloved charts—to his right, and made hazy by the lightest of coastal fog, lay the rocky coastline. To his left, the open sea stretched out four thousand or more miles toward the Spanish coast.

The thoughts he had tried to cast out came back; he could not be distracted by the distance to Europe or the rocky coastline of Maine. Rather, it was the woman who stood just outside his cabin, staring off into the distance who commanded his attention.

His most immediate thoughts were of the pleasure they had shared last night. She was intelligent, beautiful, passionate, and mysterious. Any one of those characteristics might have

attracted him, but all four made her irresistible—even dangerous, especially for a man dedicated to remaining on course.

For at least the tenth time, he warned himself to go slowly
with her and to maintain control of the situation. He was in
no position to let his fancy dominate him, especially now.
There was far too much at stake. He had plans, plans he simply had to carry out.

He returned to thinking about the woman's mysterious
qualities. She had told him she was a time traveler and she
had spun a detailed tale of the future, a tale his own imagination made easy to accept. Still, was she really a time traveler? Or did she have some strange dark past she was afraid
to reveal. To continue to involve himself with her would be
to take a chance, to veer off course, to possibly endanger Melissa or to cause him to fail to keep his sacred promise.

Unconsciously, Ben York looked down. He considered
himself to be a man whose feet were planted firmly on the
ground. Oh, he was a dreamer—sometimes even a schemer,
he thought with a smile. But he was also intensely practical.
He was a man who eschewed witchcraft and alchemy. He was
a man who didn't really believe in magic. Yet he could accept
the idea of time travel. Perhaps he could accept it because he
was a seaman. When he traveled west, he traveled into the
sun. When he traveled east, he traveled into the darkness.
And didn't the days vary in time with the seasons? Were they
not longer on the equator, and shorter in the northern climes?
If a man could travel faster wouldn't it be possible for him to
leave his present and enter his future—if a man could race
the sun and win—yes, it *was* possible.

No, the idea of time travel did not seem like witchcraft or
magic. What if one were somehow spun around many times,
caught in some sort of maelstrom or the like? If one was traveling west, one might be spun into the future. If one was
traveling east, one might be thrown into the past, he rationalized.

Was the woman below such a time traveler? More important, if she was, how could she help him with his present dilemma? He smiled to himself once again. In a few moments Black Henri would come to relieve him at the wheel. Then he would go below. Vaguely he wondered if he could restrain himself from seeking the pleasure he found in her soft perfectly-formed body long enough to talk with her, to ask her questions, to find out more of the future. But then, he wondered, would it be entirely practical to follow what she told him without real proof.

"Ah, Captain, you have the look of a well-satisfied cat."

Ben York looked up, surprised to see that Black Henri had opened the door to the pilot house so quietly he hadn't even noticed. Even young Will had not woken up. He still slept peacefully on his bed at the rear of the pilot house.

"Can't a man look bemused without assumptions being made?" he asked Black Henri with good humor.

"Aye, Captain, but there is a lady of some worth awaiting you and unless I misread expressions, she, too, has the look of satisfaction. Dare I say the look of a purring kitten."

Ben smiled and patted Black Henri on the shoulder. "Your insight is all too keen."

Black Henri laughed. "Not insight, but only nature taking its course."

Ben rubbed his stubbly face. He was growing a beard and it had gotten to the itchy stage. But he well knew that by the time they docked in New York town he would have a full-grown beard and would look quite different than the last time he had visited that fair city. "Nature runs a pleasurable course," he answered with a wink. There was no need to hold back the truth from Black Henri.

Black Henri grinned. "Have a good evening, Captain." He half saluted, and Ben returned the gesture. Then he turned and left the pilot house, making his way down the steep steps and onto the upper deck. Maddie had gone inside now. He imagined her waiting for him—nude beneath the sheets of his bed. Then he banished the thought quickly, reminding himself that he wanted to talk with her.

"You were on deck," he said as he came into his cabin. For a second he felt a bit disappointed that she was not waiting naked beneath the sheets, but was, instead, fully dressed and reading.

"Just for a few minutes. I hardly left the front of the cabin—I didn't walk anywhere."

"I know. I was watching you."

"It's difficult—staying in here all the time."

He sat down and took out his pipe. He went through the ritual of cleaning the bowl. "I know, but it won't be so much longer. Seven or eight days unless we hit a storm."

"I'll survive my boredom. How's Will?"

"He sat up most of the day and talked a blue stream. The boy is fond of you."

"Even though I almost got him killed?"

"He doesn't blame you."

"Only you blame me."

"I'm over it. As long as you do as you're told and keep out of trouble."

"I'm not used to being treated this way." The words escaped her mouth.

"What way?"

"The way you—everyone treats me. In my time women are not men's chattels. We're independent. We go where we wish, we're protected by laws."

"Ah, yes. *Your* time."

"I know you don't believe me."

"It is both an easy and a hard thing to believe. But I have been thinking about it, about how one might utilize whatever knowledge you have—both utilize and test it, if you like."

Maddie frowned. What was he getting at? "I don't understand."

"Well, lass. You are clearly educated and you claim to have been educated in your own time. This is the year 1702.

Surely you studied history at your university. What do you know of this time?"

"You put me to a test—a difficult test. The trouble is, I know general things but I hardly know anything of specifics, of everyday life. I know no more of this time than you know of life during the Renaissance. I mean *really* know."

He smiled. "I know that the artist Leonardo DaVinci could have been a time traveler. Many things he saw in his imagination have come to pass, and I belive many have yet to come."

"Flight," Maddie said. "He drew planes—he drew men flying. They will fly—they will travel the heavens the way you travel the sea, and outer space—the stars will be the place they want to conquer just as this generation wants to conquer and settle this continent."

"Fancy, intriguing tales, lass. But what do you know of this time?"

"There will be a war—it will be known in some places as Queen Anne's War and in others as the War of the Spanish Succession. But I don't know if it has begun yet. And if it has begun, news travels slowly so it may not be known to you. Besides, my memory is faulty—I cannot remember the exact dates—only that it begins in the first few years of this century."

He grinned. "This is no proof of foreknowledge. Predicting another war is like predicting the sunrise, lass. There is always another war, though to my knowledge we are at peace now."

Maddie did not look up. Her mind was wandering, searching—it was true she couldn't remember when the war started. She couldn't even remember who was on the throne of England. She hadn't majored in history. She was familiar with general things, but had not memorized monarchs and had always been bad with exact dates save the details of the American Revolution and the defeat of the French on the

Plains of Abraham. The latter she remembered only because she had visited there.

"Can you name all the wives of Henry the VIII?" she asked.

He shook his head. "A point well-made, lass. Tell me what you know of Captain Kidd."

"Only that he was a pirate. He was famous and in my time—well, in my time there is an entertainment called movies. Like a play, but preserved so that they can be shown again and again. There are lots of movies about Captain Kidd."

He raised his brow and grinned, "This is too fanciful for me. And Kidd wasn't really a pirate. He was a privateer like myself. He was accused of piracy and sent to the gallows by his political enemies."

"Political enemies?"

"He was commissioned by the Whigs, and when the Tories came to power he was persecuted pure and simple. He was sent off to the Caribbean to capture French vessels and pirates. When he returned home, he was accused of attacking friendly vessels."

"How do you know—I mean how do you know he didn't attack friendly vessels?"

"Because, lass, I was with him aboard the *Venture Galley* on that fateful voyage to Madagascar, and so were some members of my crew, Black Henri among them. Kidd was a fine captain, a man of honor. Do your movies portray him as such?"

"Some do, some don't. Most deal with his treasure."

"Really. Well, that's something we won't discuss, lass. Safer for you in any case."

Maddie held her silence. Did he think she was stupid? Surely it was Kidd's treasure that was buried on Oak Island. But she decided to say nothing now.

"Will told me Kidd was popular in New York."

"Yes, though I have suspicions about the current governor. He is a man I do not trust."

"Then why are we going there?"

"To test a theory and to get Kidd's daughter."

"Daughter? I didn't even know he was married."

Ben laughed. "Yes, lass. Kidd was quite married. In fact, he was married more than once. His daughter lives with her stepmother, Kidd's last wife, in New York. But she will come with us to Curaçao."

"And what of her stepmother?"

"Nay, lass. Sarah Oort wouldn't leave New York unless it was to marry rich or find Kidd's treasure. One she may do, the latter I vow she will never do. I promised Kidd—I promised him that Melissa would receive her fair share of the treasure."

"He didn't leave anything to his wife?"

"Not to Sarah Oort, no. And in time you will understand why."

"You mean I am to be allowed ashore?"

He grinned again, knowing by now that how he chose his words was important. He could set her mind at ease, or he could irritate her by teasing. "You'll be part of my entourage," he answered, knowing it was a comment that would light a fire.

"I might run away," she said staring him down.

Perhaps she had learned, or was learning to play his little game, he thought. Well, it would make her no less desirable. Still, he looked at her seriously, "Lass, if you really are a time traveler, it would be best for you to stay with me. If what you say is true, you have no home, no family, no money, and no way to support yourself save that of the world's oldest profession. Now I do not doubt you could garner a fine clientele, but I think that is not what you desire, so I suggest you accept my protection."

"As long as I find it convenient," she replied.

He drew her into his arms and while initially she seemed

stiff and resistant, it was only a few seconds before she was returning his kisses.

"You do verbal dueling, lass," he breathed into her ear.

"I speak my mind."

"And I mine." He kissed her neck and then her ears and then her lips. He stepped back, then pushed her dress down over her shoulders, far down so that the curve of her breasts was exposed. For a long moment he just looked at her, then he pushed the material still further down so that all but her nipples were revealed. "There is nothing more arousing than a beautiful woman half exposed," he said huskily.

She leaned against the wall, feeling as if at any moment she would slip into a faint. His eyes looked at her hungrily and the memory of yesterday flooded through her, readying her for him now, making her want him, ache for the pleasure she knew he could give. Whatever else she thought of him, she knew he was an extraordinary lover. In some ways she still wanted to say no, still wanted not to want him. But it had gone beyond that. She did want him, the memory of last night was not enough, not when his eyes toyed with her, not when she so clearly remembered his experienced, tantalizing movements. Last night she had discovered something new about herself, something that had been hidden before. He had aroused her and satisfied her as she had previously not known was possible. It was as if he knew secrets about her body she herself did not know—knew them and knew how to exploit that knowledge.

He was forceful, yet gentle. Their lovemaking was erotic, he knew all there was to know about prolonging her pleasure as well as his own.

He bent and kissed her cleavage, but did not yet move to fully expose her. She felt the warmth of his tongue between her breasts, then again on her neck, then on her lips.

He picked her up and carried her to bed. But this time he did not strip, nor did he strip her. He lifted her skirts and removed her undergarment, moving his hands across her over and over till she groaned with excitement.

He opened his own breeches and then exposed one breast entirely so that he might toy with her. As before, she found this incredibly erotic, it made her ache for him. When he moved inside her she shuddered. She could feel his body through her clothes, the heat of him atop her, the fullness of him in her.

Only a short time ago she had wished to be back in her own time. Now, with this man, she felt she never really wanted to see the twentieth century again—not if she had to leave him.

Again, he drew out her pleasure. Again he toyed and teased, kissed and caressed, aroused and abandoned her till she felt she would shriek with desire. Then he let her know satisfaction even as he himself reached fulfillment.

She lay in his arms, a bundle of crumpled taffeta and lace, warm and satisfied. At this moment, she thought there probably wasn't much she wouldn't do for Captain Ben York.

Chapter Six

Maddie fluffed up her pillows and propped herself up in bed. Ben was long since gone, having risen before the sun to relieve Black Henri in the pilot house. She thought he had gone sometime around four in the morning.

For a time after he left, she had been in a state somewhere between wakefulness and sleep, aware of the warm place where he had lain next to her. Then, feeling comfortable and satisfied, and having no reason to rise early, she once again fell into a deep sleep. Now she was fully awake and feeling contemplative.

No one could have a better lover than Ben York, she admitted as she toyed with the edge of the sheet and recalled last night's passionate encounters. When he held her, she knew she would do almost anything he asked. There was no question in her mind that the physical attraction between them was strong and mutual. But there seemed to be more—or at least the beginning of more.

But this is not a man of my time, she reminded herself once again. What if there was another woman in his life—not just other women, but *a* woman who meant something to him, *a* woman who was more than a temporary consort?

Not that a man of her time couldn't also have other women or be capable of emotional and physical duplicity. No, it wasn't that at all. It was simply that because this Ben York

was a man of his own time, she felt there were things about
him she might misunderstand, things she might overlook.
Historically, men of this century certainly had wives and mistresses. What if Ben York was married? And if she asked him
and he said he wasn't married, could she believe his answer?

Yes. At least she wanted to believe that she could believe
him, and again she reminded herself to try to be practical and
rational in spite of the irrational state in which she found herself. A strong physical attraction—perhaps love—was most
certainly not a rational state, she told herself. At this moment,
she knew her decision-making powers, as well as her judgment, were greatly impaired by physical infatuation. Yet Ben
York did seem honorable even if he also seemed volatile and
even if he considered women to be less than independent per-
sons.

"Am I really in love with him?" she murmured—or is what
I thought about a minute ago merely physical infatuation?
How could she tell the difference at this stage in their rela-
tionship?

"After all, this has all been very intense," she said aloud.
They had seen each other every day and every night since she
had been found on the island. There were hardly any others
she could talk to besides young Will and he was still in the
pilot house recovering. And the most important of all questions filled her thoughts now. What if she were to really, truly
fall in love? What if she were to fall in love and suddenly be
whisked back into her own time? What if this were some
elaborate dream or hallucination? "What if the world is flat?"
she said, annoyed with herself.

This was not a dream nor an hallucination. She was in the
year 1702, and she was aboard a ship captained by one Ben
York, a privateer. Perhaps when they got to New York it
would all become more real . . .

And he was a good lover—*no*—last night wasn't simply
the result of practiced lovemaking. It was pure ecstasy,

magic, passion—it was the result of mutual desire and she hoped, something deeper.

"Would I give him up to return to my own time?"

She posed the question again in the silence of the cabin, but even posing it caused a sudden wave of apprehension to flood over her. *No!* At this moment the answer—almost to her own surprise—was a resounding "no." No, at this moment she couldn't bear the thought of leaving Ben York.

Maddie climbed out of bed deciding not to consider the next logical question which was, what if something happens between us—what if I fall out of love?

"Too much introspection," she muttered as she pulled on her undergarments. I need a distraction. She wondered if Will was well enough to return to his studies. That would take her mind off Ben York and off her dilemma. Surely it wasn't right to fall in love with him—to let him fall in love with her unless they could remain together. Had he thought of that too? Probably not, she decided, because after all, he only half-believed she was, indeed, a time traveler.

Maddie stopped dressing and while still in her chemise and pantaloons began exercising. Each and every morning she had gone through the routine in order to keep in shape.

She stretched her long leg out to the brass rail that ran around the room. It was obviously there in case of a storm at sea, but it was ideal for her ballet stretching exercises.

She leaned forward and touched her toe, then she leaned backward as far as she could, with her left hand over her head. She performed this movement twenty times slowly, then she changed legs and performed it twenty more times.

Then she stood with her heels together and her hands above her head. She bent her knees and slowly went up and down. These were her ballet exercises, exercises she did every day of her life. Oh, how she had wanted to be a ballerina!

But it seemed that both time and nature combined to deny her girlish dream. Nature dictated her height, and she was a good deal taller than most women who became ballerinas.

Secondly, she was sent away to private school and while they offered ballet lessons, the lessons were quite ordinary. Had she been truly groomed for ballet, she would have had to take professional lessons every day of her life, and she would have had to have attended a special ballet school.

She was only twelve when she discovered she did not have the single-minded ambition to become a ballerina. She enjoyed practice, but not to the exclusion of everything else. There was just too much to learn, too much to see, too much to do.

But she did enjoy the exercises and when she was fourteen, she settled on a sport that combined ballet exercises with an excitement that dance lacked. That sport was fencing. She fenced one or two hours a day, and by the time she reached her senior year in college, she had achieved a level of excellence that qualified her for the National Women's Fencing Team. She smiled now at the irony. Fencing was the one eighteenth century skill she possessed.

She finished her stretching exercises, inhaled deeply and checked the lock on the cabin door. It was locked from the inside. She drew the curtain over the window and then she carefully took Ben York's sword from the place where it hung.

Regrettably, there wasn't much room in the cabin, but nonetheless, she went through a series of moves designed to keep her in shape, to keep her agile.

On the morning before Will was wounded, he had found her practicing and she had sworn him to secrecy.

Perhaps Ben York would not be distressed to discover this talent of hers, on the other hand, he might be furious. It seemed that only men were supposed to fence in this time period. Nonetheless, it seemed to her that this was not the worst possible thing to know how to do.

Her problem, she lamented, was that as she had been educated as a generalist, she knew a little bit about a lot of things. She wished now, as she had before, that she had become more expert in the details of history.

Then, for the second time this morning, the question of her permanency in this time and place flooded over her—would she be taken back, just as she was beginning to make all-important adjustments—just as she had begun to fall in love?

Black Henri was dressed in tight knee-length black breeches, an open necked snow white shirt, and a bright red vest. He wore a scarf of many colors round his neck, and his legs below the knees were black, smooth, and bare. He was barefoot too, seldom bothering to wear shoes aboard ship. His skin glistened with perspiration and when he smiled his teeth were as white and as strong as any shark's. But his smile was not menacing, it was warm, friendly, and most often he seemed filled with laughter. He had come once again to the pilot house because Ben had gone below to eat.

"Well, young Will McNab, you be on the mend! Black Henri can tell!"

Will was out of bed and dressed. His arm was still in a sling, and while he appeared to have lost some weight, his color had returned.

"I'm feeling a lot better. How is Miss Maddie?"

"She's in top form, that one. And now she obeys the Captain's every word. But she worry about you. She wants you to come and see her today if you are up to those stairs, boy."

Will grinned. The little place they had made for him in the pilot house was excellent. He vastly preferred it to being below the deck with the rest of the crew. But he was feeling fine now, and he was bored and even anxious to get back to his studies.

"Am I to go anytime?"

"I think you can go when you wish, she did not prescribe any hour."

Will nodded. "I'll go now then."

"And leave Black Henri to do his watch alone?" Black Henri winked and Will knew he was only joking.

"I'll stay if you want . . ."

Black Henri laughed, "Go ahead, Will McNab. Go and do book learning."

Will went down the steps slowly, holding on to the rail with one hand so as not to fall. He knocked on the door and Maddie opened it.

"Oh, Will!" she hugged him tightly. Normally, had it been any other woman, he might have struggled to free himself from such a display of emotion. But truth be known, being hugged by Miss Maddie was not an unpleasant sensation, and she smelled wonderful—like a field of heather.

"Are you all right. Does it still hurt?"

Will shook his head. "It's healing well. It doesn't throb anymore. In fact, where you sewed it, it itches."

"Oh, that's a very good sign indeed. I should look at it, in fact, I should take out the stitches."

Will looked dubious. "Will that hurt?"

"It will sting a little, but it shouldn't really hurt."

"Then do it now and get it over with," he said, sitting down.

Maddie carefully removed the sling from his arm and then she carefully unbandaged him. She smiled; there was no festering or redness around the wound—the stitches had indeed healed. She took a tiny pair of scissors and cut the stitches, then using tweezers, she pulled the thread away. Each pull elicited a small noise from Will, but it was clear that he was not in real pain.

"Are you going to rebandage it?"

"No, it's better for the air to get to it now. Tell me how it feels. Move it around for me."

Will did as she bid. First he moved his arm one way, and then the other.

"Very good! I'm so pleased."

"Does this mean I'm all well?"

"I think it does."

The expression on Will's face turned to a frown.

"You're not happy? I thought you would be overjoyed to be well."

"I am," Will insisted, then shifting his weight from one leg to the other, "But this means I will have to return below deck to sleep."

"You like it in the pilot house?"

"Yes, ma'am. It's small, but the bed under the side suits me and it's a private space. When Black Henri is on the night watch, he tells me stories till I fall asleep, and if I waken, I hear him singing softly. When Captain York is on the night shift, he is as quiet as a mouse."

"I'll talk to Captain York. Perhaps he'll let you stay there. I can't think why he would object."

Will grinned from ear to ear. "Thank you," he said. Then, more seriously, "When I was hurt—the Captain gave me the pipe so I wouldn't feel the pain. It made me dream—real, real dreams.

"You mean vivid dreams, like real life."

"Yes, ma'am. But I thought I heard you and the Captain fighting. Were you fighting?"

"Not really. I mean we were, but it's all over now. He was angry with me. He was mostly angry because you were hurt. Captain York is very fond of you, Will."

Will beamed. "Can we go to studying now? I want to make the Captain proud."

Maddie smiled and reached for the Bible. "I think he's already very proud of you, Will. You're a brave boy, I don't know what would have happened to me if you hadn't helped me."

Again Will smiled. He sat down beside her and opened the Bible. "I'm ready."

Maddie turned to the twenty-third psalm and Will began, "Yea though I walk through the valley of the shadow of Death ..."

He had some of the words memorized, but others she knew he wouldn't recognize out of context.

Will continued reading and when he had finished, Maddie hugged him, "Oh, that was very good."

"David was young, wasn't he?" Will suddenly asked.

Maddie nodded. "I suppose he was about your age."

"And he didn't have parents either, did he?"

"I guess not . . ."

Will looked up at her with sad eyes. "That's what I always wanted most."

Maddie put both her arms around him and this time hugged him more tightly. *How selfish I've been,* she thought. Will also was alone in this world, and although he had been born into it, it was no easier for him than for her.

"You've got tears in your eyes," Will said looking at her with alarm.

"It's all right, Will. I was just thinking how lonely it's been for you."

"I'm all right," he assured her.

"I know you are. Will, I can't be your mother, but can you think of me as a kind of sister—I mean, I have no family either and if I'm to adopt a family—well, I'd want to adopt you."

Will fairly beamed. "Could I really be like your brother?"

"Yes, of course."

Will snuggled close. "We'll always be friends," he said softly. "Always."

Sarah Oort looked intently into her sterling silver-edged mirror. "Forty," she whispered as she moved her hand across her face and then across her still smooth neck. No one would have believed her age. Men often mistook her for a woman in her late twenties, and even when she was with her beautiful eighteen-year-old daughter, Katra, they were more often taken for sisters than mother and daughter. Not that she was seen with Katra that often, indeed Katra had been away for almost two years and only just returned to New York.

Sarah silently blessed her Dutch and Scandinavian heritage for her good looks and the fact that she wore her age well. She was tall compared to other women, nearly five-foot seven. She was also blessed with a superb figure—long legs, graceful arms, a magnificent torso with small hard breasts, and a long slender neck. Her hair was white-blond, and her eyes a devastating, deep blue. Once, when she had been younger, she had worn her hair loose to her waist. But now, more mature, she bound it back into two elaborately woven braids.

Sarah took great care with her appearance. She exercised with great regularity, ate sparingly, and each night covered her entire body in scented whale oil. The oil kept her skin soft, youthful, and supple. In addition, Sarah imported the finest cosmetics from Paris. When the occasion demanded, she made her pupils larger with Belladona, and she used mascara, powders, and seductive perfumes.

Sarah was also known for her fine clothes. Her wardrobe was the envy of all of New York's women.

Her clothes were imported from all over the world. She had rare embroidered silks from the Orient, vivid printed cottons from Holland, lush taffetas and velvets from Paris, Chantilly lace-trimmed undergarments, and even rich furs from the wilds of Russia. In winter, when the cold winds swirled and the city was buried in snow, Sarah Oort dressed in fine woolen gowns, wore a seal skin cape trimmed in sable and a matching sable hat. She rode about the city in a colorful red sleigh drawn by four black stallions. Everyone knew Sarah Oort, if not personally, then by reputation.

Sarah was not only beautiful and well-dressed, she also lived like a princess, surrounding herself with luxury. Her home was a three story stone house located several blocks from Trinity Church. It was furnished with Oriental screens, hand-carved tables and chairs, silk cushions, and inlaid mother-of-pearl tables.

Sarah begrudgingly admitted that each of her husbands had contributed to her wealth. But she thanked only herself for doubling their legacies and for holding on to every penny.

All of her husbands had been seagoing men who had brought her booty from the four corners of the earth.

Sarah Oort was a wealthy woman, perhaps the wealthiest woman in the New World. Her last husband, Captain William Kidd, had made her the richest of all, but she cherished the thought that in death, he might make her richer yet.

Sarah wanted for nothing, but those who knew her well knew she desired even more in spite of her already elevated economic state. In matters of gold and precious possessions, Sarah Oort was insatiable.

On this particular morning, Sarah Oort had been lounging about. Such was not her usual habit. Ordinarily, she would have been up and dressed and overseeing the several businesses she managed. Money made money. It was not enough to inherit and spend. It was necessary, even pleasurable, for her to watch money multiply. Whatever else she was, no one had ever accused Sarah of being lazy.

But today she did not call in to check over the books of the tavern she owned near the battery, nor did she go to the warehouse to check the stock of her trading company. Today she had altered her usual routine in order to be available for the final fittings of her costume for the Governor's Ball to be held on the weekend. Yes, she had vowed not to work today. Fittings were tiring, and she certainly felt she had earned a day's rest. In any case, she was also to see Katra today, and she deemed her meeting with Katra to be quite important.

Thus Sarah, dressed in rouge silk embroidered Oriental pyjamas, was lounging about when her maid knocked on her bedroom door.

"Come in, Gerda," she called out imperiously.

Gerda, a girl of fifteen years, entered cautiously. Her mistress was a woman of many moods and her temper flared more often than her generosity.

"Your daughter is here," Gerda reported as she bowed ever so slightly.

"Show her in," Sarah requested with a wave of her hand.

Katra was the only child fathered by Sarah Oort's first husband, a wealthy older man who had been thoughtful enough to die when Sarah was still a young woman under twenty years of age. Katra never knew her father and was thus Sarah's child alone.

Like her mother, Katra was tall and ramrod straight. She had the same long, lovely torso with high full-blown breasts as her mother, her legs were long, and she had a sculptured face. She also had blue eyes and long blond hair. *She takes after me in other ways too,* Sarah thought. Katra was practical, intelligent, independent, and dedicated to increasing the family fortune.

"Mother . . ."

Katra sailed into her mother's room. Her blond hair was loose, falling over her bare shoulders. She wore a pale blue cotton day gown trimmed in eyelet.

"Have I come too early?" Katra asked.

"No, I'm glad you're early. I most certainly wanted to see you before the dressmaker arrives."

Katra smiled knowingly, "I suspect this is not a social call. You seem to have a reason for wanting me to come."

"As much as I enjoy your company, you're quite right."

"And where is the mysterious Melissa, Mother? I've been back from Europe for some time now and our paths have never crossed. Here I am with a stepsister I have never seen. I begin to think this is by design rather than a mere accident."

"I've kept you apart for a reason."

Katra laughed. "I have suspected as much. You seldom do anything without reason, Mother."

"I intend to explain. It is all part of a plan I've devised, a plan in which you would play a major role."

"I see. Ah, Mother you are mysterious."

"It's about William's treasure."

"Tell me your plan," Katra urged.

"I have been doing a little research."

"Research?"

"Yes, knowing one's prey is half of catching him."

"And who do you plan to catch?"

"Captain Ben York. I believe he is the only one of William's friends who are loyal enough to have hidden the treasure and to see to it William's wishes were observed."

"Let me guess," Katra said smiling. "You think William Kidd would leave his treasure to his daughter, Melissa."

"I consider that likely. That's why I've kept her here with me and why I've kept you two apart. If you are to help me, she must not recognize you as my daughter."

"Are you sure this treasure exists? Some doubt it does."

"I plan to find my late husband's treasure trove. I'm certain he took the Portuguese galleon and just as certain that more than a King's ransom is buried somewhere."

"On one of the Caribbean isles?"

"Most likely."

Katra sat down on the end of divan. "Tell me more, Mother. Tell me about this Ben York who is so loyal."

"Ben captains his own ship, the *Wilma*. He lives in Curaçao and will most certainly winter there."

"But how can we be certain he knows where the treasure is located?" Katra asked.

"We can't. But we must do everything to find out. Ben York has not made port in many a month, so I think he must be in, or headed for Curaçao. He would feel safe there."

"What do you want me to do?" Katra asked.

"I have discovered that Ben York has a brother—a Rob York. He lives in Curaçao and looks after Ben's interests. He is keeper of Ben's treasure and he runs the house. But I think he is a bit of a lay-about and I know he likes women."

"Of which I am one."

"Ah, yes. You are such a woman as to make him forget all others. You know how. If you are willing, I will send you to Curaçao tomorrow. You will find, meet, and allow yourself to be wooed by this Rob York. When Ben returns you will practically be a member of the family and if he is already there, then you can become a member of the family in any case. You will be able to discover all."

"And if there is nothing to discover?"

Sarah shrugged. "Then you will have missed winter in New York."

"And what may I expect if I succeed?"

"Then we share and share alike. I, of course, will finance your voyage and all the necessities of life while you are away."

Katra got up off the divan and began to move around the room like a spider doing a dance. "And what of dear little Melissa? She is, after all, Kidd's natural daughter whilst I am not. Even if I find out the treasure exists and where it exists, we still shall not have it."

Sarah scowled. Melissa was seventeen and William Kidd's daughter by his first wife. She was an attractive young girl and she had been annoyingly close to her father. Sarah had long suspected William would leave her everything but thus far nothing had materialized save a small stipend which paid for the girl's keep at a school to train young ladies for marriage. Sarah did not envy the stipend. She was grateful for it because it kept Melissa nearby and it cost her nothing.

"If William's treasure is real, and if indeed it is willed to Melissa, then Melissa would have to meet an untimely death," Sarah answered.

Sarah deemed herself a generous woman. She would not kill or have someone killed for less than life was worth. The stipend fell into that category but alas, the treasure did not.

"Even so, wouldn't this Ben York still have the treasure? If Melissa were dead, would he not keep it?"

"He would want to keep it, I'm sure. But if we know

where it is—well, there is no need to worry. I have friends. Ben York might end up dangling from the end of a rope just as William did or he might meet a sudden death in battle over the treasure. Once we know what we need to know, I will take action."

Katra sat down. The expression on her face revealed deep thought.

"I know you're thinking things through. You're a smart girl to do so. Not that I haven't already thought things through. You've been in Europe for several years. No one knows you are my daughter, not even Melissa, no less Ben York or his brother. And of course I have arranged a new identity for you—complete with Royal Papers. You shall be called Katra Cross."

Katra smiled. "And to seal our bargain?"

"This gold amulet, one of two. I always wear the other round my neck." Sarah displayed her own amulet and then pressed an identical amulet into Katra's hand. It was on a heavy gold chain just as was the one around her own neck.

"I'll go," Katra agreed.

"Then you must pack now. The ship leaves on the high tide tomorrow morning."

Katra embraced her mother and Sarah gave her a trunk.

"All you need is in here. Money for the voyage, your papers, and a new wardrobe." Sarah pointed to a trunk in the corner.

"You've thought of everything."

Sarah moved to Katra's side. She hugged her. "That's what mothers are for."

"On what ship do I sail?"

"On the *Catcher*. You leave early, so perhaps you should board tonight."

"Will you see to having the trunk delivered?"

"I'll summon my carriage now."

Katra kissed her mother's cheek. "I'll just stop by home and pick up a few things, then I'll go directly to the docks."

Sarah nodded. "I hear this Rob York is most good-looking."

Katra laughed. "Ah, Mother you do think of everything."

Chapter Seven

"Miss Maddie! Miss Maddie!"

Maddie opened the door of the cabin to find Will standing outside. He was smiling from ear-to-ear and was animated with excitement.

"Come out on deck, Miss Maddie. Come outside! Land's in sight! We're coming into New York Harbor."

Maddie felt a surge of anticipation as she reached for her shawl, wrapping it around her shoulders. It was late August, and already she sensed a nip of fall in the early morning air.

"This way," Will instructed. "Captain York said you could come up to the pilot house to see!"

Maddie followed Will, climbing the steps that led to the pilot house. Inside, Ben steered the ship toward what appeared to be the docks. The water was a trifle choppy, and there were at least ten other ships at anchor offshore and as many more dockside.

In the distance Maddie could see land. Not just the barren New England coast, appearing then disappearing through the fog, but New York.

"There she is," Ben said with a grin. "Thought you might like to have a look."

Maddie peered into the distance, past the vessels at anchor which bobbed in the blue water, like children's toys in a tub. Maddie could see New York Harbor—a denuded New York

Harbor from that she had last viewed. There was no great lady with her torch held high to welcome them. There were no dramatic skyscrapers reaching for the heavens, and there were no factories belching out the smoke that had previously served to remind her that New York was about trade and commerce. The water that flowed around their vessel was clear and unpolluted, churned by the offshore wind, and much of Manhattan seemed shrouded in greenery. To Maddie's eyes, the sight was stunning; no, more than stunning, it was shocking. It was the proof that she truly had traveled back in time—the wagons along the shore, the sight of the dirt roads, the huddle of buildings all seemed to speak to her. The whole panorama seemed to be saying—accept this, it has really happened to you.

"You look a bit taken aback," Ben observed, glancing at her.

"More taken aback than you can imagine."

"Is it the biggest place you've ever seen?" Will asked, his voice filled with enthusiasm.

Will couldn't know, or perhaps even imagine how she felt. He didn't know her secret. How could she even begin to describe what a magnificent place New York City would become? For now she had to find an answer that would satisfy him. Maddie shook her head, "No, I think Boston is bigger." It was as honest an answer as she could give and still keep her secret. Though she thought silently that Boston was certainly bigger in this time period, while in her own time period, New York was far larger.

"One day New York will be the larger of the two cities," Ben predicted.

He glanced at her, as if he was waiting for her to confirm his prediction.

"I think you're right," she replied. As soon as she said it, she knew he was testing her in front of someone else. He wanted to make sure she kept her story to herself.

On the deck below, the crew worked feverishly. "They all

seem to be working hard now," Maddie said, indicating the activity below the quarter deck. "Even the troublemakers."

"They know full well that in a matter of hours they can fulfill their desires. Whiskey, women, and all manner of diversions await them in the many pleasure houses that line the bowery."

"To each his own," Maddie said in a near whisper. She felt desirous of other pleasures. She longed to step onto land, to see other women, to walk in a park, and most of all to feel the comfort of a warm bath in a proper tub. But she warned herself not to expect twentieth century amenities. Whatever else, she had to remember the time period. She had to be careful even if she was with Ben York most of the time.

Silently, she lectured herself, thinking that after all, the atmosphere in which she'd existed for the last month had not been unlike the atmosphere she might have expected in any strictly male group in any time period.

If she'd been captured by some motorcycle gang or marooned with a large group of men in her own time she knew it probably would have been the same. Under such circumstances, twentieth century attitudes toward any given woman would no doubt have fled. In fact, in the twentieth century, she might not have been so lucky, she thought to herself. She might not have found a man like Ben York, a man who could be rough and ready, and yet who had honor. That he could also be erotic, passionate, and gentle was something that made him very special. She might not have found a young Will McNab either. Will had responded well to his studies. He was a bright lad. And she thought she and Will needed each other, that no matter what, they would always be friends because they were both orphans of a sort.

Yes, she knew she had grown used to life on the ship. That she had grown to accept her surroundings and the restrictions placed upon her. But now the reality of it all flooded over her anew. Stepping ashore, meeting new people, having to talk with strangers all presented a new set of difficulties.

"Will, go down to my cabin and bring up my sword."

Maddie glanced at Will. He knew full well she used that sword daily to practice with, but he said nothing. Indeed, his expression didn't even change.

"Yes, sir!" he said proudly, and then he hurried away.

"You do look distracted. Are you not as glad to make port as you thought you would be?"

Maddie tried to smile. "Something like that. It just looks so different—it reminds me of how many things I must get used to—of all the changes."

Again he did not take the opportunity to say he believed or disbelieved her, he just looked sympathetic. Then he turned toward her. "I want you to go below and put on that fine green gown," he requested.

"Is it the sort of thing I should wear ashore?"

Ben laughed. "Indeed, and I want to make an impression. As soon as we dock, the governor's representative will be piped aboard to negotiate mooring and other privileges."

"It's hard for me to tear myself away from looking at New York."

"Do as I say, and we'll see it up closer, much sooner."

Sarah Oort was dressed in a fine brocade day dress and her huge hat bore a splendid feather and several large ribbons. She stood in front of her desk, gathering up papers, preparing for her day's work. A gentle knock on the door, which was ajar in any case, caused her to look up. "Yes, Gerda?"

Gerda bowed ever so slightly. "A messenger has brought a message, Mistress Oort."

"And where is this message?"

" 'Tis oral, mistress. I've been bade repeat it."

"Then please do, preferably before the sun sets," Sarah snapped.

"The message is, Captain Ben York's vessel, the *Wilma* has rounded New York Harbor and is about to moor."

Sarah jumped to her feet. "Are you certain, girl?"

"Yes, ma'am. 'Tis a short message, I could not be mistaken."

"Is the messenger still here?"

"Yes, Mistress."

"Tell him to wait. I must pen a note to Michael Faraday. Hurry, go downstairs before he leaves. It will only take me a few minutes."

Gerda nodded and fairly flew out of the room.

Sarah hurried to her desk and took out a piece of fine linen parchment. She hurriedly wrote, "Please see to it that Captain York receives an invitation to the Governor's Ball. It is worth our while to be hospitable." She signed her name with flourish and quickly folded the parchment and put it in an envelope which she addressed to Michael Faraday, Governor's Representative. Then, she closed the envelope and tilting the candle on her desk slightly, poured hot wax to seal it. While the wax was still soft, she imprinted her own symbol onto it with a round metal seal, the raised design of which bore her name.

Gerda had returned and now paused in the doorway.

"Here," Sarah extended the envelope. "Tell him to hurry."

"Shall I return?"

"No, leave me," Sarah replied, with slight irritation.

Gerda hurried away and Sarah went to the window to look out on the harbour in the distance. If she went to the windows walk atop the house she could probably watch Ben York's ship moor.

"So much trouble," she murmured as a rare frown covered her face. Had Ben York come just two days ago, she might have been spared both considerable trouble and expense. Certainly she would not have sent Katra to Curaçao. "But still . . ." she said aloud as her fingers curled around the curtain, "Katra might prove a valuable back-up should Ben York somehow slip through my web."

Sarah's mind raced. Apart from sending Katra to Curaçao,

Ben York's timing was impeccable. He would not miss the opportunity to attend the Governor's Ball and meet the new governor, Governor Bellomont. No privateer who plied these waters could afford to miss the opportunity of a social contact with the governor. There were favors to be given and favors to be called in. Commerce was an never-ending round of negotiations and dickering. And didn't she of all people know it! Every new regime meant new arrangements. Peter Stuyvesant, albeit a man who had governed before her time, had initiated a series of "protocols" as they were known. Privateers had to negotiate for moorage rights, for protection, and even for the right to walk unmolested on the streets of the Bowery. A captain had to make certain arrangements for his men—take certain responsibilities for their actions. And the friendlier the relationship with the governor, the better the negotiations were.

True enough, the Dutch no longer ran New York, but the English were at least as oriented toward commerce as were the Dutch. The two groups had always gotten on well, and little had changed in the city's administrative rules since the English took over.

"And when you go to the Governor's Ball," Sarah whispered with a smile, "you will stumble into my web, Ben York."

"Ah, good. You look just right in that dress." Ben walked around her appraisingly as Maddie modeled the green dress he had asked her to wear. It was both more modest than the other dresses and more seductive. It had a tight leather bodice that fit over it, pinching in her tiny waist and pushing her breasts up. But Ben had assured her that this was a "daytime dress" the sort of dress worn in the city during the afternoon.

"Just right for what?" she asked looking back at him. She had never seen him dressed as he was now. The transformation was quite startling. He wore snow white tight breeches and long royal blue stockings. His shoes were black and had silver buckles. He wore a ruffled shirt and a blue waistcoat that matched his stockings. It was trimmed with gold and had large gold buttons. Beneath his waistcoat, atop his shirt, he wore a blue brocade vest. He also had a gold-trimmed hat.

His beard was not long past the stubbly stage, but it was neatly combed and trimmed. He looked incredibly handsome, tall and strong. And dressed in this manner he also looked influential—a man about town or what she imagined a man about town in this time period would look like.

He smiled mischievously at her. "How can you ask, 'dressed for what?' You're dressed for New York, dressed for trying on clothes, dressed to be the woman on my arm."

Because he seemed to be teasing her, she refused to take the bait.

"You have grown silent on me, lass."

"I've learned not to lose my temper when you try to taunt me."

He laughed. "Well soon Michael Faraday will draw up to the dock in his fine carriage and we'll begin to negotiate our little mooring."

"I don't understand."

"And do ships dock free in your time?"

Maddie frowned. If truth be known, the cost of docking a vessel at any given location had never even occurred to her. But she supposed the Port Authority of New York certainly did charge a fee. "No, they pay," she replied.

"And we will pay, too. But it will be a percentage of our booty. Say, lass, when Michael Faraday sees the likes of you, he may want you."

"Stop that. You're just trying to make me angry."

Again he laughed. *A splendid lady,* he thought. She was such a hot headed little minx. He admitted he did like to tease her and in any case humor disguised the way he was beginning to feel for this unusual woman. No, it wouldn't do at all for her to see through him just yet. A woman whom he intended to make his woman would have to pass through certain tests, undergo certain experiences. She would have to be at least as unusual as this woman appeared to be. But he warned himself to make certain first. After all, what did he really know about her? Moreover, could she possibly be telling the truth? No, before he confessed his feelings to her, he had to know more. He had to be certain of himself for both their sakes. He pulled her into his arms and quickly kissed her cheek. "Well, rest assured I'm not prone to part with you."

"And I have nothing to say about this?" She drew back and studied him with her deep green eyes.

"Nothing, lass. But come along. We should not be lingering in the cabin when Michael Faraday arrives."

"Who is this man? Is he very important?"

"Aye, lass he's the man with the keys to the Kingdom of New York Town. He's—to put it crudely, Governor Bellomont's Chief Thief—politely called, "The Governor's Representative."

"The governor takes a percentage of the booty you have in the cargo hold?"

"The governor and the merchants of the town. Things are quite well-run here. At least one gets to pay a single person instead of having to negotiate with ten or more."

And you don't mind?"

"I would only mind if the price were unreasonable. In any case, I would not be here were it not necessary.

"As I told you, I long ago made a blood bond with William Kidd to come to New York and get his daughter, Melissa, to look after her, and to see to it she receives her portion of the treasure."

"Tell me about this Sarah Oort—the last wife of Kidd."

"She is a rich woman and, if I may say so myself, a shrew such as to make the bard wince. He confided to me that he made a mistake, that Sarah is a hard, wily woman; a woman who would stop at nothing to gain more and more wealth. I should not, in truth be surprised if she were not, in some way, involved in his demise." Ben shook his head, then added, "It was his feelings toward and suspicions of Sarah Oort that made him ask me to promise to see to it that young Melissa was looked after."

"Ben, how can you trust your crew? They were all with you when the treasure was hidden."

"There are a few men I would trust with my life. They know all, but in general the crew knows little. We retrieved our own treasure trove and left three chests of little value. Kidd's treasure is on the island, but not in the obvious place. As for finding the island, I assure you none of them could possibly locate it without a detailed map."

Maddie slipped into silence, then just as he reached for the door handle, she drew him back. "You said you were going to involve me. How?"

"I have to find Melissa and take her back to Curaçao. She needs another woman—someone who can at least be a big sister to her. And like Will, she may need some education. We'll winter in Curaçao and when I'm certain we're clear of Sarah Oort, I'll see to it that Melissa receives her legacy."

"You think Sarah Oort will try to interfere?"

He grinned. "I think she would stop at nothing to achieve what she desires, and she most certainly desires Kidd's treasure. She is a powerful woman who can muster powerful resources to obtain what she wants. It is my task to convince her that what she wants is myth, not reality."

Maddie nodded. It was all beginning to make sense. Especially in the light of history and what she knew. Kidd's treasure was never found. It most certainly had led to much controversy as the argument concerning whether it was myth or reality continued.

"I want you to take Melissa under your wing, so to speak."

Ben smiled engagingly at her and Maddie smiled back. She supposed it was flattering. He seemed to respect her intelligence and clearly wanted her to tutor both children—Will and little Melissa. And they would be together. A barrage of questions popped into her head, questions about Melissa, about this Sarah Oort, and even about Curaçao. What would her future on the lovely island be like? But everything was uncertain—even her future in this time period. There seemed little to do but take things as they came.

"Very well," she agreed. "But no more about selling me or trading me for mooring rights."

Again he kissed her lightly, furtively. "I don't know a man with enough money," he whispered into her ear.

At that moment someone in the pilot house—probably either young Will or Black Henri hit the great brass gong.

"Come, my lady. Our guest has arrived."

He took her arm and led her down the steps and out onto deck. Maddie felt taken aback by what she saw.

The crew, even those who had molested her, were cleaned up and clearly wearing their best clothes. They lined either side of deck, standing at attention.

Just as she and Ben reached the deck, a tall, well dressed gentleman was being piped aboard the *Wilma*.

He wore black shoes with large silver buckles, white stockings, and black breeches trimmed in gold braid. Over a ruffled white shirt, he wore a red three-quarter length vest which was also trimmed in gold, and a black jacket with a red lining and red cuffs to match the vest. It also dripped gold braid. His hat was the usual three cornered colonial style, trimmed in gold. He carried something that looked close to being a modern briefcase, and he wore a monocle which dangled from a gold chain. His face, she noted, was most angular, giving him a bird-like appearance.

"Ah, Captain York! What a pleasure to see you again! How many months has it been?"

The man spoke to Ben, but his eyes rested on her and she felt somehow as if she were being dissected. She now realized that his face was angular because he was so thin, almost gaunt and that his sharp features were indeed bird-like, in fact, he reminded her of a sharp beady-eyed crow.

"Nearly a year," Ben replied.

He seemed to be ignoring the fact that the man, whom she assumed to be Mike Faraday, was staring at her. She looked back, though not directly into his eyes. Yes, everything about this man from his clearly expensive clothing to his gold pocket watch chain, seemed to proclaim his station in the community and his wealth.

Upon greeting Ben, he bowed ever so slightly. Now he smiled—an ingenuous smile, Maddie thought.

"I see you have a lovely new companion, Captain York. May I have the pleasure of an introduction."

Ben smiled. "May I present, Miss Maddie Emerson."

"Pleased, I'm sure."

Mike Faraday's dark eyes flashed and he bent from the waist and took her hand and kissed it. When he straightened up he leered at her cleavage for a single second then, for the first time, looked at Ben.

"As usual, my friend, you exhibit excellent taste."

Ben did not acknowledge the comment. "Shall we turn ourselves directly to business?"

"Certainly."

"Then let us take some sherry in my cabin and go over the ship's manifest. Then if you care to inspect the hold . . ."

Mike Faraday's eyes grew feral as they darted about, then again he smiled. "The manifest will do. I know you to be a man of honor. In any case, we're fair and you know better than to hold back."

"Indeed," Ben said, ushering Faraday toward the steps that led up to his quarters.

Both men stepped aside, and in the end, it was Maddie who led the way.

* * *

Ben and Mike Faraday sat down at the same small table where she and Ben usually ate supper. But now the white damask cloth was gone, and in its place, papers covered the table, long parchment papers covered with lists.

Maddie did not sit at the table, but instead sat off the to the side, refilling the wine glasses when they were emptied. She noted that Ben did not drink as fast nor as much as Mike Faraday.

"Ah, I see you carry cloth from India! It is much coveted by the merchants of New York."

"Taken off a French galleon, near Madagascar some time ago."

"Forty bolts—a goodly amount. Tell me, is this the fabric used for Saris? Is it gaily colored and woven with threads of gold and silver."

"Indeed," Ben said.

Mike Farraday's little animal eyes fairly glistened. "Five bolts . . . ?"

"Done," Ben said, as he wrote "five bolts of Indian cloth," in a round hand.

"And Oriental spices—mmm," Mike Faraday said, rubbing his chin. "One container of ginger?"

"Done," Ben agreed, adding the ginger to his list.

"And sugar," Mike Faraday said, as he allowed his finger to come to rest midway down the ship's manifest.

"We've a goodly amount of sugar," Ben said, grinning. "After all, we've come from the Caribbean."

Maddie was glad that Mike Faraday could not see her face. They had not come from the Caribbean! But certainly Ben York did not want it known where they were coming from—or going to for that matter.

"A hundred pounds of sugar should do it," Mike Faraday announced.

"That's a goodly amount of a valuable cargo," Ben said, rubbing his chin.

Was it? Maddie was fascinated. It hadn't even occurred to

her yet that what was reasonable, even cheap in her time, was valuable in this time period. But of course, sugar must be very valuable, she realized. It came from far away. Besides that, there was no refrigeration and sugar and salt were the great preservatives.

"How long will you be in port, Captain?"

"A week, ten days at most."

"And you think the sugar too much?"

Ben shook his head. "No, it will be fine as long as nothing more is added to this list."

"No more," Mike Faraday agreed. "Please ask your men to load these items into my wagon."

Ben got up and went to the door. He called out and Black Henri appeared almost instantly. Ben told him what to get from the hold, and he was gone.

When Ben returned to the table, he signed the document and so did Mike Faraday. Then Mike Faraday rolled it up and put it into a long metal tube, a device it seemed to carry about scrolls and parchments.

A second copy was quickly made and signed. This one was taken by Ben.

Mike Faraday stood up and stretched. "Ah, one other thing! Good heavens, I almost forgot. Oh, the Governor and Mrs. Bellomont would be furious if I'd been remiss."

With those words, Mike Faraday withdrew a large white envelope sealed with wax from his vest pocket. "An invitation for you and your lady to the Governor's Costume Ball on Saturday night."

Ben took the invitation and bowed slightly. "We're pleased to accept."

Again Mike Faraday turned to Maddie and again he took her hand and kissed it. "Such a pleasure, my dear. And I do hope you will save a dance for me? Tell me, how will you be dressed so I will know it is you?"

Ben circled Maddie's waist with his arm. "We have no costumes aboard—we'll have to find something when we go ashore. But we'll identify ourselves to you, my friend. Tell me, how will you be dressed?"

"I always come as the Prince of the Night," Faraday answered with a twisted smile, "Yes, my friend. I come as the devil himself."

Ben's expression did not even change, though Maddie felt a chill run down her spine. *Frightening,* she thought. *Yes, this Mike Faraday was a frightening man.*

An hour later, Ben York helped Maddie down the gangplank and then lifted her onto dry land. How odd this was! They were moored by a dock at the end of a dirt road. All around was virgin bush and beyond was New York. Not the megalopolis she had known, but a truly small town by modern standards. Maddie tried to visualize Manhattan. She decided they were docked slightly to the east of what was today Broad Street.

Even before they left the *Wilma,* Ben had posted a skeleton crew of trusted men to watch the ship and given the rest of the men liberty. They had been loaded into wagons and carted into town, there she supposed they would vent their pent up desires on drink and women of the night.

"Come, we have much to do," Ben said, helping her almost immediately into a plain carriage which waited for them dockside.

Maddie waved to Will who stood on deck with Black Henri, then Ben gave the signal and the carriage moved away, clattering down the rutted dirt road toward the town. They turned onto a better road, and Maddie was surprised to see that it was still called Broad Street.

"And what are these many things we have to do?" she asked.

"First we must go to Sarah Oort's to try to find Melissa. Then we will go shop for you. Since Mr. Faraday was good enough to give us invitations to the Governor's Ball, it is best we attend."

"I thought you didn't like the Governor? I thought you were in a hurry to be off to Curaçao?"

"There are some things which are more or less mandatory. When I receive an invitation from the Governor himself, well, I cannot refuse. This is not the last time I shall have to dock here."

"Protocol."

"Precisely."

The carriage rambled on till it turned onto a cobbled road. The road was lined with taverns and inns. Even this early in the day she could tell what kind of area this was, but in present day New York it was the center of the financial district.

Then the carriage rounded the corner and the scenery changed radically. Only then did Maddie realize they were moving from east to west across the tip of Manhattan on Bridge Street.

A huge green expanse marked the fort at the tip of the island and as they traveled in a northerly direction, up Broadway which was now spelled Broad Way. Ben pointed out the jail, the Governor's mansion, and finally Trinity Church. Maddie felt spellbound. In her mind she could see Trinity Church as it was in her time, guarding the entrance to Wall Street, a tiny building dwarfed by all those that rose around it. But now, Trinity Church was a giant building, the largest one in the area.

Trinity faded from her view, and soon there were streets lined with stone houses and several that were lined with establishments that clearly belonged to merchants.

Maddie was fascinated with all she saw out of the carriage window as they drove along. She inhaled deeply of the fresh, cool air and took in everything with the eyes of a child. This world was wonderful! Suddenly she felt the challenge she was sure her forefathers must have felt—the challenge of a new world.

A few more corners were rounded, then the carriage drew to a halt in front of a large stone building on Princess Street. Over the wide doorway on the first floor hung a green and gold sign that proclaimed it to be, *The New Amsterdam-York Inn and Tavern.*

"We'll be staying here," Ben said, as he alighted from the carriage and quickly turned to offer his hand and help Maddie down.

"You didn't tell me we'd be staying away from the ship."

"I had Will pack a few things for you, the rest we'll be buying. Come, come now, don't tell me you won't be happy to be out of that cabin for awhile, to be in a real room, to sleep in a real bed!"

"Oh, I will be. Do they have bathtubs here?"

"Ah, I knew you dreamt of more than simply spending your nights with me. Yes, I'm sure a proper bath can be arranged."

Maddie smiled and he took her arm to escort her inside. "I see the owners have a combination name."

"The best of both worlds. I do believe New York is English to stay, but it did seesaw back a forth several times. Even so, the populace is quite friendly. The Dutch and English here get on well. It's not a problem."

"I'm glad to hear it," she said, honestly.

He guided her along. "Here, let's go in the side door so as to avoid the drinking clientele."

"This isn't a dockside area—is the drinking clientele dangerous?"

"Not at all, and quite right, this is a better neighborhood. It's just that overnight guests usually use the side door and it is all the better to do so if you should come and go on your own."

Maddie digested the information as he opened the door and stepped aside for her. Inside the entryway it looked almost as if it were the lobby of a small and quite proper little hotel. There were a few comfortable chairs arranged near the fireplace and along one wall, a kind of desk where she presumed the guests registered and paid. Behind the desk, on the wall there were about ten large keys hung on wooden pegs.

"This hotel is run by Madame Molly Merriweather, but everyone calls her Mother Molly. She's an old friend, a woman who can be trusted."

"Is that important?"

He grinned. "In a town run by the likes of Governor Bellomont, Mike Faraday, and Sarah Oort, I'd say it's a distinct advantage. With that explanation he picked up a brass bell and rang it. In a moment a large round woman bustled through a door to the left of the desk. She had great huge thick gray-blond braids wrapped in huge circles over her ears so that she looked as if she were wearing braided earmuffs. She wore a dark dress with a crisp white apron and her face was as round as her body. For a long moment she looked at Ben, then she burst into a great wide smile and held out her arms.

"Ben York! As I live and breath! Is that you under all that bushy hair! You're growing a beard! I hardly knew you."

He laughed and gave her an immense bear hug. "Ah, Mother Molly you haven't changed one bit."

"You're such a liar, Ben York. But your lies always please me. Where's Black Henri and that rogue Lopez de Vaca? Oh, yes, and that lad, Will?"

"They're standing the first watch. But they'll be round tomorrow night."

"I suppose the others are staying dockside?"

He grinned. "Closer to the action."

"That kind of action I can do without. I run a respectable establishment. Now, you better be telling who this beauty on your arm is?"

"This is Maddie Emerson. Maddie, this is Mother Molly."

"Just 'Mother' will do, dearie. My boys tease far too much."

Maddie smiled. "I'm pleased to meet you."

"Well, now, I imagine you'll be wanting number ten. It's the finest room in the house."

"That's the very one I've dreamed about," Ben said with a wink. "And Maddie will want a bath tonight."

"I hardly blame her. I'll see to it myself."

The woman grinned and then winked. "I think I should bring the extra large tub, I'm sure you need a good scrub, too."

Maddie felt her face flush with Mother Molly's words and intonation. Her implication was quite clear.

"A good idea," Ben joked back. "But now we must go to see Sarah Oort. By the way, save room number nine. I have an idea we may need it, too."

"No trouble at all."

Mother Molly took down the key for room number nine and ten and handed it to Ben. "It's yours when you need it. As long as you don't bring that Sarah Oort here. I don't like to see the likes of her around here." Mother Molly shook her head, then turned to Maddie. "Terrible woman, that one," she said half under her breath.

"I promise, I won't bring her here," Ben answered. He had a bemused look. "In any case, it's not her I want to see."

Mother Molly arched her thick brow and crooked her finger, beckoning Ben to lean closer. "Be careful, Ben York. You may not want to see Sarah Oort, but rumor has it, she wants to see you. Rumor has it you know the location to Kidd's treasure trove and that Sarah means to have that treasure at all costs. She's a greedy bitch that one, and dangerous, too."

"Thank you for the warning. It comes as no surprise."

"I thought it wouldn't. But take care anyway."

Ben took Mother Molly's hand and squeezed it. Then he motioned to the wicker basket the coachman had brought. "Have someone take that upstairs," he requested. "We'll be back in a few hours."

"Will I fix you supper?" Mother Molly asked.

"Not tonight. Tonight we'll supper at *The Inn of the Three Feathers.*

"So fancy!" Mother Molly exclaimed.

"It's our first night ashore."

"Well, you be sure to heed my warning and not get caught up in celebrations."

Mother Molly shook her finger at Ben who only responded with a smile and by hugging her round her ample waist.

Mother Molly turned to Maddie. "Take care of him. He doesn't take me seriously."

"I'll try." But she had barely gotten the words out of her mouth before Ben had whisked her about and back into the waiting carriage. He shouted instructions to the driver and again they clattered off.

Chapter Eight

It didn't seem to Maddie that they traveled far, but then she was forced to remind herself that the developed part of Manhattan in this year, 1702, was only a fraction of the city she knew. The most number of buildings were between the docks and what she knew as Wall Street. The area between present day Wall Street and Maiden Lane was largely residential and beyond that, it was farmland. The house they stopped in front of was, nonetheless, quite elegant. It too was made of huge stones and it had small dormered windows. It was three stories high and surrounded by a surprisingly well-cared for garden consisting of four distinct sections. By the side of the house was a gardener's cottage with a thatched roof. Again, Ben helped her down from the carriage. They walked along a pebble-strewn path, and when they reached the door, he banged the ornate brass knocker.

"This is a very large house—and would be a large house even in my time," Maddie commented.

"As I told you, Sarah Oort is a woman who is both powerful and rich."

Maddie held her silence, though Ben's words raised many questions in her mind. Surely women with Sarah Oort's power and fortune were few and far between. Maddie wondered how Sarah had prospered so in a man's world. Was it only through convenient marriages? But she did not ask at this moment, there was time later to learn about how such women came to be in a time when women seemed to be excluded from almost everything.

The door opened and a young girl curtsied. "Madame Oort is not at home," she announced.

Ben was tall enough to look over her head and right into the house. Without actually looking at her, he asked, "And where might Madame Oort be?"

"I'm not at all certain, sir. She did not tell me where she was going."

He took Maddie's arm and pushed past the young girl, more or less pulling Maddie into the house.

"Sir, Madame did not tell me to . . ."

"Melissa! Melissa! Are you here!" His voice boomed through the house and the maid timidly looked at him, her mouth slightly open.

"Melissa! It's Ben York, are you here?"

"Ben!"

Maddie's eyes followed the sound of the feminine voice to the top of the winding staircase. At the top stood a strikingly attractive strawberry-blond. Her red-gold hair tumbled below her shoulders, and she wore a russet dress that clung to the curves of her slim, yet curvaceous young body. Could this ravishing *femme fatale* be "little Melissa"? Maddie felt thunderstruck.

Melissa lifted her skirts and hurried down the stairs. She had beautiful brown eyes with long lashes, white skin, and a heart-shaped face. She was even prettier up close than she had appeared at a distance. Maddie felt stiff—as if she had been lied to—this was certainly no child!

"Ben, oh, Ben! It's wonderful to see you! Oh, I thought you'd never come!"

"But I promised I would. And you know I always keep my promises."

Maddie watched in silent annoyance as Melissa threw her arms around Ben, cuddled up to him and kissed him not on the cheek, but fully on the lips. Worse, he did nothing to break the kiss or discourage her from what seemed a somewhat shameless display of affection. *Men,* she thought in disgust. *It mattered not to him that this girl was half his age.*

Melissa let go of him and glanced at Maddie curiously. "And who might this be?"

"This is Maddie. Maddie, this is Melissa Kidd."

Maddie nodded without smiling. Melissa half smiled and turned her head away and back to Ben immediately.

"I thought you would never come. I thought you would leave me here with the witch forever."

"Has Sarah mistreated you?"

"No, not mistreated—well, not exactly. She wants me to write down everywhere I ever sailed with my father. She wants to know everything. She's wild to have his treasure, she's greedy. No, she hasn't mistreated me, but that's only because . . ."

Melissa stopped speaking in mid-sentence and she turned to the little maid. "Don't stand there listening you little dolt. Sarah will make you tell her everything. Go away before you hear more than is good for you."

The little maid scurried away, seemingly glad to be dismissed even if she was dismissed so rudely.

Melissa turned back to Ben, and in a much lower voice said, "She hasn't mistreated me because she needs me. Without me, you wouldn't return. Ben, take me with you now. Take me out of this house. Sarah is not to be trusted."

Ben smiled. "Don't worry, I don't trust her."

Maddie noted the fact that Ben was still holding Melissa's hands. He turned to her. "Maddie, please help Melissa pack. If we work quickly, we can be on our way."

Maddie stared at him wondering if her look conveyed her annoyance and hoping it didn't reveal her jealousy. Why had he led her to believe Melissa was a child no older than Will? Had he said that, or had she just assumed it? Damn, it didn't matter, he should have warned her. "Well, let's get packing," she snapped.

Melissa did not smile. "This way," she said, pointing Maddie toward the stairs and adding, "We must hurry. Who knows when she'll come back?"

Melissa led and Maddie followed. They went into a large airy room on the third floor. Melissa took out a large wicker trunk. "You can begin with those drawers—I'll go down and talk with Ben."

Maddie scowled for the first time. "You'll do no such thing!" she said harshly. "I am not a servant. Get to work yourself. We'll do this together or not at all."

Melissa opened her brown eyes widely. "How dare you talk to me that way?"

"And how dare you talk to me the way you just did? We're equals, is that understood?"

Melissa blinked at her, then flung open the closet door and began pulling out dresses and stuffing them into the wicker trunk.

"You had better be more selective," Maddie warned. "There won't be room for everything."

"Pooh!" Melissa said. "I have more trunks."

"Well we don't have more room on the carriage. Nor time for you to pack everything you own."

Melissa turned and tossed a small wicker bag to her. "Use this for the things in the drawer. I don't suppose two trunks will be too many, do you?"

Maddie didn't answer. She silently threw undergarments and night clothes into the basket, aware of just how angry she was—angry and yes, jealous.

I should be able to handle this because I'm older, Maddie reminded herself. But Melissa seemed annoying—spoiled to say the least. But it was the more important questions that really plagued her, what exactly did Melissa Kidd mean to Ben York? What did he expect of her? And what did Ben mean to Melissa? Clearly more than he realized. *Ben York is a typical man,* she thought. *And Melissa is very attractive.* "Damn," she muttered.

"Did you say something?" Melissa asked, arching a perfectly shaped brow.

"No! Just pack!" Maddie answered, wanting nothing more than to stomp right out of this house. But again confusion flooded over her. *To where and to what?* And she did want Ben—that was precisely the trouble.

Room nine in *The New Amsterdam-York Inn* was smaller than room ten which Maddie and Ben occupied even though it was directly across the hall. Their window looked out on a small garden, but the window in room nine overlooked the street.

Melissa ran her hand through her strawberry-blond curls abstractedly as she looked about room nine. The bed was single and the wardrobe was small as was the dresser. "I really should hang my gowns," she announced, looking a trifle pouty, "At least those that I can hang."

"I'm sure Maddie will help make you comfortable," Ben assured her.

Maddie was still standing in the doorway. She smoothed out her own skirt and then said sharply, "It would be absurd to unpack everything here. After all, we'll be leaving in a few days."

"Quite right," Ben agreed. "Why don't you take out just what you need and I'll have the other things stored on the *Wilma.*"

Melissa looked at Maddie in annoyance, but when she turned to Ben, her face was radiant. "I suppose I could do that. Of course it will be a terrible decision. I mean I'd have to decide now what I'm going to wear to the Governor's Ball on the weekend and then if I change my mind, well, all my clothes will be on the ship."

"It's quite simple," Maddie said, well aware of the sarcasm in her words, "you just can't change your mind."

"I suppose not," Melissa murmured with a shake of her curls.

Maddie turned to Ben. "I thought we were going shopping."

He smiled with what Maddie felt was maddening calm . . . no, worse than that, it was amusement! He was amused! Confronted with two women he seemed to be enjoying the subtle undercurrent of mutual distrust between them, their sparring, the fact that both clearly cared for him. *The bastard,* Maddie thought angrily. *He's using us against each other, each to make the other jealous! And he loves it all!*

For her part, Melissa did not actually look at Ben York. Instead, her large brown eyes fell on Maddie. *Who was this woman? Was Ben taking her shopping? Could this woman be his mistress?* She felt hurt. She'd been waiting for Ben York for so long! Melissa turned her eyes toward Ben at that moment. She fluttered her dark lashes ever so slightly. "Please go ahead without me. I don't want to keep you from whatever you have to do. I mean, I know how it is—especially when you've been a sea for a long while."

Maddie bristled. The implication was that she was on Ben York's arm because he'd just docked and like the rest of the crew had wasted no time finding a woman to bed. "We were at sea together," she said icily, trusting the reality of her relationship with Ben would dawn on Melissa the child-woman.

Melissa expression changed just enough to satisfy Maddie.

"Really? Where did you find her, Ben?"

Maddie felt truly angry. Melissa's tone was syrupy when she spoke to Ben.

Ben grinned. "On an almost-deserted island."

Melissa turned toward the mirror that hung over the dressing table. "I see," she said, looking at her image and again toying with her hair. "Well, I am tired. Please go right ahead with your shopping."

"We'll be back in time for us all to dine together," Ben promised.

Again Melissa smiled devastatingly at him. "How very charming. I will look forward to it."

"I'll have someone come for the trunks you want put aboard ship."

"You are a dear!" Melissa whirled around and danced into his arms, planting a kiss on his lips. *"Adieu,"* she whispered. Then, "Till later, dear Ben."

Ben only smiled. Maddie thought it was an idiotic smile of self-satisfaction. *How delightful! He must simply relish in it all,* she thought angrily. She lifted her skirts and walked purposefully down the hall, aware of his footsteps behind her.

"A wonderful girl!" Ben said as they settled in the carriage and he gave the driver directions.

"She's very young," Maddie said evenly. She stared out the window, partially forcing herself to ignore him.

"Seventeen—old enough. And I daresay she's developed beautifully since I last saw her."

"Old enough for what?" Maddie snapped.

"Old enough to be quite a beautiful young woman. It's been over a year since I've seen her. As I said, she's matured a great deal and I'm certain under your tutelage she will mature even more."

"Perhaps she doesn't even want me to tutor her."

"I'm sure she does." He turned to her and touched her on the arm so that she was forced to look at him. "You do like her, don't you?"

"I really don't know her well enough to make that judgment."

"Well I know you will like her and I know she will like you. I shouldn't want my girls fighting."

The look on his face was absolutely galling. His eyes twinkled and his mouth twisted just ever so slightly. He was teasing her! He damn well knew she was jealous. Unconsciously her fists doubled. Half in anger with him, half in anger with herself. She was making it too easy for Ben York. He knew she cared. "I am not necessarily your girl," she announced.

"Really?" He was smiling now.

Unable to keep it in, her anger and jealously both surfaced. "Well, I have no intention of being part of a cast of thousands!"

He burst out laughing and let his arm drop around her shoulders, giving her a hug. "Ah, my dear, the green-eyed monster has come to inhabit you. You're jealous. I like it."

"I am not! She's just a girl."

"Right you are. But she is a very pretty girl and soon she will be a very rich girl."

Maddie opened her mouth, but he leaned over and kissed her suddenly. It was a deep kiss, a kiss that made her relax in his arms, even though she wondered if the driver knew what was going on, or if people could see inside the carriage through the little windows.

"Don't worry," he whispered. "If I had wanted her inheritance, I wouldn't be giving it to her in the first place. And if I wanted her, you wouldn't be here."

Maddie said nothing. She just leaned against him, and again she felt she didn't want to leave him. Not even to return to her own time. Still, even if he were telling her the absolute truth, Melissa clearly wanted hm. Being in close quarters with her was going to be a problem, Maddie decided.

After a short time, the carriage came to halt in front of a long, low, wooden building. "We're here," Ben announced as he opened the carriage door and jumped to the ground. Rather than bothering to pull down the little steps, he held out his arms, and smiled at Maddie. "Jump!"

Once again feeling light hearted, and leaving all thoughts of Melissa behind, she smiled and jumped into his outstretched arms.

"This is it," he said with a sweep of his arm.

"This is what? It hardly looks like a fashion salon."

"Nor are we in Paris or London where I might have taken

you to a couturier. In any case this unassuming building holds far more than clothes."

"It doesn't look like Macy's either."

"What is a Macy's?" He looked at her questioningly.

"A department store," she answered with humor. "In my time a New York department store. A place where you can buy clothes or furniture or cosmetics or whatever . . ."

"Ah, you do have details of this future world, don't you?"

"It's because I'm telling you the truth."

"Truth or imagination, it's amusing. And make no mistake, even if I can't quite accept your tale, I believe you believe it."

"One day I hope to be able to prove my story, but till then I suppose you'll just have to be satisfied in being entertained."

He laughed and shook his head. "Well, you may think of this place as a sort of place like your Macy's. It's a warehouse for the booty taken off various vessels. It's booty that can be bought."

"And there are clothes?"

"Clothes fit for a Queen. Indeed, some of the clothes may have been intended for a Queen. I understand that a Spanish ship from the Orient bearing fine woven cloth and gowns of embroidered silk was intercepted and that its cargo is here. There was also a French ship taken—on its way to Quebec with gowns for the ladies of the upper-classes."

"But why are all these goods here?"

"Because each privateer or pirate's vessel that seeks docking privileges has goods taken from it in payment as mine did. Some goods go to merchants, but many go to the city fathers. They put their goods here and sell them to merchants or anyone else interested in paying in gold."

"Will the items that Mike Faraday took from your ship this morning be here as well?"

"I doubt they've made their way here yet, but eventually what is not taken by the governor or Mr. Faraday will be brought here. They have first choice. I suspect the sugar and ginger spice will not end up here, but that at least some of the cloth will."

"The governor had first choice? Naturally, I should have guessed," Maddie said somewhat sarcastically. On the face of it, graft and corruption seemed more blatant than in her time, but in reality she wondered if there was much difference save the actual quantity. Naturally, in the modern world, money had replaced goods as a form of payment, but in essence, it seemed the system had changed little in two hundred years.

Ben led her into the building around which guards had been posted. "Things are a bit of jumble," he said good naturedly. But we'll find the clothes and you can just rummage through them."

She did not ask what would happen if she couldn't find anything she liked. The time was too short to have something made in this pre-sewing machine era. "This is a costume ball," she reminded him.

"I've not forgotten. I know where masks can be obtained, so look for something simple."

She hadn't the vaguest idea what sort of things constituted a costume—save the fact that Mike Faraday had already mentioned he was coming as the King of the Night. "Do you have any ideas?" she asked.

He stepped back and looked at her appraisingly. "Come as Diana the Huntress, the Roman Goddess. Yes! That's perfect! A simple white dress without the bodice and some gold leaf for your magnificent hair and a bow and arrow."

Maddie smiled. It wasn't a bad choice by any means, and certainly she could manage such a costume. "And you?" she asked.

"I shall come as your brother, Apollo."

"And am I to behave toward you in a sisterly fashion?"

Ben squeezed her round the waist tightly. "Certainly not." Inside, the light was dim as there were no lamps or candles and the only light came through the windows high along the walls. *Not windows really,* she thought as she looked at them.

"Why does this place have the windows so high on the wall? And why aren't they bigger?"

He shook his head at her question. "Because my dear, they are not really windows. Indeed, only recently have houses been built with proper dormered windows. This old relic used to house troops. Those windows, as you call them, are slits for rifles. First off, this isle has been fought over by the Dutch and the English, second, there were once Indian raids till the island was properly bought."

Maddie smiled. "For the equivalent of twenty-five dollars in my time. Considering this island will become the largest and most powerful city in the New World, it was cheap."

He lifted his brow. "Is that so? And what of Mexico City? What of Havana? What even of Boston Town?"

"All smaller, save Mexico City," Maddie answered confidently. "New York will have eight million people living on the island and many, many more nearby."

He roared with laughter. "That's more people than on all of the earth, lass! I think an island would sink under the weight!"

She wished she had a picture or that she could whisk him forward in time just as she had been whisked backward. "I know you don't believe me, but it is true," she insisted. He wouldn't—no perhaps couldn't understand if she told him what would happen to the population of the earth. He would never believe that it would mushroom to ten billion.

" 'Tis not a world I would want to live in," he said thoughtfully touching his chin. "No, far too many people. But come along. We have booty to explore. You don't have much jewelry, I think I must find you some necklaces and bracelets—emeralds, that's what I want! You were meant for emeralds."

Maddie blushed because his eyes were so bold, his

thoughts so evident. He kissed her lightly on the cheek and squeezed her once again, "Come along."

Maddie set all the bundles down on the big double bed. It was, she admitted, a collection. She rather felt as if she had been rummaging in a costume shop all afternoon, though in fact there were far more than clothes.

In the end she had chosen an exquisite white silk dress which without its bodice and with a little work done on the top, could easily be turned into a Greek-style draped dress. She had even found some gold leaves for her hair. They appeared to have originally been part of some military uniform.

In addition to the dress, Ben had insisted she take a collection of seductive undergarments made of lace and eyelet, one diaphanous nightgown had tiny seed pearls sewn into its boarders at the sleeves, neck, and around the bottom.

Ben also purchased several day dresses as well and he bought her an expensive looking necklace and some earrings. When they left, he paid in gold coins.

For a time, Maddie fought the feeling of "being kept". What, she asked herself over and over, was her choice? She had arrived in this century with nothing but the tattered clothes on her back. Ben had a few dresses on the ship and those she had worn day in and day out. Moreover, she had arrived ill-equipped to support herself in any way—not that many women did support themselves in this era. That, she supposed, was why Sarah Oort so interested her. Obviously Sarah Oort had married money in the first instance, but somehow she had managed to parlay her inheritance into more money. Perhaps she was, as Ben and Melissa indicated, an untrustworthy and miserable woman, but she clearly had brains, too. Brains enough to be able to maintain her independence in a time when an independent woman was truly a rarity. Maddie glanced at Ben and wondered if there wasn't some way in which she could feel more independent, some way in which she could earn her keep, so to speak. *That way,* she thought, *I could come to him as a lover and feel truly free. And I want that,* she admitted.

Ben sat in a chair and watched her as she unpacked her new finery and carefully hung it up.

"You have a very smug look on your face," she observed.

"Ah, lass, you may claim be a time traveler, but it is evident to me that you are no different than any woman I know in at least one respect. You like to buy fine clothes."

Maddie looked up. "I admit it. And I admit I'm tired of wearing the same two or three dresses day in and day out."

"When we get to Curaçao, I'll take you to the place where my own treasure trove is stored. I did not make a heavy investment in jewels today because I have far better stored away. I've only been waiting for the right lily white neck on which to hang my emeralds, sapphires, and diamonds."

"I hardly know whether to take you seriously or not. In any case, I'm not a gold digger." She turned to him almost imploringly. "Ben, I may be different than others you have known even if you can't see it. I want to earn my own way—I don't just want to be your mistress."

He frowned. "And what is a gold digger? It's a term with which I am not familiar."

"A woman who only likes a man for his wealth."

He laughed. "Ah, lass I know you like me for more than that. Money is not an end in itself. It's a convenience."

Maddie smiled at him as she hung up a yellow dress. "This is a pretty dress. Everything is pretty. Thank you." She decided to leave her twentieth century thought for awhile. Maybe later she could make him understand what she meant, what she wanted.

"On you it will be ravishing. But tonight, after dinner when we return here, I expect at the very least you will model some of those silken undergarments . . ."

Her face flushed at the thought—they were the most lacy and seductive of articles. Two of them he had picked out himself, holding them up for her to view with a thoroughly wicked gleam in his dark eyes. And then, to embarrass her even further he had whispered in her ear, "I will cause you to suffer the agony of a thousand pleasures."

The very promise had sent a chill of pure wanton desire down her spine.

"I'm taking you and Melissa to the finest inn in New York Town for dinner. Wear that green dress I like so much."

Maddie nodded. It was the dress she had been wearing when they first . . . she shook her head to dispel thoughts of their lovemaking and reminded herself once again of Melissa's presence. She sincerely hoped she would not feel so put out with the girl at dinner as she had when she had first met her. *At least,* she reminded herself, *the shock of discovering Melissa was not a child was over.*

The Inn of the Three Feathers was near the water, but not near the docks. It appeared to be a rather more sophisticated place than where they were staying, though Maddie wasn't sure if it had accommodations for overnight guests or whether it only served meals. Hotels and restaurants as she knew them, did not yet exist. Still, once they were seated in the small private dining room overlooking the wild bushy landscape with the water seemingly below them and lapping up against the rocks, it seemed much like any restaurant she had ever been in, save for the fact that in some ways it was more elegant than most.

The table was set with a white damask cloth and had silver candlesticks. The silver was real and the china was real china from China.

"A fine red wine to celebrate our reunion, Melissa." Ben poured the wine into the silver goblets.

"To us," Melissa breathed.

Maddie remained silently put out. Melissa acted as if she didn't exist. Melissa's eyes glowed when she looked at Ben.

She was coquettish and Ben accepted it—*no,* she thought, *he is basking in it.*

"When will we sail for Curaçao?" Melissa asked.

"At dawn, the day after the Governor's ball. We will need a day to recover and I will need a little time to find a few new crew members. There are men I won't be taking." He glanced at Maddie who knew just the men he meant.

"And then?" Melissa's brows lifted expressively as she leaned across the table.

Ben lowered his voice to a near whisper. "We'll winter there. Let matters cool off a bit, then we'll collect the treasure and you will have your inheritance."

Melissa smiled. "My father was right to trust you, Ben York."

Much to Maddie's consternation, Melissa had reached across the table and covered Ben's hand with hers. Maddie felt like an outsider, as if she didn't belong. *I won't let her force herself between us,* she vowed silently.

"Your father was my friend, Melissa."

"My father made a terrible mistake when he married Sarah," Melissa confided, as she took a sip of her wine. "He even told me he had made a mistake. He was going to divorce her."

Ben nodded. "Sarah will be furious when she discovers you're gone."

"I imagine she knows by now that I'm gone. She'll be more than furious. But then, she only wanted me to stay so you would come for me. And now you have. You're so brave, Ben."

"Bravery has nothing to do with it."

"If what Melissa says is true, aren't we all in some danger now?" Maddie asked. Then she added, "You yourself said Sarah Oort was a dangerous woman."

"Dangerous but not foolhardy. And yes, there is some danger," Ben admitted. "That's why we're staying where we are. It's what you might call more secure."

"What can she do?" Maddie asked.

Ben half smiled, "Any number of things. But nothing too overt. She'll be careful because as powerful as she is, she too has enemies."

At that moment the innkeeper and his wife appeared with a wooden cart filled with food. It held dishes of green vegetables and baked potatoes. It's centerpiece was a large roast beef. With a flare, the innkeeper sharpened his knife and began carving. He gave each person what they asked for, trimming the fat carefully and adding juice from the finely cooked roast.

"I've been looking forward to this," Ben said. "What a lucky man I am, dining alone with the two most lovely young women in New York, and having the finest rare beef, too!"

Melissa smiled at Maddie who forced herself to return the smile.

She's very much prettier than Ben's other mistresses, Melissa thought as she looked at Maddie carefully and tried to take her measure. And she seemed smarter too . . . smart in a strange way. But she reminded herself, Ben had known many beautiful women and remained a bachelor all these years. *Waiting for me,* she thought to herself. It was no secret. She had been telling Ben York she loved him since she was four. And now she thought, looking at him fondly, now the time had come when he could tell her he loved her, too. Again she looked at Maddie. They were together in the same room, obviously they were lovers. Well, his infatuation would wear off. If not before they left New York, than after they arrived in Curaçao. *We are destined for one another,* Melissa thought as she gazed at Ben fondly. Perhaps her father had suspected as much when he left his fortune with Ben to give to her.

"Captain York?" A fresh-faced young man poked his head through the door just as the innkeeper was putting her plate in front of her. Maddie looked down on it wondering how anyone could possibly eat so much food, and then she looked up when the young man spoke.

"Aye," Ben replied.

"I've brought a message. The innkeeper at *The New Amsterdam-York Inn* said I'd find you here."

"And so you have." Ben held out his hand to receive the rolled parchment. Ben unrolled it and read it quickly. It did not surprise him that it was from Sarah Oort. He looked up at the messenger. "Tell Madam Oort I will be there at two. Alone."

"Thank you, Captain." The messenger turned on his heel and hurried away.

"Speak of the devil," Maddie said. "Well, she knows where we're staying."

"Ah, that's not what matters," Ben replied. "Well, I'll see her and find out what's on her mind."

"You already know," Melissa put in.

"Then I shall see her and we'll play a little cat and mouse."

"See to it that you're the cat," Maddie advised.

"Good advice," Ben laughed. "Let's eat, ladies. Let's eat."

When they returned to *The New Amsterdam-York Inn* a little after eleven p.m. Maddie felt comfortably full and ever so slightly aglow from the wine.

As they opened the door to their room, the first thing that greeted them was a huge copper tub sitting in the middle of the floor. Steam rose from its surface then disappeared in the dim pinkish light given off by the lamps which had funnels of tinted glass over their oil burning flames.

The huge four poster bed was covered with a quilt that had been turned back, and the bed, tub, and lighting all combined to make the room seem wonderfully warm, cozy, and romantic.

"How's that for a tub of hot water?" Ben asked as he

walked around it. "Ah, and look at this, Mother Molly has sent up fragrant soap and some perfumed oils."

Maddie felt her skin glow, not at what he said, but of how he said it—how he looked at her. "I've been day dreaming of a hot bath for weeks."

He smiled at her and then walked to her. Without another words, he began undressing her. He unlaced her bodice and slipped it off, then he removed her dress and petticoats. He looked at her for only a second, then he lifted her and set her into the warm water.

Maddie leaned back and closed her eyes, enjoying the sensation of the warm water. When she opened them, Ben had climbed into the tub, positioning himself so that he faced her.

The feel of the water and the nearness of him brought back that first wonderful night, and all thoughts of Melissa were forced from her thoughts by the sensations that surged through her.

In moments they were both covered with the lather of the fragrant soap. Ben's hands slid over her body, tickling and taunting her as she did the same to him.

Then, after a time, they rinsed off and climbed out of the tub. They dried each other off, and then Ben carried her to the bed.

Without a word, he began applying the perfumed oil. They had laughed and teased in the tub, but now they fell silent as the heady aroma filled the room. Maddie felt incredibly relaxed as Ben rubbed the oil into her back, over her buttocks, and then down over her legs.

Then gently he rolled her over. She moaned at his gentle touch, when he rubbed the oil on her breasts. It was deeply sensual, and her nipples hardened as he rubbed them, though barely seeming to touch them. Then his hands, smooth and soft, coated her stomach, her hips, and then her legs as he spread each droplet over her skin, drenching her in the fine oil.

She felt feverishly aroused by his movements, by the sweet smell of the oil, by the texture of her own skin as his hands slipped from one part of her to another, sailing over her, taunting her with sweet torturous movements that made her forget everything save the fact that he bent over her, touching her while barely seeming to touch her.

When at long last he joined with her, she lifted herself to him, holding him close, kissing him frantically as she fell with him into throbbing fulfilment. In his arms, her face buried in his chest, there was nothing else. No past, no present, no future. There was only the intensity of the moment, the enduring feeling she had that they were somehow destined to one another's arms.

Sarah Oort's receiving room had all the comforts of such a room in upper-class London or even Paris. The furniture was exquisitely upholstered in rich tapestry and many of the chairs and tables were from the Orient.

Ben perched somewhat uncomfortably on the edge of the divan, an ornate and large piece of furniture perched on four spindly legs.

Sarah, wearing a flowing silken gown reclined comfortably on a brocade chaise lounge.

"You do look like a bird about to fly away," she commented dryly. "Really, dear Ben. Please feel free to lean back and light your pipe. You do still smoke, don't you? I always loved the smell of your tobacco."

"I do and thank you." He produced his pipe, feeling instantly better. The ritual of preparing the pipe gave him something to do. It was an incredible tension reliever.

"I presume you came to New York for dear little Melissa."

He saw no necessity to lie, and in any case she certainly knew Melissa had come with him. "And to see you as well, Sarah."

"How charming."

She smiled devastatingly and he warned himself not to let down his guard. Her blond hair was loose, and she had positioned herself seductively on the lounge so that the curve of her angular hip could be seen. Sarah Oort could purr like a kitten, then claw like the cat he knew her to be. "Melissa is not here, I presume you've already spirited her away."

"I did no spiriting, Sarah. She left here of her own free will."

"Oh, gracious, I did not mean to imply otherwise. She's been waiting for you Ben. You're all she talks about."

"I hardly think so."

"Then you think incorrectly. Melissa's been in love with you all her life. She's been waiting for you to come and take her away."

"How flattering a picture you paint. Melissa is young enough to be my daughter. Were she waiting for me in the sense you imply, she will be sorrily disappointed. She is with the woman I love at this very moment."

"Ah, you've taken a new lover! How utterly delightful!"

"More than a new lover, I think. Much more."

"My, is this the same Ben York I've known? You do seem changed."

"In a way. I've brought something for you, Sarah. Something William bade me give you."

Ben watched as Sarah's eyes flashed and she leaned forward in anticipation. "That is a surprise, I thought his treasure would all go to little Melissa."

"He bade me give her gifts as well."

"And the bulk of his treasure . . ."

"A myth, Sarah, you should know that."

"I know no such thing. If it is a myth why are you taking Melissa away?"

"Because she wishes to come to Curaçao. I promised William she would be tutored. I intend to keep my promise."

"And am I deserving of nothing? I've spent a lot on the

girl, I've looked after her for three years now and she isn't even my own child."

Ben forced himself to remain poker-faced. He knew full well about the stipend, but there were things better left unsaid. "I know that, and so did William. I'm sure that's the reason I've been told to deliver these to you." He stood up and withdrawing a leather pouch from his pocket, handed it to Sarah Oort.

Sarah took it and quickly opened it. She shook out its contents into her hand. "Ah," she said with a sly smile. "My, my, what beautiful stones! And so well-matched." She held four large diamonds, six sapphire, four emeralds, and two rubies.

"They're fine jewels," he reiterated. "A small fortune."

"*Small* being the key word—they are but a fraction of the so-called 'myth', yes?"

"But the total of the reality," he lied, wanting her to believe, but sure she wouldn't.

"Well I am pleased that dear William remembered our better moments together. I'm quite satisfied, Ben. Thank you."

Her eyes stared into his, but no matter how straightforward her stare he did not believe her for a single second. Sarah Oort could never be satisfied. And the truth was, the jewels were valuable. But of course Sarah was right. They were indeed, a fraction of the whole.

He stood up then. "I must be leaving."

"So soon. You won't even sip a brandy with me?"

"I can't really. But I will see you at the Governor's Ball."

"Oh, what a delightful surprise to learn you've been invited. But of course, darling, I do hope you will dance with me once, at the very least."

"I shouldn't miss it, Sarah. It would be my greatest pleasure."

"And mine will be to meet your lover—what is her name?"

"Maddie Emerson."

"Quaint," Sarah purred.

She extended her arm, offering him her tiny hand. He kissed it and gave it a squeeze just to let her know she did not unnerve him. "Till Saturday night."

"Till Saturday night," she repeated.

Chapter Nine

Governor Bellomont's residence was located in the center of a large square that comprised Fort York at the foot of Broad Way. Across the way from the Governor's Mansion was the Secretaries Office, and on the other side, King's Chapel. The other buildings housed troops although the Custom House, the City Hall, and the Jail, all at the foot of Broad Street, also had a compliment of troops.

Sarah Oort had no difficulty entering the compound as she was well-known to the guards as a frequent visitor. She was escorted down the long corridor and shown into the reception room. There, as was the custom, she waited for the governor's wife.

Sarah Oort ran her hand abstractedly over her white blond hair, brushing wisps of it off her forehead. Then, while still waiting, she took stock of the governor's reception room, mentally appraising each and every item. It was, she quickly concluded, furnished no better than her own reception room. But then, the governor's wife was considerably younger than she—younger and less experienced in decorating, dress, and the accumulation of wealth.

She herself had married young and well to William Cox. The home she moved into was completely furnished and when he died she inherited everything. She took her inheritance into her marriage with the already wealthy John Oort, who also died. Then she married William Kidd, recently executed in England for piracy. Kidd had enriched her ten times over. And she thought, unable to suppress her smile, he would make her even wealthier once his treasure was found.

Beatrix Bellomont glided into the room. She wore a rich lace petticoat with a gold overdress. Her sleeves were embellished with lace. Beatrix was also a blond of excellent proportions. She had darting brown eyes and full lips. Beatrix also had an obvious kind of sexuality, a kind of plump readiness that intrigued many a man. Not that she was fat, it was merely that she had a look of ripeness about her, a soft fleshiness that men found nearly irresistible.

"Sarah! How glad I am to see you. I grow so lonely."

Sarah smiled tolerantly. She supposed that Beatrix was to be pitied. Lord Bellomont was much older than she—older, careful, and jealous of his possessions. He most certainly considered Beatrix one of those possessions, she was his pride and joy.

Not that being married stopped Lord Bellomont from enjoying dalliances. Not at all. In fact, Sarah thought, she'd been in bed with him several times in the last month. Not that Beatrix suspected, and not that it was an affair that meant anything. Going to bed with Governor Bellomont was, Sarah reflected, rather like taking out an insurance policy. The premiums were high, but they lessened risks taken. But at this moment, it was not the governor she cared about. It was Beatrix. She had carefully cultivated Beatrix's friendship over the past year, and now it was time to ask a few favors.

"I'd come more often, but my businesses keep me occupied."

"How fortunate you are to have businesses—I get quite bored myself."

Sarah smiled. "Sometimes they keep me too busy. I wasn't home when Ben York came for Melissa."

"You mean he kidnapped her?"

"No, she went with him of her own free will. But of course I wanted to see Ben York myself."

"And now you've missed him?"

"No. I learned where he was and sent him a message. To my surprise he came to see me. He brought a small legacy from my late husband."

"Oh! That's wonderful! What did he bring?"

"Jewels—lovely jewels, really. But I'm sure they're only a portion of what is hidden somewhere."

"And he intends to keep the rest? That's illegal. Besides, it isn't nice."

"I can prove nothing, dear Beatrix, nothing. Ben is a handsome thief."

"We should tell my husband. He could have Ben York arrested."

Sarah smiled sweetly. "Oh, I know. But there's always a danger when one gets arrested. Sometimes the interrogators are too—shall I say vigorous—in their interrogation."

"You mean they might hurt him?"

"My dear, they might kill him."

"Oh, dear. I'm sure my husband wouldn't . . ."

"Intentionally—no, I'm sure he wouldn't. But still, there would be witnesses and far too many people would learn the secret. No, the fewer who learn where the treasure trove is, the better."

"But how will you find out?"

Sarah touched young Beatrix's arm. "With your help, I hope."

"My help? Oh, Sarah, how could I possibly help?"

"Beatrix, you're young and you're beautiful. I know you have wiles that you can exercise."

"But I'm married."

"Men are not faithful nor do women need to be. John Bellomont is old, Ben York is young and exciting. He'd be a challenge for you, Beatrix. In any case it would be a short liaison—a tender union with important pillow talk."

Beatrix smiled. "Do you think he might like me enough to confide in me?" Her eyes twinkled.

"I'm quite sure he would find you irresistible. And of course we could ensure his pliability with a little of your husband's special cognac."

"You're so naughty, Sarah. But where will I meet him, I mean when will the opportunity to offer him the cognac arise?"

"At the ball on Saturday. Ben is coming with his mistress."

"But what about her? And whatever will John think?"

"Darling, John will be much to busy to notice, and I'm sure Ben's mistress is no match for you."

"You're so flattering."

"Truth is no flattery. I know he'll like you, and properly questioned after drinking enough of your cognac and I'm sure he'll talk."

"It does sound like fun."

"Lucrative fun," Sarah said leaning even closer. "I'll share William's fortune with you, Beatrix. You could be independent."

Beatrix smiled radiantly. "I'll do it," she agreed.

Sarah leaned over and kissed her young protege on the cheek. The bored and the frustrated always made good accomplices, she thought. In any case, far from putting all her eggs in one basket, she had neatly divided them and would indeed divide them further.

Phineas Pike was a short bear of a man whose height belied his strength. He had small dark feral eyes and a large, red square nose that was so pig-like in appearance that it might better have been called a snout. The rest of his face was obscured in a dense black beard which was greasy and unkempt. His teeth were rotting stubs which caused him days of pain and added to his natural bad temper. Phineas Pike was a dangerous man for he was both untrustworthy and dishonest in the extreme. There was blood on his hands, murder in his heart, and hatreds, new and old, plagued his soul.

At this moment, Captain Pike's ship, the *Whippet*, was anchored not at the foot of Dock Street with the other vessels, but rather on the east side of the island several miles past the new docks that lay opposite Great Queen Street, and offshore so that the vessel could be reached only by rowing out to it.

Phineas Pike himself was in his cabin sitting at a table in front of a half-empty whiskey bottle. Opposite him sat a handsome young man named Jason Richards and two old crew members—men who had not sailed with him for several years, yet men who were well-known to him. One was Riffen Moore and the other was Digby Daws.

"More?" Pike questioned as he held up the whiskey bottle.

"Two fingers," Riffen answered, making a gesture to indicate just how much he wished.

"Two fingers it will be and I'll wager you never sat at Captain York's table and drank whiskey."

"Not us," Digby put in. "No, Captain York is too fancy for the likes of us, but he's known to have taken whiskey and even broken bread with that black bastard, that Black Henri."

Riffen made a guttural noise and Captain Pike made a face.

"Soon they'll all be dead and we'll be rich," Riffen added.

"Our days of sailing with Captain York are over," Digby intoned, taking a swig of his whiskey. "We were told when we went ashore not to come back. He called us troublemakers. Well, I for one am prepared to show him real trouble."

Pike laughed. "He ain't seen half the trouble you can make, hey boys?"

"Not half," Riffen muttered. "Not half."

"I always thought that bastard York knew where Kidd hid his treasure," Pike muttered.

"We don't know the exact location. We only know he intends to give it to Kidd's daughter."

"Aye, that should make Sarah Oort his dear bereaved widow a happy woman," Pike sneered sarcastically.

"York won't talk," Digby said.

"He'll talk if we have the girl—Kidd's daughter," Pike sneered, rubbing his chin.

"And where might we find her?" Digby asked.

"She's staying at Mother Molly's—*The New Amsterdam-York Inn* on Princess Street."

"I'll fancy York is there, too, with his dark-haired wench."

Pike laughed. "I've seen Kidd's daughter. She's a tender little morsel."

"If we know where she is, what keeps us from grabbing her?"

Pike spit on the floor. "The desire not to get caught. Jason, you've been as quiet as a lamb."

"I've been listening, Uncle."

"Good. Now listen to this. York, his wench, and Melissa will be going to the Governor's ball on Saturday. You'll be going too Jason, and you will take up with Melissa and lure her away. We'll be waiting."

"And then we'll have our fun!" Riffen sneered.

"We'll keep her in one piece till we have what we want. She's more than just a tender morsel, she's the ticket to Kidd's treasure," Pike reminded them.

"What makes you think Ben York will tell where the treasure is to save her?"

Pike spit. "I know York. He promised Kidd he'd look after little Melissa."

Riffen roared. "We'll look after her! We'll look after her good."

Pike poured some more whiskey, then he turned and picked up a parchment. "I have a plan of the governor's house and a map of the city. We'll make our plans tonight."

"Good," Riffen and Digby both said together. Then they raised their glasses toward young Jason. "To a handsome young man who'll catch us a tender young morsel."

Pike laughed. "Makes me glad I educated ye, lad!"

* * *

Governor Bellomont walked around his study purposefully, his hands clasped behind his back. Walking helped him to think and thinking matters through was essential if one were to succeed.

Michael Faraday was, on the other hand a sitter. He watched Bellomont move around the room. Bellomont was a portly man who was built like a large ball atop two spindly legs. He was, to be sure, a well-dressed ball—all trimmed in lace and dripping with gold chains.

"Tell me about his mistress," Governor Bellomont urged. "What have you learned?"

Faraday smiled. "Rather a lot, though generally his crew is not talkative. They were on some island, though the crew doesn't seem to know where. It was summer and it was hot and from the description I would say it was north rather than south. Perhaps off Maine. In any case it was a rocky island. Most of the crew would not speak of any island but one or two disgruntled crew—who are not sailing with York when he leaves—told us what we know."

"If he leaves," Bellomont interrupted.

"If he leaves," Faraday amended. "In any case, they spoke of this nameless island and of pits. But they said that only a few things were retrieved and three trunks were buried."

"I see. And the wench?"

"She was found on the island. She's a mystery. But apparently there was trouble on the ship. Some of the crew wanted her and York stopped them."

"One can hardly blame him. She might have been killed," Bellomont said.

"And that would have been a pity. She's a real beauty," Faraday said, steepling his hands.

"I see. Well the solution to our little dilemma seems quite simple. As soon as they arrive at the ball I will take Captain York's mistress in tow. I think we can count on Sarah Oort to keep Captain York occupied. I'll drug the wench and see what I can get out of her. If I learn what I hope to learn, we can arrest Ben York and make him talk."

"So, you'll get information out of her—is that all you intend?" Faraday laughed wickedly, and Bellomont grinned.

"Why not have a little fun? If she's half the woman you say she is, I shall have great trouble resisting. A governor must have his pleasure, too."

Michael Faraday laughed again. Saturday night had all the makings of a fine night. He decided it would be most entertaining. His spies in the mansion had told him of Sarah's visit and her conversation with Beatrix. What with Beatrix cornering Ben and the governor cornering Ben's mistress, he felt he himself would have no difficulty with the most satisfying Sarah Oort. Yes, all in all, he thought, Saturday would be truly the most entertaining of the Governor's Balls.

"You both look breathtaking," Ben said as he helped Maddie and Melissa out of the carriage. "I'm going to be the envy of every man here since I'm escorting the two most ravishing women in all New York."

Melissa, looked youthfully lovely in a low cut snow white gown with an overskirt patterned to look like snowflakes. She wore a sparkling tiara studded with tiny diamonds and a half silver mask to complete her costume of a winter princess. She smiled radiantly up at Ben and fluttered her eyelashes. "You should make no judgments about beauty till you've met Katherine Bellomont."

"I'm sure she couldn't compete with either of you."

Maddie smoothed out her dress and said nothing. She felt as if she looked good, if somewhat exposed by her Roman costume which was draped over one shoulder and clung to her body. Still, it was better than the actual clothes of this period. There were restrictive and generally a bother. Small wonder women were so helpless, they could neither run nor kick. Her costume was an improvement. Its folds were at least graceful and its long skirt was not full and awkward because it wasn't held out by paniers and stayed petticoats. Unlike Melissa's hair, which was elaborately coiffed, her own hair fell loose, and was crowned with a ring of gold leaves. She wore a plain white half mask

As they approached the great double doors of the Governor's Mansion, the doors swung open and they were ushered into a large wide hallway. Maddie looked about curiously.

Ben whispered to the butler who then announced in a loud voice, "Captain Benjamin York, Miss Melissa Kidd, and Miss Maddie Emerson!"

They moved down a long reception line and then they passed into a huge room lit by silver candelabras.

Everything about the houses and their furnishings interested Maddie. To her the furnishings seemed priceless. She had only begun to realize that material possessions were more precious than in her own time. A person's wealth, she learned, was judged not so much by what he or she had in gold, but how many precious belongings one had accumulated. Dishes, silverware, furniture—all were handmade rather than mass-produced, and all were apparently counted and taxed.

Mother Molly was considered rich because she owned one hundred ounces of silver, sixteen chairs, eleven tables, twelve beds, and three Turkish rugs. The idea that financial worth was measured out in teaspoons, cups, and saucers had never occurred to Maddie. Gold and jewels were naturally valuable, but household items were precious, hard to come by, and they were both treasured and measured. Moreover, value was accorded in strange ways. A cup and saucer were seen as more valuable than a small inlaid mother-of-pearl fan from the Orient. It was all very odd and all because mass production was as yet unknown.

Maddie was pondering these things as she stepped into the ballroom on Ben's arm.

"Ah, Captain York, I presume."

A gregarious humpty dumpty-looking man decked out in rich silly looking clothing and dripping with gold and jewels smiled at them. "Governor Bellomont at your service."

Ben bowed from the waist. " 'Tis I who am at your service," he answered.

The governor smiled and withdrew a gold snuff box and sniffed of its contents. "You bring not one, but two lovely ladies to my home, Captain. I'm both flattered and grateful."

Again Ben smiled. "I'm certain you know Miss Melissa Kidd. And this is Miss Maddie Emerson."

"Yes, of course I know Miss Kidd.

He turned immediately to Maddie and took her hand. "My dear, I'm so very happy to make your acquaintance. And where are you from, sweet lady?"

"Boston," Maddie replied.

"A wonderful city! A truly wonderful city! Ah, listen, the music has begun. Please my dear, come and dance with me."

Ben let go of her arm and actually spun her toward the Governor. Clearly she was to dance with him and she assumed that saying no to someone in his position was not allowed.

Maddie was not certain just what she had expected, but within seconds she realized that the music was slow and stilted and that this dance consisted of formal movements, rather like the minuet, but not quite as formalized. She tried to do as the others did, but succeeded in feeling nothing less than awkward.

Nonetheless, she persevered. Then, across the dance floor she saw Ben. He was not with Melissa, but with another blond. A very pretty blond who somehow seemed to be pouring out over the top of her gold lamé dress. Ben was dressed as a "highwayman" and he looked nothing short of dashing.

"Oh, I do hope you're not jealous," the governor said. "I see you've spotted Captain York and my wife, Beatrix. She's come as King Midas's wife."

Maddie forced a smile because the governor seemed to be looking at her hungrily. But surely a man with such an attractive younger wife was satisfied! At least she hoped so. It seemed to her as if all the men she'd met were incredibly lecherous. Not that twentieth century men weren't lecherous, too—but somehow they didn't always seem so obvious. She supposed that was because these men were allowed to be obvious, while twentieth century men were bound by different customs as well as by law.

"I'm not a very good dancer," Maddie said, hesitatingly. "We don't have much time for dancing in Boston."

"Oh, don't I know it! So Puritan! But surely you're not a Puritan, are you?"

"No," Maddie answered truthfully. She hoped he wouldn't ask her what she was.

"Tell me how do you spend your time in Boston, my dear?"

Maddie wasn't sure how to respond. "I read a lot," she finally said, and immediately she regretted her honesty, remembering how few women in this time period read.

"Read! How perfectly wonderful! I have quite a library, the largest in New York. May I show it to you?"

Was this some rouse to get her alone? Maddie hesitated, then decided she was being foolish. The house was full of people and with this man she could certainly take care of herself. "I'd like very much to see the library."

He led her out onto a balcony and then along the side of the house and through a set of glass doors into a large room filled with leather bound books.

"Oh, it smells wonderful in here," Maddie said looking around. The fact was, she was glad to escape the sight of Ben fawning first over Melissa and then over the governor's young wife. He hadn't looked at her since they had arrived. Was Ben really a womanizer? The question plagued her. Melissa never stopped flirting with him, and seemed to enjoy it. Yes, Maddie knew she was feeling annoyed. Annoyed with

Ben and annoyed with herself for letting a young girl like
Melissa bother her.

"Please, please feel free to look about. I'll pour us a spot
of fine French cognac."

Maddie began examining the books. It was incredibly exciting. It was like discovering a rare bookstore, not that they
were rare yet, but they would be and they seemed so expensive to her.

Governor Bellomont went to the sideboard, and since he
was standing with his back toward her, he did not bother to
hide the smile that covered his face as he poured her cognac
from a special bottle, and his from another. The bottle from
which he poured her drink was laced with a wonderful potion. It would render her silly and pliable for a time, and then
it would send her into a deep sleep. He hardly knew which
stage he relished most.

"Here you are, my dear."

Maddie took the cognac off the silver tray. She sipped it
and felt it immediately, as it warmed her throat, then her
chest. It relaxed her wonderfully. She withdrew a book from
the shelf. "Oh, this looks very interesting."

"Please, take it with you. Let it be my gift to you."

Maddie smiled up at him. "Oh, thank you."

He bent over and refilled her glass and smiled.

Maddie took another drink, and then another. One sip made
her seem to want more. "Books—book—they must be
expen—expensive." She finally forced the last syllable out of
her mouth. Then she giggled. She felt strange, lightheaded,
and silly. *Why?* she forced herself to try to think, but she
couldn't. She felt nothing short of giddy.

She took another sip to clear her head. But it was no use,
she only felt like laughing even though the room was spin-
ning, her knees felt weak, and she knew if she tried to stand
she would surely fall. "The dr—drink," she finally managed.

"Is a delightful cognac," Governor Bellomont replied as he
leaned over her.

His face looked so round she was suddenly obsessed with her earlier image of Humpty Dumpty and she burst into uncontrollable laughter, murmuring, "all the King's horses and all the King's men—couldn't, no they couldn't put, put . . ."

Governor Bellomont seized her shoulders and shook her ever so slightly. "Tell me, where exactly did you meet Ben York?"

Maddie stared at him. She had no idea where she was, nor who he was, but somehow she understood the question. "Oak Island. I went on a mystery tour."

She watched uncomprehendingly as Humpty Dumpty's brows lifted in surprise. "A mystery tour?" he repeated.

"Buried—buried . . . ah, treasure," she slurred just as she slipped off the divan and onto the floor. Her last incoherent thought was that she would wake up in the twentieth century and she shook her head and cried, "No, Ben—Ben!"

"Shh, poor dear girl," Governor Bellomont muttered as be bent over her unconscious form. A smiled crept across his face. "Ah, I can hardly wait to undress you. And when you're quite undressed, well, we'll have a little talk and then I'll have a little entertainment."

Governor Bellomont ran his hand lightly over Maddie's bare shoulder, then he touched her breast almost furtively. "Oh, it's so hard to wait," he said aloud. But then he sighed. Women had their place, but money was more important.

Governor Bellomont tinkled a little bell on the table and in moments two large men entered. "So much easier than I thought," he announced. "Take her to my quarters and tie her to my bed."

One of the men lifted Maddie and tossed her over his shoulder. They left quickly, by the back entrance. The governor, humming to himself, put away the brandy and returned to the ball, dancing with some undistinguished-looking woman, then he headed, humming to himself, off to his private quarters. Below, the liquor flowed like water. Absolutely no one would miss him.

He lit the lamp in his quarters and looked at Maddie on the bed. "Trussed up like a little piglet," he said with a smile, as he bent over her. "Humpty Dumpty, indeed," he muttered in irritation. "I'll teach you a lesson or two." He sat down on the edge of the bed and fiddled with her dress, undoing it at the shoulder. Then he slipped his hand beneath the soft fabric and cupped her breast in his hand. "Oh, what lovely breasts, you have," he said aloud. Quickly, he removed her dress, leaving her only in her petticoats. Then he shook his head and forced his bulk up. "You're going to be quite a delight, my dear. But you'll be here as long as I want you here, and I really have things I must see to first."

He went to a chest and returned with a long silk scarf. He tied it round her mouth so she couldn't scream if she awoke, then he gathered up her dress. "Just to show your Captain in case he doesn't believe that you're in my bed and told me the facts that lead to his arrest."

Lastly, Governor Bellomont blew out the lamp leaving Maddie bound, gagged, and unconscious in the darkness. He hurried off into the night. First to write an arrest order, second to question Captain Ben York when he was brought to the police station.

Beatrix Bellomont wore a gold half-mask that did nothing to disguise her true identity. Her dress was gold and studded with shimmering sequins. Cut daringly low, it revealed her swan-like bosom while the color made her hair seem even blonder and her skin even whiter.

Beatrix had taken Ben to an alcove between dances. She stood close to him, so close he could smell the perfume in her wild golden hair. "Please, have another glass of wine, Captain."

Ben sipped the dark red wine. Beatrix Bellomont was indeed beautiful, and he admitted, seductive. She moved closer to him and moved against him suggestively, clearly offering herself. Not that he blamed her for desiring another man—her husband was three times her age, and hardly a dashing man. Still, Governor Bellomont was a powerful man and some women were attracted to power.

He looked down into Beatrix Bellomont's eyes—eyes which begged him to take her. It was then that he knew for certain that something had changed for him. Only weeks ago he would have accepted her unspoken, but nonetheless, brazen invitation. He would have whisked Beatrix Bellomont away and known immense pleasure with her. But then, weeks ago he might even have looked a second time at Melissa who had changed mightily since he'd last seen her. But all that was before Maddie, his mysterious woman of the island. Strange though she was, and even if he couldn't quite accept her tale of time travel, he was bound to her. He looked at other women, but he knew he did not really see them as he once had. Instead he heard in his mind, Maddie's musical laugh, he remembered their talks, and he relived their wild passionate encounters. She was a tiger of a woman; she was his woman, and for the first time in his life, he wanted no other.

But protocol was such that he could not be rude to the wanton Beatrix Bellomont. He wanted only to get away from her. He searched the crowded room, looking over her blond head. Maddie and Governor Bellomont were no where to be seen and equally puzzling was the fact that Melissa seemed to have disappeared, as well. It was as if both of them have been somehow spirited away—it was then that he realized it had been well over an hour since he had seen either of them.

"What is it, darling Ben?" Beatrix cooed.

"I haven't seen the ladies I'm escorting for some time."

Beatrix laughed. "Oh, I'm certain Melissa Kidd can take care of herself. She was dancing with a very handsome young man. Perhaps they went into the garden together."

"Perhaps," he agreed. "But where is Maddie?"

"Maybe they're together. In fact, perhaps they're in the ladies powder room. Shall I investigate for you?"

"Would you?" Perhaps his mention of Melissa and Maddie had made her realize he had no intention of being unfaithful.

"Of course, darling. Come along. I'll deposit you in the library while I check on the whereabouts of your ladies."

She took his hand and led him out of the alcove, across the main ballroom, and then down a long corridor and into the library.

"Here we are. Now, let's see, I'll pour you some cognac and then go and look in the powder room."

"I've really had a lot to drink already," Ben protested.

"Nonsense! The governor had a very special old, imported cognac here. Ah, yes, here it is. I'm sure he would want you to sample it."

Ben sank into a comfortable chair and watched as she poured the cognac into a silver goblet. There were two goblets on the sideboard already, he vaguely wondered who else had come to sample the governor's cognac.

"Now you drink it all down, and I'll be right back."

Ben waved at her as she disappeared, then he took a long sip of the cognac. It was all she had promised, smooth as silk, a truly fine cognac.

Beatrix glided through the library door, leaving it ajar. She paused outside, looking through the crack. Her husband had shown her the drugged cognac months ago so she would not drink it unwittingly or offer it to guests.

Beatrix waited, then murmured, "No, no . . ." Ben York was supposed to stay awake long enough to answer questions, long enough to make love to her! But he had not! He had slumped down in the chair and appeared to be quite dead to the world. She hurried back inside the library and looked him, jostling him ever so slightly.

His eyes did not open. "Damn!" Beatrix whispered. It must have been all the wine. Combined with the drug in the cognac, it was too much. Beatrix sighed. Sarah Oort would be angry. And come to think of it, she was angry too. He was so handsome! And he hadn't even kissed her before falling into this—this drunken stupor. Abstractedly, she kicked the chair and swore under her breath. "You were going to be my stallion!" she breathed. "But now it's back to my big pig!"

Melissa walked by young Jason's side. He was very suave, but of course he lacked Ben York's maturity and experience. Still, a woman should have some experience, too, Melissa rationalized. Yes, every conquest was nothing but a step toward the fulfillment of her dream to marry Ben York.

She wondered if she and this handsome young man had been gone long enough to make Ben jealous. And where on earth had Maddie disappeared to? Not that she really cared. In fact, she could hope that Maddie would never come back. Ben did seem all too attached to her. Well, she thought, he would get over it. Then it occurred to her that Maddie might be playing the same game she was playing. Was she also trying to make Ben jealous?

Melissa tossed her strawberry-blond curls in silent annoyance then she turned to Jason. "We've walked a good distance now. We're practically beyond the garden. In fact, I'm not sure we're still in the garden at all. I think we better head back."

Jason suddenly grasped her wrist. "I think not, Miss Kidd."

"Let go of me! Let go of me this instant! I'll scream and the guards will come! I'll have you arrested!"

"I think not!" Jason answered menacingly.

Melissa opened her mouth in surprise. He held a long glittering blade, and he held it dangerously close to her throat. The scream she was about to utter died inside her, and she suddenly felt a wave of real panic surge through her.

"Scream and you will never scream again! Now, come, hurry!"

He pulled her along. They were suddenly off the path and in a thicket. "My dress is tearing!" Melissa gasped.

"Shut up, or I'll tear it off!"

Melissa began to shake. Then Jason whistled through his teeth and suddenly from out of nowhere, two large ugly and foul smelling men appeared.

"Oh, she is a pretty little morsel. Your uncle was right." Digby grinned lecherously at Melissa.

"Don't touch me! I'm Melissa Kidd!"

"Aye, the daughter of a hung pirate. You're soon to be the pleasure of his much ill-treated crew."

Melissa felt as if she were going to faint. What were these horrible men going to do to her? Did they intend—Oh, dear heaven—she wanted to scream, but she couldn't.

"No time for that now. Money first and women after," Riffen muttered. "Here, gag her and tie her up. I've got a big sack right here. We'll just put her in it and take her to Captain Pike."

The ugly man hadn't even finished speaking when the other man gagged her. They tied her hands and feet and then put a huge sack over her. They tore off her skirt so the sack would fit, then one of them tossed it over his shoulder, and carried her away as if she were a sack of grain.

They quickly tossed her into a wagon and after a long bumpy ride, she was carried along a rutted path. They were near water, she could smell the salt air. Then she knew they tossed her in the bottom of a boat. She felt the boat being rowed across the water. Then, after a time, there was much yelling and she was put into a rope basket and hauled aboard some unknown vessel.

"Git her out of the sack!" someone shouted. "She'll smother and she ain't no good for nothing dead!"

The sack was taken off and her gag removed. Melissa gasped for air, and looked around her. A collection of ill-dressed, foul smelling cut-throats leered back at her. Not one of them, not a single one save Jason looked even decent. And clearly he was no better than the others since it was he who had delivered her to this fate worse than death.

"Aren't you the pretty little thing," Captain Pike said, chucking her under the chin.

"Don't touch me!" Melissa shrieked.

"Well, I won't for now, my dearie. Got to keep the merchandise in good condition, eh? Take her to the room behind me cabin and lock her in."

Melissa staggered, then mercifully, she passed out.

scarily he was not some from the pliers shack ...

"Ain't you the pretty little thing," Cantrel like said ...

Cora ... good Melissa snarled ...

"Well, I saw the how ... quanta? ... to keep the ...

the table and left her in ...

Melissa ... more Hally, Chu ... of ...

Chapter Ten

Governor Bellomont went directly from his private quarters to his office on the main floor of his mansion. He stormed in the door and stopped to look with disgust on a relaxed and half-asleep guard. The guard jumped to his feet, smoothed out his uniform and still looking utterly flustered to see the governor at this hour while the ball was still in full swing, snapped to attention.

"Summon Faraday! the governor blustered.

"Yes, Governor!" The guard stood still, then revealing his confusion, "And where might I summon him from?"

"From the ball I imagine, and if he's not there, try his private apartment. He might well be with some wench."

The guard nodded and hurried away. Personally, he hoped to find Faraday dancing the night away. It had been his experience that men summoned while in the midst of a sexual liaison were seldom in a good mood and in fact, could be out and out dangerous.

"And tell my wife to come in here, too!" Bellomont shouted after the guard.

"Yes, Governor."

Bellomont opened his desk drawer and shuffled about for parchment, then dipping his ornate quill pen into the ink, he began to write the arrest order for Ben York with a flourish.

It was twenty minutes before Mike Faraday appeared. Governor Bellomont looked up in annoyance. Faraday was practically still dressing, a sure sign he had been with some woman and not attending to business.

"Yes, Governor. At your service." Faraday straightened up and tried to look less dishevelled then he felt. Sarah Oort was nothing less than insatiable and he felt utterly spent.

"Good thing you're young," the governor grumped. "Well, I believe I have sufficient information—that is I have sufficient cause to issue an arrest order for Captain Ben York and his crew."

"Have you written it yet, Sir?"

"Yes, I have only to affix the official seal."

Mike Faraday turned to the cupboard, opened it, and handed the governor the heavy metal embosser which would imprint the document with the official seal of New York.

He watched while the governor embossed the document and then he took it.

"Well, what are you waiting for?" the governor asked.

"Just where might I find Captain York?" Faraday asked, lifting his brow. "I don't believe he is in the ballroom."

"How should I know? I don't even know where you might find his crew."

"Find whose crew?" Beatrix Bellomont asked as she glided through the door.

"Captain York's crew. Have you seen him?"

"Indeed. He's in our library quite unconscious."

"Drunk?" Bellomont asked.

"No, I gave him the wrong cognac—it was all a mistake."

Bellomont grinned. "Mistake or no, it's most fortunate, my dear. Well, Faraday, that makes a part of your task a bit easier. Beatrix, you return to our guests and I'll see to Captain York."

Beatrix made a pouty face and then turned and left in search of Sarah Oort.

"Come along, Faraday." Bellomont guided Faraday down the long hall.

"Where's the woman?" Faraday asked.

"Tied up in my quarters awaiting my pleasure," Bellomont answered with a slight wink. "She will simply have to wait till I've questioned Ben York. Business before pleasure, right Faraday?"

"Right, Governor."

"It's a lesson you should learn."

Mike Faraday turned red, but said nothing more. The governor was in a good mood because everything was going well for him, and according to his plan.

Will McNab had remained on the ship for one night, then he had gone to *The New Amsterdam-York Inn* where Mother Molly had allowed him to sleep on the sun porch.

But tonight, with Captain York and the ladies gone, he accompanied Bob Tanner and Lopez de Vaca to the dockside pub, *The Crown and the Anchor.* There, the three of them met up with seven other crew members for an evening of eating and drinking. Not that any of them allowed young Will to drink. But he was allowed to sit with them and partake in the conversation now and again. All of Captain York's loyal crew had vowed to protect young Will and each treated him as they might have treated a younger brother.

Black Henri, Lopez de Vaca, Samuel Harrowsmith, Bob Tanner, Yan Ould, Juan Corso, and Jack Hacket were all like family to Will, though he was closest to Black Henri. Black Henri did not come to *The Crown and The Anchor* because he was staying with friends some miles away.

It was near midnight and Will, who had moved away from the table and positioned himself in a corner by the hearth, was nearly asleep. Then there was a great commotion which jolted him into frightened consciousness. The King's soldiers poured through all the entrances of the pub, muskets and swords drawn as if for a pitched battle.

"Hold still and no one will be hurt," an officer said, stepping forward.

The innkeeper looked horrified. A normally robust man, Will noticed that all color had drained from his face. "What have I done?" he wailed.

"Nothing. We seek only members of the crew of the *Wilma*. Be there any here?"

"Over there!" The man who shouted pointed to the long table where Bob Tanner, Lopez de Vaca, and Runner Jim sat.

The three of them stood up. Will felt frozen to the spot, he crouched down, hoping to be overlooked.

Seeing no escape, his three friends didn't go for their swords, but stood stark still. Then Bob Tanner spoke, "Why are you seeking the crew of the *Wilma?*"

The officer unrolled a parchment. "I have here an arrest order signed by the governor." He didn't read the document, but only waved it imperiously.

Will watched in horror as his three friends were marched out of the tavern. No one seemed to notice him but still he did not move right away for fear they would. For what seemed a long time to Will, the room was ominously silent, then gradually men again began to drink and the serving girls again began to laugh.

Will eased his way from the corner of the hearth toward the back door. Then when everyone was distracted by a fat buffoon who was drinking a tankard of ale straight down, he slipped out the door into the darkness of the night. He leaned against the building for a second, trying to think.

If there was an order from the governor to arrest the crew, then most certainly there was an order to arrest Captain York. He had overheard a few conversations—now they made sense to him. There were people after Captain Kidd's treasure—those people must believe that Captain York knew its whereabouts.

Will frowned and raked his memory. Just before he'd gone to sit by the hearth, where he now realized he had in fact dozed off, the others must have left to go to another tavern. Then he remembered that Jack Hacket said he would be at *The Windmill* tavern. Perhaps the others would be with him. Will scurried down the street, picking up speed as he ran. He turned a corner and then ran through a field. He jumped over a stone wall, and was soon standing in the shadows of *The Windmill* tavern, pressed flat against the side of building, scarcely daring to breathe.

A group of soldiers was just coming out of the tavern and they marched Jack Hacket before them. They stopped in front of a tall thin man—a familiar man. Will squinted at him. It was Mike Faraday, the man with whom Captain York had negotiated docking privileges.

Will strained his ears to listen.

"Only one?" Faraday asked the officer with annoyance.

"Yes, sir. They don't seem to be staying all in one place."

"I suppose this will take all night. We have to get all of them, everyone connected with the *Wilma*.

"I heard Captain York had a comely wench with him," the officer said.

Will strained to hear still harder. Maddie! They were talking about Maddie!

"Ah, yes, the lovely Maddie Emerson, allegedly from Boston Town. Well, no need to worry about her. She's trussed up in the Governor's personal quarters."

The guard laughed wickedly, "What a fate awaits her! I hope the old man doesn't crush her."

Faraday too laughed. "He has yet to crush Beatrix."

"Well, where to next?"

"The Bull Tavern, I think. What about the vessel itself?"

"There were two guards. We took them in already."

Will waited till the soldiers had all climbed in their wagon and until the wagon was clattering down the street. Then he whipped away.

Black Henri was neither at a tavern nor an inn. The color of his skin prevented him from staying at such a place. But he was not bothered by this. Indeed, he had confided to Will that he had rather stay with his friends, the Antonys, who were free blacks and who lived in the Negro Quarter near the Bowery. In any case, his beloved Angela lived with the Antonys and it was she he yearned to see.

Will bit his lip, trying to imagine what Captain York would do if he were him. It would take the soldiers a long time to find Black Henri and certainly it would take him a long time to make his way to the Bowery—especially on foot. The city, he well knew came to an end at the street called Wall. Beyond that, stretched unknown fields all along the High Road to Boston Town.

But he did know where the soldiers were headed. They were now on their way to *The Bull Tavern.* He turned quickly then, and scampered off down the deserted cobbled streets. He would go directly to *The Brideshead* and hope some of the crew were there and that he arrived in time to warn them.

It was a nightmare run and by the time he reached his destination, Will felt like his lungs might burst. He paused for only a second outside the door, then he edged inside, looking furtively about till he saw Juan Corso who sat in a corner with another Portuguese crew member, Gabriel Vagas.

"Hold there, boy!" A giant had seized his shoulder and jerked Will back toward the door.

"What's the matter? Let me go!" Will wrenched free only to be grabbed by the arm—his wounded arm which was still sensitive. He winced in pain.

"We'll have no little pickpockets in here," the man said, shoving him roughly toward the door.

"I'm no pickpocket. I've come for my friends, over there!"

"Friends indeed," the man continued to push him back toward the door.

"Juan! Juan Corso!" Will shouted as loudly as he could so as to be heard in spite of the din that rose up from the drinkers.

Juan Corso looked up and a flash of recognition showed in his face. He was up in a flash, hurrying toward Will.

"Let him go!" Juan ordered.

The innkeeper dropped Will's arm and Juan, unusually large for a Portuguese man, motioned him away from Will.

"Get Gabriel! Hurry, come with me now!"

Juan saw the panic in young Will's face and he motioned Gabriel to the door.

"You must come with me now," Will implored.

"But I've half a roast left on my plate," Gabriel complained.

"What is it?" Juan asked.

Will pressed his lips together. "Outside," he hissed. "Hurry, hurry it's a matter of life and death."

The two crewmen went outside with Will who immediately pulled them round the side of the building. "There's an order to arrest the whole crew. The Captain's in jail and Miss Maddie is held prisoner by the governor!"

"Madre de Dios!" Juan Corso muttered.

"We must hurry. The soldiers have gone to another tavern. But they'll be here soon, they're going to every tavern in New York town."

"Yan Ould is at his sister's," Juan said. "She lives on Petticoat Lane."

"Black Henri is in the Negro Quarter, near the Bowery," Will revealed.

"We need horses," Juan said. "Come along, I know where we can get two. You, young Will, can ride holding on to me."

Maddie opened her eyes and wiggled in absolute discomfort. She looked around, almost relieved in spite of her predicament. Oddly, she remembered her last thought before passing out. It was that she was back on Oak Island, and that was followed by a terrible fear that she would awaken to find herself once again in the twentieth century. But she had not.

Instead she appeared to be in some man's bedroom, tied to bed with a silk scarf in her mouth.

She looked down at her loosened undergarment. One thought after another shot across her mind. Her dress was gone and she was in her petticoat! The governor! He was responsible for this! The lecherous old bastard! Anger filled her and she swore under her breath.

The first time she had been tied to a man's bed had been bad enough, but this was entirely too much! She was sick and tired of men treating her this way, she thought defiantly. She wasn't an after-dinner mint to be placed on someone's pillow!

She moved her hands. The bonds did not feel all that tight. Both hands were tied together to the headboard of the bed. She began to manipulate them and to her pleasure, she felt them loosening. After a a few minutes she was able to dig at the knot with her finger and in a moment, she had loosened it sufficiently to wriggle free.

She quickly undid her gag and took a deep breath. Stupid old man! He had probably undressed her, caressed her, and then gone off to do whatever deed he intended doing. But surely he would be back. And where the hell was Ben? Off with Melissa or the governor's wife, no doubt!

She shook her head which felt awful. Something must have been in the cognac. Still, her anger now caused adrenalin to surge through her, bringing her to a fully alert state.

She looked around the room. Damn! Where was her dress? She could hardly run away wearing only a torn, filmy petticoat. She stormed to the wardrobe and flung open its door.

Inside, a collection of men's clothing hung neatly. She searched it and finally withdrew a pair of breeches—tight and far too small to fit the governor. "Fine," she muttered. Next she withdrew a silk shirt with ruffles. "Good," she whispered. Next a bright red cummberbund and after that, a red brocade vest. In no time she uncovered long red stockings and in a trunk at the foot of the bed, she found some smallish knee boots. The clothes must have belonged to some young boy, she concluded.

Well, there was no time to waste pondering just whose clothes she had found. Maddie ripped off her stupid petticoat. "Goodbye to this ridiculous clothing!" In truth she was thinking more of her everyday clothes rather than her costume, but no matter. She felt she had had enough. She rolled it all in a ball and threw it into the wardrobe. She put on the silk blouse and the breeches. Then she adorned the vest, the stockings, and finally the boots.

She walked to the full-length mirror at the far end of the room and looked at herself. "Not bad," she said with satisfaction as she fastened the cummerbund.

Quickly and efficiently, she pulled her long thick black hair back and tied it with yet another scarf she found in a drawer. "Now, one more thing," she said looking about. "Ah, yes."

By the hearth was a long narrow cupboard. She opened it up and looked in with delight. There were four swords, all different weights. She tried each and selected one together with the belt and scabbard that went with it. She fastened it round her waist. "To the hell with how I'm supposed to act," she said, feeling thoroughly rebellious. Quickly, and just for practice, she drew her blade and stepped back into parrying position. Then she slashed at the air expertly. "Take that!" she said, imagining the fat governor before her. "I'll teach you to drug me and take liberties."

Maddie turned suddenly, sword in hand toward the door that lead to the balcony.

"Hold!" Juan Corso looked pale.

"Miss Maddie?" Will peered out from behind Corso in awe.

Maddie smiled. "Oh, Will."

"We came to rescue you," Juan said, then he smiled broadly, "It hardly seems necessary."

"Rescue me? Where's Ben?"

"He's been arrested. We have to get out of here. Hurry, I'll tell you everything on the way to get Yan and Black Henri."

"Would you like to dress first?" Juan asked. Gabriel who stood behind him had been unable to speak a word. Clearly the sight of a woman dressed as a man was too much for him.

"I am dressed," Maddie answered. "I intend to stay this way."

Neither of them said anything. They simply motioned her to follow as they slipped back out onto the balcony and quietly across the garden toward the governor's stables.

Maddie moved along with them feeling for the first time in months as if she were herself, free of full stiff skirts and clothes that made life all but impossible.

The stable was totally unguarded when Juan, Gabriel, Will, and Maddie tiptoed inside.

"Will you ride with me? Juan asked.

Maddie shook her head. "I know how to ride. And just for once I'm dressed for it."

Juan said nothing, but he selected five of the best horses in the stable. Maddie took a beautiful coal black stallion. She saddled it herself much to the amazement of her three male companions, then she mounted, sitting easy in the saddle.

Juan took Will with him, and Gabriel road alone with the other horses in tow for Yan Ould and Black Henri. They guided the horses out into the night and rode off, avoiding Broad Street and traveling instead up Broad Way which had no taverns past Beaver Street.

"Much faster than one foot," Will said, as they came to Maiden Lane. It was virtually the last street within the town, running east and west between Great Queen Street on the east and Broad Way on the west.

"Do you know which house?" Juan asked.

Will nodded. "Yan brought me here with Black Henri the

first day we docked. Black Henri was on his way to the Bowery and I came with him this far to see the sights."

"Good thing," Maddie remarked. It was a bright moonlit
night and she reckoned it must now be at least one a.m. "We
must hurry," she urged. "We must get Black Henri and Yan
and get to the jail before dawn."

"It's that house!" Will said, pointing to a small neat stone
house. He slipped off the horse and hurried to the door on
which he pounded.

After a few minutes, a woman wearing a long white gown
and dust cap came to the door bearing a lantern. "Whatever
is it, boy?" she asked, peering at Will.

"We've come for Yan. It's an emergency."

"Oh, yes. You're the lad who came a few days ago with
the black man—I recognize you now. Trouble? Is there trouble?

"Yes, ma'am. Please call Yan. Tell him to dress and to
hurry!"

She turned then and called out Yan's name. In a few seconds Yan appeared, rubbing his eyes sleepily.

"There's trouble, Yan. Get your clothes, hurry!" Will said.

Yan hurried back upstairs; barely a minute later returned
ready to ride, buttoning his shirt as he flew out the door.
Soon they were off again, this time with a guide who knew
his way. Yan, among all the crew members, had the distinc-
tion of having been born in the colony when it was Dutch. In
his lifetime it had expanded from a huddle of buildings
around the docks to a well-populated and prosperous little
town of some nine thousand people.

Now they rode four abreast with the extra horse running to
one side. They rode along a dirt wagon road. Maddie mar-
velled at it all. They were headed for what today was the
Lower East Side. A short trip from Wall Street in the twentieth century, but a long ride through semi-wilderness in the
year 1702.

Within forty-five minutes they entered a neat but clearly

separate little community. A sign on its outskirts proclaimed it to be "The Free Black Community of the Bowery."

Juan was the one who made the decision to wake someone up in order to find Black Henri. It was a providential choice. Black Henri was a guest in the house next door.

Black Henri answered the door with Angela at his side. Will and Juan explained to him what had happened and for a long moment Black Henri thought. Then he smiled, his white teeth gleaming in the dark. "By now the whole crew and the Captain must be in the jail. Most of the soldiers will be sleeping. We'll go now, we'll try to free them all at once."

"But we're only four."

"Five," Maddie said firmly. "I know how to use this sword."

"She does," Will quickly confirmed with some admiration. "I've seen her."

Black Henri was not concerned that Maddie was a woman. "Good, we can use another sword." Then he paused momentarily, and called out for Angela. She hurried down the stairs, holding her robe together, and looking apprehensive.

"You're leaving so soon?" Her dark brows lifted, and she touched him imploringly.

"Angela, pack your bag and go to the *Wilma*. You wait there for me, no matter what happens. I'm taking you to Curaçao with me, I will not leave you again."

A smiled suddenly covered her face, and she stood on her tiptoes to kiss him. "I'll be there," she whispered.

And then they were off, headed back into town toward the jail located on just the other side of the fort where the Governor's Mansion was located.

A quarter mile from the jail, Black Henri raised his hand to bring the riders to a halt. He gathered them in close so that each could hear. "We'll tie our horses by the rail near the courthouse and from there we'll go on foot."

"But we'll need them to get away," Will whispered.

"Aye, lad. That we will. And we'll need more horses as well. Fortunately, the soldiers keep a large number of horses near the jail. They're tied in the back. Now, we'll ride to the jail one by one, tie our horse, and stay in the shadows of the custom house till we're all together. Is that clear?"

"I'll go in first," Maddie volunteered. "I'll distract the guards and then the rest of you come in from behind. We'll free the crew and put the soldiers in their cell."

"It'll be dangerous for you to go in first," Black Henri continued, scratching his chin thoughtfully.

"Yes, but I can distract the guards as none of you can."

Black Henri nodded. "Can't argue with that. All right, but be careful. Now go, our hours before daylight are numbered."

Ben forced open his eyes and looked about. It was pitch black except for a line of dim light under the door. And the floor was hard and cold. Somewhere water was dripping into this dank tomb. Gradually, his eyes adjusted to the blackness and saw that high on one wall there was a slit-like window. Grimly, as he became more fully awake, he realized he was in some sort of cell. He shook his head and then put both hands to his temples. His head throbbed far worse than he remembered it throbbing from any previous hangover. And then, the evening began to return to him. He was not drunk! He had been drugged!

Ben was just contemplating the moments before he passed out from drinking the cognac when he heard footsteps outside the door. He strained to listen.

"He's probably still out cold," one man said with disgust.

"Better for him. When he comes too, the governor will have his secrets beaten out of him."

Ah, that was it! Ben pressed his lips together and made no attempt to move. As he heard the door open, he closed his eyes.

"See, dead as a doornail."

"I expect he'll be out for an other hour at least."

"Then he'll talk to us. We'll make him."

"What about the rest of his crew?"

"They've quieted down now. Still some at large, but we should have them all by tomorrow night. The governor said they'd be locked up for some time."

The two men turned, closed and locked the door, then shuffled off. Again Ben opened his eyes. The crew! They'd rounded up his crew? But they had some were still at large—maybe they would rescue him. And what had happened to Maddie? He fairly shook with anger. *If she was hurt God help them!* He would find a way to punish them. He cursed silently and reminded himself to remain quiet for the time being. As long as they thought he was unconscious, they wouldn't torture him. And time, he judged, was important. Yes, the more time he could buy the better.

Together Maddie, Black Henri, Will, and Yan huddled in the shadows of the custom house.

"Are you sure?" Black Henri questioned.

"Quite sure," Maddie answered. In her mind she had it all worked out. She didn't hesitate, but strode across the darkened square to the front door of the jail. She paused for a moment outside and undid the top three buttons of her blouse, pulling it down slightly to expose her bare shoulder. She fluffed out her magnificent hair and then walked straight in the front door.

The soldier behind the desk looked up at her as if she were some sort of vision. Maddie quickly took stock of the situation.

Behind a wooden desk, there were four other soldiers. Behind them, on a great hook, was an iron key ring with huge keys hanging from it. There didn't appear to be anyone else around.

"What! Who are you?" The soldier finally managed.

"Who indeed!" one of the others said.

Maddie smiled, but said nothing.

Two of them came from behind the desk. "What a rare beauty you are!"

"I've never seen a woman dressed in such a manner," the other said lifting his brow.

Maddie waited an instant till the second of the two took another step toward her, then she whirled around and ran outside with the two soldiers in quick pursuit.

Out of the darkness, Black Henri and Yan Ould appeared. The two surprised soldiers never knew what hit them. Black Henri seized one tightly around the neck from behind and rendered him unconscious. Yan Ould hit the other over the head with his sword hilt and achieved the same result.

The two were quickly tied up.

"I'll go back now," Maddie whispered. "Stay ready. I'll bring the others out."

She hurried back inside where now there were only three. "Come!" she commanded. "Your friends are in trouble! Hurry!" She ran outside and all three of the remaining guards followed. Once outside in the darkness, they were immediately set upon. It was no battle. Sheer surprise gave Black Henri and Yan an advantage. Using a three-foot board he had found, Yan Ould, with two well-placed blows to the shins of one and chest of another, had both on the ground, one gasping for air and the other grasping his shins in agony. Yan quickly wound rope around their feet and chest. Black Henri grabbed the other one by the arm as he went by and blindsided him with a mighty punch to the face. There was a loud groan as the jailor crumpled to the ground drawing his pistol in his right hand as he went down to his knees. Black Henri quickly moved out of the line of fire to the right, and knocked the pistol out the guard's hand with a sharp blow down on the arm. He then punched him again in the face. This time there was no getting up for the jailer. All three were tied up just like the two who had come before. Black Henri stuffed their mouths with their own kerchiefs and stacked them by the side of the building.

Black Henri and Yan relieved their prisoners of their pistols and stuffed them in their own belts.

"This way." Maddie led them inside. She hurried and took the keys, ran down the corridor opening the cell doors. Black Henri and Yan went into another room looking for weapons.

"I'll be damned," one of the crew said, looking at Maddie as she opened his cell door.

Maddie paid him no mind. She flung open the last door. "Ben!"

He looked at her, his mouth opening in sheer surprise.

"Are you all right?"

For a moment he toyed with pretending he was hurt simply so she would hold him, but seeing her dressed as she was in male clothing so surprised him that he was incapable of subtrafuge.

"I was drugged," he said.

"I too—but we must hurry, there's little time, I fear."

He nodded and they hurried outside. The crew had found Black Henri and Yan who handed out the weapons they seized from the jail's armory. Ben quickly retrieved his own sword, returning it to its sheath.

"You look quite stunning, my darling, but ever so silly with that sword."

Maddie frowned at him. She almost felt like drawing it and parrying with him just to let him know how well she could use it, but instead she simply shrugged. He would find out in time that she was dressed as she was for a reason.

No sooner had the thought of a demonstration crossed her mind when the door burst open and soldiers appeared, armed soldiers—apparently those who had been sent to find the rest of the crew.

"On guard!" Ben cried. Swords were quickly drawn and Maddie also drew hers. She held it in position expertly—her

whole body tensed. It only took a single second for her to realize that this was no polite fencing session with rule and
points accorded. This was an absolute melee with no holds
barred. Still, she knew she could fight, she knew how to handle her weapon, she knew she was good at it.

Ben lunged at a soldier and cut his arm forcing him to drop
his weapon. At the same time Maddie parried a second attacker who was coming at Ben from another angle. She skill-
fully flicked his sword out of his hand and slashed his
breeches so they fell down and he tripped over them. Yan
dragged the fallen soldier off to one side and Black Henri finished another off with a blow to the head executed with his
pistol butt. The doorway became jammed with soldiers trying
to get in. Three more soldiers pushed their way in. Ben,
Maddie, and Yan engaged them immediately with flashing
steel. Other members of the crew attacked soldiers as they
tried to enter. Maddie once again parried and thrust and
pressed her opponent, finally wounding him in the arm and
chasing him into a crew member's waiting grasp. He was
rendered unconscious.

Ben also overwhelmed his opponent by skewering him in
the ribs with a feint parry and thrust. Yan just avoided being
run through and managed to cut his attacker's ear and leg
which sent him to the floor writhing in agony.

The fight continued till what was left of the contingent of
soldiers was caught between Maddie, Ben, and Yan on the
one hand, and the now well-armed crew on the other. One by
one, the soldiers lifted their heads and dropped to their knees,
surrendering.

"Lock them all up, and make haste!" Ben ordered.

He withdrew his kerchief and wiped the perspiration off
his brow as he looked at Maddie in awe. She was beautiful,
intelligent, and one of the best swordsmen he had ever seen.
She had moved artistically and knowledgeably, almost as if
she had been born with a blade in her hand. She knew all the
positions, all the rules, and she was brave and wonderful. He

wanted her more than he had ever wanted any woman. But at this moment what had to be done crowded both desire and admiration from his mind.

"You were breathtaking," he whispered.

Maddie smiled.

Then Ben turned. "Go to the ship and make her ready to sail at dawn's first light." He spoke to the crew and he pointed to those whom he wished to go back to the ship. "The rest of you come with me."

Two-thirds of the men rode off the ship. They were led by Yan Ould. The remainder went with Ben and Maddie to *The New Amsterdam-York Inn* to get Melissa.

Lopez de Vaca drew his horse close to Ben's. "I've heard your old enemy Captain John Pike has weighed anchor off New York."

Ben nodded. Pike was a formidable enemy. Vaguely he wondered if Pike's arrival had anything to do with tonight's events.

They reached the inn and dismounted, tying their horses outside. Ben bade Maddie to wait. He vaulted up the stairs two at a time and flung the door to Melissa's room open. As he had feared, she was nowhere to be seen.

He shouted to one of his men to take her belongings to the ship, then he returned downstairs to question the old man who had been on duty.

"She never came home at all," he said crinkling up his nose, "but last night there was a scar-faced man skulking about."

"Pike," Ben said under his breath.

"What will we do?" Maddie asked.

"We'll sail—we'll board Pike's vessel in the early morning fog and do battle. We must get Melissa back. Pike is a killer."

Maddie nodded. However much she disliked Melissa, there was no question she had to be rescued.

"To the *Wilma!*" Ben ordered.

They dismounted at the dock, slapped their horses' rumps

and sent them back from whence they'd been taken. "Take up your positions," Ben ordered. "We'll slip out now and head north to near where Pike's vessel is anchored."

The great anchor was pulled up and the ropes that moored the vessel to the dock were severed. Men seemed to be running everywhere and soon the *Wilma*'s sails were unfurled and they caught the pre-dawn breeze.

The *Wilma* cut through the water as Ben guided her through the fog. Maddie stood by his side.

"Normally, I'd curse the fog," he said. "But now it's a blessing. It means we can't be seen by the keeper of the dock light."

"It's so quiet," Maddie said in a near whisper.

Ben momentarily set the wheel and then he turned to her, drawing her into his arms. He circled her slender waist, then touched her buttocks, pressing her to him. "You were truly wonderful tonight. I never dreamed a woman could be so exciting!"

His lips kissed her neck and then her lips. She pressed against him, eager for him, desiring him. But in a moment he pulled back, his own face flushed with his desire for her, "We'll have to wait," he breathed, "or we'll run aground."

Maddie, her own face glowing, looked up at Ben lovingly. There was still work to be done this night.

Melissa sat miserably on the wooden floor in the pitch black darkness of her tiny prison. She shivered, wondering what horrible things might be crawling about. So many ships were infested with rodents. "Oh, please don't let there be any in here," she murmured. Then, she shook her head. "I just can't sit here," she added, aware that the sound of her own voice was comforting in the darkness and equally aware that either there was no one in the room adjacent, or that this hole in the wall of a closet was soundproof.

Sniffing, Melissa struggled to her feet and held out her

hands in front of her as she moved forward till she came to the wall. She felt around and soon found the latch of the door. She hugged the door and began moving to her left, counting the steps, and feeling the wall with her hands. She walked some ten measured steps before she reached the corner. She continued the process and walked six measured feet before she found another corner. She began again, but pulled back her hand suddenly realizing she had touched something soft—it wasn't alive and so she picked it up and felt it more carefully. It appeared to be a rag. She felt along the shelf and then screamed slightly as with a terrible clatter, she knocked a huge bucket to the floor together with several long-handled mops.

"I must be in a cleaner's closet," she surmised. She did the best she could to pick up the mops and the bucket. Then she lifted one of the mops in her hand and holding it high over her head, prodded the ceiling of her little prison. To her enormous surprise, on the fourth prod, a part of the ceiling moved.

"A trap door!" Melissa said with joy.

Hastily, she pushed and prodded some more, moving the wooden cover aside. She was rewarded with a gush of fresh air and a square of moonlight on the floor.

She moved to the side of her prison, waited, and listened. No one seemed to be patrolling anywhere near where this door opened onto the deck.

Quickly, Melissa stripped off her cumbersome dress, then she looked about trying desperately to see what she could use to climb up and out. She turned the large bucket upside down and put it on the floor, then she piled some loose planks atop it. Finally, she climbed up and reached the opening with her hands. But it was no use, she couldn't lift herself up and out of the hole; it was still too far away.

"Stupid storage closet," she muttered. "Why can't there be anything useful stored in here?" She began ransacking the shelves and boxes in the semi-darkness. "Ouch!" She withdrew her hand quickly and sucked her finger. Then, more carefully she examined what she found. She picked it up and held it to the slight light that came through the trap door. It was a grappling hook! It was perfect!

Melissa found a length of rope and she tied one end to the jigger, then she tossed the wicked looking thing up, through the opening. She pulled on the rope slowly till she felt it tighten. The large sharp prongs of the jigger caught on something. She tested it and it seemed strong enough.

Using her feet to climb up the side of the wall, she held fast to the rope and climbed up, hand over hand the way she had seen sailors do it. Then, she firmly grasped the sides of the opening and swung herself through out onto the damp, foggy deck.

Melissa looked around and listened. She heard nothing. Quietly, she set the hook down and replaced the trap door, then keeping to the shadows, she moved swiftly to one of the tethered long boats. She moved the canvas aside and crawled inside, deeming it a good, warm hiding place. There was no use trying to escape the ship till it was lighter. Then, God willing, she thought, she could slip overboard and swim for shore, hopefully undetected.

Chapter Eleven

The *Wilma* cut through the calm waters of the East River past the new docks at the end of Great Queen Street.

"The fog is with us," Ben said, turning slightly toward Maddie. "It's just thick enough to veil our movements, but not so thick as to inhibit our navigation."

"The sun will burn it off rapidly," Maddie warned.

"Aye, but we'll have boarded Pike's vessel and made off by then."

He seemed absolutely confident and she wished she felt the same.

"There . . ." Ben said, pointing ahead. "There lies Pike's ship, the *Whippet*. It looks to me as if everyone is asleep. I think we'll have the element of surprise."

Ben gave a signal with his hand and Maddie watched as the men assembled on deck took their places. The boarding planks were in place, and when the distance between the two vessels was right, heavy ropes with great grappling hooks on the end would be hurled across open sea to the deck of the *Whippet*. The hooks would attach themselves to the gunwales or rigging and when the men pulled on the ropes, the two ships would be joined. Then planks would be dropped and the crew of the *Wilma* would swarm across them yelling their battle cries, invading the deck of Pike's ship with flashing steel and pistol fire.

It seemed like an eternity as the *Wilma* edged over closer—then, suddenly a cry went up from the deck of Pike's ship. There was a guard posted and he had seen them—though to Maddie it seemed a miracle they had gotten as close as they had without being seen.

Grappling hooks silently arched through the air and landed with a thud. Men pulled on the ropes and the hooks, each holding fast to the gunwales of Pike's ship as Ben's crew drew in the slack rope bringing the ships closer together as the river churned up between them.

When they were only yards apart Ben ordered, "Drop the planks!"

Hardly had the alarm been sounded aboard Pike's ship when the planks were dropped and the crew of the *Wilma* began boarding.

It was an extraordinary sight. The silence of the night was filled with the screams of men and the clash of steel. The few men who landed first defended themselves from those of Pike's men who had made it to deck, but they also stood in front of Yan Ould who fastened the ropes. In moments larger numbers of men were swinging aboard Pike's ship on ropes even as half-naked members of Pike's crew stumbled from their quarters, half-asleep, but with swords and pistols.

Ben was gone as soon as the ropes bound the two ships together and Maddie followed in spite of protestations.

"Go back! I know you can fight, but his is no place for a woman!"

"I'm a better swordsman than half the crew, I'm going!" she shouted back defiantly.

Ben did not have time to answer her. He scrambled onto the deck of Pike's ship and was immediately engaged by Riffen.

Maddie too scrambled aboard, sword drawn and ready to fight.

"Me God! Will ye look at that!" Digby shouted. He had his sword drawn, but his amazement at recognizing Maddie gave her the split second she needed. There was no polite parrying here, no artistic swordsmanship. She thrust her sword forward, penetrating his shoulder.

"Me God! The she-witch has wounded me!" he screamed, dropping his sword and clutching his shoulder. Maddie advanced on him and he fell to his knees. "No! Don't kill me!"

"Get up and jump!" she shouted angrily. Against a man she didn't know, she doubted she could be merciless. But against this terrible man she felt personal anger. "Up and over the side or I'll run you through!"

Digby wasted no time. Still clutching his shoulder and wailing, he scrambled up on the rail and then jumped into the water where he joined others who had been forced over the side.

"Ben! Ben!"

Maddie turned to see Melissa crawling from beneath a long boat. She was dressed only in her petticoats, and her strawberry-blond hair blew in the breeze.

As Ben turned toward the sound of Melissa's voice, Riffen dove overboard.

"Oh, Ben, I knew you'd come!" Melissa ran across the deck toward Ben while the crew of the *Wilma* rounded up the last of Pike's men.

"My God, what have they done to you?" Ben held out his arms to receive her and she fell into them, and then into an apparent faint.

Maddie scowled and walked toward them.

"Pike's nowhere to be found, "Black Henri reported.

"Probably hiding," Ben replied without looking up. "Oh, poor little Melissa."

"Should we search the vessel?" Black Henri inquired.

"It'll take too much time. Disable her and then we'll set sail for Curaçao." Again he turned to Melissa. "If they've touched you, I swear I'll kill them."

"She's just fainted," Maddie said, wondering if he had

even noticed that she had dispatched Digby to the water below.

"Poor child, God knows what she's been through."

Ben seemed truly distraught and he looked at Melissa with love in his eyes. Maddie felt suddenly mystified by his obvious feelings for Melissa. Perhaps Ben York wanted them both—perhaps she had been foolish to accept his words of love as meaning he intended to be faithful.

"C'mon," Ben said, still holding Melissa in his arms. "I'll carry her back to my cabin and you can care for her."

Maddie stiffened. She fought the desire to snap back, "Care for her yourself." Instead, she followed silently.

Ben put Melissa down on the bed and Maddie watched, wondering if indeed Melissa was unconscious. Then her brown eyes fluttered open and she smiled up at Ben, throwing her arms around his shoulders. "Oh, you saved me!" she breathed, kissing him hard on the lips.

It was a long kiss and Maddie scowled at them.

"Did they hurt you?" Ben asked, brushing her blond hair off her forehead.

"They took my dress and locked me in a closet with rats. They were going to—to—oh, I just can't talk about it. Oh, hold me, Ben!" Tears gushed from Melissa's big eyes and she hugged Ben, forcing him to hold her closer.

"But they didn't . . ." he asked.

"They were going to . . ." she answered.

"I'm sure she'll be fine," Maddie said coldly.

Ben turned around as if he had forgotten she was there. He stood up awkwardly. "Maddie will care for you. I do have to take the wheel now."

"Come back soon," Melissa murmured.

Ben took Maddie's hand and led her outside onto deck. "She's been through a lot, Maddie. Look after her, will you?"

"Ben, Melissa is perfectly all right. Frankly, we've all been through a lot."

"She's young and innocent, Maddie. She doesn't have your strength."

With that mild reprimand—or at least she assumed it was a reprimand, he turned and headed for the pilot house. He knew she was jealous and she felt angry and hurt.

Maddie whirled around and went back into the cabin. She looked at Melissa harshly, "He's gone, you can stop acting now."

Melissa sat up and smiled like a kitten. "He loves me, you know. He's always loved me. You're just a temporary attraction. I don't suppose he's ever known a woman who could handle a sword as you do, so he's intrigued. But that's not what a man like Ben wants, he wants to take care of a woman. He knows he can take care of me."

Maddie looked at Melissa in wonder. At least she was blatantly honest, and Maddie thought, there might well be something in what she said. *Well, I am what I am,* she thought, *and I can't change. If Ben doesn't love me as I am* . . . she couldn't finish the thought because she was too anxious about his real feelings. And if he didn't really love her? If he did love Melissa? What then?

They had been at sea two days now, and every now and again, Ben looked at the two women as they leaned over the ship's rail watching the sea as it foamed around the ship. They were there now, in spite of the stiff wind and fog.

He personally thanked heaven for both the strong winds and the fog. The winds would carry them on their way and the fog would obscure the ship. His Dutch flag fluttered in the breeze as he set a sure course for the Caribbean, for his home port of Curaçao.

Again he glanced at Maddie and Melissa. Perhaps they would become friends after all. Melissa did have a girlish, immature crush on him, but it would pass. As for the wildly beautiful Maddie, she had stolen his heart and he admitted it to himself. What a woman! She rode like the wind and she handled a sword as if she had been born with one in her hand. She had risked her life to save him and she had earned the respect of every man aboard. In fact, she had probably even earned the respect of the two trouble makers he had let go—the two that had joined Pike, Riffen and Digby. If she had not earned their respect, then at least they had good cause to fear her. Digby would be nursing his wounded arm for some time to come and Riffen—well, it would be awhile before Riffen would again sit comfortably. He had seen to that.

Yes, Maddie was quite a woman and he knew he loved her to the exclusion of all others. Whoever she was, and wherever she came from, it mattered not to him. As soon as Melissa had her inheritance and he had seen to her care, he would take his share of the treasure and marry Maddie. Then, he thought happily, they could sail away to some peaceful place there to live out their lives with one another. He thought briefly of what had happened to Kidd. No, he did not want his life to end with a hangman's noose. It was, he reasoned, almost time to leave his life of privateering. It was not as if he didn't have a valuable skill. Perhaps he and Maddie could go back to Boston and he could work at the newly founded university. He could teach cartography and spend time redrawing maps. It was his passion and it seemed a good way to retire from privateering.

But not yet, he thought to himself. Right now he had a million odds and ends to clean up. He had a house to put in order.

Sarah Oort sat before her dressing table brushing her hair, expressing anger in each stroke. She stared hard at herself, ever mindful of the fact that anger caused wrinkles and wrinkles would turn her into an old crone.

How could Beatrix Bellomont, the governor's wife, have been so stupid! Indeed, how could Bellomont himself have been so inept? His wife, unwittingly—of course she was always unwitting to Sarah's way of thinking—had delivered Ben York right into his hands, and he in turn had actually had Ben York behind bars, drugged and completely helpless.

And there was *that* woman! Sarah's blood boiled when she thought of Maddie Emerson. How could she have made such a fool of Bellomont? And what were all these stories about her dressing as a man and taking part in pitched battles. "A master of fencing," someone had said. Where did this Maddie Emerson come from? Who was she? What was she to Ben York?"

Sarah tossed the brush down on the table and got up, walking across the room to the window. To make matters worse, that stupid little wretch Melissa had disappeared. No doubt Ben had her.

"Not exactly what I'd planned," Sarah said to herself.

She bit her lip and forced herself to think of Katra. Katra was both smart and beautiful. Smart, beautiful, and greedy. Katra wouldn't fail. There was simply too much at stake.

At that moment Sarah Oort was distracted by a knock on the door.

"What is it?" she replied with irritation.

"Begging your pardon, madame. There is a Captain Pike to see you."

"Pike?" Sarah repeated. As she spoke his name, she conjured up his unkempt image. A ruffian—an unpleasant, dirty little man. A disgusting man but nonetheless, an old enemy of Ben York.

"Well, I've done business with disgusting people before," she said to herself. "Men like Captain Pike are sometimes useful, but naturally they should be kept off the furniture."

"I beg your pardon, madame."

"I was talking to myself, Gerda." Sarah glanced out the window. The weather was fair enough. "Tell Captain Pike to go and sit in the garden," Sarah instructed. "Tell him I'll be down in a few minutes. And for heaven's sake, don't let him in the sitting room."

"Yes, ma'am."

Sarah listened with satisfaction as the little maid pattered off. Then she turned to her closet. What to wear for a boor like Pike? Not that it mattered, there was no need to impress him. Without further thought, she chose a mauve gown trimmed in antique lace. Pike she deemed was too ill-bred to appreciate her taste, too ill-educated to understand her repartee, and too crude to become overly involved with—even if the scheme centered around trapping Ben York. But if he had something simple in mind—well, what was there to lose?

She smoothed out her skirt and looked fondly at herself in the mirror one last time before joining Captain Pike. It was so hard to find a suitable man with whom to seek diversions. On the whole, the current crop of available men in New York was a sad lot. The governor was a pig who was married to a stupid goose of a woman. The commander of the army unit was a boar who actually snorted before, during, and after lovemaking. Mike Faraday was just barely adequate. And all of them—the whole lot as Ben York had just proved—were bungling idiots. "And no better in bed," she muttered.

Sarah glided down the walkway and into her private garden. It was an exquisite garden, well-laid out and scattered with benches and ornate bird baths. "Ah, Captain Pike," she said, forcing a smile but not offering her hand to him. He looked like an ill-tempered, grubby little frog. Certainly no kiss would turn him into a prince.

"Madame."

He grinned, displaying a disgusting mouthful of decaying teeth as he attempted to bow in greeting, though his girth would not allow anything like a proper greeting.

"And what brings you to visit?" she asked, careful to avoid getting too close to him. God knew what vermin his ill-washed body carried.

"I've come to seek your help."

"My help? What could I possibly do for you?" Sarah lifted her brow. It just seemed as if men couldn't do anything for themselves these days. They all needed propping up, probing, or financing. They seemed devoid of gumption, empty of ideas, and broke. It was at moments such as these that she lamented the loss of William Kidd. At least he was a real man.

"I have cause to believe we have mutual interests, Madame. I have cause to believe that you would like a part of your late husband's treasure."

"Some say the treasure isn't real. That it does not exist," Sarah responded with care.

"It exists, Madam. You know it and I know it. If it did not exist, Captain Ben York would not have made away with Melissa. He would not have boarded my ship and wrecked it to rescue her."

"You had Melissa?" Sarah said, somewhat surprised. She certainly wasn't prone to feel sorry for Melissa, but if Pike had her that was cause for some sympathy.

"Indeed. She's the key to the location of the treasure. Ben York will take her to it."

Sarah felt both annoyed and intrigued. But perhaps this little horror of a man could be of some help. If Katra failed—she had to keep the possibility in mind—even if she succeeded, she might need some kind of help. Could Pike be both an insurance policy and a help to Katra?

"Just what is it you propose?"

"I need some funds to finance immediate repairs to my vessel."

"And would you then pursue Ben York?"

"I would."

"I have taken some steps of my own—you would have to fit yourself into my plans."

"That only seems fair."

Fair? Sarah wondered if he knew the meaning of the word. Well, he wouldn't double cross her, she would see to that.

"We'd have to split even. And you'd have to pay me back out of your half."

In answer he made a begrudging grunt.

"And you would have to take some crewmen loyal to me with you."

Again he grunted.

"When you get to Curaçao, you will contact my daughter, Katra. By then she will doubtless know the location of the treasure."

"Your daughter?"

"I'll describe her to you and show you how she can positively be identified. She wears an amulet identical to my own."

Pike nodded. This was like making a deal with the she-devil herself. He wondered now if he ought to trust Sarah Oort. But then, he didn't have the funds to repair his vessel and if it wasn't repaired, he was out of the game all together.

"Is it agreed?" Sarah asked.

"We should shake hands," Pike said, offering his paw-like hand.

"Ladies do not shake hands," Sarah replied icily. "Come, we will set out a contract and I will see to it the repairs to your ship are made in haste."

"Shall we go inside?"

Sarah shook her head. "Unnecessary. Meet me in two hours' time at the custom house and we'll settle everything."

Pike grinned. "Good."

With that he doffed his hat and then turned to leave. Sarah watched him amble through the gate and back to his carriage outside. He was truly a dreadful little creature.

Jamaica was the home port of many, if not most, of the pirates who sailed the Caribbean. It had belonged to Spain since its discovery by Columbus in 1494. But there was no gold in Jamaica, so the Spanish neglected the island, using it primarily as a supply depot while a few settlers took up cattle ranching. In 1655, it became the first colony in the Americas to be captured by a formal British expedition. The Spanish freed many a slave, armed them, and took them to the mountains of Jamaica. These people became known as Maroons and encouraged by the Spanish, they continually harassed the invaders. But the British continued to hold Port Royal, and from Port Royal which was both corrupt and rich, the British buccaneers made relentless attacks on Spanish vessels and on other Caribbean ports.

Katra thought of Port Royal with a shudder. It was filled with pirates, privateers, and buccaneers. It was filled with women of all types—mostly mulatto beauties who plied their profession as prostitutes in the hundreds of brothels that lined the streets of Port Royal. Port Royal was dangerous for decent women and equally dangerous for men. Every night there were murders and brawls. What justice there was seemed to be the vigilante justice of the mob or of the corrupt governor of the island.

The ship on which Katra traveled had docked in Port Royal for one night. She had locked herself in her cabin and huddled in fear most of the night listening to marauding bands of raucous men and the screams of women on the nearby docks.

Several days later, she arrived in Curaçao, relieved beyond measure to discover it far nicer than Jamaica or even Cuba. It had a genteel charm the other islands of the Caribbean lacked, and certainly it was far safer for a woman. There was simply no question in Katra's mind. The English and the Spanish were not to be trusted in matters of settlement and administration. The Dutch were clearly superior, it seemed. Peter Stuyvesant who had governed New York for the Dutch, had also governed Curaçao, and he had left his mark on it. A few privateers called Curaçao home, but they had to obey the laws and respect the peacefulness that generally characterized the place.

Jamaica was a pirate's den, pure and simple. Its inhabitants were primarily on the run from the law of one or more countries. Jamaica was a refuge, but in a sense it was also a prison without wall or bars. Many who were there could not leave because they had nowhere else to go.

But Curaçao had a permanent Dutch population; it was a real settlement. Farmers plied the land of its rolling hills while Willemsadt, a small miniature Dutch City thrived under the tropical sun on the southern coast. The climate was far more pleasant than the Jamaica she remembered, and the populace far less rowdy. The only major problem was that the island was subject to raids by the Spanish, but it was now better fortified, and as far as anyone knew there was peace between Europe's warring royal houses. As a result, there hadn't been a raid in some time.

Katra unpacked her trunk, carefully hanging up the simple garments she had brought with her. She paused, now and again, to look into the mirror, pleased with the transformation in her looks. Her silken blond hair was no longer no ornately coiffed, but was now braided into one thick golden rope which hung down her back. She wore a simple blue dress and crisp white over-apron. Her dress was low cut, and her tight bodice pushed her white breasts upward. She smiled at herself indulgently. She looked both desirable and innocent. In fact, she looked the epitome of the innocent young Dutch milkmaid.

While on the voyage, she reviewed her mother's plan. Her mother had provided her with information—the names of William Kidd's loyal crew members as well as his friends. The plan was to seek out Rob York and pretend to be looking for her long, lost father, a Dutch seaman named Karl Cross. She would approach Rob and tell him that someone told her he might be able to help. She knew full well he wouldn't be able to help, but her disappointment and obvious state of destitution would cause him concern—she would be the damsel in distress and she was sure of herself—sure of her ability to arouse the proper emotions in him—and just as sure her ploy would work.

"And not soon enough," she said looking about her room. The Van der Voort family ran this inn and while it was clean and reasonably quiet, the rooms were also small and hot. The inn did not face the right direction to take advantage of the trade winds which might have cooled its rooms.

"We can only hope," Katra said, looking once again into the mirror, "that our Mr. Rob York can offer us better accommodation."

She smiled and then sat down at the tiny writing table. Rather than seek out Mr. York in person, she decided to send him a note and ask him to meet her here, in the inn. Yes, it was always better to have a man seek you out—and most certainly his curiosity would be peaked. She smiled again, thinking how much more pleasant her task if the Rob York looked anything like this brother, Ben.

The table inside Ben's cabin was bedecked in a white tablecloth, and had been set with silver and fine china. Ben and Maddie had finished their supper, the first meal they had had alone since leaving New York. Usually, Melissa joined them. But tonight she had complained of not feeling well and taken to her bed with what appeared to be a head cold.

Ben poured a goblet of red wine and looked across the table at Maddie. "You look delectable tonight. It's been awhile since you've worn feminine clothing." Then he grinned wickedly. "I'm not sure if I like you best in low cut gowns or when you wear a man's breeches."

Maddie ignored both his leer and his tone. "Men's clothing is more practical," she replied. "In my time women wear men's clothing—as you call it—much of the time."

He laughed. "I agree, it is more practical. But no matter what you wear, I daresay you'll have no trouble with this crew. First, the troublemakers are gone and these are better men, and second, well, my lady, you've built a reputation for yourself as a swordsman."

"Swordswoman," Maddie said, firmly. She was feeling combative and somewhat assertive. She was testing her own pride, she was not going to be part of a cast of hundreds of women, she wasn't even going to be one of two.

He laughed, thinking her correction colorful, even original. "Very well, as a swordswoman. Nevertheless, your reputation has bought you the freedom of the ship and the respect of every man aboard."

"Melissa seems to go where she wishes. Surely not because she can handle a sword. In fact, if anything, she enjoys being helpless."

"She commands respect because she is Kidd's daughter. Were she anyone else, she might be treated differently. As for being helpless, well helplessness can be attractive."

Maddie looked back at him coldly. Did that mean he liked helplessness, or did it mean others liked it? She felt he was playing word games with her, teasing her.

"She puts it on," Maddie insisted. "As for the rest, you just said the troublemakers were gone."

"Aye, but men will be men. Fortunately, this is not such a long voyage and the men know that they'll have many months ashore.

Maddie sipped her wine. They hadn't been intimate since they'd left New York. She felt it was because Melissa was always around. At least once Melissa had deprived Ben of the opportunity to be alone with her. Maddie was angry that Melissa continued to flirt and he did nothing save enjoy it.

Ben stood up, wine in hand and walked to the back of her chair. He set his glass down and put his warm hands on her neck, moving them slowly, seductively over her bare skin. "I've missed you," he said, bending to kiss her ear.

Maddie shivered at his touch. She had missed him too, missed him and longed for him. But she was also angry and now she was cautious.

He straightened up and drank some of his wine, then he returned his hands to her throat, moving them again over her neck, then downward to her shoulders, and then finally slipping them beneath her dress, to caress her breasts.

"Don't!" she said, tensing.

"Come, come, you don't mean that."

He made no move to stop and she drew in her breath, fighting her own reactions, her undeniable desire. He knew her too well. It was no use saying no. She didn't mean it. She leaned against him, stiffly at first. But he did not stop and soon she no longer even cared to resist. She closed her eyes. It was like magic. He was standing behind her, taunting her and she felt her whole body responding to his seductive touch, to the movements of his fingers.

He lingered on her nipples, toying with both till they were hard in response to his teasing. Then he pulled her up and turned her around in his arms, kissing her passionately. "Yes, I have missed you," he whispered as he swept her into his arms and carried her to the bed.

He undressed her slowly, caressing her as he did so. She in return kissed him and unbuttoned his shirt, longing for the feel of his broad chest against her own flesh. He hurriedly finished disrobing and then they were next to each other, naked and writhing in the heat of one another's bodies.

They made love for a long while, then he curled around her. Maddie lay still beside him, happy and satisfied, yet still troubled by the thought that he might also love Melissa.

At that moment, she thought of home, of what she had left behind when she was transported back in time. At first she had been frightened, then it had become something of an adventure. But here in Ben's arms it seemed as if fate had somehow granted her an unspoken wish—she had been delivered into the arms of a man to whom she felt overwhelmingly drawn.

But what if Ben loved Melissa more than her? Would she want to stay in this time period then, or would she want to be taken back? Not that it was a real choice. Nothing had happened to indicate she could go back. And suddenly she felt afraid again, afraid that fate might once again interfere in her life—that it might sweep her forward just as it had swept her backward, that she might lose him forever in time. It was then that she suddenly realized that no matter what, she didn't want to go back. She wanted to stay here with him, no matter what the hardships or the challenges. If Melissa were her competition, so be it. Maddie decided she would fight for Ben York's love.

"You're silent," he whispered sleepily.

"I was thinking—thinking I want to stay here."

He laughed in semi-amusement, "We are surrounded by ocean, where else would you go?"

"I meant I want to stay in this time."

"Ah," he replied, noncommittedly.

"You still don't believe me, do you?"

"Neither do I call you a liar. As I have told you before, I believe you believe—but what if I told you such a story?"

"I probably would not believe you. But in time, I promise I will find a way to prove my story."

He didn't answer, but only nuzzled her. "True or not, I'm glad you want to stay."

She almost asked him about Melissa then, but she squelched the question. This was not the moment.

Rob York stood outside the Van de Voort's Tavern and Inn. He reread the mysterious note that had been delivered to him that afternoon, then he pushed the door open and entered.

The dining area was filled with the usual array of customers and he walked through it to the foot of the stairs. Then he climbed up, aware that a number of people below were staring at him. Doubtless, they thought he was on his way to a liaison with a lady of the evening. That was certainly the usual reason for coming to the inn.

He reached the second floor and then walked down the hall, stopping outside room eight. He knocked lightly.

The door opened a crack and he glimpsed at a beautiful young girl, her blue eyes looking up at him expectantly. "Miss Cross?" he asked hesitantly.

"Mr. York?"

"Yes."

The door opened wider. "Come in, please."

Rob peered into the tiny room. It was crowded and somewhat airless. It looked quite uninviting. The girl on the other hand, was quite inviting. She was pretty and modestly dressed. She had lovely blond hair and big blue eyes. She looked innocent and he thought it a pity to ruin her reputation even if she were a stranger to Curaçao.

"Perhaps we would be more comfortable downstairs," he suggested. "I should be pleased to buy you some supper if you haven't already eaten."

"Oh, I should be most grateful. Truth be known, I haven't eaten for several days."

He frowned and offered his arm. "Then you shall eat now," he said, feeling entirely gallant.

He escorted her back down the winding staircase and then selected a table in a secluded corner. He ordered wine and a beef dinner.

"You are most kind to a total stranger," Katra said, being sure never to take her eyes off him and fairly commanding he look at her.

"I cannot allow you to starve. Now please tell me, how can I help you? Your note said you were seeking my assistance in a personal matter, Miss Cross."

She smiled beguilingly. "Please call me Katra."

"Very well, Katra."

"My father, Karl Cross is a seaman—a first mate to be accurate. He sailed with Captain Kidd. I was told you might know of his whereabouts. I am quite desperate Mr. York. I have no money—in one day's time I shall be forced to leave the inn and—and—well, I don't know how I shall end up."

Katra forced tears to flood her eyes. How well she knew that Karl Cross was dead—long gone and fortunately not well-remembered.

Rob frowned. "I didn't know Karl Cross had a daughter," he said, studying the poor girl. Oh, how he hated being the bearer of bad news—especially when encountering someone beautiful and young and alone.

"I am his only daughter—his only child."

"Oh," Rob answered. Then he reached across the table and took her small white hands in his. "I'm sorry to be the one to tell you, Katra, but your father is dead."

"Oh, dear heaven!" She bit her lip and forced more tears to her eyes. They tumbled down her cheeks and she wiped at them, with her hand, trying to appear brave and congratulating herself on her fine performance. "Whatever shall become of me, Mr. York? Is there a pauper's home on Curaçao? I shall surely have to go to one."

Rob still held her hands. "Please don't cry."

But it was too late. Katra had opened wide the floodgates and she continued to cry and now wailed, "What shall happen to me? I shall have to—to—sell my body or—oh, what shall become of me?"

"You'll come home with me," he suddenly said. He was certainly not going to let an innocent young woman sell herself. Then added, "There are many rooms and servants. You shall be quite safe and somehow I'll find something for you to do. Perhaps you could assist me . . ."

"I couldn't allow you to keep me," she said, sounding somewhat incoherent.

"Heavens, no! I promise you Katra Cross, this is an honorable invitation. I shall find honest work for you."

She looked up through her tears. "I can keep accounts."

"There, see? You can help me keep accounts. Come now.

Please cry no more. Just eat your dinner and then we'll get your things and take them to *Castaway*."

"*Castaway?*" she questioned.

"Our estate—my brother's and mine."

Katra nodded. "Oh, you're so kind. Kinder than I ever imagined a man could be."

He smiled warmly, trying to put the poor girl at ease. "Everything will be just fine, Katra."

She looked into his eyes bravely. "Oh, I must believe you."

Chapter Twelve

Castaway, the York estate, would have been called a hacienda had it been in Cuba rather than in Curaçao. It was a mile east of Willemstad and built on a hill above the ocean. It had a broad tile terrace that looked down on the surf and the white sand beach below. The house itself was built of stucco and had a tile roof to help keep its airy rooms cool. But unlike estates on other Caribbean isles, this estate was not built in the Spanish type of architecture even though the building materials themselves were the same. The rectangular house was built around an indoor patio. But a second floor jutted from the front of the house and there was a single third floor room in the very middle of the front. The facade of the house resembled houses in Amsterdam and was painted a characteristic pink pastel and all along the second floor were tiny little wrought iron balconies.

The huge main floor room in the center of the house served many purposes. It was a parlour, a study, and living area. It had a tile floor, a multitude of plants, and two large cages containing an array of tropical parrots. There were several divans draped in colorful prints and a large Spanish-style credenza, a great writing desk, and many smaller tables and candelabras. The room was open, spacious, and airy. In fact, the indoors was so much like the outdoors, it was often hard to tell where the room ended and the flower-filled patio began. In the center of the room, a stairway wound its way upward to the second floor which held three bedrooms and onward to the top floor which was a single large suite.

To the left of the center room there was a spacious dining room and next to the dining room a kitchen. To the right, there was a library, and beyond that more bedrooms each of which opened onto the patio. The bathroom had a large sunken tile tub which took many pails of water to fill. It also had an ornate toilet which was Ben York's pride and joy. He said it had been taken from a Spanish vessel on which the King of Spain had traveled. It was a throne-like object of considerable comfort. A pail, set in the floor beneath it, could be emptied from outside the house.

At this moment, Rob York was in the center room, working at his desk, though in fact his mind was not all together on his accounts. Indeed sitting down to do the accounts brought to mind last month's unpleasantries.

"You look distracted," Katra said as she glided into the room. "Not at all as if you're concentrating on those accounts you told me you had to do."

He looked up, almost glad to have had her interrupt him. "It's a bore," he admitted. Then added, "I resent paying so much to our fatuous governor."

Katra made her blue eyes wide. "I don't understand. Why must you pay him?"

Rob turned about to face her. He loved explaining anything—it made him feel important, which, truth be known, was not a feeling he had often. Ben was the important one in the family. Ben was the older, and he made all the decisions. "We have booty and oft times that booty is traded to passing merchants. In order to maintain our privateering license and in order to have the protection of the government, we must pay a percentage of each sale and indeed a percentage of what is in our stores to the governor of this fair isle."

"I see," Katra said, then pouting prettily, "I can see why you find it a bore and why you resent it."

"Last month the governor decided I was holding back on him and he had me arrested."

"Arrested?" Katra said in mock alarm. "Oh, poor Rob," she said, as she touched his arm lightly.

"Aye, but he is much too impressed with Ben, my brother to cause much trouble. He let me go. But damn, it made me angry—oh, I'm sorry. I'm not used to having a lady around."

Katra smiled. "It's all right. I understand. Do you always stay ashore and do the accounts?"

Rob nodded. "I'm not that fond of sailing. But at times I do envy Ben because he gets to have all the adventure."

Katra walked to the back of his chair and placed her hands on his neck which she began rubbing gently. "It must be a great strain," she said softly. "Let me help you relax. You're such a kind, good man. I want you to know how much I appreciate your helping me."

Rob closed his eyes. Her fingers were taunting on his skin and he felt almost hypnotized. And she was a lovely wench— but he was a man of honor. Again, he reminded himself of her terrible distress and of the fact that it would be wrong to take advantage of her. Better to warn her of her effect on him. "Please, if you continue so, I may desire more."

Katra moved in front of him, her hands now resting on his shoulders. Her blue eyes fastened on his. "Perhaps I desire more," she offered suggestively.

Rob looked longingly up at her. She had a ripeness about her that made her even more desirable. He stood up and pulled her into his arms. She had been in the house nearly a week now and each day he had wanted her more and more. It was almost too good to be believed! She had stumbled into his life, and now she was offering herself to him. Desire overcame him, as he leaned down and nuzzled her neck.

"Are you sure?" he asked as his lips touched her bare shoulder.

"Oh, yes," she sighed, pressing herself to him. "Oh, I feel

you strong against me," she sighed, clinging to him. "I do want you, I do."

It was enough. Rob swept her into his arms and carried her to the second floor. The accounts could wait. It had been eons since he had a delectable woman in his bed, eons since he had explored and plundered a divine female.

He lay her down and fell down beside her, stunned by the fact that she began undressing him immediately. She seemed more than willing, yea, she seemed anxious and surprisingly experienced.

"You're bolder than you appear," he breathed, plunging his hand down her dress, discovering her full white breasts.

"And you're wanton," she whispered back, touching him in a way which he found unbearably pleasant.

"This shall be over far too soon if you touch me so," he said as he loosened her dress and slipped it down and pushed it away.

She only giggled as she continued to caress him. Feverishly he removed the rest of her clothes and toyed with her breasts. But she was far too active for him. He parted her legs and entered her just in time. But she didn't seem to mind. She sighed and groaned, moaned, and thrashed about. He devoured her with kisses, and could only promise, "I'll be slower next time, sweet maid."

Maddie alighted from the carriage that had brought them from the quay into Willemstad. It was far from what she knew it would become in less than twenty-five years. Soon, she thought, the Dutch would build a real city here, known primarily for the pink and white spun-sugar ornateness of its structures. A few years ago she had vacationed at Aruba, but not even the oldest of the island's standing historic structures had yet been built in the year 1702. In five years time, the first Jewish House of Worship in the hemisphere would be built here, and that would be followed by many other buildings.

But now it was a virgin island. The main street was a simple dirt road along which were a ramshackle of dwellings, shops, and stalls. There were three or four taverns and at the end of the street, a reasonably stable-looking building which was the town's only inn. For the most part, the buildings were stucco with thatched palm roofs. The largest of buildings were the two fortresses which guarded the entrance to Saint Anne's Bay, thus protecting the city. These, Maddie noted, would be enlarged in a few years and part of them would endure.

"You seem familiar with this place," Ben commented.

"I was here in my own time," she whispered.

He smiled tolerantly and she knew he still could not believe her. But some way, she thought, I will prove it sooner or later. Just how had not yet occurred to her.

"Where do you live?" she asked curiously.

"In the hills not far away. We'll go there soon, but first we must get some provisions."

"And the crew?"

"Will, Black Henri, and Yan Ould will stay at *Castaway* with us. Some others will stay in town and still others have homes outside of town. This island has many small bays and coves. A man can virtually live on the beach. This island is protected, storms never seem to hit it. But then, since you have been here before, you must know that."

Maddie nodded. "I also know that those mountains in the distance, across the ocean, are the peaks of the Andes and the coast of South America lies only twenty-eight miles from here."

He smiled, "You might have read that. It is of course, correct."

"Come, I'll send Will and Black Henri to buy the provisions. I'll take you and Melissa to the inn for some lunch.

We'll wait for my brother there. He'll come to fetch us and our luggage in the wagon."

At that moment the second carriage drew up and Melissa alighted. She hurried up to them, a trifle put out that they hadn't waited for her before leaving the ship.

"See, it didn't take me that long to pack."

"No harm done. You had so many trunks we'd have needed two carriages in any case," Ben said cheerfully.

"If you had waited we could have all ridden together," she said, admonishing Ben and looking at him steadily with her big brown eyes.

Maddie said nothing. It pleased her when Ben treated Melissa like the child she was and, during the last few days of the journey here, he had done just that much to Melissa's chagrin.

"It's time for sustenance, not remorse," Ben said good naturedly. "Ah, it is good to be home, to be where it is safe. Come, ladies."

With that, he took each of them by the arm so that Maddie was on his left and Melissa on his right. They entered the tavern and without exception, all the customers greeted him. It was clear that Ben York was not just well known, but a kind of local hero returning to his home.

He escorted both of them to a table and ordered drink and food.

The tavern owner himself brought the drink, then he sat down with them.

"It's been too long," he said, patting Ben on the back.

"So it has Peter, my friend. Ladies, may I present the owner of this tavern, Peter Drukka. Peter, these two lovely ladies are Mistress Maddie Emerson from Boston Town, and Mistress Melissa Kidd from New York."

Peter bowed from the waist. "My humble establishment is honored with your presence. It is rarely that my establishment is blessed with two such beautiful women."

"Have you seen Rob?" Ben asked.

"Ah, everyone has seen Rob. Everyone is talking about him as well. But perhaps I should keep silent and allow him to tell you his—'news'."

Ben lifted a brow. "Is it so special?"

"It is a lady," Peter replied.

"Ah, so my brother Rob has a new lady friend. And who might this be?"

Peter shrugged. "A mystery woman. She stayed in town for several days at the Van der Voorts. Then your brother came and she's been on your estate ever since."

Ben grinned. "And is this all the gossip?"

Peter shook his mop of dark hair. "The maid who tends your estate, as well as the cook, all say he had taken this mysterious woman to his bed."

"And is this mysterious woman beautiful?"

Peter smiled at Maddie and Melissa. "Not as lovely as these two, but fair, nonetheless."

Melissa ignored Peter and addressed herself to Ben. "How old is this brother of yours?"

"Younger than I am, and a bit of a rogue."

Melissa smiled and Maddie wondered what she was thinking. Melissa was young, but it was obvious that she was one of those women who loved the hunt. She was tiring of trying to convince Ben she was right for him. Maddie could almost read it in her expression, Melissa was thinking that wrenching Rob free of this mysterious woman might well prove entertaining.

"Oh, goodness. They've arrived," Peter said, standing up quickly. "Now don't betray me, you must act as if you know nothing."

"You have my word," Ben answered with a wink.

Rob strode toward the table with Katra at his side. "I'll bet I've caught you telling all my secrets to my brother," he guessed, looking at Peter.

Peter blushed and bowed. "I have much work to do. I'll return with your lunch."

Peter hurried away and Melissa looked up at Rob and smiled a devastating smile.

Rob looked into Melissa's lovely heart-shaped face. Her face was extraordinary—reddish blond. And her eyes were like that of a beautiful doe. He felt thunderstruck.

Katra stood stiffly on his arm, though she fairly felt the electricity between the two of them. "I'm Katra Cross," she announced, even as she pecked Rob's cheek to make sure everyone fully understood their relationship.

Maddie felt the sudden electricity between Melissa and Rob York. What a complicated set of circumstances, she thought, looking from one to the other. This Katra Cross was very pretty, and there was something familiar about her too. Something Maddie couldn't quite put her finger on at the moment.

Melissa barely acknowledged her. "You are quite as handsome as your brother," she cooed, blinking her wide brown eyes, eyes even larger than those of Katra Cross.

In all, Melissa quickly took stock. Katra was older and trying to appear younger. And she thought, her waist was thicker than mine, her breasts smaller, and her legs shorter. Still, she would be a worthy opponent. Ben did seem quite attached to this Maddie person, but Rob was younger and no doubt more easily seduced. Furthermore, Rob was just as good-looking as Ben York, just as good looking and perhaps more rakish in his ways, or at least less staid. Besides, Ben always treated her like a little girl. Perhaps his brother would know enough to treat her as the woman she was.

"Please sit down," Melissa invited. She squeezed over. "Here, Rob, there's room next to me."

Maddie looked from one women to the other in mild amusement. Vaguely she wondered if Ben saw what she saw and realized that Melissa had just set her cap for his brother. One had to admire her, Maddie thought. She wasn't at all put off by this Katra Cross. Something inside of Maddie wished Melissa luck. Not just because she wanted Melissa to leave

Ben alone, but because there was something not quite right about this Katra Cross—but like her familiarity, Maddie couldn't capture just what it was. She only felt somewhat uncomfortable, as if this Katra Cross were an enemy of some sort.

Ben sat at his roll top desk, slowly he closed the account books and looked up at Rob. "Everything seems to be in order."

Rob who stood a few feet away shifted his weight from one foot to the other. "The governor didn't think so. He had me arrested a few weeks ago."

Knowing Rob as he did, and knowing the governor, as well, Rob's admission was not surprising. The governor was persistent and meticulous about receiving his share and about seeing that the books were in order. Rob, on the other hand was an adequate bookkeeper, but he was far from a perfectionist. Moreover, he resented paying the governor. Ben looked his brother in the eye. "Were you holding back on his share?"

"Yes—well, just a little, I thought . . ."

"Don't. We're well-protected here. The peace we enjoy is well worth the money."

Rob shrugged. "Sometimes it seems a lot."

Ben didn't bother to argue. Rob was young. He made mistakes. Instead, he changed the subject. "So tell me, brother. How did you come to meet this comely wench, this Katra Cross?"

"Ben, I've made a mistake—I've been trying to think this through since yesterday in the tavern, I doubt I slept all night."

"Start at the beginning," Ben suggested. He turned around and motioned his younger brother to sit down.

"Katra's the daughter of Karl Cross. She's been looking for

him. She came here in search of him and when I found her she was destitute."

"I didn't know Cross had a daughter," Ben said, rubbing his chin thoughtfully. "Still, it's possible."

"Are you suggesting she lied to me?"

Ben laughed lightly. "No, not at all." Then he shook his head. "When I first say her, I thought her quite young. But now I think she is older than she looks."

Rob's face reddened. "You're most observant brother. I thought the same and your observation is bourne out by her experience in bed."

"So, she knows her way around the mattress, is that it?"

"Certainly she is not the virgin maid I took her for. Still, I found her most enjoyable."

Ben laughed. "And now suddenly you don't?"

Rob shook his head. "I can't get Melissa out of my head. It's not right for me to go on with Katra."

Ben couldn't help smiling. "I'd say Melissa finds you quite attractive, too. Ah, to be young. To be the object of two women. Better you than me, brother. Take care or they will tear you limb from limb dividing you. I had a taste of that on the voyage, but as might be expected, Melissa's lost interest in me since discovering you it seems."

"You're laughing at me. What should I do?"

"In spite of her age or her experience, you must tell this Katra the truth."

"Yes, I know you're right."

"I sympathize," Ben said, "even if it is a problem I don't ever expect to have again."

"Is it that serious with you and Maddie?" Rod felt quite surprised. He'd thought his handsome suave brother would never really find just one woman.

"Never have I felt so toward a woman," Ben confessed.

Rob studied his brother's expression. "Well, I confessed all to you. Tell me how you met this perfect woman. She's both beautiful and mysterious. Your men tell me she can handle a sword as well as you."

Ben grinned. "So she can."

"And that she can read, too."

"Yes, she is well-educated."

"And you just stumbled on this extraordinary creature?"

"Exactly. I found her in a hole—fallen into an excavation on our deserted northern isle."

Rob's eyes widened. "How on earth did she get there?"

Ben immediately decided not to tell his brother Maddie's all too fantastic time tale. "She claims to have been marooned following a ship wreck."

"Is it possible?"

"Anything is possible, brother."

"And does she make you happy?"

"Yes. I intend to say with this woman for as long as she will have me."

"You intend to marry?"

"Eventually. All things in good time."

"So tell me, what are the immediate plans."

"To winter here. In the spring we'll return to the north and I'll see to it Melissa gets her inheritance."

"And then?"

"Retirement," Ben announced. "I've had enough. I've no desire to end my life at the end of a rope as Kidd did. And somehow, if I continue, it seems almost inevitable. One's good fortune cannot hold forever."

"That seems a wise decision. Ben, can we return to my dilemma?"

"You mean the two women?"

"Yes. I'll be honest with Katra, but what shall I do with her? She's destitute and though she is experienced, I don't think she is the type to earn her living by selling her body."

"Then give her some money and send her to New York where she can find honest work."

"There are few ships going to New York till spring."

"As long as you tell her the truth about your feelings there is no reason why she can't stay here. It is a big house. Just move her to the bedroom on the far side of the house."

Rob nodded. "I'll have to think about all of this."

Ben smiled at his younger brother. "The sooner you're truthful with her, the better."

Rob returned his brother's smile. "Right now I have to meet Melissa. She waits for me on the beach."

Ben shook his head, "And so the courtship begins, one enters before the other exits. Only one so young could have such a problem," Ben laughed as he waved goodbye to this brother.

"Two women," he said shaking his head and in a second he was thinking about Maddie. He could all but smell the perfume of her body and feel the heat of her passion. She was wild and reckless, everything any man could desire. He desired her now and he thought, *she is woman enough for any man.*

Maddie stared at her image in the mirror. Outside, just down the hill, a long deserted white sand beach beckoned. What did women in this century wear to go swimming? Did women in this century go swimming? A wave of homesickness suddenly swept over her. She thought of summers—summers spent vacationing in the Caribbean or on Martha's Vineyard. She thought of hours spent on the beach soaking up the sun and reading. But women in this time were constrained by unspoken rules, by absurd clothing and by men's attitudes. But Ben *was* different. He treated her with respect even if he didn't believe her story.

As she often did, Maddie once again began to think about the past, the present, and the future. Did she want to go home? Did she want to return to crowded vacation resorts and to the hustle and bustle of the twentieth century? No, none of that was really the question. She could adjust to everything, and the truth was, both the pace of life and the smaller population of the eighteenth century were attractive. The real question was, did she dare love Ben? What if she was suddenly returned to the future? A terrible pain filled her, a dreadful fear. No, she didn't want to leave him. There were no choices about how she felt about him—it was too late, she already loved him and she didn't really want anything to change.

Maddie was snapped out of her reverie when the door to her boudoir opened and Ben stepped in. He was naked to the waist and the hair on his chest glistened.

"You look lovely with your hair loose."

"Thank you. Ben, do you ever go swimming?"

He looked at her quizzically. "Sometimes," he allowed.

"Do women ever go swimming?"

"I shouldn't think they know how."

"I know how—Ben, I want to go swimming."

He frowned at her and then grinned. "Can we wait till nightfall? There'll to be a full moon tonight."

Maddie smiled back because she knew they were both thinking the same thing. "Yes," she whispered. "At midnight."

Katra Cross sat on the edge of her bed and unwrapped the package that the messenger had brought. She felt vile. Rob York who had been putty in her hands just a few days ago had not been near her bed since his brother returned home. Instead, he stood about in some sort of trance-like state drooling over Melissa Kidd.

How fortunate that she had been in Europe and narrowly missed meeting her stepsister till now. Melissa hasn't the slightest idea who I am, Katra thought. Katra narrowed her eyes and shook her head in irritation. Melissa was ruining everything, and if not ruining it, making it ten times more difficult. Still, she was in the house and Ben York had returned.

No matter what her relationship with Rob, there was still a good chance she could find the map that showed where Kidd's treasure was buried.

Katra looked at the little box and then opened it. On receiving it she had presumed it was from her mother, but now as she lifted the lid, she realized it was not. Carefully, and filled with a sense of puzzlement, she unfolded the parchment inside the box.

> *I've been with your mother in New York and I know about your mission here. I know you are sent to find out the location of Kidd's treasure by seducing young Rob York. I had thought to enter into partnership with your mother, cunning witch that she is, but I prefer to enter into a partnership with the party of the first part, yourself. My ship is docked on the far side of the island at Crescent Bay. Meet me there by the sea caves tonight. Bring a lantern and signal two and one-half swings, then wait. You have the brains to find out where the treasure is, and I have the means to go and get it. There's no need for your mother in this arrangement and I suspect she would expect you to be practical. Make no mistake, if you fail to cooperate with me, I'll tell Ben York who you are and that will end it for all for you.*
>
> *Tonight,*
> *Phineas Pike*

"Damn!" Katra muttered as she tore the note into tiny bits and then putting it into a brass bowl, lit it with the burning candle. Another complication. But what choice did she have? If Pike told Ben York who she was, she would truly be destitute in Curaçao—her mother was a hard woman who did not reward failure. Besides, she rationalized, her mother would double cross her in a second if it meant more money, and especially if it was the only way to succeed.

Crescent Bay—Katra stood up and began gathering up what she would need. It was best to get started now so she could travel in the daylight.

The sky was like black velvet studded with sparkling jewels and the moon was full, its light shimmering on the dark waters that caressed the white sand beach with gentle waves.

"Do you really swim?" Ben asked. Maddie had brought a large square of canvas which she had spread out to sit on and Ben had brought a bottle of fine Madeira and two silver goblets.

"Of course, I do. In my time almost everyone swims and laying on the beach is a common pastime."

"Fully clothed?"

"Hardly. We wear bathing suits. Most immodest by the standards now."

"Women openly expose their flesh?"

"Yes. But most of the gowns of this day are quite revealing."

He reached over and kissed her neck, whispering, "Yes, the curve of gentle white breast is promising."

Maddie touched his hairy broad chest with her hand. His skin was soft, yet he rippled with muscles. He was wearing skin-tight breeches, boots, and a sash. His shirt had already been discarded.

"Is this way you intend to swim?" she inquired, half-laughing.

"No, lady. I will strip clean of all clothing. And you?"

"Yes. In my time we have a name for swimming naked—we call it skinny-dipping."

He laughed. "The detail you provide always tempts me to believe."

Maddie stood up suddenly, taking him by surprise. She quickly discarded her bodice, then slipped out of her gown and her petticoats. In a moment she was naked beneath the full moon. But she didn't wait, she streaked toward the sea, her hair flying in the wind, till her rounded white buttocks disappeared into the foam of the wave.

"Wait!" Ben York stood up and finished stripping himself, then he ran after her, surprised to find her swimming beyond the low breakers, parallel to the beach.

"My, God, lass! You don't lie! You swim like a fine fish!"

"I love swimming."

"You're the first woman I've ever known to swim."

She laughed and turned on her back. He was beside her now and she uprighted herself to tread water. He did the same and then she felt his hands on her, moving over her beneath the water. They were tantalizing, like hot fire beneath the water's cool surface.

"I'll race you to the beach," she challenged.

"Run, lady!" he replied.

Maddie broke away and stroked at the water till she felt the sand beneath her feet. She ran toward shore. But she reached only the hard packed sand where the waves lapped ashore when she felt him seize her round the waist. They both tumbled to the sand, laughing.

"You are a wild and lovely creature," he breathed as he suckled her salty breast while gently rubbing the other.

Maddie softly stroked him in return. He was a sword of fire, his breath coming in excited, ready gasps. Yet for her he was willing to wait till his knowing movements caused her to writhe in his arms and open her long legs to receive him.

He lifted her buttocks and entered her just as a cool, low wave washed beneath her. He filled her with warmth while the water cooled her hot flesh.

They were as tangled together as knotted seaweed, as they rolled in ecstasy on the sand till she lay atop him while he held her breasts. Maddie moved as he usually moved till he arched his back and the two of them tumbled into throbbing release while the ever breaking waves washed over them.

He rolled her on her side, then began devouring her with kisses. "I love you, I love you," he said over and over.

Maddie clung to him. "I love you, too."

Katra Cross stood by the entrance to the caves. It was still and all she saw was her horse, tethered to a palm tree a few feet away. It was a clear night, a still night. She signaled with her lamp.

Then, emerging from the palms, she saw the heavy set Captain Pike. He trudged toward her and the smell of him floated before his rotund body on the night air.

"Ah, Katra Oort, I presume. What a fair woman you are. It must run in the family."

"Have you come to discuss my looks or Kidd's treasure?"

"Cold and direct like your mother, I see. Looks are not the only thing that runs in the family. Bitchery as well."

"Neither insults nor flattery will accomplish anything."

"I have nothing to accomplish save the finding of Kidd's treasure. Are you accepting my terms?"

"What choice have I?"

"None that I can think of."

"By bargaining with me alone, you've betrayed my mother. I need some sort of guarantee you won't betray me, too."

Pike rubbed his chin. "You have the guarantee that I won't tell York who you really are."

"If you tell York, I won't have time to locate the maps. No, I want something of value to hold till you've kept your word."

Pike spat on the ground. This Katra Oort was even smarter than her mother. "Aye," he agreed. "Come tomorrow night and I'll bring a bar of gold for ye to keep."

Katra smiled. Yes, that would be good enough. Even if he betrayed her, she could use it to get back to New York and she would have plenty left over. "Tomorrow night," she agreed. "But after than, we'll not see each other till I've found the maps."

"Agreed," Pike said, even as he considered just how to trick her.

Old Inez was a mottled black and grey horse who usually pulled a plow, but who tonight was the means of Will's first solo horseback ride.

For over a week now Black Henri had been giving him lessons, and he took them with enthusiasm, remembering their swift ride through the streets of New York. During the day, Maddie made him and Melissa study, but in the evenings, Black Henri took him to the stables and taught him to ride.

"Now you head out on this path," Black Henri had told Will. "Old Inez knows her way, even if you don't. She'll go a few miles, then she'll remember it's feeding time and amble home with you."

Will mounted as he had been taught, and he took the reigns in his hands. Old Inez lopped off and Will imagined himself astride a great black stallion, the wind in his face as he rescues some lovely maiden in distress.

Old Inez slowed after a while, but she did not yet turn around. Will let her choose the way, and to his surprise, she climbed a slight knoll over looking the sea.

At the top, Old Inez stopped to graze on the new green shoots of grass and Will sat astride her, looking out over one of the hundreds of secluded bays.

He squinted off toward the sea. Was that a boat anchored offshore? He strained to see it, but even in the moonlight, he could only make out the silhouette because the vessel was shrouded in darkness.

Then Old Inez stopped grazing. In the distance another horse whinnied. Will was suddenly alert, too. He looked around and he listened. Voices—somewhere below on the rock strewn beach, he heard voices. Then he heard the sound of a horse galloping away.

"C'mon Inez!" Will urged his horse on, but she wouldn't move. Her mouth had once again sought the tasty new green shoots of grass. Will strained, then he saw a rider was galloping down the beach. A rider with long hair that blew in the wind. But it was too dark for him to make out who the rider was. He looked toward the vessel at anchor and now saw a boat in the water being rowed toward the larger vessel.

Someone had met someone from the ship at anchor. And that someone, he suddenly realized, was heading back toward *Castaway*. Will shivered. It all might be nothing, it all might be none of his business, but he still felt apprehensive. He prodded Old Inez in the ribs and as suddenly as she had stopped, she started. She carried him down the hill and back along the path toward home. The closer they got, the faster Old Inez galloped.

I oughta tell someone, Will thought. But who? If it were nothing, he didn't want Black Henri or Captain York to laugh at him. On the other hand, if it were something important, he wanted to make sure someone knew.

Should he tell Mistress Maddie? No, he decided against it. He adored her and always had. But he also adored Captain York and he knew that Captain York was in love with Mistress Maddie. Soon, he felt, they would get married and have sons of their own. Then, he thought sadly, Captain York and Mistress Maddie might not want him about. But if in someway he could prove useful—show them he could always be a help—well, then they might decide they needed him, just a little. In that split second, he decided he would tell Melissa. He would let her decide if what he'd seen was of importance or not. After all, as Captain Kidd's daughter, she had more experience than he while at the same time, she was younger than all the others and wouldn't laugh.

Chapter Thirteen

Rob York walked through the lush garden toward the terrace that overlooked the sea. There, he knew, Melissa waited for him.

He paused momentarily to pick a wild tiger lily, then he hurried on, anxious to meet and talk with her alone.

He saw her before she saw him. Through his eyes she was a beautiful vision, standing by wild white rose bush in a pale blue dress trimmed in crisp white. Her long lovely hair was tied only with a ribbon, but otherwise hung loose, a profusion of thick strawberry-blond curls. She turned when she heard his footsteps and she smile warmly. "I wasn't sure you were coming."

He felt like a school boy, she made his heart pound and his mouth go dry. She was cool and warm at the same time, she was outgoing and yet reserved. She was shrewd, yet somehow soft and vulnerable, she was above all else beautiful and he felt drawn to her as if he were a pin and she were a magnet. It was as if Katra had never existed.

"I would never fail to show up for a meeting with you," Rob said, allowing his eyes to feast on her.

"You shouldn't say such things. You never know what terrible circumstances might force you to postpone a meeting . . ."

"They would have to be terrible indeed. Here, I've brought you a flower—a tiger lily."

"It's lovely."

Melissa took the flower from him and examined it slowly. "This island has so many exotic blooms."

"None that match your beauty. Forgive me for speaking so boldly, but from the first moment I laid eyes on you, I knew you were someone special. I know it hasn't been long, but it's been long enough for me to discover my feelings for you. Melissa, I want to court you."

Melissa looked into his eyes. "Are you free to court me?"

"You want to know about Katra Cross, don't you?"

"I want to know what you are willing to tell me. But most of all, I want you to be honest with me."

"I could not be otherwise. Katra Cross came to this island less than a month ago. Her father was a shipmate of your father. She was destitute. I took her in—and well—I admit that we became lovers."

"I see," Melissa said softly, though in fact she was not surprised at all. Still, his honesty showed he really cared, and she waited for what would follow.

"We are lovers no more, Melissa. I swear it."

"But she is still here."

"Only because she is destitute. I spoke to Ben about her. She's been moved to a room on the extreme other end of the house. As soon as a ship comes which is headed for New York, she will be put on it. It is over between us, I told her it was over."

"And just what did she say?"

She seemed to understand. Katra is older than she looks, more experienced than she appears."

Melissa suppressed her smile. "If you are certain it is completely over between you . . ."

"It is. I swear it to you."

Melissa smiled shyly and looked into his eyes. "Then you may court me.

Rob stepped closer and took her hand, lifting it to his lips. He kissed it, and moved toward her to claim a kiss from her lips, but she held out her hand to restrain him.

"We'll go slowly," she cautioned.

"Are you not certain of my feelings?"

"It is you who must be certain."

"I am," he protested.

Melissa only smiled. "Then you will be just as certain in a few weeks time."

He nodded. She was right to make him wait, to give him time to consider everything without the distraction of a quick physical liaison. Melissa, he decided, was wise beyond her years.

Maddie sat and stared out over the ocean. Before her the white sand beach stretched to the sea, and as far up and down as she could see, towering coconut palms swayed in the tropical breeze. Between the palms and the sand was a natural wall of giant boulders. She sat atop one now and thought about last night when she and Ben made wild passionate love in the cool surf beneath the full moon.

All that bothered her now was Melissa. She was ninety-nine percent certain Melissa meant nothing to Ben, but the fact that Melissa was always there, always flirting with him, unnerved her, and she knew that at times she had been jealous and indeed still harbored some resentment.

"Maddie!"

Maddie turned at the sound of her name. Melissa had discarded her shoes, lifted her full skirts and was headed toward her. How odd that she should appear just when I was thinking of her, Maddie thought.

Melissa scrambled up the rocks and sat down beside Maddie. "Oh, it's warm from the sun," she commented, then added, "It feels good."

"And it's peaceful here," Maddie added.

"I suppose I'm disturbing you."

Maddie turned quickly. "That's not what I meant." But as soon as she said it, she wondered if indeed that was what she had meant.

"Oh, of course it is. I see how you feel about Ben, and I know you resent me."

Maddie started to protest even though the girl had read her mind with maddening accuracy. What did Melissa want? Why was she suddenly being so honest. "I won't deny that I . . ."

"Don't say anymore. Hear me out," Melissa interrupted.

"All right."

"Ever since I was a little girl I've thought Ben York was the most handsome, wonderful man alive. I think in some way I've been in love with him since I was a small child. Then, after my father was killed—well, Ben was the only man I could trust."

"I understand that," Maddie said.

"Well, I resented you, too. I thought I'd have Ben to myself and then there you were—beautiful and brave and intelligent. And the truth is, he didn't even see me—except as that little girl."

"You don't resent me anymore?"

"No and you have no reason for resenting me. I realize that my feelings for Ben were childish and immature. He's too old for me. Maddie, it's Rob I want."

"Rob? Do you really want him? I thought you only wanted to take him away from Katra."

"At first that was it, of course. But I've come to know him. I see we're more alike than Ben and I. I think I'm falling in love with him."

Maddie smiled, feeling a sense of relief. "I'm sure he feels the same. He's always admiring you."

"Oh, I know he feels the same. He's asked to court me."

"Oh, that's wonderful, Melissa." Maddie turned toward the younger woman and took her hand. She felt grateful that Melissa had sought her out to tell her all this, to explain her feelings. "I was jealous of you," Maddie confessed.

"Well, no need to be. But there is a problem."

"Katra Cross," Maddie guessed.

"Yes, Katra Cross. I don't trust her one bit. Rob says it is over between them and I believe him, but I don't trust her."

"I don't blame you," Maddie replied.

"Maddie, you must help me keep an eye on her. I keep feeling she is here for some reason other than what she told Rob and even for some reason that goes beyond her involvement with Rob. I think she was using him."

"For what purpose?" Maddie asked, puzzled.

"For the purpose of finding my father's treasure. She lives here now—Ben has said she can stay till a ship sailing to New York comes. Ben and Rob feel sorry for her, but I'm suspicious."

Maddie nodded. "I also find her suspicious and untrustworthy."

"Then you'll help me?"

"I'll do whatever I can," Maddie agreed.

Darkness enveloped the estate as the large English clock in the main floor room struck the hour of three a.m.

Fully dressed in dark colored men's clothing, Katra crept down the hall from her isolated room in the east wing, through the deserted kitchen, and dining room, and finally into the main room.

She paused for a moment to get her bearings. Her eyes had already adjusted to the darkness, though in fact the main floor living room was not pitch black as the long corridor had been.

The living room had windows, and because the day had been warm, the shutters on them remained open, as they often did at night. Thus the light from the moon and stars cast an eerie light on the tile floor and Katra could easily make out the pieces of furniture and the covered cages that held the colorfully feathered tropical birds.

She hurried to the desk, walking silently with cat-like stealth. She carefully tested the rolltop, then eased it open, making as little noise as possible and stopping at almost every inch to listen for signs of detection. But there was only silence and Katra felt assured the household slept.

She listened and looked about. Nothing. Feeling bolder, she took a candle and returned quickly to the kitchen where she lit it from the ever present embers on the cooking stove. She then returned to the darkened living room with her tiny light.

She thrust it back in the holder on the desk and began looking through the papers which were neatly put in each of the desk's small cubby holes. Nothing.

She went through the drawers and then began feeling of the desk, observing it. Such desks had, more often than not, a secret compartment. That would be the logical place to hide a treasure map.

Annoyed, Katra prodded and pushed. Atop the desk, Ben's pipe holder teetered dangerously close to the edge then fell to the floor with a loud crash.

It was as if the crash began a chain reaction of sudden noise and dreadful confusion. "Ahhhhh!!!" shrieked one of the parrots.

Katra straightened up instantly in terror. She blew out the candle, but as she spun around in the darkness she overturned one of the cages.

"Ahhh! Help! The ship's on fire! The ship's on fire! The ship's on fire!" a screetching imitation of a human voice screamed in the darkness.

Katra, unnerved by the voice hurriedly fled just as she heard footsteps coming down the stairs.

"Who's there?" Ben called out in the darkness.

Maddie followed carrying a lantern and silently cursing the fact that there were no such things as flashlights.

The light from the lantern cast long shadows in the otherwise darkened room.

"The ship's on fire! The ship's on fire!" the parrot continued to scream.

Katra, in the meantime, reached the door of her room which she had wisely left ajar. She hurried in, closing the door silently. Then, in a flash she was beneath the covers, ever listening for footsteps.

Back in the living room, Maddie and Ben looked about. "Ah, there," Ben said, pointing to the pipe stand and mess on the floor. "Damn, my meerschaum pipe shattered on the tile."

Maddie uprighted the cage and peeked in. "Shh, Polly, it's all right."

"His name is Toby," Ben said.

Maddie paid him no mind. "Someone's certainly been in here," she concluded.

"It was on the edge. Look, a stiff wind's come up and all the shutters are open. It might have just fallen."

"And the parrot?"

"He could have caused the cage to tip in agitation."

Maddie shook her head and sniffed. "I think not." She raised her lantern toward the candle. "This candle was recently lit," she observed.

Ben touched it. The wax was still soft from the heat. "You're right. We've had a would-be thief. I don't think he had time to take anything."

Maddie did not ask what made him so certain that their thief was male. Instead, she decided to test the waters. "What might a thief have been looking for in this desk? There are valuable artifacts around, it seems to me a thief would take those."

"Perhaps. In any case, we must close and lock the shutters at night. I guess we are not as safe here as I assumed. I will also have to place guards."

"Is there anything in the desk that might be of value?" Maddie asked.

"I rather imagine our thief was looking for a map."

"A treasure map?"

"Yes. But don't worry, it's in a safe place."

Maddie frowned, though in the darkness he could not see her. As she recalled, many had been killed in search of Kidd's treasure. "Perhaps Captain Pike is here," she ventured.

"I'll check on it, though I doubt he would be brave enough to come here."

"Perhaps he sent someone."

"Possibly—but he is not the only one looking for the map."

"Are you sure it's safe?"

He looked at her and then reached out and touched her lips with his fingers. "Quite safe, don't worry."

"I do worry for you. Greed is a formidable enemy."

He smiled at her in the darkness. "Indeed it is. Come, let's go to bed. We'll further investigate this mystery in the morning light."

"Time, time, time," Katra muttered to herself. She needed more time to find the map, to explore the house. But she needed more than time, she needed the trust of those in the house. And it would be more difficult now because the house was guarded and the shutters were closed and locked. She had failed utterly the other night. Maddie and Ben had found the candle still warm and in the morning, they searched the outside of the house. No one seemed to be suspicious of her, but still she thought with horror, she might have been caught. If she failed, her mother would not pay to bring her back to New York and heaven knew what that vile, horrid man Pike would do to her. Without the map, she would have to chose between devils.

There was, in Katra's way of thinking, only one solution. That solution was to get Rob back, to make him take her back to his bed. If she could prod him for information, perhaps she could short cut the search.

Yes, there was no question about it. She had to do something to protect herself and to make this whole thing easier. After all, she came perilously close to being caught the other night.

"Protection," she whispered. At the moment Rob York and the word protection seemed almost synonymous.

Will stepped out from behind the stall where Old Inez was kept. He had fed the old horse along with the others, and now he was about to get them all some water. Normally One-Eyed Jake, who was a retired seaman, and who lived on the estate, saw to all the work in the stables. But One-Eyed Jake was getting old, and Ben York had suggested that while they were here, Will help out, giving One-Eyed Jake the leisure to take some time off and visit his daughter who lived on the other side of the island.

This particular morning, Will had gotten up early in order to get to the stables early. Melissa came every morning and went for a short ride before breakfast. He hoped this morning she would be alone so he could talk with her.

Will had just rounded the corner of the stable when he saw Melissa coming across the field.

"Miss Melissa!" he called out. He set down his bucket and ran toward her.

"Good morning, Will. My you're up early. I'm so glad, you can help me saddle my horse."

"I'd be pleased to," Will answered. He turned about and fell into step beside her. She was dressed in a riding habit, a sort of long full skirt that was divided as men's trousers were divided. She had it specially made because the available saddles were not proper saddles intended for ladies who usually rode sidesaddle.

"Miss Melissa, before you go riding, I have to talk to you. I have something to tell you."

"And what might that be?"

Will kicked his foot in the dirt. He had rehearsed his speech several times, but now he felt awkward and wondered if he hadn't made a mistake. Maddie was easier to talk to and, on reflection, she probably wouldn't have told the Captain if he'd asked her not to.

"Well, what is it," Melissa said a bit impatiently.

Will still didn't look up. "Well, I haven't told anyone else yet—I was afraid they might laugh. But you being Captain Kidd's daughter and all, well, I thought you might know if what I saw was important."

Melissa's facial expression changed and became more serious. She touched Will's shoulder gently. "Tell me what you saw."

Feeling more confident, he looked up. "Well I was riding on Old Inez the other night. I went clear up to the rocky point that overlooks that bay just the other side of the island."

"And?"

"And I saw a ship at anchor. Sort of a familiar ship, to tell you the truth, it looked a bit like Captain Pike's ship, but I couldn't swear to it."

"Did something else happen?" Melissa felt intensely interested.

Will nodded. "A rider came. It was a she. It was too dark for me to see much, but she had long hair, I saw that much in the moonlight before the moon went back behind the clouds. Anyway, the rider met someone from the ship—at least I think that's what happened 'cause right after the rider left I saw a small boat headed out for the larger ship. And the rider, well the rider left really fast. Mistress Melissa, I'm sure that ride was headed for *Castaway* on the low road that follows the shore." Will waited a moment, then added, "I haven't told anyone else cause I thought they might laugh at me. You're not going to laugh at me, are you?"

Melissa put her arm around Will's shoulders and gave him a sudden hug. "No, of course not! Oh, Will you're very smart, and you're probably right to have told me."

"Should we tell Mistress Maddie and Captain York?"

"Not yet. Will, I want you to take me to where you saw all this."

"Now?" Will asked in a bewildered voice. He was surprised she seemed so intent. "I have to get the horses some water."

"I'll help you so you can finish sooner. Then you'll take me this very morning."

"So you think it's really important," Will said proudly.

"Yes, Will. I think we have a spy in our midst. I think we'll have to be very clever to catch our spy, even though I think I know who it is."

Will's eyes widened. "Do you think it's the same person who broke in?"

"Yes, Will. And I think that person is Mistress Katra. I don't trust her at all."

"Why would Mistress Katra do that?"

Melissa hugged Will again. "I don't know, but you and I are going to find out."

Rob walked toward Katra Cross who stood in the distance, her loose golden hair blowing in the brisk ocean breeze. It was late afternoon and she had asked him to meet her by the rock wall.

He felt apprehensive. He had told her it was a mistake between them and he had also told her she could stay until a ship came and that he would pay her way to New York. At the time, she had taken it better than he had expected, but now he wondered if she wouldn't try to begin their affair anew. A small voice inside warned him that she might prove difficult.

He pulled himself up onto the one of the large rocks and

sat down. It was always pleasant here; it was the perfect place to talk, especially in the late afternoon when the house sometimes grew too warm from the intense sunlight. "Did I keep you waiting?"

Katra sat down. She looked across at him. "No. I like it here. It's always cool, and usually there is no one about."

Immediately, Rob felt ill at ease. Her eyes seemed to hold some terrible sadness and she looked softer and more vulnerable than she had looked since the first day they'd met. Perhaps it was the way she was dressed, perhaps it was deliberate. Sometimes he felt like a fool around women. He was never sure of his own perceptions.

"Do you still feel the same way about that young girl, Melissa?"

She looked as if she were going to cry and Rob steeled himself. This was his fault. He shouldn't have been so hasty to have her, he should have waited and gotten to know her better. Still, she had been willing and it was true that she was experienced.

"I can't lie to you," he said, searching her eyes. "I am deeply attracted to Melissa. You're very beautiful Katra. It's just that I . . ."

"Please, wait." She spoke so softly he could barely hear her, and he was compelled to lean closer. She sounded very emotional, almost shattered. Then she turned to him with something like terror in her eyes. "What am I to do," she whispered. "I've not had my monthly blood. I'm quite certain I'm carrying your child."

Rob felt so stunned he could hardly move. His mouth went dry and he felt weak as the true meaning of her shattering confession crashed in on him. "You're with child," he gasped.

"Your child," she reiterated. "It's true there was a man before you, but that was several years ago. You're the only man I've been with—I've been here for two months now. It could only be your child."

He knew he could not dispute that. She had not left the estate, there was certainly no other man.

"I have no family, no friends, no money. What will become of me? What will become of our child?"

Great tears were falling down her cheeks, and her bountiful breasts fairly shook with emotion. He felt terrible and he knew no matter how much he loved Melissa that this changed everything. He reached out and put his arm around her shoulders and drew her close to him. "I shall have to make new plans," he managed. "Please, don't worry. I'll take care of you, of our child. I'll take care of everything."

Katra looked up at through tear-filled eyes. "Will the child have your name?"

He nodded and pressed her to him. He looked over her shoulder, staring into the distance, trying to think, even as she leaned against him. Then he decided. He would have to tell Melissa immediately, anything else would be unfair.

"Come," Rob said, climbing down from the rock and lifting Katra down. "Let's walk back to the house."

Katra slipped her hand into his. Her stage training held her in good stead. She had always been able to cry at will. Now, in addition to her abilities as an actress, she could congratulate herself on being able to predict how people would act. She had thought Rob York an honorable young man. His reaction to her tale of pregnancy was honorable indeed. He intended to make an honest woman out of her even at the expense of his own happiness. It took all of her ability to suppress a smile of supreme triumph. Melissa would be furious.

Melissa dismounted and walked along the sand, leading her horse. "I suppose the tide washed away the imprint of the horse's hooves," she lamented.

"Two tides," Will said. "There was one last night and one this morning. And she was riding on hard packed sand, by the water's edge."

"I was just hoping there would be some clue."

"I was hoping the ship at anchor would still be here."

Melissa shook her head, "Pike is too smart to stay so close. If they have set times to meet, then he is probably anchored off one of the nearby islands or in some difficult to reach place. Anyway, were he anchored offshore he would see us and grow suspicious and far more careful."

"Do you think they always meet here?" Will asked.

"Probably. I think we'll have to watch Katra carefully."

"Do you really think she works for Captain Pike?"

"Yes."

"But she was here when we came and we did leave Pike in New York."

"I know, it's very puzzling. Still I'm sure it was Katra you saw." Melissa, who had been looking down, searching the sand with her eyes as if she expected some clue to magically appear, straightened up. "Come Will, take me to where you saw all this, and take me home along the second trail you followed so I can learn how to get here."

"Are you coming back alone?" he asked.

Melissa raised one of her eyebrows and looked at him. "Will, you and I are going to take turns watching this place till Katra and Captain Pike meet again. We must make sure."

"I'll come tonight," Will promised.

"And I'll take tomorrow night," Melissa said. "We better get back now, or someone will begin to wonder about us."

Will smiled at her. He felt excited, as if he were part of a mystery. Captain York would be proud of him if he helped Melissa catch a spy, perhaps he would be proud enough to keep him around even after he married Mistress Maddie and had sons of his own.

The long days were wonderful, Maddie thought as she walked through the palm grove. Everything about life here with Ben York was like a dream. He loved her and she knew she loved him. She wanted to stay with him always, to marry him, to be the mother of his children. But one thing stood between them, one thing which troubled her.

For a long while after she knew she loved him, she had feared being taken back to her own time period, but now for reasons of which she was unsure, those fears had receded.

What troubled her was the fact that he still could not accept the truth about her, that he still did not believe she was a time traveler. How could they stay together always if he did not accept her reality? Not that he called her a liar either. He admitted he believed in the possibility of time travel, and spoke in scientific terms of how it might be possible. But he still doubted her. Instead, he made up an elaborate excuse for her claim. He believed she had amnesia, and that her claim of having come from the future was the result of some dream she had while unconscious. And it was true that as the months passed, the future from which she had come seemed to grow more distant and less of a reality. But still, however fantastic, she knew what had happened to her, and she was beginning to feel strongly that all could not be complete with Ben until he too understood and believed. Everything, she thought, would be perfect if only she could prove her origins to him. They might never speak of it again, but to have him really believe her was beginning to mean more and more to her.

"Maddie!"

At the sound of her name, Maddie was drawn out of her reverie. Ben was following her down the path and he quickened his step to catch up with her.

"And where might you be headed, my love?" He reached her side, drew her into his arms, and kissed her.

She leaned against him, comfortable, happy, and wondering a little why everything couldn't be absolutely perfect between them. "To the mango grove. I wanted to collect some fruit for lunch."

"Ah, let me show you a fruit you have not yet tasted. It should be ripe now."

Maddie took his hand. "And what fruit might that be?"

"The berry of a lovely flower. We call it passionfruit."

"You jest," she suggested, laughing.

"No, I do not. It is tasty and succulent."

She followed him beyond the mango grove into a tropical thicket. "There," he said, pointing to the berries. He picked a few and handed them to her. Maddie tasted them. They were a delicious fleshy fruit.

Then he leaned over. "I shall taste them on your lips."

This kiss was long and probing. It sent chills through her body and she did not protest as he lay her on the soft ground and began with maddening slowness to undress her and make love to her. And once again, just before she became lost in the pure pleasure of his caresses, she wished he really believed her story.

Melissa fairly flew into Maddie's room and she slammed the door behind her to emphasize her fury.

Maddie looked up with a start, Melissa, hands on hips and her brown eyes ablaze looked as if she were going to explode. "I hope I'm not the object of your anger," Maddie said.

"You're not!" Melissa flounced down on the bed and kicked at the floor with her shoe. "I'm going to kill her! I don't believe a word of it! She's a whore and a liar!"

"Don't believe a word of what? And who is a whore and a liar?"

"Katra Cross!"

"You know I don't like her either, but why are you so angry with her?"

"Rob! Before I came she and he—well, no matter. He gave her up, he wanted to court me."

"Yes, I know. Has something happened?"

"Everything has happened!" Melissa returned. "Everything!"

"What has Katra done?"

"She told Rob she is carrying his child! Can you imagine?"

"No!"

"Of course, he said he'd take care of her, keep her here and give the child his name."

"Oh, Melissa, I'm so sorry."

"Sorry? Sorry? You don't believe it do you? I don't! She's lying. She's made up this story to stay here, to keep Rob. I don't believe it for a moment. She's too smart to just get pregnant."

"You know, Melissa, it could be true."

Melissa looked into her eyes. "No, I know it isn't. I feel it. I know she's lying and I'm going to prove it."

"Well, you did say just a few days ago that you didn't trust her."

"And you said you'd help me. Will you still help me?"

"I'll do anything I can. I told you that the other day. Do you believe this still has to do with your father's treasure?"

"Of course, just as you and Ben believe that someone broke in the other night looking for something."

"We didn't know you were awake."

"I wasn't till I heard the pipe stand crash to the floor."

"We couldn't find any footprints outside the house in the morning."

"And had someone broken in from outside there should have been footprints because the ground was moist from the afternoon rain. No, whoever it was, came from inside the house. I think it was Katra Cross."

Maddie smiled at Melissa who was smart as well as pretty. "I think you could be right, she crossed my thoughts as well."

"I'm just going to have to nap in the afternoon," Melissa said, "so I can get up and watch her at night."

"Melissa, you must be careful. We don't know who her accomplices might be."

Melissa smiled. "Oh, I'll be careful." She held her silence for the moment, because she was, in fact, quite sure who Katra's accomplices were.

Katra sat on the side of the bed. She wore a princess style night gown that displayed her large white breasts. Rob sat in nearby chair, a wine goblet in his hand.

Katra was desirable, of that there could be no question. He thought back to the nights he had spent with her, nights of ribald lovemaking. He had loved her billowy breasts then, indeed he had been drawn to them, had lost himself there seeking pure physical pleasure. How was it that now, as he sat close to her, he felt absolutely nothing? He did not feel even the slightest bit aroused.

"Do you want me?" Katra asked in a deep throaty voice. She walked to him, leaned over and kissed his forehead. His nose touched her cleavage. She smelled nice, but still there was nothing.

"I think I've had too much to drink," he said, offering the only excuse he could think of to cover his lack of arousal.

She sighed. "You have drunk a great deal lately."

It was true. He had wine for dinner, then he has some island rum, then he had more wine. Finally, in an alcoholic stupor, he was able to sleep. Ben had said nothing yet, but Rob felt a lecture would soon be forthcoming.

"It's all right," Katra said, sadly. Then in a small pitiful voice, "I know you don't love me. I know you're only with me because of the child."

Rob looked into her eyes and felt like crying. He had ruined her life, his life, and perhaps Melissa's life. He felt contemptuous of himself, and he took another large gulp of wine.

"It's all right," Katra said. "I understand."

She took the goblet and walked across the room with it to where the bottle stood on the credenza. Back to him, he heard her refilling the glass. She seemed to understand that he wanted to get drunk, indeed needed to get drunk. He looked at her and felt even worse. Somehow he wished she didn't understand. He wished one of them—either Katra or Melissa—would be furious with him. But neither of them seemed to be angry. Katra seemed understanding, and Melissa seemed angry at Katra rather than angry at him. Women. Rob decided he did not understand them.

"Here," Katra said, handing him back the goblet.

Rob drank it down and slumped into the chair. Katra returned to the bed and sat down. She was still sitting there in silence when he passed out.

Katra leaned over and jostled his arm. His eyes remained closed, but he groaned slightly.

"Can you hear me?" she demanded.

"Huh?" Rob's head rolled slightly.

Katra shook him a little harder. "Can you hear me?" she asked slowly and clearly.

"Y—yes . . ." he slurred.

"Where does Ben keep the map?"

"Map?"

"Where does Ben keep the map?" she asked slowly, leaning near him and speaking in a thick syrupy voice.

"Sword handle—in his sword handle."

Katra could not suppress her smile as she put on a long dark robe, and quietly leaving her room, moved once again through the living room like a black cat. Silly Rob, she thought. He had drunk too much wine, but just to make certain, she had drugged him heavily.

She passed the room where Maddie and Ben slept. She

stopped and listened. They were also fast asleep. She heard Ben snoring and quickly moved on.

The living room was darker than when she had been here before because the shutters were now closed and locked. She stood and stared into the darkness. Where else? Where indeed? And she knew she would never have thought to look there herself. She moved down the hall toward the sword rack. Ben's sword was there, he kept it at the very end of the rack. She remembered admiring it one day, admiring its long silver blade, and its fine gold braid. In the darkness she reached out for it, and lifted it from the rack.

She held it by the handle and then, knowingly, turned the handle. She had heard once of a man who had a secret compartment in the handle of his sword. The handle moved and Katra, elated, turned it again and then again. On the fifth twist, it opened with a little click. In the darkness she reached in and with drew out a small rolled parchment. Her heart was beating a mile a minute. This was surely the prize! This was most certainly the map to Kidd's treasure.

Quickly, she stuffed the scroll down her dress, then she twisted the sword handle back on, and silently placed the sword back on the rack. She lifted her robe and sped up the curved staircase. Once in her room, she lit a candle and then unfolded the paper.

"It is the map!" she whispered in triumph. Katra smiled. Her mother wanted it, Captain Pike wanted it, and she alone had it!

Katra thought for only a moment. Yes, she would arrange a meeting with Pike. But first she would change the map ever so slightly. If he double crossed her she could see to it he was punished. Katra smiled to herself. She was definitely going back to Europe and there, she would live in style with her share of the treasure.

Chapter Fourteen

Maddie and Ben walked barefoot along the sandy beach. It was after lunch, but the tropical sun still shone brightly overhead.

"I can't believe we've been here almost three months," Maddie said, kicking at the sand, and enjoying the feeling of it between her toes. She wore a plain cotton skirt with a white peasant-like blouse. Her dark hair was loose and wild, falling on her bare shoulders in a profusion of thick rich dark curls.

"The days pass quickly here."

"It is beautiful."

"But deserted. I long for both beauty and access to a cosmopolitan city," he confessed.

"You sometimes surprise me," Maddie replied. "I miss some of the things a city had to offer."

"I built this house here because it's a safe haven. But it's not where I intend to live out my days."

"Where do you intend to live out your days?"

"In Havana, with you."

"Havana?" Maddie said in surprise.

"It's a city and it's beautiful. The island is beautiful and yet it has everything. And if you are with me, then it will be perfect."

He stopped walking then and pulled her into his arms.

"Maddie, I love you. I love you as I could love no other woman and I want to marry you."

Maddie's lips parted in surprise. She had felt comfortable with his love, safe in his arms, but she was still taken aback by his unequivocal declaration. He hadn't seemed the marrying kind. "Are you sure, Ben York? Are you certain you want to give up your freedom?"

"For you, yes. I want to love you and hold you. I want you to be with me always, to be the mother of my children—to be my lover, my wife, my love."

His dark eyes were locked on hers and he bent and kissed her. It was a long, slow, deliberate kiss. A rare kiss, a kiss that made her want to cry with happiness.

"I love you, too," she said, leaning against his broad chest.

"I have money and several years ago I began construction on a house outside Havana. It's on a hillside, it's breathtaking."

Maddie looked into his eyes and he saw her distress.

"What is it? Can't you share my dream?"

"Ben, we can't go to Havana," she said slowly. "At least not now."

Ben's brow furrowed. "Why not?"

"There's a war," Maddie said. "There's a war. England and the Netherlands are at war with Spain and France."

"How can that be? We've heard nothing of such a war."

"Ben, the news just hasn't reached us yet. I know because . . . I know because in my time I studied the war. It will last for a very long time, but it won't begin here just yet."

He looked almost relieved and she knew he didn't believe her. "It'll be all right, darling."

Maddie shook her head. "It won't be. Everything would be perfect between us if you just believed me—I wish I could convince you somehow."

"As I've told you before, I believe that you believe—it's

true I don't know from where you came, but I know there is some sort of explanation."

"There is. I have given it to you."

"I cannot accept it," he said still holding her close. "But that doesn't mean I don't love you. I don't care where you came from or how you came into my life. I only know I want you to be with me forever."

Suddenly an idea overwhelmed Maddie. This was her chance. "Ben, I remember a detail. If I tell you and I am proven right, will you believe me?"

"It will have to be more detailed than a war . . ."

"It is. Ben, I don't know the exact date, but I do know that this European war will reach the new world in 1702 and that Saint Augustine, in Florida, will be attacked and burned to the ground."

"That seems specific enough—yes, Maddie, if this comes to pass, I will have no choice but to believe you."

"Then I must abstract one promise. Promise me we won't go to Havana till next year. That's all I ask."

Ben smiled at her. "We couldn't go before then in any case. We have to go north to get Kidd's treasure. We won't be free till that is done."

Maddie nodded. "Then I will say no more."

He sat down on the sand and pulled her down beside him. "Say you love me one more time."

"I love you," she said willingly.

He cupped her chin in his hand and kissed her lips, then her ears, then her neck. In a moment they were lying in the sand and his hands were roaming beneath her skirts and she was moaning with pleasure at his persistent caresses. She felt him hard against her and then he freed himself and lifted her skirt. He pulled down her blouse and toyed with her breasts while she undid his shirt and pressed against him. His lips seemed everywhere, and then he joined with her, moving against her till she cried out with joy. They seemed to be falling, tumbling, rolling all at once as the throbbing release of their passion filled them both with mutual happiness.

"I shall always lust after you," he whispered.

Maddie kissed his ear. "You had better."

Melissa crept along the hall till she reached the door of Maddie and Ben's bedroom. Then she stood stark still and waited, her ear to the door. Yes, Ben was sound asleep. She could hear the rhythm of his snoring through the door.

Ever so carefully, she opened the door and tiptoed inside the room. When she was near the bed, she whispered urgently, "Maddie, wake up. Maddie . . ."

Maddie opened her eyes and blinked into the darkness.

"Maddie, wake up."

"Melissa?"

"Come quickly. I have clothes for you, don't ask questions now. Just come!"

Maddie eased out of bed and wrapped herself in her robe. She followed Melissa into the hall. "What do you mean you have clothes—what's going on?"

"We must hurry. I'll tell you on the way. Here, put these on right now and we'll be off."

Maddie did as Melissa suggested. They were men's clothes and even in the darkness she could see that Melissa was dressed the same way.

Maddie was still buttoning her vest as she followed Melissa, who paused only to take Maddie's sword from the sword rack and to take a pistol for herself.

"Where are we going?" Maddie asked again as Melissa led her through the house and out into the garden.

"We're following Katra," Melissa hissed.

"But she must be long gone by now. How do we know where to go?"

Melissa fairly beamed up at Maddie. "I followed her last week. I know where she's going. Come along, hurry, I know a short cut as well. If we move swiftly, we'll be there before her, in plenty of time to watch and see just what she's up to."

"Don't we need a lantern?"

"No. The moon is bright. If we carried a lantern someone would see us. Katra might even see us—Katra or whomever she is meeting."

Maddie didn't argue but instead simply followed Melissa to the stable where, to Maddie's surprise, Will waited with three horses.

"Will?" Maddie said in surprise.

"Will is the one who first found out about this," Melissa explained.

"Something wicked is going on," Will announced.

They quickly mounted their horses and rode through the mango grove, then they followed the trail above the beach. Once they were out from under the trees, it was bright enough to see. Both the half-moon and the stars were bright in the cloudless sky.

"Is it far?" Maddie whispered.

"A fair ride. But we won't go all the way, just close enough to see. I'm telling you, she's up to something, Maddie. I knew she'd make her move soon. It's spring and soon we'll be sailing ourselves."

"I know, Ben says we'll be ready to leave in two weeks."

"Pregnant indeed," Melissa hissed. "She's not showing at all, Maddie. She might be able to fool Rob, but she can't fool me."

"You think Mistress Katra isn't pregnant?" Will asked, wide-eyed.

"It's a certainty," Melissa returned confidently.

"Have you told Rob what you suspect?"

"Not yet. I want to have proof, otherwise he'll just think I'm jealous. Not that he really cares for her. He certainly doesn't sleep with her. But, of course, that's how she continues to fool him. He doesn't know if she's had her blood or not, because he isn't intimate with her."

Maddie glanced at Will, but mercifully he was riding ahead of them and hadn't heard Melissa's forthright assertion.

"I'm sure you're right," Maddie agreed. "She doesn't look pregnant to me either."

Maddie thought of all the women she knew. When they were pregnant, they glowed with happiness and almost immediately they seemed to grow pleasantly round. And a few had morning sickness by the third month. But Katra Cross had none of these symptoms. She was still slender and flat of stomach. She was definitely not sick in the mornings, and she seemed sullen and withdrawn. True, Rob was not making love to her, but otherwise he showed her every consideration and certainly he stayed away from Melissa. Rob was a young man of honor. Even Ben commented on how much responsibility he was showing.

Melissa suddenly put out her hand. "Shh!" she cautioned. "The coast is very rocky here, there's a hidden cove. We'll have to dismount and climb down a bit. Follow us."

Will had already dismounted and was tethering his horse. Maddie and Melissa followed suit. Then they began to climb down the rocks.

Maddie thought that one had to admire Melissa, she climbed like a cat.

"There—over there . . ." Melissa pointed and then lifted the slender glass from her belt. She peered through it expertly, then handed it to Maddie.

There, down on the beach Maddie could just make out the silhouette of Katra Cross. She was building what looked like a small fire. In a moment, it was lit.

"Now just you watch carefully," Melissa instructed.

Katra seemed to be holding something into the fire—a torch, Maddie realized. In a moment it was lit, and Katra was swinging it up and down, right, then left.

"She's signalling someone," Melissa said in triumph.

"Look, point your glass that way . . ." Maddie stared out

across the black ocean. There was a vessel and though it was far away, she could see the light flashing in answer.

"I knew it. I just knew it!" Melissa said angrily. "I'd like to go right down there and tear every single hair out of her head!"

"You'll do no such thing. We have no way of knowing if anyone else is around. We'll go back now and we'll tell Ben."

"Will he believe us?"

"Of course he will."

"He just might think I'm jealous."

"And pray what motive would Will and I have? No, he'll believe us. I think he has doubts about Katra himself. Come on, hurry. We'll want to get back before Katra does."

Melissa was up in a shot and soon the three of them were climbing back up to where the horses were tethered. They mounted quickly, then headed back to the estate.

"Ben, wake up," Maddie said, standing by the side of the bed.

Ben opened his eyes and stretched. "God, what time is it? It's still dark."

"I know, wake up."

He blinked at her uncomprehendingly. "Why are you dressed like that, what's happened?"

"Something very strange."

At that moment there was a knock on the door and Melissa poked her head in. "I have Rob and Will, we're here."

"Come in, close the door," Maddie replied.

Ben had swung his legs over the bed and pulled on his breeches. He was now buttoning his shirt. He peered out the window and noted that the thin line of dawn was just appearing. He then turned to Maddie. "Well, what is this about and where have you two been?"

"Following Katra Cross," Melissa said quickly.

"Katra?" Rob's expression was filled with puzzlement. "You mean she isn't here?"

"I'm sure she's back by now," Maddie replied.

Maddie looked at Will, his eyes wide with excitement. "We'll let Will tell you. He's the one who made the discovery."

Will beamed. "Captain York, Mistress Katra's been meeting someone. She went out tonight—up the beach several miles to where that cove is—she signaled a ship."

"I don't understand," Rob muttered.

"I do," Melissa said, turning to him. "She's lied to you. She's no more pregnant than I am. She's someone's spy and she's after my father's treasure."

"Melissa's probably right," Maddie confirmed. Will saw her first, then Melissa followed her twice, now all three of us have seen her."

Ben rubbed his chin. "I think it's time we confronted Miss Katra Cross."

Rob said nothing but he followed as Ben led the way downstairs. He lit a lantern and handed it to Rob. "Go to her room and fetch her. Tell her we want to talk to her this moment."

Rob strode down the hall. Could all this be true? He knocked on Katra's door and when she didn't answer, he opened the door.

"Get up!" he ordered.

Katra blinked open her eyes and Rob bent over and pulled her out of bed.

"Don't pretend with me. Here, put on your robe and come along."

"What have I done?" Katra asked, imploring him with her eyes. "Why are you angry?"

"Just come," he said, prodding her forward. He felt vulnerable and stupid. She must be an accomplished actress to have convinced him of the depth of her feelings. He now realized how skilful she was, and he knew now he had been duped by her.

He pulled her down the hall and into the main room which was ablaze with lights form the several lamps which had been lit.

"My, all ready back in bed were you?" Melissa said, meanly.

"I—I don't know what you mean."

"Yes, you do," Maddie said. "We followed you, Katra. We saw you signal your accomplice. We know it was you who prowled through the house some weeks ago."

Katra opened her mouth to speak, but words did not come out.

"Who are you?" Melissa said. "I know you're not who you say you are, and I know you're not pregnant."

"I won't tell you anything," Katra said, pressing her lips together.

"You aren't pregnant, are you?" Rob said, stepping closer.

"Of course not!" Katra snapped. "But that's all I have to say."

Maddie moved closer to Katra and then suddenly reached out and touched the amulet around her neck. She had seen the chain before, but usually the amulet itself was hidden beneath the laces of Katra's bodice. Now Maddie saw it for the first time. She saw it and recognized it.

"This is the same amulet I saw on Sarah Oort."

Maddie studied Katra—God, there was a resemblance. Perhaps that was why she hadn't trusted her from the beginning.

But it was Melissa who suddenly put it all together. "You're Katra Oort!" she blurted out. "You're the stepsister I never met!"

Ben shook his head. "Katra Oort. I suppose your mother sent you and I suppose it is the good Captain Pike you've been signaling."

"Hell!" Rob muttered. "This is all my fault."

Ben reached out and put his arm around the shoulders of

his younger brother. "It isn't your fault, it's the fault of greed."

"But how do we know how much damage this little witch has done?" Rob asked. "We should check our stores on the far side of the island."

"Indeed we should," Ben agreed.

"What are we going to do with Katra?" Maddie asked.

"Hang her," Melissa suggested without a smile crossing her lips.

Ben laughed. "Oh, I think not. I'll decide on something later. For now we'll lock her up. We've just the place—that little room off the kitchen. It has a good solid door and no window. Still, plenty of breathable air comes in."

Rob tossed a shrieking Katra over his shoulder. She cursed all the way to the kitchen. He dumped her on the floor of the room and then left, bolting the door behind him.

"Damn, she scratched me," he muttered.

Melissa stood on her tiptoes and kissed him. "I'll be waiting for you, Rob York."

Ben kissed Maddie. "We'll take Black Henri and go check our cache. Then we'll be back to deal with Katra and decide what to do. We may have to leave early for the North."

He reached for his sword and then slipped into its sheath. "Take care while we're gone." He bent and kissed Maddie again. "We'll be back before nightfall."

Then Ben turned to Will. "You've done a fine job, lad. Look after the women for me, will you?"

Will beamed. "Aye, aye, Captain."

Maddie stood on the terrace with Melissa and Will as they watched Ben, Rob, and Black Henri ride off on their way to the caves where, as Maddie well-knew, Ben stored many valuables.

It was only a few weeks ago, Maddie recalled that she and Ben had ridden alone toward the caves. They had ridden for more than an hour, then tethered their horses in a grove of trees. He had led her up a rocky path on foot, and midway there, had whistled out a secret code to the guards who stood on duty.

Then, when the sound of another whistle answered, they climbed some more till they reached the hidden entrance to a cave.

Ben went first, climbing over a huge boulder, then sliding down out of sight. She followed, and when she slid down the other side, he caught her in his waiting arms.

"How will we get out?" she asked nervously. She had never liked caves.

"There's a rope ladder. No need to worry, my love. There are several ways out as well as in."

With that, he took her hand and led her through the dark, down a narrow passage, then into a larger cavern. It was well-lit by torches that lined the walls. There were trunks in every corner as well as ropes and rope ladders, and much of the paraphernalia one would find around sailing ships. "I've both riches and things practical," he said, opening one trunk and carefully unwrapping a crystal goblet. "There are these and dishes galore, as well as silver."

Maddie looked at the crystal goblet. It was beautiful and glistened in the light from the torches on the walls.

"And that my lady is only the beginning . . ." He took her hands and pulled her toward another trunk. This one he opened with a key and when he opened the heavy lid, a treasure trove of jewels sparkled before her eyes. Pearls and silver, gold and semi-precious stones.

"Oh, they're beautiful," she gasped.

"Not as beautiful as they will be around your neck. But these are paltry treasures . . ." he leaned over and picked up a small black velvet box and opened it, holding it out toward her. Inside on a satin lining, lay an exquisite emerald necklace, earrings, and bracelet.

Maddie was speechless as he took the necklace out of the

box and fastened it round her neck. Next he put on the bracelet, then the earrings.

He held her by the shoulders and looked at her and smiled. "Whomever these were intended for could not have been half as lovely as you."

With that, he kissed her tenderly. "These are for you, my beauty."

"I don't know what to say," Maddie whispered.

"Say you will stay with me always."

"I will."

"Did you say something?" Melissa asked, turning toward Maddie and jostling her slightly.

"Oh, no. I was just thinking."

"I can hardly see them now," Melissa said, staring off down the beach.

They rode on the hard packed sand, and soon they appeared very small, and then they disappeared where the beach curved and a jetty of high rocks blocked the view.

"You look troubled," Melissa said. "I'm certain everything will be fine. I doubt Katra discovered the stores. Will and I've been watching her carefully."

"I'm sure you're right. But it's not the stores about which I'm concerned."

"What then?"

"With the map that shows the location of your father's treasure. That's surely what she was really after."

"Ben said it was safe . . ."

"I know, I just wonder—perhaps she found it and copied it."

"Oh, I don't think so. I don't even know where it is. Do you?"

"No, but I just can't get over the idea that Ben and Rob should have gone off in search of Captain Pike rather than to check the stores."

"Do you really think so?" Will asked.

Maddie caught the look of worry on young Melissa's face, as well as the tone of Will's question. "It was just a thought," she answered, trying to make light of her own concern. "I'm sure everything will be fine. Let's go back inside and fix ourselves something to eat."

Melissa made a slight face. "I suppose we have to feed *her.*"

Maddie laughed. "I suppose we do."

Maddie began cooking some eggs while Will sat at the table watching.

"I know what I'm going to do," Melissa said in a slight whisper. She walked to the door behind which Katra was, and said in a loud voice. "I don't think we should give her any food or water! I think perhaps we should do away with her before Ben returns. I don't suppose he'll want to boil her in oil either!"

Maddie smiled. Melissa was venting her anger, trying to frighten Katra.

"Here," she offered, putting the scrambled eggs on a plate. "Will, bring the bread."

Will brought the bread and leaned near the door, deciding to play Melissa's game. "We sure don't need to feed her yet. I heard once every couple of days was often enough."

Maddie smiled and whispered. "Enough for now. Let's go out onto the terrace."

It was mid-afternoon and Maddie sat with Melissa and Will at the desk. Both of them were progressing well with their studies. They could read quite well now and oddly, Melissa had a natural aptitude for mathematics.

"You're reading has improved a hundred percent," Maddie praised.

"I suppose reading does have some advantage," Melissa

conceded. "But I confess, it's not really what I want you to teach me."

"And what do you want me to teach you?"

"Fencing. I want to be able to handle a sword as well as you."

"Me, too," Will announced.

Maddie laughed lightly. "It will take years of practice. But I will gladly teach you. It's very good exercise."

Melissa's eyes sparkled. "Oh, when can we begin?"

"Not now!" a rough male voice shouted.

Both women jumped, and Will whirled about in terror. Maddie was about to try to reach her sword when she realized it was to no avail. Captain Pike stood in the doorway, sword drawn and ten or so men were entering through the windows.

"Where's Katra?" he questioned, narrowing his eyes and walking closer to Maddie and Melissa. He pointed the tip of his sword at her throat. "Not so brave now, are you, my lady?"

Maddie struggled to sound unafraid though in fact she could feel Melissa trembling at her side. "Katra's locked up—in a room off the kitchen, near the back door. Will, show them where she is."

Pike waved his sword at one of his men. "Take the boy and find her and release her. Bring her here."

The man wasted no time carrying out the order. He grabbed Will roughly by the shoulder and they disappeared instantly.

Will tried to think. What had Maddie meant? He was sure she was trying to tell him something. The door, that was it! She wanted him to try to run away. They reached the kitchen.

"There." Will said, indicating the door.

"Open it!" the man shouted.

Will went to the bolt. He made a face of strain. "I can't. It's rusted, it must be stuck."

"Out of the way!" The man nearly kicked Will, but he relaxed for just long enough, putting both hands on the bolt he believed stuck. In a flash, Will bolted out the door running like lightening for the stable and a fast horse.

"Damn!" the man cursed. The bolt lifted easily and Katra sprang out of the closet. The man realized it was too late, the boy was long gone. He grabbed the startled Katra by the arm and pulled her forward, returning to the living room with her.

"Ah," Pike said smiling toothlessly. "My lovely accomplice."

Katra looked from one to the other, sensing this was the worst of all possible outcomes.

"Where's the boy?" Captain Pike shouted.

"Got away, he tricked me."

Maddie and Melissa exchanged quick looks of relief. But the relief was short-lived.

"Stupid bastard!" Pike snarled. He drew his pistol, pointed it at the errant and now terrified man, and shot him point-blank. A terrible silence enveloped the room.

Pike then turned back to Katra. "Hand it over!" he demanded. He now held the tip of his sword to Katra's throat.

Katra dipped her hand into her bodice and withdrew the folded paper. She handed it to Pike. "I was going to give it to you tonight anyway."

"I doubt that," Pike replied as he glanced at the map. "I suspect you've had it for some time."

Katra said nothing in her own defense. Pike had just killed one of his own men in a fit of temper. He was clearly not the type with whom one argued.

"Well, now what a dilemma—three lovely ladies and I've only room to lock up two. You two!" he said, whirling back toward Melissa and Maddie.

Melissa had paled and Maddie held her arm, afraid she might faint.

"No need to worry my lovelies. I wouldn't dream of harming a hair of your lovely heads till the treasure is mine. After that—well, after that, I think I'll enjoy ye both."

"Ben York will kill you," Maddie said, narrowing her eyes.

"But he'll not sink my ship while you're aboard. Come along ladies, time is wasting."

"What about me?" Katra said, walking boldly to Pike's side.

"And just what do I need you for, lass? No, old Phineas Pike doesn't need the likes of either Sarah Oort or her daughter, Katra. Stay here, I'm sure Ben York will find your story entertaining. Here men, take these two!" Then Pike turned back to Katra, his pistol pointed at her, his beady eyes glaring. "Before I go, I'll have me gold bar," he gruffed.

Katra began to shake, but Pike grabbed her arm. "Take me to it," he hissed. "Or I'll forget me manners."

Two large men seized Melissa and Maddie. They tossed them over their shoulders and headed off.

Melissa screamed once, but Maddie motioned her to silence. Damned if she'd give them the satisfaction of acting frightened, she vowed silently even though inside she really was frightened. Captain Pike was a proven killer.

"Captain York! Captain York!" Will rode like the wind, holding on for dear life and shouting as loudly as he could. He knew where the caves were, but he wasn't sure if Ben York was still there, or on his way back already.

Then in the distance he saw the dust of the horses. "Captain York!" he shouted again, spurring his horse on.

"Will! What is it?"

Will pulled in his horse. He felt tight in the chest just as if he and not the horse had been running. He was also frightened. "Captain Pike! He's here! He's come to your horse!"

Ben felt himself tense and he saw Rob visibly pale.

"Mistress Maddie told me to escape—I rode as fast as I could."

"Good, lad," Ben said. "Hurry! We must get back to *Castaway*."

* * *

Katra sat in a chair silently staring into space. What was she to do now? Pike was gone with the map and the gold. Without knowledge of where the treasure was, her mother certainly wouldn't want to see her again.

She considered her options carefully. And then she decided to wait. Better to bargain with Ben York. At least he would keep his word. And she thought, owing it to her own good sense that she did, in fact, have one bargaining chip left. A small chip to be sure, but nonetheless, a chip.

The sun had just dropped like a flaming ball into an ocean made pink by its glow, when Ben and Rob York returned with their men.

Katra did not wait, she greeted them as they dismounted.

"Where's Maddie?" Ben demanded. His face was white as if he knew instantly on seeing her free that Maddie wasn't there.

"She's been kidnapped," Katra said without hesitation. "She and Melissa were taken by Pike. He sailed on the afternoon tide."

Ben's face contorted slightly as he slid off his horse and went to Katra. He took her arm roughly. "I swear if you're lying you'll be punished, woman or not I'll have you hung from the yard arm."

"I'm not lying. He double crossed me. He has the treasure map and he has Maddie and Melissa. He left me here."

Rob stomped his foot and swore.

Ben looked at his sword.

"It's gone," Katra said.

Ben undid the compartment quickly and his heart sank when he saw it was empty and the map was indeed missing. "You took it, didn't you?"

"Yes, but I copied it. Pike has one of the copies and the copy he has is not quite right. It goes to the hidden island by the longest route possible."

Ben looked at Katra hard. She was certainly not stupid. "So, if we left now, we might get their first, is that it?"

Katra nodded.

"I wouldn't believe a thing she told you," Rob cautioned.

But Ben thought otherwise. Katra had nothing to lose by telling the truth now. "It's good of you to tell me this."

"I ask only that you take me with you or give me enough money to get back to Europe. It's little enough."

"It seems a lot for one who caused this in the first place," Ben reminded her. "You realize of course that I do not need the map. I kept it only in case something happened to me."

Katra looked at him pleadingly, though this time she was not acting. "I didn't have to tell you that Pike has an altered version."

Ben looked at her for a long moment in silence. Then he nodded his agreement. "Let's hurry! We must ready the ship and sail on the midnight tide."

Ben stared upward, first at the star studded sky, then at the *Wilma*'s magnificent sails as they caught the wind. Maddie had told him that in her future, ships were powered by great engines run sometimes by gasoline and sometimes with solar power, which she described as the power of the sun. He knew he wouldn't like her future—if indeed it were real. He loved the look of his sails when fully unfurled, he liked the feel of the wind and he felt invigorated to battle the elements. Something, he thought, was missing from this future she described, something he knew he would not want to lose.

Still, he would give up anything to have her back, to have her safe. No matter where she came from, no matter what, he knew he must find her. "I love you, Maddie," he whispered to the wind, and in his mind, he could almost hear her answer.

"Captain York?"

Ben turned about to see Will. "Yes, lad?"

"We will find her, won't we?"

Ben pressed his lips together. He had seen what Pike had done to one of his own men, he could only pray that Pike wouldn't harm either Maddie or Melissa. "We will find her," Ben answered, trying to sound as if he himself were positive. Then he added, "Both of them."

For a few moments neither of them spoke and then Ben said, "You're very fond of Maddie, aren't you?"

"I'm fond of both of them, sir. But I'm especially fond of Mistress Maddie."

Ben nodded. "I don't know what you have become of all of us if it hadn't been for you, Will. You've been a real hero."

Will beamed, as he always did when Ben complimented him. "Mistress Maddie has—sir, I hope you don't mind if I say this . . ."

"Say what you want."

"I never had a mother, sir. Mistress Maddie has sort of been like a mother, I think. And Mistress Melissa has been a little like a sister. It's the first time I've ever felt like I had a family."

Ben looked at Will, then he reached out and put his arm around the boy's shoulder. "And do you see me only as Captain York?"

Will looked up, his face a little flushed, but his expression very serious. "No, sir. I sometimes dream about your being my father. I always wanted a father."

Ben smiled and wondered if Will could see the tears in his eyes. He hugged Will. "You flatter me, son. Let me tell you, no man could wish for a better son than you. You don't have to worry, I'll be a father to you. I promise."

Will also had tears in his eyes. He hugged Ben York back fiercely and then he pressed his lips together tightly, "We'll find them," he said confidently. "I know we will."

Rob climbed the steps to the pilot house. He looked from Ben to Will. "I'm sorry to interrupt."

Ben grinned. "Rob, I think I'm going to adopt young Will, here. What do you think?"

"I think it a good idea."

"Are you really going to adopt me?" Will asked.

"I am, and you will be called, Will York."

"I don't know what to say."

Ben smiled. "But you still have chores. Go down to the galley and rustle us up some food. We've a long night ahead of us."

Rob sat down. "We won't catch Pike's ship for a long while, Ben."

"I know."

"I'm afraid for them both. They're spirited and Pike is—I swear, if he lays a hand on them I'll tear him from limb to limb."

"You'll have to fight me for the pleasure," Ben replied.

"You don't think he would . . ."

Ben shook his head. "Not now. He'll want to keep them in good condition. If he doesn't find the treasure, then he has them to bargain with."

"You sound so confident, I almost believe you."

Ben did not answer. The truth was, he didn't feel confident at all.

Chapter Fifteen

Melissa paced around the small cabin like a caged tigress. "This is outrageous," she fumed. "What are we to do? Does that pig actually expect us to survive a month's voyage penned up like this?"

Maddie would have smiled at Melissa's temper if she hadn't judged their situation to be so serious. Nonetheless, she felt a good sign that Melissa had gone from terror to anger. "It isn't very big," she agreed.

The cabin was no more than nine feet by ten feet. It held two bunks and a small table with two chairs. There were hooks to hang things up on, and a chamber pot under the lower bunk. There was one small window, too small to escape through. But as Maddie reminded herself, there was no place to escape to—they were at sea.

"I suppose we should be grateful not to be below deck," Maddie said after a few minutes.

"We need water," Melissa said, looking about. "And what will we do about our clothes? We can't wear the same clothes for a month."

Maddie sank into one of the chairs. She shook her head. "I don't suppose Ben can catch up to us and somehow rescue us at sea."

"Oh, God he might not catch up with us at all! Pike has a head start! What's to become of us!"

Melissa's facial expression contorted and she began to cry again.

"It was better when you were mad," Maddie said. "We mustn't let Pike know we're frightened. Somehow—I don't know how, Melissa, but somehow we've got to get control of the situation. Somehow we have to scare him into treating us decently."

Melissa looked thoughtful. "I suppose you're right," she said slowly. "But right now, I don't have an idea in my head."

Both of them fell silent as they heard footsteps outside the door. Then the latch turned and Captain Pike strode in, a twisted smile on his stubbled face. The foul odor of the man filled the small cabin.

"Ah, ladies! I do hope you're enjoying my hospitality."

Melissa straightened up. "See to it we're brought some water," she ordered imperiously.

Captain Pike slapped his leg and roared with laughter. "I see ye'r old Kidd's daughter! A royal bitch! It's I who make the rules on this ship."

Melissa folded her arms in front of her and thrust her chin out defiantly. "Dear Captain Pike, it is true that I am my father's daughter, and you would do well to remember it. I suggest in the quiet of the night, you consider how many friends my father had and how many friends you have. I daresay that if anything happens to either of us, you will have to answer for it."

Pike had no opportunity to answer. Maddie moved to one side of him, an ironic smile now covered her face. Melissa—who hadn't an idea in her head a second earlier, had accidentally or otherwise, hit upon a strategy. Maddie thought it was a strategy that just might work.

"She's right you know," Maddie added, sounding mature, calm and logical. "Ben York has many friends, too. And naturally if anything happened to us, either one of us, Ben would never rest till justice was done."

"I'm not scared of Ben York nor all of Kidd's friends," Pike blustered. But even as he spoke, his face had grown red and was screwed up in thought.

"Perhaps that is because you have never been hunted," Maddie said, lowering her voice for effect, so he would have to strain to hear each and every word she spoke.

"Like an animal," Melissa hissed.

"Yes," Maddie agreed. "Exactly like an animal. You'll always have to look behind you, you'll always have to have guards you can trust, you'll never be sure when you close your eyes that you will live to wake—Ben and Kidd's friends will hunt you down and have you killed."

"Horribly . . ." Melissa whispered as she too moved behind Captain Pike. "Your nails will be torn out, you'll be skinned alive, strip by strip, and then you'll be either drawn and quartered, or boiled in oil!"

Maddie kept her eyes on Pike. Melissa's predictions were so graphic and so terrifying that Pike actually looked shaken and Maddie saw his hand tremble ever so slightly.

"Yes, I should think twice about how we're treated," Maddie added.

"Yes, you had better consider the possibility that you'll need us if you wish to go on living. And what's more you'll have to keep us in good condition."

"It is you who are my prisoners!" Pike yelled. "I'll not listen to ye bitches for another minute!"

"You're right to hide from your future, Captain Pike. I should not like to face it either if I were you," Maddie added.

"I'll consider what I like," he huffed. But Maddie thought he sounded much less confident than he had earlier. Pike spun around, but no matter in which direction he turned one of them was staring hard at him. He lurched toward the door and pulled it open. Then he bolted through it, and slammed it behind him. In a moment they heard the bolt slip into place.

Maddie hugged Melissa and whispered, "I'll wager he won't sleep well tonight."

Melissa giggled ever so slightly. "I feel less miserable now. How long do you suppose it will be before we get water?"

"Not long," Maddie answered.

Melissa looked thoughtful. "What shall we ask for next?"

"We'll need fresh clothes and deck privileges and—good food of course," Maddie suggested.

Suddenly Melissa hugged her tightly. "Do you think this might work?"

Maddie nodded. "I think it might. We'll see and anyway, what have we to lose?"

At that moment the bolt on the door was once again opened. A grubby crew member came in with a large bucket of steaming water and another container filled with regular water. Behind him another crew member held out a basket of cloth, some sewing needles and thread.

"Captain said to have this brought to you," he mumbled sullenly.

Maddie looked at Melissa and Melissa looked at Maddie, both suppressed a smile.

"Tell Captain Pike," Maddie said, "that he has earned three points."

"Beg your pardon, Mistress?"

"Tell Captain Pike he has earned three points," Maddie repeated.

"Will he know what that means?" the crewman asked.

"No, but we shall be pleased to explain tomorrow."

The crewman muttered a reply and left quickly, locking the door behind him.

Melissa danced about the bucket of water. "It's working!" she said happily. Then she stopped. "But I don't understand the points myself."

"Oh, I think we'll tell him he needs one hundred points. When we don't get the things we need we'll subtract points and when we do get the things we'll need we'll add points. If he gets one hundred points we'll tell Ben not to kill him."

Melissa sat down and clapped her hands. "What a splendid idea!"

"I think we'll want a lock on our side of the door," Maddie suggested.

"Oh, at the very least," Melissa agreed. "I'd be locked in, and everyone else locked out."

Maddie sorted through the large box of cloth. "I suppose we can make some undergarments at least," she suggested.

"And sewing will help pass the time."

Maddie looked down. Theirs was a small triumph. It was going to be a long voyage, and she might never see Ben again. The thought almost brought tears to her eyes, but she reminded herself that she had to remain optimistic—if not for herself, then for Melissa.

Ben York leaned over his charts. Katra's altered map would send Captain Pike to an island north of the island where the treasure was buried. There were hundreds of islands, but of course Maddie knew where the island with the treasure was, and when he became lost, Pike would force it out of her. The best he could hope for was one day's lead, and he would only have that if he made up the time already lost to Pike's head start.

He shook his head. If he were to really gain time, he would have to take a short cut sooner rather than later and he would have to pray for spring fog when he reached the coast of Nova Scotia—a fog which would hide the *Wilma* from view and enable him to surprise Pike.

But it was too soon to think of the end. The beginning of this voyage mattered more and there were important choices to be made. He could sail north from Curaçao and pass between Dominica and Puerto Rico and then sail northwest through the Bahamas to the Florida coast. Once off the coast, he would simply follow it till he reached French waters off Canada. The other alternative was to sail northwest now and pass between Cuba and Haiti, then up to the coast of Florida. This route was shorter and more direct, but in the spring it was also fraught with danger. Storms arose quickly, and the currents and winds were tricky.

He closed his eyes and clenched his fists. There was so much that could go wrong—it seemed as if there were a thousand and one possibilities, situations too numerous to even list. Suppose Maddie was right, suppose there was a war. Pike could easily be captured in French waters—he was most assuredly unfamiliar with them. And then there was also the nature of the northern coast. It was dangerous, islands strewn with odd, often unchartered rocky formations extending out into the ocean. One could not count the number of grounded ships in this area because there were so many.

A terrible fear filled him. A fear that he might never see Maddie again. A fear that she might be lost to him. He shook his head, forcing himself to concentrate on the route he would take.

How would Pike go? And immediately Ben knew the answer. Pike had not taken on fresh supplies in Curaçao while he had been loading the *Wilma* and readying her for weeks. To Ben, it seemed almost a certainty that Pike would go the first route, he would sail between Puerto Rico and Dominica. Pike had connections in Mayaguez. He would almost unquestionably stop there for supplies. Yes, if that were so, then that's where time could be made up. It was how Ben could get ahead of Pike and be waiting for him when he arrived at the island, *if* he arrived. Again, he said a silent prayer. A prayer for Pike's safety—at least as long as Maddie and Melissa were his unwilling passengers.

Phineas Pike tossed in his bunk, he was drenched in perspiration and he could actually hear his heart beating as his blood seemed to surge through his veins. In his now persistent nightmares, he saw Ben York and Kidd's first mate, Yan Ould, and even York's brother, Rob. He himself was trussed up and that big bastard, Black Henri, was pulling out his nails with pliers. Pike groaned even in his sleep, then flopped onto his other side.

In a moment, he saw himself, still tied up, being dragged toward a steaming pot of boiling oil. He screamed out in his sleep, "Mercy! Mercy!" Then, in a sweat, he sat bolt upright, shaking from head to toe.

He stared out into the absolute darkness of his stuffy, airless cabin. "Aye," he muttered. The women were his prisoners. He was in command. He had the map. He had a head start. He knew where he was going. Didn't he have the upper hand? He scowled and chewed on his lower lip. What Kidd's daughter said was true. Her father's friends would hunt him down. And Ben York would follow him to the ends of the earth. He would never know a day's peace nor a night's rest.

"Women!" he spat onto the floor beside his bed. They were always more trouble than they were worth. True enough, one could have pleasure with them, too, but it never really seemed worth it in the end. And the smart pretty ones were the worst. He shook his head, thinking of the venomous Sarah Oort. "They're all alike!"

Well, he wouldn't let them know how much trouble they really were, but he decided he would treat them decently. He vowed that when he made port in Mayaguez he would bring aboard some amenities for the ladies. He also vowed that when the treasure was his, he would leave them unharmed on the island for Ben York to find.

"Then," he breathed, "maybe I'll have my old age in peace."

The Caribbean Sea had been calm even when the *Wilma* sailed through the often tricky Windward Passage between

Cuba and Haiti, but now he was north of Cuba, sailing between Cuba and the Bahamas Islands, and the mottled buttermilk sky told Ben York that his luck was running out, and that somewhere a tropical storm was rising, a storm of unknown power. It could be mere rain and wind, or as he wellknew, it could be a storm of swelling waves and wind strong enough to carry a man through the air.

The night passed uneventfully, and at four, an hour before dawn, Black Henri appeared, ready to take the wheel. "The sun, she won't come up today," he predicted glumly.

"I'm afraid you're right."

"Two weeks makes a difference," Black Henri commented.

Ben knew his old friend and companion was right. Normally, they would not have sailed for another two weeks, possibly three depending in the winds and the weather. But Pike had forced them to go early, thus risking an encounter with a late season hurricane.

Black Henri pointed off in a northwesterly direction. "Out there," he said shaking his head.

Ben let Black Henri take the wheel, but he did not leave the pilot house. He waited, sitting nearby, drinking soup that Will brought from the galley, and waiting for the dawn.

As the time came for the sun to rise on the eastern horizon, the light changed only ever so slightly. Now, unlike an hour earlier, swirling dark grey clouds appeared on the distant horizon. Black Henri was right, the storm would come from the northeast.

They sailed onward and Ben's heart sank as the clouds grew into dark mountains beneath which he was certain a bank of wind and water from the heavens would envelope the *Wilma*.

Within the hour, the sea that washed against the side of the *Wilma* no longer lapped gently and was no longer a bluegreen color. Now the water was choppy, and the white foam looked like little teeth napping at the sides of the vessel. Moreover, the sea swirled black, in ominous warning. Then,

when the clouds stretched from one horizon to the other, the
wind dropped, then ceased all together, leaving the *Wilma* be-
calmed, bobbing in the black water, beneath the darkened sky.
Nothing stirred, the ship merely floated restlessly in the water.

"It could be hours," Black Henri predicted.

"Or just minutes," Ben answered. At another time, sleep
might have claimed him, but the threat of danger caused
adrenalin to pump through his veins, jolting him into an alert
readiness.

He walked outside onto the deck and took up his bullhorn.
He shouted out his orders, sending his crew scurrying in all
directions. He ordered the sails lowered and the ship secured.
The crew scrambled to tie down all moveable objects, checking and rechecking their knots. The hatches that led to the
hold were bolted down, the barrels of fresh water covered except for those that were only partially full. Those were left
open to catch the rain when it came.

An hour passed, then two. As Ben suspected it would, the
wind began to come up gradually, this time from the south.
Within minutes, it was gale force, and Ben could no longer
judge from which direction it came as it seemed to swirl
about moving in a great circle. The ship moved with it, tossing this way and that way in a sickening series of rapid mo-
tions.

The sky was as dark as night, yet it was high noon, and the
ship moved where the sea carried it.

Using both hands, and hanging on for dear life, Ben
climbed down from the pilot house and walked around the
deck, checking the ship. This storm was only beginning, and
he well knew the real danger lay in the *Wilma* being
swamped by the high seas.

Ben made his way back toward the pilot house holding on
to the rope that circled the deck. The wind washed white-
crested waves over the deck now, and the ship dipped suddenly forward, then insanely backward. A clap of thunder

sounded, the heavens parted as a sudden lightning bolt split the black sky in two.

Soaked to the skin, Ben staggered into the pilot house where Black Henri held the ship on course, a grim expression on his face.

There was another clap of thunder, another bolt of lightning, and suddenly they were being pelted not just by the high waves, but by rain. It fell as if in sheets, pounding on the deck and mixing with the salty waves causing a frothy foam to ooze over the hatches.

"We be all right," Black Henri said confidently. "We bobbing like a little wooden box, but we be all right." He crossed himself.

Ben nodded. Black Henri's native language was French, so his English was broken. But he knew the sea and hearing him express such confidence made Ben feel better. Still, he could not help wondering where Maddie and Melissa were in this storm. Had Pike already made port in Mayaguez? God, he hoped so.

Maddie stared out the little window of the cabin she shared with Melissa. "All I can see is the dock. I think supplies are being brought aboard."

Melissa was sewing. Together they had made several sets of undergarments so that they could rotate at least that part of their clothing by washing and drying what was soiled. And, as on the first night, water was delivered regularly so they could wash. Meals left something to be desired, but it seemed obvious that the two of them were eating better than the crew. Most significantly, Captain Pike had not reappeared to torment them. Or, as they suspected, to avoid being tormented himself. Instead a sullen crew member came, delivering food and water, and listening to their varied complaints. As a result of one, a lock had been installed on the inside of the door as well as the outside of the door.

"Where do you suppose we are?" Maddie asked, turning to Melissa.

Melissa shrugged. "I've sailed the Caribbean a lot, but frankly, one place looks much like another. I looked out, but from what I can see, I really can't tell where we are. Except I know it's not Havana."

Maddie sat down and picked up the sewing piece she had been working on. "Ben's ship was already supplied for the first leg of the voyage, so he won't have to stop. It must be a good thing that we've made port. It means Ben will have a chance to catch up."

Melissa nodded. "This must be Pike's home port, the way Curaçao is Ben's."

There was a knock on the door and Maddie got up. "What is it?" she called out.

"Something from the Captain," the now familiar voice answered.

Maddie unbolted the door and the same sullen crew member bent down and pushed a large trunk into the room. Then he bent over and handed them a big basket of fruit. "From Captain Pike," he said, a trifle begrudgingly, then he added, "Captain says when we leave this port, you'll be allowed out on deck in the mornings—but just here on the quarter deck."

Maddie looked unimpressed, certain that their reactions to everything would be carried directly back to Pike. "Tell the Captain that simply will not do. We want to be able to go out in the cool of the evening as well. Weather permitting, of course."

The crew member nodded dumbly and then turned his back and left, forgetting altogether to lock them in.

But Maddie closed the door anyway, locking it from the inside.

"Oh, oranges!" Melissa took one and began peeling it immediately.

"Save the peel," Maddie said.

"Why?" Melissa asked as she raised both eyebrows.

"We can make tea using the peels. It will keep us from getting sick."

"I never heard such a story," Melissa confessed, as she studied the orange.

"Let's see what's in here," Maddie suggested as she opened the lid of the trunk. Then she laughed. "Well, well, look at this!"

Melissa came to her side and peered in. The trunk was full of clothes. Skirts and blouses, some shoes, some nightclothes, and even several rather decent-looking dresses. And for their amusement there were some picture books and a deck of cards.

"Dear Captain Pike must indeed be having nightmares," Maddie mused.

Melissa smiled. "I do hope so."

And then both women looked at each other and their expressions grew serious. Their victory over Captain Pike was temporary, and based only on his fear of retribution. But the truth was, if something happened to Ben, if he couldn't catch up, if he didn't find them, Captain Pike could easily turn vicious once again. Vicious and very dangerous.

Melissa took Maddie's hands. "Ben and Rob will come," she said steadily, as if she had to say it just so she would believe it.

Maddie closed her eyes, still holding Melissa's hands tightly. When she closed her eyes, she could conjure up Ben's image. All of her longed for Ben York. Being separated from him was more terrible than she had imagined it could be, she felt as if she had lost a part of herself.

"Please be safe," she whispered. "Please be safe."

Sarah Oort walked in her garden, leaning over now and again to observe the progress of her prized tulips which had burst into bloom only a few days ago, filling her garden with brilliant red, yellow, and white blossoms.

"Another spring," she said aloud. She felt resentful of the season and inside, she knew she felt resentful because it was the season of youth, the season of young love, and above all, the season of hope. But for Sarah it was none of these things and feeling sorry for herself, she began to think how she had come to her present state.

Her first two husbands had been older than she. They had been stodgy and set in their ways, interested only in plundering her young body and showing her off. She was yet another of their worldly possessions, yet another jewel in their collection. Still, she had not had to put up with either of them very long. They had died and left her a small fortune in property.

She pressed her lips together and sat down on the hard wooden bench, opposite her bed of prize tulips. Her thoughts settled on her last husband, the famous Captain William Kidd.

He had come to live in New York City twelve years ago in the year, 1690. He was already known as a famous captain and as the owner of several vessels. He sailed the coast, sometimes paid by New York, sometimes paid by Massachusetts. His mission was to rid the coastal waters of pirates, though of course, English and Dutch privateers were welcome as long as a share of their booty was given to the city fathers.

Sarah first met Kidd at the home of Governor Fletcher, the Governor of New York before the Earl of Bellomont took over. Kidd was a big man with broad shoulders and massive muscular arms. When he held her, Sarah felt fragile, as if she might break. It was a feeling she enjoyed, but seldom knew.

He was a widower and she a widow. He began courting her immediately and soon they were entangled in as passionate affair as one dared imagine. Kidd had taken her as he took everything. He had virtually ravished her and she had been swept to the heights of passion by his rough ardor. Unlike her other husbands, William Kidd had a youthful vigor.

But alas, he left her too often and when he was gone, she could not remain faithful.

"Dear Governor Bellomont," she whispered. Before coming to New York to become governor, thus taking over from Fletcher, Bellomont had arranged for Kidd to be outfitted and licensed as a privateer. He was one of the investors who raised the money for the voyage of the *Venture Galley*. Kidd was to sail the Indian Ocean and his letter of marque empowered him to capture French vessels. He also had a special commission authorizing him to seize certain pirates. But the emphasis was on enemy prizes.

Off the Malabar Coast, Kidd took his most valuable prize, a Moorish vessel with a cargo valued at £710.000. It was this vessel that was the reported source of Kidd's lost treasure. "My treasure," Sarah said, clenching her fists in frustration.

Everything had gone wrong then, just as it had gone wrong now. A new government was elected in England and Lord Bellomont was sent to be Governor of New York and to rid the area of pirates. The new government claimed Kidd had taken ships he should not have taken. Seeking refuge, Kidd came to New York and was immediately arrested by Bellomont who had funded his activities in the first place.

He'd been held in jail for months, and during all that time, Sarah had visited often, attempting with all her wiles to pry out of her husband the whereabouts of his treasure. But he would not tell her. After six months, he was sent to England, and there, tried and hung. The documents that could have proved him innocent were kept by Bellomont.

Sarah dipped into her pocket and withdrew the letter she had just received from Katra. Again she reread it, again she trembled with anger over its contents.

> *Dear Mother,*
>   *I have left this day to return to Europe. Ben York left me sufficient money to do this. Our plan utterly failed. Captain Pike betrayed you and me. He has kidnapped*

*Melissa as well as Captain York's lover. He is on his
way to retrieve the treasure, and Ben York is in pursuit.*

*I might have succeeded if you had not made a deal
with Pike. He was my undoing and he most certainly
will not share the treasure with you if he finds it.*

*I don't know when, or even if, I will return to New
York.*

> *Your daughter,*
> *Katra*

The letter's content was disappointing enough, but Katra's
curtness made it even worse. The letter was not signed,
"love, Katra." It was simply signed, "Katra."

As for Pike, he was clearly a raving idiot. If Ben York captured him, he would have him for breakfast.

"Well, I know where to find Ben York when he's done in
Pike," she muttered to herself. Ben would no doubt eliminate
Pike, and then go to Havana where she knew him to be build-
ing a house.

"I will be waiting for you," Sarah vowed. "You and dear
little Melissa."

The sea had rolled and then roared as the heavy winds
whipped up the water and lashed the *Wilma*. The storm had
lasted for the better part of two days, and then it stopped not
suddenly, but with maddening slowness. The sky went from
black to grey, and finally, on the third day a patch of blue appeared, a patch which hourly seemed to grow larger. And the
wind changed. It was no longer a cool northeasterly wind, but
was now a humid southerly wind, a wind which barely carried the *Wilma* along.

Black Henri had gone to his cabin and there fallen into a
deep sleep of sheer exhaustion. Ben, soaking wet and bone
tired, finally handed the wheel to Yan Ould, and staggered to

his own cabin where he stripped, dried himself off, and then fell across the bed.

His dreams turned back into the nightmarish storm and in his sleep he could see the *Wilma* as he chased Pike's vessel across the open sea.

"Maddie!" he called out her name in his sleep and she appeared in the distance. "Maddie!"

Her thick dark hair was loose, a tangle of wind blown curls falling on bare white shoulders. Her green eyes searched for him, and she held out her long graceful arms.

Her diaphanous white robe seemed to blow away on the wind, leaving her naked before him. She was a smooth, white alabaster statue with rose tipped breasts and rounded, firm buttocks.

In his dream he pursued her across the choppy water, almost touching her, almost within grasp of her wonderful hair. But always, just as he almost reached her, she seemed to float just out of reach.

"Maddie, Maddie!" He ran faster and faster across the water and finally he succeeded in grasping her hair and pulling her to him. She smelled like the sea, salt fresh. Her flesh tasted cool, yet she burned beneath his touch—"Maddie"—he tossed, trying to pull her back as she disappeared, then he opened his eyes and found he was embracing his pillow, and whispering her name in his sleep. In the darkness he felt his eyes fill with moisture. She was everything to him. He had to find her.

Sarah Oort wore an elegant lavender dress made of taffeta. Her skirt was decorated with ruching and her sleeves were caught up with darker lavender garters studded with pearls. Around her shoulders she wore a light cape and she carried a small velvet satchel.

She paused at the foot of gangplank and looked up at the *Western Star.* Then she turned to the ship's officer who stood nearby. "Have my trunks brought to my cabin," she requested. Two of her own servants had already unloaded two trunks from Sarah's personal carriage.

Mike Faraday, dressed in brown breeches, wore a matching vest, and a gold trimmed jacket. His three cornered hat, a bicorne, made him look more bird-like than usual. "I can't believe you are really embarking on this wild goose chase, Sarah."

"It is permissible to chase wild geese if one knows where they nest," Sarah retorted.

Mike Faraday shrugged. "I should know better than to spar verbally with you. You always win."

"I intend to win more than simply a verbal battle. I intend to have what is rightfully mine."

"But this trip is so sudden! And to go alone, dear Sarah. How will you win? I simply don't understand."

"I am a woman of means and influence. Money buys friends in high places, as you of all people should well know."

"Did I ever ask you for money?"

"No, but the same cannot be said of your governor."

Mike Faraday grasped both of her hands. "I implore you not to go Sarah. I desire you, I shall ..."

"Easily find another to lie in bed beside you."

"You misjudge me."

"I don't think so, you're an opportunist. I don't hold it against you, but I don't misjudge you."

He raised his brow. "I still do not understand why you are suddenly going to Havana."

"Because eventually Ben York will turn up there. I shall reveal him to the Spanish authorities and offer certain bribes. I wager I'll end up with a portion of the treasure and Ben York will end up at the end of a hangman's noose."

"I don't believe he's ever taken a Spanish vessel. He's always taken Portuguese vessels."

"No matter. His guilt or innocence of no concern to me.

All I care about is getting my rightful share of William's treasure."

Mike Faraday looked at her for a moment, then lifted her hand and kissed it. "I can't stop you. You're a stubborn woman."

"I'll be back," Sarah vowed. She lifted her skirt and walked up the gangplank.

Mike Faraday stood stiffly at the bottom. A strange feeling swept over him.

The feeling that he would never see Sarah Oort again.

Chapter Sixteen

A soft white fog shrouded the island that lay off the star-board side of the vessel. Maddie stared out at the island, searching for something familiar, but nothing looked as it should or had on her last visit.

Melissa stood by her side on the quarter deck, and finally, unable to stand the suspense any longer asked, "Do you remember it? Does it look familiar?"

"No. Melissa, I'm sure this isn't the right island. I'm sure we passed it yesterday."

Melissa glanced down on deck where the lone guard had been posted to watch them. The rest of the crew was ashore. How can it be the wrong island? It was Ben's map."

"I don't know unless . . ."

"Unless what?" Melissa said impatiently.

"Unless Katra altered the map to somehow protect herself against Pike."

Melissa's eyes suddenly came alive. "It's just the sort of thing Sarah Oort's daughter would do! Oh, dear heaven! Ben will be looking for us in the wrong place! I mean, if he's looking at all. How would he know the map Pike has has been altered? I mean, he doesn't need a map at all."

Maddie gripped the rail, trying to think. This might not be a negative development. They had wasted a day and a half sailing around Mahone Bay. That surpassed the head start

they had on Ben—or at least the head start she supposed they
had on Ben. He would have left immediately, of that she was
certain. She looked up, searching the fog and thinking of how
many fog shrouded islands there were. Was the *Wilma* out
there somewhere? Was Ben waiting? Perhaps he was waiting
at Oak Island for them? Her heart fairly pounded at the
thought that he might be so close, that their ordeal might be
drawing to a close.

"Look!" Melissa said, pointing off toward the island.

Through the fog, Maddie saw the long boat approaching.
Pike was standing at the prow, his face studded with droplets
of water, his expression angry. The oarsmen, with their shov-
els beside them, cut through the water, each stroke shortening
the distance between them and the ship.

"He doesn't look happy," Melissa said. It was a vast under-
statement. "I guess you're right, I guess this isn't the right island."

"I'm sure it isn't."

Maddie and Melissa watched in silence as Pike and his
men boarded the ship, muttering and cursing.

Pike, wasting no time, scrambled aboard and walked purposefully toward the quarter deck where Maddie and Melissa
waited.

He stopped a few feet from them, panting from the exertion of having climbed the rope ladder. Then he took a filthy
kerchief out of his pocket and wiped the perspiration and salt
water off his face. He pulled the crumpled map from his
other pocket and unfolded it, waving it toward Maddie.
"Look at this! For three hours we've scoured that island!
There's no pits as shows on here!"

Maddie took the map from his fingers and studied it. It was
a copy—this was not Ben's writing.

"You've been here before, wench! I'll wager ye know
where the right island is! I'll wager I can make ye take me
there!"

With a swiftness that surprised even Maddie, Pike grabbed

her hair and wound it round his hand, yanking on it and pulling her close to him. "Ben York or no Ben York, I'll have ye stripped and beaten!"

Melissa also moved swiftly. She kicked Pike hard on the back of his short legs, then she raked his scalp with her long nails, causing him to cry out in pain and let go of Maddie.

"Leave her alone!" Melissa screamed.

Pike whirled around and back-handed Melissa, sending her flying across the deck and into the door of the cabin. She sunk to the floor, stunned and half-unconscious.

Maddie jumped to avoid him. "You stupid little man!" She shouted loud enough for Pike's crew to hear. "If you'd shown me this map sooner I'd have told you this wasn't Ben York's writing! You've been made a fool of by Katra Oort. I'll take you to the island," she said evenly, "but leave Melissa alone."

Pike cursed and wiped blood off his head. "I'll gladly leave both ye bitches alone forever as soon as I have me treasure trove."

Maddie held out the map. "It's this island. We passed it yesterday."

Pike snatched the map from her fingers. "Get back in your cabin!"

Maddie hurried to Melissa's side. She lifted her up and Melissa groggily took a step forward. Maddie opened the door and half-dragged Melissa inside. Then she lay her on the bed. She was about to put a wet compress on Melissa's head, when she heard Pike slip the bolt on the door, locking them in. From beyond the door she heard him order a guard placed on their cabin.

Maddie smiled to herself. They would not sail back to Oak Island till morning. Pike would not risk the uncertainties of this rocky bay at night because the chance of going around was far too great.

* * *

Dawn did not bring the sun. Instead, the persistent spring fog hung low, floating like a ghost over the shrubbery and mingling with the light green spider-like webs of northern moss that fell from the pines.

Rob and Ben York lay flat on a jagged rock, their eyeglass fixed on Pike's vessel. Meanwhile, the *Wilma* lay at anchor, in a secluded cove halfway round the island.

"They're anchoring now," Rob said as he watched through the glass.

"Any sight of Maddie or Melissa?" Ben asked anxiously. Just to see her through his glass would have given him the strength to do anything, that he knew.

"No. They're probably locked up."

"I'll kill Pike if he's harmed them—if he's . . ." Ben couldn't even say it, though in his nightmares he had seen it often enough. He dreamt of Pike hurting Maddie—he dreamt of him having her against her will. The thought of Pike's hands on her infuriated him, made him tremble with anger.

"You'll have to fight me for the privilege," Rob replied through his clenched teeth. He, too, had been tormented by nightmares, and he also had prayed for Melissa's safety while cursing Pike's existence.

"I feel as if we've been waiting forever," Ben complained.

"They're coming!" Rob hissed. "Yup, they're lowering two long boats."

"Is the whole crew coming ashore?"

"Looks that way," Rob confirmed.

Ben snatched the glass and looked through it. "C'mon," he muttered. "Let's get back to the ship."

The two of them ran down a wooded path, then out onto the open beach. They quickly waded out into the ice cold water, pushing the rowboat and then jumping in. They raced for the *Wilma.*

"What's the plan?" Rob asked anxiously.

"We'll take the men and row to Pike's ship. We'll board from the far side while they're ashore. First we'll find

Maddie and Melissa. When they're safe, we'll row back to where we just were. Then we'll take our men, encircle them, and surprise them while they're digging in the pits."

"Won't they see us when we leave Pike's ship?"

"No, they'll be at the pits. They can't see their vessel from there. We should have the advantage of complete surprise."

Ben and Rob did not even reboard the *Wilma,* they simply climbed from the row boat into the long boat with their men. Black Henri had issued arms and given the order on Ben's signal to have the boats lowered into the water.

Within minutes they were cutting through the water, headed for Pike's ship in absolute silence.

As the three long boats came alongside, Ben gave the signal. Black Henri threw up the large grappling hook with the rope attached and silently, he climbed it. When he reached the top, he threw the rope ladders over the side, and the crew of the *Wilma,* cutlasses held in their teeth, pistols in their belts, and swords at their side, climbed up swiftly and fanned out on the empty deck in all directions.

"There's a lone guard on the quarter deck," Black Henri whispered. "He's asleep."

Ben took the steps, two at a time, with Rob following on his heels. Ben drew his sword and poked it gently into the protruding belly of the snoring seaman, then he yelled, "Up!"

The crewman's eyes snapped open and filled with instant terror.

"Get up slowly, and don't even blink if you want to continue breathing," Ben ordered.

Mindful of the sword against his skin, the man pulled himself up. He was shaking violently. Rob disarmed him, and Ben dropped his sword and pushed the frightened man toward Black Henri. "Have him locked up below!"

Ben grappled with the bolt, even as he heard a lock being lifted on the other side. He flung open the door—"Maddie!"

"Oh, Ben!" Maddie flew into his arms even as Rob pushed

past them to go to Melissa who was sitting on the side of the bed.

"You did get here! I was so afraid we'd be gone!" Maddie leaned against him.

Ben held her close, stroking her hair, even as he buried his face in it. "I was so afraid for you. Tell me you're both all right—Pike didn't . . . ?"

Maddie shook her head. "We're fine now that you're here," she whispered. She knew half the crew was staring at them, but she didn't care. "Just hold me a second longer," she asked.

Ben drew her back and kissed her. He wanted to do more. He wanted never to let her go. But both of them knew there was more to do, that there were scores to be settled as well as unfinished business.

Sarah Oort sat before her mirror in her spacious cabin aboard the *Western Star,* the ship she owned.

She pulled a silver-handled brush through her blond hair and thought that Havana was certainly not the worst place to spend the spring. Heaven knew it was better than New York. And naturally her waiting would have a purpose. Ben York would most certainly triumph over Captain Phineas Pike, a man whose brain she judged to be no larger than a small pea.

Yes, Ben would triumph and he would come to Cuba with his beloved so that they might move into the charming house he was building. Doubtless, she thought bitterly, they intended to live on Ben's share of William's treasure while Rob and Melissa lived on Melissa's ill-gotten inheritance.

"Well, you shan't win," Sarah vowed. She intended on arriving first and on seeing the Spanish governor of the island. She would tell him exactly who Ben York was, and she would offer a considerable bribe to have Ben and his brother locked up. Whatever became of Ben's mistress and Melissa was none of her concern. She supposed the two of them were good-looking enough to make a fine living as prostitutes. Certainly Spanish seamen would pay a pretty penny for Melissa whose copper-colored hair never failed to attract Mediterranean men.

As part of her arrangement with the Spanish governor, she would get the *Wilma* which no doubt would have the treasure aboard. Then, Sarah thought happily, she would sail off with William's treasure leaving them all behind, destined to whatever the fates decided for them.

Just at that moment there was a terrible noise and a dreadful jolt. The fine French perfumes that lined Sarah's dressing table went flying to all corners of the cabin, while she, stool and all, were sent off into the wall with a resounding crash.

"We've been rammed!" a panic-filled voice on deck shrieked.

Sarah forced herself up, shaking her arm. No, nothing seemed broken. She quickly laced her bodice and hurried toward the door of her cabin.

She flung open the door of her cabin and looked down on the deck. The sight that greeted her eyes stunned her.

The crew of her vessel ran in circles, panic-stricken and totally disorganized.

A much larger ship had rammed the *Western Star*, and armed men were now in the process of boarding. Most came across the great planks that had been dropped, but others jumped, swords drawn and cutlasses ready.

Sarah held on to the side of door to steady herself. Her blue eyes traveled upward. In the wind, atop the mast of the vessel which had rammed them, a Spanish flag fluttered in the afternoon breeze.

"We surrender!" Captain Hartfield shouted. He was waving a huge white flag. "Men, surrender your arms!"

Sarah squinted meanly at Captain Hartfield. He was a weasel of a man. Certainly William Kidd would never have surrendered. And no blood had even been drawn! Surrender, indeed!

She turned again toward the melee. Those who had boarded were in uniform. Spanish uniforms! This, she quickly surmised, was not a pirate vessel. Something serious was going on. Something she did not understand.

She picked up her long skirt and stomped to the edge of the quarter deck. She looked from the Spanish soldiers to her cowering crew who were already being disarmed. Then focusing on Captain Hartfield, she narrowed her blue eyes.

"How dare you surrender my vessel!" she shouted.

He turned toward her. "We cannot fight the Spanish army!"

No sooner had he finished speaking than an elegantly dressed officer stepped forward. He had thick dark wavy hair, a long moustache, deep brown eyes, and swarthy skin. He was dressed immaculately in a white uniform dripping with gold braid. The sword at his side was silver with a pearl handle. He bowed from the waist. "Senora!"

Sarah watched as he bolted up the stairs to stand in front of her. He took her hand and kissed it. "Perhaps I should say, Senorita! Am I to understand this splendid vessel is yours?"

"It is and I should like to know just why you have boarded? I sail under a Dutch flag, are not our nations at peace?"

The handsome young officer smiled. "Captain Juan Jose de la Madrid, at your service, Senorita."

"Why have we been rammed and boarded?" Sarah repeated impatiently, as she ignored his flattery.

Captain Madrid smiled and pointed upward at the Dutch flag that flew from the mast of the *Western Star*. "Senorita, our two nations are at war. I regret to inform you that you and your fine ship are my prisoners."

Sarah's mouth opened, but no sound came out. She was too stunned. War? What war? "Are you also at war with the British? This vessel sails out of New York."

"I fear so, Senorita."

He smiled, fingered his moustache and raised his brow. "I

really cannot tell if you are a *senora* or a *senorita*—you have a ripe maturity as well as girlish beauty."

Sarah felt as if a rug had been pulled from beneath her feet. His flattery was meaningless in view of the facts. "What shall become of me?" she managed.

The captain smiled again. "You are a prisoner, my fair blond beauty. I fear you will be spending the duration of the war on Cuba . . ." His dark eyes looked her over slowly and his smile twisted ever so slightly, "as my personal prisoner."

"But I own this vessel. I can pay handsomely for my freedom."

"No, no, Senorita, I own this vessel and all that is on it. I do not bargain for what I already have."

"You're no better than a pirate!"

"Come, come, let us go into your cabin and discuss terms. I think you will find your personal surrender—pleasurable indeed."

He advanced on her and Sarah retreated. He slammed the door behind them and seized her round the waist, pulling her roughly into his arms. He kissed her and as he did so, he began to undo her dress. "I do hope it will be a long war," he breathed, lowering her to the bed.

Sarah closed her eyes. No doubt it would be a long war. It was best to make the most of things, that was a lesson she had learned long ago.

"We'll take you and Melissa back to the *Wilma,*" Ben said as they rowed away from Pike's ship. "You can wait with Will till all this is over."

Maddie shook her head. "I'll not be parted from you again, Ben York. Give me a sword."

"And me a pistol," Melissa added.

Ben had no time to argue. Maddie had grabbed a pair of breeches and she was even now struggling into them, pulling them on underneath her skirt. When they were on, she pulled down her skirt and threw it in the water.

"You're determined, aren't you?"

"Yes, I'm determined to be at your side, always."

Ben looked lovingly at her, then he turned his attention to the task at hand. He gave the signal and the boats headed for the sandy beach.

When they reached shore, they dragged the long boats onto the sand, then Ben divided them into three groups, intending to send each in a different direction. "All Pike's men will be by the pits. We'll come from three sides and take them by surprise. Attack when you hear the cry of a coyote." Ben put his hand near his mouth, then he did a surprisingly realistic imitation of a wild dog.

Silently, they broke into their groups. In seconds they were dispersed and moving through the woods silently.

Ben, Maddie, and nine men moved through the bush as quietly as possible, hardly daring to breath as they approached the sound of voices.

Maddie peered through the bushes. As Ben had predicted, Pike and his crew were all around the pits. They were stripped to the waist and all were covered with sweat from the arduous task of digging. Most had laid their arms in the sand nearby.

Ben waited. Then after what seemed an eternity, he again made the sound of a coyote. One or two of Pike's men looked up momentarily, then returned to work.

Suddenly, and from all three directions at once, the crew of the *Wilma* sprang forward, swords and pistols drawn.

Pike's men scrambled for their weapons, but for many it was too late and they raised their arms in surrender or dropped to their knees.

But Pike had drawn his sword and he advanced to do battle with Ben.

Riffen drew his sword and ran toward Maddie. "I always wanted to do battle with a woman," he shouted.

By the time Maddie looked up again, others had found their weapons and at least ten or so of Pike's men, including Pike himself, were engaged in battle.

Maddie easily leapt away from Riffen, but he too leapt and in a second, their swords clashed.

His lips were pressed together, his eyes flashed with hatred, and it was instantly clear to her that he meant to kill her if he could. He pranced about, moving her ever closer to the edge of the pit just as Pike maneuvered Ben in the same direction.

Riffen thrust forward and slashed her blouse, but Maddie jumped aside and slashed back, not only hitting flesh, but severing Riffen's hand at the wrist. It fell, still clutching his sword into the pit. Riffen himself wailed in pain, and clutching his bleeding stump, fell to his knees to beg for mercy.

Maddie dared not look down—but a sudden recollection crossed her mind as she remembered what the guide had said when she took the tour. He had spoken of how a television camera had been lowered into the pit in 1971 and how it recorded the image of a severed human hand.

At that moment she heard a terrible scream and she whirled around as Pike tumbled backward into the blackness of the same bottomless pit.

"He's triggered the flooding mechanism!" Ben shouted.

The men all moved away from the pit seemingly afraid that it would somehow swallow them, too.

Maddie inhaled deeply. Then she walked to Ben's side. The battle was over. Black Henri and the others were putting Pike's men in irons.

Ben's arm circled her waist and he hugged her ever so slightly. "The sun's coming out," he observed.

"Is the treasure flooded?"

Ben shook his head. "It's not in that pit. We'll get it now and go back to the ship."

To Maddie's surprise, they didn't go to any of the other

pits. Instead they walked inland, toward a rock formation. There, in a cave, were all the chests holding Kidd's treasure.

"You mean there is no treasure in the pits?" Maddie asked in amazement as the men carried the caskets to the shore.

"No, not one chest."

"But how did the pits get here? Did you dig them just to make people think that's where the treasure was?"

Ben shook his head. "I'm afraid the pits are as much a mystery to me as they are to you. We found them when we came here. They're all secured with trap after trap. Someone who knew mining techniques must have built them. We looked, but we found nothing."

Maddie laughed. "In my time they're still looking."

"Ah, yes. Your time."

His eyes twinkled and she knew he still did not believe her. But for the moment she was so glad to be with him it did not matter.

He looped his arm through hers and they walked together down to the shore. "Maddie, I want to talk to you about Will."

"I'll be glad to see him," she confessed.

"Maddie, I want to adopt the boy. I want him to have a real family."

"Oh, Ben, that's wonderful! Yes, I'd like that, too."

He spun her around and kissed her again. "You're perfect. I love you."

That night, they had a feast aboard the *Wilma*. Two of the men had gone ashore and shot a deer. The venison was cooked to perfection. The ship's cook also made bread and they had beans and some greens they picked ashore.

Rob drank from his goblet of wine and then he turned to his brother. "I assume you'll want to head off to Havana."

Ben nodded. "I certainly want to take Maddie there."

Maddie stiffened slightly. How could they go there? Certainly it was not safe. But she didn't say anything just now. She would wait and plead with Ben later, try to convince him it was unwise to go to Cuba. They had wintered in Cuba, this was the spring of 1702, this was the year the war of the Spanish Succession came to North America.

"I for one want to go back to Curaçao," Melissa said.

"We'll be getting married there," Rob put in.

Ben winked at his brother. "Waiting all that time are you?"

Rob's face flushed red and Melissa giggled and pressed his hand. "You're a captain, Ben. Why can't you marry us now, right now, tonight."

"I can do that," Ben said.

Melissa leaned over and took the goblet away from Rob. "Stop drinking this minute. You'll be useless if you're drunk."

Melissa's forthrightness caused them all to laugh, although Rob again turned the color of a fine cooked beet.

"I sensed you will reform my brother," Ben said, looking at Melissa.

"I shall indeed," she replied.

Ben went to his bookshelf and took down his copy of *The Book of Common Prayer* which stood next to his Bible on the shelf.

"Are they really getting married?" Will asked, wide-eyed.

"Really," Maddie answered, giving him a hug.

Ben turned to the page that held the marriage ceremony in the liturgy and Melissa and Rob stood up and held hands.

Ben began reading and Maddie held Will's hand and listened as Rob and Melissa pledged themselves to one another.

"I now pronounce you man and wife," Ben concluded.

Rob took Melissa into his arms and kissed her. It was such a long, probing passionate kiss that Will's face turned red and he moved restlessly in his chair.

When Rob let Melissa go, he turned back to Ben. "A toast, my brother!"

"To a long and happy marriage for you both," Ben said, holding his wine goblet high.

They all drank some more wine. "You know, brother, Melissa and I don't want to go to Havana. What would you say if we divided the crew and Melissa and I took Pike's ship to Curaçao. Then you and Maddie could sail where you like."

"I have no trouble agreeing to that. In fact it's a fine solution to a difficult problem. We would either have to do as you suggest or scuttle it. Frankly, it would be a strain on supplies to have two full crews on one ship. So, you take Pike's ship and half the prisoners and I'll take the *Wilma* and the other half of the prisoners."

Rob grinned. "Doesn't that make me a captain too?"

Ben laughed. "So it does and I think I know why it is you ask." He turned to Maddie. "Will you marry me now?"

Maddie felt like crying with happiness. She already felt married to Ben York, and she knew that having the words spoken wouldn't make her feel more married. Still, it was important for both of them and she thought, looking at Will, it was important for him, too, because then they could be a real family.

"Yes," she answered looking into his dark eyes, "Of course, I will."

Ben looked back at her. He didn't kiss her, but still she could feel his lips on hers because she knew he was thinking of kissing her.

Rob took the book and read from it and when he finished, Maddie and Ben did kiss.

Ben bent over and gave Will a big bear hug. "Maddie and I want you to be our son, Will. We'll be a family, even when there are other children."

Will's eyes grew moist, but he didn't cry. He just nodded silently feeling as if all his dreams had suddenly come true.

* * *

Maddie leaned over the rail. She had lost count of the days they'd been at sea, lost count of all the times Ben had made love to her, and lost count of how many times she thanked the fates for bringing them together.

She looked at the ocean as it broke against the *Wilma*. Days ago in the northern part of the Atlantic, the sea had been a cold sea blue but now that they had traveled so far south, it had turned into a sea green color and it was calmer.

If only they weren't headed for Havana—what would happen when the fact that war had broken out reached Havana. Would they be arrested?

"Ship ahoy!"

Maddie looked up as she heard the resounding shout from the crow's nest.

High in his perch, Yan Ould held his glass to his eye and pointed off into the distance. "Ship ahoy!" he shouted again.

Ben stepped out of the pilot house. "Can you see her flag?" he called out.

"Not yet, Captain, but she's closing fast!"

Maddie searched the horizon. She could see no ship. She lifted her skirts and ran around the other side of the ship. There, coming toward them, was a magnificent sailing ship.

"A Spanish flag, Captain!" Yan Ould cried from his crow's nest. "Captain, I believe her guns at the ready! Captain!"

Yan Ould said no more. Ben was out of the pilot house, bull horn ready. "All hands on deck! All hands on deck!" he shouted. Then, "Battle stations, men! Man the guns!" Ben then gave the order to arm Pike's crew, he knew they would rather die than be taken prisoner by the Spanish.

For a moment Maddie stood spellbound. She had never seen the *Wilma*'s big guns at the ready. She ran at breakneck speed to the cabin and as quickly as she could, she changed into men's clothing and armed herself. When she burst out of the cabin and onto deck, the two ships were closer yet.

Maddie was halfway up the steps leading to the pilot house when the approaching vessel fired its first volley.

A wave of fire flashed across the deck and the *Wilma* turned, slowly, but nonetheless in time to avoid being struck by the second volley.

Then, with a shudder, the *Wilma* returned fire.

Maddie clung for a moment to the steps leading to the pilot house, then she forced herself up them.

Ben was at the wheel, his face set. He didn't turn toward her, though she knew he knew she was there. "We're going to be boarded," he muttered. He tore open a cabinet and tossed her a pistol. "Protect yourself," he said.

This was not like the fight with Pike. Ben looked concerned as well as bewildered. The other vessel was larger, clearly its actions had taken him by surprise.

Maddie looked from Ben out onto deck. The distance between the vessels had decreased dangerously and then she saw the great hooks being thrown, and she knew the crew of the Spanish vessel was preparing to board.

"I should tell you to hide," Ben said breathlessly.

"I will fight with you," she whispered.

He looked at her and pressed his lips together, as tears seemed to fill his eyes. "I love you," he said under his breath, then he burst out the door to join his men on deck and Maddie followed, not hesitating to enter the fray.

There was no time to look and see what was happening to any of the others. This was a one-on-one battle, a pitched battle. This, Maddie realized with sudden clarity, was war.

The Spanish soldiers were not disorganized as Pike's men had been. They were highly-trained and well-disciplined. They were excellent swordsmen, and they fought bravely.

The first man she engaged seemed mesmerized by the fact she was a woman. But after a few parries, he realized she was also a worthy opponent, and he fought with valor till she forced him over the side and into the blue-green waters of the Caribbean.

Maddie took on three more swordsmen, and she suffered a slight wound on her left arm. But she did not abandon the fight, she continued, trying now and again to spot Ben. But it was no use, there were too many, they came too fast, and she could not look about or even attempt to assess the total situation.

Perspiration poured off her forehead and then she realized that there was less noise, less shooting. The man she fought suddenly dropped to his knees.

Maddie paused. Halfway across the deck she saw Ben. He grinned at her and the wiped his brow. "We've taken them!" he shouted, throwing his hat in the air.

Maddie ran to his side, tears running down her face.

"God, you've been wounded!" Ben pulled her toward him, even as Black Henri leaned over.

"It's just a scratch, really. I'll be fine."

Ben pulled her into his arms and kissed her and the whole crew clapped. "Ah, they love you as much as I do," he whispered.

"We have the captain," Black Henri announced.

Ben turned away from Maddie momentarily and looked into the eyes of the Spanish captain. "Why did you attack us?" he demanded.

The Captain's eyes narrowed, "We're at war, Senor Captain. A week ago British forces burned and sacked Saint Augustine. We're at war with Britain and the Netherlands."

Ben said absolutely nothing, but he turned and looked at Maddie. Then in a near whisper, he said, "Saint Augustine."

"What is your wish, Captain?" Black Henri asked.

"Disarm the ship. Disarm the crew and take anything of value, then set them off. I've no desire for the vessel. We sail for Curaçao immediately!"

"You show us much mercy," the Spanish captain said, bowing slightly.

Ben turned away and took Maddie by the hand. "Best I see to that scratch," he said, a half smile creeping round the corner of his mouth.

He closed the door of his cabin behind them.

Maddie looked up into Ben's eyes. "Does this mean you believe me?"

"Absolutely, you've given me proof of what I couldn't quite accept before." He touched her hair, and drew her close. "It's a miracle that brought you to me."

Ben bolted the door and turned again to her. "Can you forgive me for not believing your tale before?"

Maddie leaned against him and circled him with her arms. "Of course, I can forgive you. It was a hard tale to accept."

"I should have known, I should have believed," he said holding her tightly.

There was something different now, something Maddie could not describe. Ben began to undress her, slowly as always, devouring her with his eyes, as always, touching her tenderly as before. Yet he saw her with new eyes, looked at her in a different way and touched her more sensuously, more lovingly, more with his whole self. It was as if an invisible barrier had been removed.

He carried her naked to their bed and caressed her into moaning passion, as he kissed her entire body. "You are my wife, my love," he whispered. "You are a timeless gift."

Maddie felt joined with him completely, joined as they had not been joined before. "Now it is perfect," she whispered.

FOR THE VERY BEST IN ROMANCE—
DENISE LITTLE PRESENTS!

AMBER, SING SOFTLY (0038, $4.99)
by Joan Elliott Pickart

Astonished to find a wounded gun-slinger on her doorstep, Amber Prescott can't decide whether to take him in or put him out of his misery. Since this lonely frontierswoman can't deny her longing to have a man of her own, who nurses him back to health, while savoring the glorious possibilities of the situation. But what Amber doesn't realize is that this strong, handsome man is full of surprises!

A DEEPER MAGIC (0039, $4.99)
by Jillian Hunter

From the moment wealthy Margaret Rose and struggling physician Ian MacNeill meet, they are swept away in an adventure that takes them from the haunted land of Aberdeen to a primitive, faraway island—and into a world of danger and irresistible desire. Amid the clash of ancient magic and new science Margaret and Ian find themselves falling helplessly in love.

SWEET AMY JANE (0050, $4.99)
by Anna Eberhardt

Her horoscope warned her she'd be dealing with the wrong sort of man. And private eye Amy Jane Chadwick was used to dealing with the wrong kind of man, due to her profession. But nothing prepared her for the gorgeously handsome Max, a former professional athlete who is being stalked by an obsessive fan. And from the moment they meet, sparks fly and danger follows!

MORE THAN MAGIC (0049, $4.99)
by Olga Bicos

This classic romance is a thrilling tale of two adventurers who set out for the wilds of the Arizona territory in the year 1878. Seeking treasure, an archaeologist and an astronomer find the greatest prize of all—love.

Available wherever paperbacks are sold, or order direct from the Publisher. Send cover price plus 50¢ per copy for mailing and handling Penguin USA, P.O. Box 999, c/o Dept. 17109, Bergenfield, NJ 07621. Residents of New York and Tennessee must include sales tax. DO NOT SEND CASH.

HISTORICAL ROMANCE FROM PINNACLE BOOKS

LOVE'S RAGING TIDE   (381, $4.50)
by Patricia Matthews

Melissa stood on the veranda and looked over the sweeping acres of Great Oaks that had been her family's home for two generations, and her eyes burned with anger and humiliation. Today her home would go beneath the auctioneer's hammer and be lost to her forever. Two men eagerly awaited the auction: Simon Crouse and Luke Devereaux. Both would try to have her, but they would have to contend with the anger and pride of girl turned woman . . .

CASTLE OF DREAMS   (334, $4.50)
by Flora M. Speer

Meredith would never forget the moment she first saw the baron of Afoncaer, with his armor glistening and blue eyes shining honest and true. Though she knew she should hate this Norman intruder, she could only admire the lean strength of his body, the golden hue of his face. And the innocent Welsh maiden realized that she had lost her heart to one she could only call enemy.

LOVE'S DARING DREAM   (372, $4.50)
by Patricia Matthews

Maggie's escape from the poverty of her family's bleak existence gives fire to her dream of happiness in the arms of a true, loving man. But the men she encounters on her tempestuous journey are men of wealth, greed, and lust. To survive in their world she must control her newly awakened desires, as her beautiful body threatens to betray her at every turn.

Available wherever paperbacks are sold, or order direct from the Publisher. Send cover price plus 50¢ per copy for mailing and handling to Penguin USA, P.O. Box 999, c/o Dept. 17109, Bergenfield, NJ 07621. Residents of New York and Tennessee must include sales tax. DO NOT SEND CASH.